# *Unforgettable Hungers . . .*

He stepped closer. In the moonlight, Natalie could see the expression on his face, and even before he spoke, it frightened her. "Can I see you again?

She licked her lips. "No, I don't think that would—"

"I do." His mouth was taut, and he spoke in a harsh whisper.

She opened her mouth and that was when it happened, out of the blue, so fast that she was unprepared for it and couldn't have stopped it even if she'd wanted to.

In a fluid move, he placed his hand around her neck, bent and crushed her mouth against hers. At first, she was too dumbfounded to respond. But then she clung to his wide shoulders in order to keep her rubbery legs from giving way.

Finally he pulled back, then said in a strained voice, "Damn, I didn't mean for that to happen."

"Like hell you didn't!"

"Natalie—"

She didn't wait to hear any more. She jerked her car door open, got inside, and drove off. But she couldn't leave behind the smell and touch of Stone McCall.

*Also by Mary Lynn Baxter*

Priceless
Sweet Justice

Published by
Warner Books

**ATTENTION:**
**SCHOOLS AND CORPORATIONS**
WARNER books are available at quantity discounts with bulk purchase for educational, business, or sales promotional use. For information, please write to: SPECIAL SALES DEPARTMENT, WARNER BOOKS, 1271 AVENUE OF THE AMERICAS, NEW YORK, N.Y. 10020

# HOT TEXAS NIGHTS

★

## MARY LYNN BAXTER

**WARNER BOOKS**

A Time Warner Company

WARNER BOOKS EDITION

Copyright © 1996 by Mary Lynn Baxter
All rights reserved.

Cover design by Diane Luger
Cover illustration by Matzura
Hand lettering by Carl Dellacroce

Warner Books, Inc.
1271 Avenue of the Americas
New York, NY 10020

W A Time Warner Company

Printed in the United States of America

First Printing: February, 1996

10 9 8 7 6 5 4 3 2 1

*This book is dedicated to my dear friend
and loyal fan
JACKIE McGRIFF*

A special thanks to John Watson
in return for help, advice, and patience

# One

Natalie Whitmore eyed herself in the mirror. Did she look all right? She'd chosen a short, simple black cocktail dress that emphasized her slenderness and her flawless skin. To buoy her spirits and her courage, she wanted to look her best tonight.

When the family entertained, it was done in style. But why not? she asked herself. After all, they were one of the most prosperous and influential families in the community. To be invited to a dinner party at the Whitmore ranch was tantamount to being invited to the governor's mansion.

She smiled at that last thought, then scrutinized her image. Natalie decided that she did indeed look her best. She then swept her curls away from her face and added diamond studs to her ears.

She walked into Clancy's bedroom; her fifteen-month-old daughter should be asleep by now, but she wasn't. Clancy lay on her back, kicking her little feet in the air, playing with the mobile hanging over her head. Her teddy bear snuggled close under her arm, the baby looked up and smiled when she saw her mother.

"Ma-ma," she cooed.

"You're supposed to be asleep, you little minx!" Tears formed in Natalie's eyes as she leaned over the bed, looking at her daughter. Her throat constricted as she touched the baby's cheek.

She was pleased that Clancy had cooed her name in baby talk, but she would never say "Da-da," to her father, a fact that hurt every time she thought about it. She knew the day would come when Clancy would ask what happened to her daddy.

What would she tell her? Could she relate the story the police and Phillip's family—her family—believed to be the unvarnished truth? Would she mention the publicity frenzy that had become a way of life this past year? God help her, she couldn't tell Clancy about that or anything else, because she wasn't entirely certain herself what had happened. But that would change, starting tonight. She'd made up her mind.

"Natalie?"

She turned and saw Daniel, her brother *and* brother-in-law, leaning against the doorjamb. She wondered briefly how many families that relationship applied to.

"Oh, hi, Danny," Natalie said.

She was the only Whitmore who could call him "Danny" and get by with it. From the first moment she had been taken into this household, she and Daniel had bonded as brother and sister. While everything else had changed around her, that had not.

Dr. Daniel Whitmore held an endowed chair in British literature at the University of Texas at Austin and had always been a more sensitive soul than the other Whitmore men. He was also the best looking, with nearly perfect features—almost too good-looking for a man—and a short but well-proportioned body.

"I knocked, but . . ." Daniel was grinning at her now.

"Sorry. Guess I was woolgathering." Natalie turned back to Clancy and tousled her curls.

"You are coming down to dinner, aren't you?" Daniel asked.

"Of course." Natalie straightened, then leaned against the wall. "Why do you ask?"

"Because you've been acting so withdrawn lately."

When Natalie didn't respond, Daniel went on, "Actually, 'weird' is a better word." He paused. "I know something's bothering you, and I think it's time you coughed up." He smiled. "You've always come to me before with your problems."

"I know," Natalie said, purposely shifting her gaze back to Clancy, who was still awake, playing with her toys. "But this time I have to figure things out on my own."

"So in other words, butt out?"

"You're putting words in my mouth, Danny. That's not what I meant at all."

"Yeah, right," he scoffed, and suddenly Natalie wondered if he was indeed miffed with her for not confiding in him or if he was teasing her good-naturedly, as usual.

Did he now expect her to rely on him for everything just as the Whitmores had done since she had married their eldest son? Did the entire household expect her still to give in to their every demand? That thought was utterly ridiculous, she knew. Or was it? If so, then again she had no one to blame but herself. For more than a year she had depended on the family for the strength to carry on. She'd recently learned that that had been a big mistake.

"Natalie?"

"I've got a lot on my mind, but I'm slowly but surely working it out." Natalie made her tone light, then she walked over and kissed him on the cheek. "Anyway, don't you think it's about time I grew up, handled a few of my own problems?"

"If that's what you want," he said, his gaze now on Clancy.

He looked so dejected that for a moment Natalie was tempted to blurt out everything that was festering inside. But she couldn't do that; she knew she'd choke on the ugly words if she tried to repeat them. Besides, she had something else to tell not only Daniel, but the entire family. She planned to have her say at dinner.

A moment of uncomfortable silence followed, during which Natalie realized that he hadn't completely forgiven her for her evasiveness. Daniel, she had learned from experience, didn't like to be thwarted. That was one Whitmore trait he hadn't evaded.

To combat the awkwardness, Natalie said, "I'll see you downstairs in a minute."

He threw up his hands. "Okay. Have it your own way." He turned on his heel and walked out of the room without another word.

Moments later Natalie met Josie, the housekeeper, on the landing.

"Miz Martha sent me to sit with the baby."

"That's not necessary, Josie. Just looking in on her every once in a while should be sufficient."

"Oh, I don't mind. Besides, Miz Martha's having the dinner catered—" She broke off with a sniff. "There's not much for me to do."

Uh-oh, Josie's territory had been invaded and she wasn't happy. Natalie hid a smile, then said, "You're a dear. Thanks."

She walked on toward the formal living room, where the family and guests were already gathered. She paused in the doorway.

The room fell silent as all eyes riveted on her. Had they been talking about her? Intuition told her they had.

"Am I late?" she asked, feeling awkward and hating it. Maybe that awkwardness stemmed from a guilty conscience. She brushed aside the thought. She didn't have anything to feel guilty about.

"Of course you're not late." The booming voice and smile of her father-in-law, Fletcher Whitmore, seemed to have the effect of a puppeteer yanking the strings of his puppets. Everyone suddenly jumped to life. "We're just early."

Everyone laughed, then began to talk at once.

"Want your usual?" Daniel asked, walking over and offering her his arm.

"Yes, please," she said as he ceremoniously escorted her to the couch.

"I'll only be a moment," Daniel said as Natalie sat down.

True to his word, he returned almost instantly with a Perrier and lime and handed it to Natalie. "Can't gab, though," he said. "At least not now. I'm bartending tonight. Our usual barman is in Barbados on vacation."

"Must be nice."

After Daniel left, Natalie's eyes circled the room. Stanley, Daniel's brother, dressed in a western suit, stood against the mantel, looking out of place, as though he didn't fit into the posh surroundings.

Physically he didn't look like a Whitmore. His skin, leatherlike from so much exposure to the sun, made him look rougher and older than his twenty-eight years. The fact that someone had broken his nose in his youth didn't help his appearance either.

But it was his small, wiry stature that set him apart from his brothers and father and which he seemed to resent the most. Natalie thought he compensated for his lack of stature by being the most vocal and pushy of the bunch. It was obvious he was determined not to be overlooked, unless he was drinking. Then he turned quiet and sullen.

Watching Stanley finish his drink, Natalie knew that he wasn't far from reaching the drunken stage. She turned away, disgusted, accepting that Stanley despised her. Natalie had always sensed his underlying contempt; she'd seen the smoldering looks of jealousy he had always thrown Phillip's way over the years when he'd thought no one was looking. However, in front of the family he treated her with respect, proving himself a true hypocrite.

She didn't care what Stanley thought about her; she'd made peace with that long ago. Still, he gave her a creepy feeling. Thank God he didn't live in the house.

Paula, Stanley's wife, stood next to him, looking presentable for the first time in a long while, Natalie thought. She had on a peach silk dress, and her usually stringy hair was pulled back and clipped at the nape of her neck, though she, too, was obviously drinking excessively.

Neither she nor Stanley acknowledged Natalie's entrance, which was just fine with her. The less she had to do with them the better.

Martha, her beloved mother-in-law, winked at her from across the room. She appeared deep in conversation with one of the guests, the Whitmores' business and financial adviser, Sam Coolidge.

Sam acknowledged Natalie with a smile and a lift of his martini glass. She smiled in return, thinking about the way he dressed. "Flamboyant" was the word that came to mind. Tonight, though, a flare for the outrageous would be more appropriate. Her gaze fell on his tie, and she almost laughed out loud. She couldn't be absolutely certain of the design, but she'd swear from a distance it looked like painted clown faces.

Outrageous or not, he had been loyal to her and the family, and for that she would always be grateful.

"You look lovely, my dear."

The low voice brought her head back around. "Why, thank you, Ben. I needed that." Ben Byers was her favorite family friend, a crackerjack attorney.

"I'm glad to see some color in those cheeks for a change."

"Estée Lauder does wonders."

He looked confused for a second, then a slow grin broke across his lips. "Sorry, it took me a minute."

Natalie chuckled, almost forgetting that Ben Byers was a bachelor and not up on women's cosmetics.

"I understand from Fletcher that you're doing well in your real estate business."

"As a matter of fact, I am." She smiled. "Or at least that's what my boss thinks. But I can't believe Fletcher told you that. I'm surprised. He usually ignores the fact that I even have a job."

Ben's lips twitched. "I think that's because he has a hard

time adjusting to women working. Martha's always stayed home."

"Only I'm not Martha," Natalie pointed out.

Ben flushed. "No, no, you're not, and times have changed. It's just that my old friend hasn't changed with them."

"You're right." Natalie chose that moment to look at her father-in-law, who was in a conversation with Stanley and Sam. Martha looked on with an indulgent smile, while Paula wobbled on her feet, drink in hand.

Natalie wanted to turn away, but she couldn't. Fletcher, at sixty-nine, with those piercing eyes and striking features, had that same commanding persona she had always admired in Phillip. When he spoke people listened, then listened some more. That was why no one had doubted, given Fletcher's power and financial resources, that Phillip *could* have been president of the United States. It was what Fletcher had intended for him since boyhood.

"How's Clancy?" Ben asked on a brighter note, as if he realized he'd upset her.

Natalie faced him with a sincere smile. "She's a mess, that's what she is."

"Well, you can't blame her, not when everyone in this household dotes on her."

"Are y'all talking about my grandchild?" Martha asked, having made her way to the chair adjacent to the couch.

Ben chuckled. "That we are."

In her own way, at sixty-five Martha still commanded attention herself. To Natalie she was as close to an angel on earth as one could get. Not only was she the most considerate woman she had ever met, her face was still relatively unlined and her innocent nature led some to believe she hadn't a care in the world.

Yet when one looked closer, the ravages of pain were there in her eyes for all the world to see. She had loved her oldest son with a passion that was missing in her relationship with her other sons.

"I don't know what I would've done without Clancy," Martha was saying. "She's been my lifeline."

Ben reached out and covered her veined hands. "I understand."

"Ma'am, dinner is ready."

Martha turned and faced the woman who was in charge of the catering service and smiled. "Thank you, Hannah. We'll be right there."

Dinner was a delicious affair, carried out to perfection, and Martha beamed. The Whitmore family china, crystal, and silverware graced the huge dining room table, as did lovely arrangements of fresh flowers.

Tonight was the first time Martha and Fletcher had formally entertained in over a year, and, no one could fault their understated but elegant style.

After the salad, the succulent prime rib cooked with tiny new potatoes and carrots, and fresh peach cobbler à la mode had been consumed, Fletcher stood and *ping*ed his glass. "I'd like to propose a toast."

Everyone's eyes focused on him, an expectant look on their faces.

"To my son, Phillip." He paused and swallowed. "And to what might have been."

Natalie didn't dare look at Martha or anyone else while they sipped their drinks.

Sam Coolidge was the first to break the uneasy silence. "I read that article in the paper, Fletcher. You'd think those newspaper hounds would leave well enough alone. Goddamn vultures, is what they are."

Before anyone could respond, Natalie spoke. For the second time in the evening, she became the focus of attention. "Sam's right. The media hasn't let up in fifteen months. That's partly why I feel the investigation into Phillip's death should be reopened," she said, her eyes on Fletcher.

No one said a word.

Fletcher's face turned purple with rage, but the others stared at her as if she'd just landed from an alien planet.

*"What did you say?"*

Natalie didn't flinch in the wake of her father-in-law's deadly tone.

"Natalie, what the hell—" Daniel began, and stood.

Without so much as glancing in his direction, Fletcher said, "Shut up and sit down, Daniel."

Daniel closed his mouth and sat down.

Fletcher's features remained twisted in rage, and when he spoke, it was through clenched teeth. "Our son and your husband's death was an accident, pure and simple. The media is known for its sensationalism. It's the way they handle things nowadays. They have no right to question what was and is an open-and-shut case. And don't you ever question that again, you hear?"

Even though her tongue felt like dry plaster, Natalie said, "I have no choice but to pursue another investigation because I've come to believe his death was *not* an accident."

"Why, you're crazy as hell!"

"Fletcher, please," Martha said in an unsteady voice.

He glared at her, then back at Natalie. "And just how do you plan to carry out this crazy scheme of yours?" he demanded in a jeering tone.

The silence that followed was explosive.

"I intend to find the cop who killed my husband."

# Two

The day was gloomy. Rain pelted against the window of the hospital room, but Stone McCall scarcely noticed, except to compare the weather with his mood. They were compatible in every way.

He'd been in the hospital, beside his daughter Sally's bed, for nearly a week now and she still hadn't regained consciousness.

He stared at his daughter. He hadn't realized just how precious she was to him until he'd first walked into this room. The last time he'd seen her, she had looked like a typical preteen kid. Now, at thirteen, she barely resembled herself. Gone were the animated pixielike features, the shiny light hair, and the twinkle in her brown eyes. She was a shrunken image of her former self.

A lump so large he couldn't swallow lodged in Stone's throat. But he couldn't cry; his heart felt dead inside. He turned and stared around the room. Though neatly carpeted and wallpapered, it was still a hospital room, with a smell that couldn't be disguised despite the many flowers. There were shadows in the room in spite of a subdued light over the bed. He wanted to turn away from that huge bed. Or was it because Sally seemed so fragile as she lay unmoving on the white sterile sheets?

He leaned closer and stared at the thin arm next to him. Her other arm was connected by a plastic tube with an IV bag suspended upside down from a metal stand next to the bed. Her veins looked like tiny blue strips. Her fingers were coiled like a baby's, which made her small bones almost visible through her transparent skin. Had she always been so small? He couldn't remember.

Rosy cheeks, her trademark, were gone. She looked drained and seriously ill. *She looked as if she were dying.*

His breath snagged in his throat as he turned away and tried to get up. He found he couldn't. His legs were like rubber. His stomach was somewhere around his ankles. His mouth was acid. His mind was utter chaos.

Yet there was nothing he could do that wasn't already being done. They had the best medical care possible. His ex-wife Connie's new husband had seen to that, for which Stone was grateful. As soon as he could, he intended to pay his fair share or more.

Sally was *his*, and he blamed himself as much as Connie did, though in his heart Stone knew she was looking for a scapegoat. Still, he couldn't deny that if he'd been the kind of parent he should've been, then maybe Sally wouldn't be lying unconscious with needles in her arm, a point Connie had driven home with words as sharp as knives.

That encounter had taken place shortly after he'd arrived at the hospital. Connie had been sitting beside Sally's bed. When she saw him, she'd gotten up and walked out of the room, gesturing for him to follow.

"She's not—" Stone couldn't finish the sentence. He couldn't find the words.

"No, she's not dead, if that's what you're asking," Connie said, her once attractive features pinched in pain and bitterness.

"Thank God," he wheezed.

"Since when did you believe in God?"

"Don't start, Connie. Not now. Can't we call a truce for now? Think what you want about me. You have every right. But for now, let's forget about us and think about our daughter."

"Don't you think you're a trifle late for that?"

"No, goddammit, I don't. Besides, you called me. Remember?"

"Only because Sally cried for you before she lapsed into unconsciousness!" Connie's lips quivered.

"Please," he pleaded, then jammed his hands into his pockets so that she wouldn't see them shaking. God, if only he could have a drink and a cigarette. "Let's don't fight. I know you hate me."

"That goes without saying." She looked him up and down. "When you first walked in, I didn't recognize you."

"I've lost weight, among other things. I've changed."

"Yeah, right," she said in a jeering tone.

"Just tell me what happened, okay?"

"Sally's been giving me . . . us trouble for a while now." Connie paused and looked back into the room.

"How's that?" Stone pressed urgently, aching to see his daughter, yet fighting the thought of actually walking into that room.

"She got in with the wrong crowd."

"Drugs?"

"No."

"Drinking?"

"Yes."

"Was Sally drinking?"

"I don't think so."

"You don't think so! Don't you know?"

"Don't you dare question me like that, you son of a bitch. I did the best I could."

Which wasn't damn near good enough, he wanted to lash back. But he pulled in his claws. Hell, he didn't have the moral right to judge her or to challenge anything Sally might have done, due to the fact that *he'd* had a rather slipshod attitude toward his own life and his work. That was what had gotten him in trouble in the first place.

It was a classic case of "monkey see, monkey do." She was just taking after her daddy.

Not long ago he'd looked in the mirror to shave and had been more repulsed than ever by the image that stared back at him. His green eyes had looked as though someone had splattered them with red paint. The lines around his eyes and mouth were so deeply grooved, they appeared to have been gouged with a knife. And his gut, still full of beer, had protruded over his belt and was in an uproar to boot. He blamed the latter on the vending machine; it had been the chef around the station.

Summed up, he'd been a goddamn mess. That was when he'd decided he had to try once again to lay off the booze. A sour taste invaded Stone's mouth; he swallowed hard.

If only he'd been around, if only he'd stayed in Austin and fought for himself, for Sally's sake, if nothing else, then maybe he wouldn't be living this nightmare.

"So, go on," he said at last, his voice low and harsh.

"If she was drinking, I didn't know it. But the boy who was driving the car *was* drinking."

"So let me get this straight. She was riding with someone who was drinking. Jesus, Connie, at thirteen what was she doing with that guy in the first place? She's too young to date."

"What would you know?" she countered vehemently, her eyes wild. "Lots of girls date at thirteen. Besides, she told me another couple was going with them."

"And that made it all right?"

"Yes, damn you, it did."

His guilt and the brutal reality of the situation formed a pocket of agony inside him that nothing could penetrate. His daughter might die because this stupid woman had used such poor judgment. He shouldn't have been surprised.

"Okay, okay, calm down," Stone finally said in a tight voice. "We can't undo what's happened, but if she—" Again he broke off, unable to voice the unthinkable. "When she recovers, then we can make things right."

"Oh, really?" Connie spat, pinning him with a stare so filled with hatred that he almost staggered backward. "Daddy dear to the rescue, huh?"

Refusing to let her bait him into another verbal slinging match, he ignored her bitter sarcasm. "I want to be alone with her for a while."

"Fine. It's about time you did something for her, even if it's sitting by her deathbed."

Once a bitch, always a bitch, Stone thought as he skirted around her and walked into Sally's room.

Now, forcing his thoughts off that heated exchange, Stone stood on unsteady legs and walked to the window just as a streak of lightning flashed across the sky, followed by a boom of thunder. He flinched, then turned back toward the bed and his daughter.

The only good to come out of his marriage was Sally. Ah, Sally. At one time she'd been the one reason he'd come home at night. Now he rarely saw her, which was best for her, he kept telling himself. If only he could reconcile that in his heart, he'd be all right. So far he couldn't. He had only to walk into his empty apartment and loneliness slapped him in the face.

Yet at the time, he had thought he was doing the right thing. Stone had always fantasized about becoming a cop, despite being raised on the "wrong side of the tracks," where cops were thought of as something less than garbage.

Through hard work, aided by a short stint in the service as a weapons specialist, his dream had become reality. He'd become that cop, but at a high cost. Soon after he'd married and fathered a child, tragedy had struck, which ended his marriage and cost him that child.

Oh, he had visitation rights, but since Connie had married again, this time snaring a man with megabucks, Stone had bowed out of the picture. Sally's stepfather could do more for her than he had ever done or would be able to do.

Still, Stone had missed his daughter, missed her smile, missed her cuddling in his arms when he read to her, missed helping her with her math. Yet he had truly believed she was better off without him in her life, especially as the bottle had become the panacea for his loneliness and the only salvation from the sewer he worked in every day.

Suddenly another expletive burst through Stone's lips. Now wasn't the time to dredge up any more of the past.

Sally's thick lashes fanned across the dark circles underneath her eyes. Would they become a permanent part of her? No, he'd make them go away when she got well.

Stone leaned his head against the cold windowpane. God, he was so tired, so full of remorse.

"Why?" The word escaped through his lips like a gut-wrenching plea.

He should've been the one lying in that bed, not her. Hell, Sally never hurt anyone in her life, while he seemed to hurt everyone who came in contact with him. For a moment he felt the urge to bang his hand against the glass. He could deal with physical pain much better than this. He'd been dealing with shit in one form or another all of his life, but he'd never let his emotions get involved, not even when he was married to Connie.

But now his child, his flesh and blood, was perhaps dying, and he wanted to kill someone. His insides screamed with the ignorant savagery and pain of a wounded animal.

A shudder ran through him.

"Daddy . . .?"

At first he thought his mind was playing an evil trick on him, that he'd heard her voice because he wanted to so badly. His body shook as though he had the palsy, and he couldn't breathe.

"Daddy . . . is that you?"

He swung around, and if he hadn't been leaning against the wall, his knees would have folded. Sally's eyes were open and she was staring at him.

With his heart in his throat, he bolted to the side of the bed and fell onto the chair beside it.

"Yes, sweetheart, it's me. I'm here."

"Are you sure I'm ... I'm not dreaming? You ... you look so different."

"Oh, Sally, love." Tears ran from Stone's eyes and splashed onto his hand. "You're not dreaming. I've lost weight, that's all. But it's you I want to talk about. I'm so sorry, so sorry."

She touched his face with the gentleness of dew falling on a rose petal. "Don't cry, Daddy. It's all right."

"No, it's not all right, but it's going to be."

"I hurt all over."

He leaned over and kissed her on the cheek, struggling to maintain his composure. "I know you do, but soon you'll be better."

"What happened?" she asked through cracked, dry lips.

Stone told her. When he finished a lone tear trickled down her face. He brushed it away with the tip of a finger. "Shh, everything's going to be just fine now."

"Daddy ... I didn't think I would ever see you again."

He touched her fingers, then placed her palm against his cheek and covered it with his hand.

"You ... need a shave," she said, trying to smile.

His heart turned over in his chest. "I'll have to take care of that, won't I, sweetheart?"

"You ... you won't go away again, will you?"

"No!" His tone was fierce. "I won't leave you again."

Her eyes fluttered. "Promise?"

"Cross my heart and hope to die."

That drew a weak smile. "I used to tell you that all the time, didn't I?"

"That you did, only now I'm telling you, and I mean it."

"I'm so tired, Daddy."

"I know. You sleep now. I'll be right here."

He knew he should run out of the room and get Connie and her husband. But for purely selfish reasons, he wanted to be alone with Sally for a few more precious moments.

Once the rest of her family and the medical personnel entered the picture, he would have to leave. But only for a while. As he'd promised, he would never disappear from her life again.

Stone watched her eyelids flutter shut, then stood, reached for his handkerchief, and dried his face. At that moment his vision and his thoughts cleared simultaneously.

His head thudded and his eyes smarted again. Yet a smile flitted across his lips, bringing relief to his exhausted features.

He would do what he should've done from the start. He would right a wrong. He would stay in Austin and clear his name, set the record straight once and for all. He would find out who had wanted Phillip Whitmore dead and why. In doing that, he would exonerate himself.

With his head held higher than it had ever been, Stone buzzed the nurse's station and then walked to the door. But he didn't open it until he'd turned back toward the bed where his daughter slept.

"I'll see you later, Sally love."

It was almost as if she heard him, for he was certain she smiled. Another tear ran down his cheek. He didn't bother to wipe it away. In that moment he knew her recovery meant he was being given a second chance. This time he wouldn't blow it.

That was his promise to himself and his gift to Sally.

# Three

Stone left his daughter's room, finally giving in to hunger. Hospital food left him as cold as the dishes they served. If he planned to eat something, though, he would have to stop by the teller machine at his bank and get some cash.

A short time later he pulled onto the lot, muttering under his breath when he saw the long line of cars waiting to use the machine. This was the same bank he'd used for years as an Austin police officer, and even after he'd left town he kept the account open with a balance of two hundred dollars. But every time he pulled up to First Austin, he was reminded of how he got into that shitstorm in the first place, how what had happened at this particular bank had sent his life down the toilet. He could still see Captain Rutgers's face turning beet red and his jowls quivering.

"Don't you dare get smart with me. You're a loaded cannon, McCall, just waiting to go off. And the only reason you're still around is that underneath all that bullshit, you're a good cop, or at least you used to be. I don't know what's happening to you, but whatever it is, you'd best shitcan it before you get *shitcanned*. Is that understood?"

"Yes, sir."

"It damn well better be. I'll cover your butt on this one, but no more. Keep your goddamn city car out of store windows. Can you live with that? This habit of doing things 'your way' has gotta stop. You play by the rules or you're suspended."

"Yes, sir," Stone repeated, jamming both hands into the pockets of his suit pants to keep from punching his superior.

Rutgers puffed on his cigarette for another moment, then said, "Go on, get the hell outta here."

Stone walked back to his office and slammed the door behind him, though he continued to feel the stares of the others in the outer bullpen. Thank God for blinds. At least they wouldn't be able to see his festering misery.

He plopped down onto the squeaky chair behind his cluttered desk and quelled the urge to add another dent to the wood with his fist. He closed his fingers into a tight ball and gritted his teeth. So what if he had a habit of doing things "his way," as Rutgers had so brazenly put it?

He got the job done, and he knew that in most instances he was respected, if not feared, by his peers. When push came to shove, his fellow officers *wanted* him at their backs. That should speak for something, McCall thought, that sour taste returning to his mouth.

Unfortunately, though, there were some who didn't bother to hide the fact that they thought he broke too many rules and got by with it. Stone refused to let that bother him. He had to do what he had to do.

The door of Rutgers's office opened again within a few minutes and he shouted, "Get in here, McCall, on the double."

Stone ground his teeth again, harder this time, thinking Rutgers would unload a fresh dose on him over wrecking the car. He trudged wearily into the captain's domain.

"Sit down," Rutgers ordered. "There's been another homicide."

Stone loosened his tie as if he were about to choke. "Where?" Did he sound as tired and disgusted as he felt?

"At a warehouse on the east side of town," Rutgers said before lighting a cigarette and inhaling.

Stone reached in his own pocket and repeated the captain's gesture. Maybe if he ever stopped drinking, he'd stop smoking, too. Now, that was a nice thought.

"The warehouse operates under the name Texas Areo Industries," another detective said. "Man, they're a big operation."

"That name ring any bells with you, Stone?" Rutgers asked.

Stone shifted on his chair. "Nope. Should it?"

"Not necessarily," Rutgers responded. "Just thought it might."

"Since it is such a big operation," Stone said, "you think it might be part of a conglomerate?"

"More than likely," Rutgers answered. He focused his attention on the black detective. "Tom, why don't you fill McCall in on the details?"

Tom faced Stone, who chose that moment to sneeze. "Bless you," the black man said with a grin.

"Thanks," Stone muttered.

"For starters," Tom continued, "they make spare airplane parts there."

"So who got waxed?" Stone prodded, deciding that summer or not, he was going to catch his death of pneumonia, especially with the air-conditioning blowing down his neck.

"An employee by the name of William Bledsoe. By the time we arrived on the scene, he was sprawled in the middle of the floor, a bullet hole in his chest."

"Dead?" Stone asked.

Tom shook his head to the contrary. "In fact, he grabbed me by the shirt and tried to tell me something. He had so much blood in his mouth, all I could make out was 'gun' and 'Whitmore.'"

The black detective grinned, adding, "And if that doesn't blow your skirt tail up, try this: The bullet drilled straight through a Whitmore business card in his pocket. Of course the damned bullet took out the first name on the card. I know of at least four Whitmores, but you can't tell from the card which one it was."

"As in the Whitmore ranching family?"

"I doubt that," Rutgers put in quickly.

Stone focused his gaze on the captain. "What makes you say that?"

For a moment Rutgers seemed to squirm a trifle uncomfortably. Finally he cleared his throat and said, "For one thing, the Whitmores are a big, powerful family with a lot of money."

"So?" Stone pressed.

Rutgers's eyes narrowed. "So, they don't go around knocking people off, for God's sake. They've got class."

Stone snorted. "Since when does having class mean you can't or don't commit murder?"

"These people don't need to commit murder; they're filthy rich. *God* borrows money from the Whitmores when He's tight."

Stone shook his head. "I've usually found that if they're filthy with it, they're just as filthy without it. Right now the name Whitmore is our only lead. We've no choice but to run with it."

Rutgers didn't say anything, but Stone knew that underneath that seemingly calm facade, the captain was steaming. For some reason he wanted to protect the Whitmores, which piqued Stone's curiosity and made this case all the more interesting.

He turned his attention back to the detective. "Did anyone see the shooting take place?"

"Not that anyone would admit," Tom said. "The head man at the plant acted shell-shocked himself, but he figures the killing's union related. The company's been battling the union for months out there."

"What did the lab boys say?" Stone asked. "Did they come up with anything?"

"They're still sifting through everything," the detective added, "but they won't find anything helpful."

They discussed the shooting for a while longer, then Rutgers told the detective to leave him and Stone alone.

Once the door closed behind the officer, Rutgers's eyes once again narrowed on Stone. "Don't even think it."

"Think what?"

"Don't play the innocent with me. You're toying with the idea the Whitmore family's somehow involved in that killing, and that's just not so."

"You know something you're not telling me, Captain?"

"What the hell does that mean?"

"It means, how do you know they're not involved?"

"Gut instinct."

"Well, gut instinct isn't enough for me." Rutgers's gut was big enough, he should know everything with a certainty.

"So what are you suggesting?"

Stone moved closer to the edge of his chair. "I'm suggesting that we check them out the same as anyone else in a murder investigation."

"Look here, McCall, you don't go accusing one of the most prominent and law-abiding families in Austin of murder!"

Stone clamped down on his jaw and hoped that what he was about to say wouldn't piss off his boss any further. "I'm not suggesting that we accuse them of anything. All I'm saying is that I check them out. If there's no smoking gun, then I'll back off like a scalded cat."

"Shit, McCall, you can stop blowing smoke up my ass. You're like a sharp-toothed bulldog. Once you sink your teeth into something, you don't know when to let go."

Stone smiled without humor. "That's why I'm so valuable to this department."

Rutgers's scowl deepened. "All right, do your investigating, but you damn well better be discreet about it, you hear?"

"Loud and clear," Stone said, rising to his feet.

"Sounds to me like you're going to relish this job. Mind telling me why?"

"Not in the least. People with money and power, who think their shit doesn't stink, make me sick!"

\* \* \*

Three days later Stone McCall's eyes read every word on the single-spaced sheet.

The Whitmore name in Austin was one to be reckoned with. It was synonymous with power and wealth acquired through land, cattle, and oil.

To most, the Whitmore family loomed larger than life, proud and private, linked by Texas history to the Founding Fathers of our country. The Whitmores were truly big land, Old West.

Amos Fletcher Whitmore arrived in the rolling, brittle woodlands of the Texas hill country in the early 1870s, only a few years after he served as an officer in the Confederate army. With him was his young bride, Kathleen. Together they built a two-story home on the remote site.

The couple's original 180-acre tract soon grew to fifteen thousand acres, and Amos and Kathleen had only one child, a son they named Vaughn Amos. They doted on him, and they had good reason. He turned out to be not only bright, but most enterprising.

In 1915 Vaughn married Tilly Milam, a "kinswoman" of Col. Ben Milam. Vaughn and Tilly were greatly admired across the hill country.

The couple had three children: two girls and a boy. The girls died tragically, leaving the one son, Fletcher, named after his grandfather.

Years later, following the death of his parents, Fletcher took over where Vaughn and Tilly left off. He married and reared three sons. Each son inherited prime land and upheld the Whitmore tradition. . . .

"Yeah, right," Stone muttered as he slammed the folder shut, reached for a cigarette, and lit it.

Staring into space, he took two long draws, then ground out the cigarette in the ashtray where numerous other half-smoked ones were stacked.

He should go home, he told himself, his eyes feeling so grainy that he couldn't blink without wincing. He didn't dare rub them; that would only make them worse. Squinting, Stone looked at the clock on the wall of his office and saw that it was after midnight.

He flung down his pencil, rocked back on his chair, and listened to it squeak, an oddly comforting sound in the deserted office. Disgusted with his idiotic train of thought, he straightened and reached for another folder having to do with the Whitmore bunch, as he'd come to think of them.

He couldn't argue with the fact that they were a formidable family, and if he had any sense, he'd handle his investigation as though he were walking on eggshells. But he knew he wouldn't. First off, he doubted he had ever had any good sense. Second, he'd never walked on eggshells in his life, and he wasn't about to start now.

What he *was* about to start, though, was an in-depth probe inside the lives of the Whitmores. In fact, he'd already begun with Phillip Whitmore's senatorial campaign. He'd placed an undercover officer as a volunteer in order to keep a close eye on Whitmore's movements.

With the help of outside sources who owed him favors, he'd put together his dossier on the family. The rest of that information stared back at him now as he reopened the folder, a trifle disappointed that he hadn't uncovered any personal dirt.

As for corporate dirt—well, that was a different matter altogether and one that he hadn't explored to its fullest. Yet. But that was the next step in his plan of action. He didn't intend to leave one rock unturned in this investigation, despite the captain's edgy nerves.

Stone's eyes scanned the top sheet of paper. Only two facts stood out: Stanley Whitmore, the youngest son, was married to an alcoholic, who had been in and out of two private sanitoriums; Martha Whitmore, Fletcher's wife, had befriended a young orphan who became part of the family and later married Phillip, the eldest son.

To the world at large, the Whitmores represented a model family. Still, Stone's gut instinct said differently. These people were the type who committed their sins behind closed doors. Their wealth ensured secrecy.

Yes, something smelled foul here, and he wasn't about to be put off. No cop worth his salt would be. When a man who'd just been shot and lay dying muttered a certain name with a business card in his pocket, what choice as a cop did he have but to investigate?

The phone at his elbow rang. He jumped, cursed, then reached for the receiver. "McCall."

"Hey, man, it's Larry."

Larry Meadows was a friend and ex-partner on the force who was in a position to return a favor now that he worked for a large insurance company with clout. The company had access to people in high places.

Larry had tried several times to get Stone to quit the force and work with him. Stone hadn't even considered the offer. He liked being a cop. Or maybe he felt more comfortable in the sewer, a painful thought he would always thrust aside.

Now, though, he was glad he had someone "in the know" like Larry to yell to for help. He had called Larry and asked him if he knew anything about Texas Aero Industries. Larry had said no, but that he'd see what he could find out.

"So what the hell are you doing up at this ungodly hour?" Stone demanded.

"Marge took the kids and went to her mother's for a few days."

"Ah, so you're rattling around in that big house by yourself, huh?"

"That's about the size of it. And I don't like it, either."

Stone chuckled. "No, I bet you don't, 'cause you're one lucky s.o.b."

"How's that?"

"Marge. She's every man's dream wife."

"Yeah, I guess you're right. But I miss the kids just as much."

Stone's gut suddenly knotted. He knew how that felt. He

missed his kid so badly at times that it made him sick. Like now.

"Stone, you still there?"

"Yeah."

"I got as much info as I could on Texas Aero and their warehouse operation."

Stone brightened. "Great."

"It's not much, but it's the best I could do."

"Whatever it is, it's better than I have. Fax it to me, okay? I owe you one."

"No, you don't. I'll always owe *you*. Don't forget I'm still kicking because of you."

"Well, thanks, anyway."

"Hope it helps."

Moments later Stone reached into the fax tray and took out several sheets of paper. His adrenaline had kicked into such a level that he was sweating and his mouth was dry as cotton.

He fell back onto his chair, then began to read. The beginning of Larry's report dealt with information that Stone already knew. He'd learned from the detective's report at the time of the shooting that spare airplane parts were manufactured in the warehouse, then sold to commercial airlines. That in itself was no big deal, at least not to the unsuspecting eye.

What was a big deal and what Stone hadn't known was that the Whitmores owned the building. He felt his excitement mount. So if they owned the building, maybe they owned a piece of the action there as well. So what did that mean?

Murder, maybe?

Stone stood, rubbed his eyes again, then called Larry and told him the information was what he had hoped it would be.

"Thanks again, old friend. If you were to walk through that door, I'd be tempted to kiss your ugly mug."

"You've been divorced too long, Stone. Get a grip."

# Four

Stone parked his unmarked police vehicle in the bank's parking lot and got out.

The bright sunlight burned his eyes, but he flinched only marginally; his stomach burned worse. He reached in his pocket for the package of Tums he kept there, never knowing when he would need them. Lately it had been several times a day. He suspected he was getting an ulcer. He just hoped that was all it was. If he didn't slow down . . .

"Ah, give it a rest," he spat as he made his way toward the steps of the bank, reminding himself that a full schedule had driven him to the bank and that he was energized by the thought that his investigation into the Whitmores could take a positive turn.

First, the undercover agent he'd placed in the campaign had overheard one of Phillip Whitmore's campaign aides say that Whitmore had an important meeting here with his attorney. Stone knew he wouldn't see or learn anything from that private meeting, but by being on hand, he just might get lucky and pick up some tidbit that could be useful.

Second, he'd received more information from his buddy, Larry, who told him that Texas Aero Industries kept their main office in this bank, his bank. And it just so happened that he needed to make a deposit to his account, as it was payday.

Couldn't have worked out better, he thought, whistling.

His plan of action was to make his deposit while keeping his eyes peeled for Phillip Whitmore, then visit one of the vice presidents, who just happened to be a woman he'd dated; they had managed to part on good terms.

He smiled again. It might cost him a dinner, but he hoped she just might be forthcoming with some information concerning Texas Aero. Yeah, dinner and a night on the town would be a small price to pay, even if seeing this woman socially was the last thing he wanted to do.

He'd sworn off relationships. Relationships, hell! He'd sworn off women, period.

Straightening the knot in his tie, then shoving back a strand of hair that the wind had blown onto his forehead, Stone made his way across the pavement. Once inside the bank, he went directly to the deposit stand. For some inexplicable reason, though, something made him pause and scan the premises.

It wasn't the man who first caught his attention, even though he was none other than the would-be senator from Texas, Phillip Whitmore. It was the woman with him—his wife, Stone presumed—who captured his entire attention.

Obviously pregnant, she seemed to exude sexual intensity, especially as she chose that moment to lick her full, lower lip, which reminded him of a pouting child's. And her hair. What the hell color was it? It wasn't blond, nor was it brown. Honey. Yeah, that was it. She had honey-colored hair.

Suddenly a woman appeared beside him. "Excuse me," she said, reaching for a deposit slip.

"Christ!" Stone said when he realized what he'd been thinking.

"Excuse me?" the woman next to him said again, this time throwing him a nasty look.

"Sorry," he said in what he hoped was an apologetic tone, though she continued to give him a judgmental look.

Screw her, Stone thought, his gaze back on the couple who

were heading toward the elevator. Determined to keep an eye on *them*, he moved from behind the table and walked toward the elevator himself, only to pull up short.

"Ah, Senator," a heavyset man said, "wait up."

Phillip Whitmore smiled, then extended his hand. "Hello, Ken." When the handshake was completed, Whitmore's smile grew. "Although I like the sound of that word 'senator,' don't you think it's a little premature?"

The man called Ken laughed, and when he did, a huge gap in his front teeth showed. "Not at all. You're gonna win. Why, hell, man, that's a given."

"Thanks. I appreciate that," Phillip said politely, then added, "Have you met my wife, Natalie?"

He extended his hand again. "A pleasure, ma'am."

"Likewise," Natalie Whitmore answered in a husky voice that was as sensual as that "pouty" lower lip.

Out of the blue, Stone felt a twist in his gut, as thoughts he ought not to be thinking settled in that lower hot spot. He swallowed an expletive, as he didn't want to be any more conspicuous.

Besides, he was here to do a job, and that job was not slobbering over Phillip Whitmore's wife.

Stone yanked his mind back under control and watched as Phillip pushed the elevator button, only to be distracted once again. An elderly lady grabbed his arm, which set the stage for another conversation.

Frustrated, Stone reached in his pocket for a cigarette, then noticed a NO SMOKING sign. He jammed his hands down into his pockets and leaned against another deposit table.

While the conversation between the Whitmores and the lady continued, Stone watched two men stroll into the bank. Every nerve ending in his body reacted. He didn't know what made him suspect them of anything out of the ordinary. They weren't dressed conspicuously. To the contrary, they were dressed like clean-cut citizens. Maybe it was the cold, deadly look in their eyes that was the giveaway, alerting him they were up to no good.

More likely it was the guns they suddenly pulled.

"Everyone freeze!" yelled the shorter of the two.

"Yeah, move and you're dead," the second gunman yelled, echoing his partner.

Luckily Stone was not in their direct line of vision, which gave him the chance to push back his jacket and unholster his pistol. He held it low, beside his leg and out of sight. Dammit, that was all he could do at this point. No way could he further endanger the lives of innocent citizens by letting these scumbags see his weapon.

He'd bide his time and maybe get a chance to make a move before—Where was that damn bank guard, anyway? Stone hoped the old man was smart enough not to try any heroics. He felt sweat begin to affect his grip on the pistol.

The tall gunman had moved closer to the elevator. The lady next to Phillip Whitmore suddenly screamed, and Stone could tell that agitated the gun-wielding thug.

"Shut the fuck up, lady!" the man hollered, and lifted his gun.

Only he didn't point it at the woman. Stone noticed the barrel was pointed directly at Phillip Whitmore, and the blood in his veins turned to ice water.

Several other patrons screamed.

Instinct and long years of training kicked in; without thinking, Stone assumed a two-handed grip on his Smith & Wesson, going into a half squat as he aimed at the gunman.

Some idiot behind him shouted, "He's got a gun, too!"

The gunman whirled, sighted Stone, his .45 automatic already raised. His eyes seemed to recognize the police crouch, and he jerked off a quick shot.

The hammer on Stone's .357 was already falling when he felt the sting of the bullet strike his forearm, knocking his pistol to the right, changing his point of aim, just as the hammer punctured the bullet primer. The heavy pistol bucked in Stone's hand milliseconds thereafter.

Instantly he realized what had happened. He watched in horror as Phillip Whitmore was slammed backward, bouncing off the elevator doors and crumpling to the floor. He'd been shot cleanly through the head.

Natalie Whitmore screamed, then also crumpled to the floor.

Instant chaos erupted, giving the two gunmen time to exit the bank.

"Someone call 911!" a man yelled, cradling Phillip's head.

"Oh, God, he's dead!" another cried. "And she's passed out. Oh, my God . . . oh, my God!"

Stone knew there wasn't one damn thing he could do for Phillip Whitmore; surely someone would look after his pregnant wife. He took off after the men, but by the time he reached the street, they were nowhere in sight.

Unwilling to give up, he ran another couple of blocks, checking all the side streets. He saw a dark-colored van in the distance, but he had no way of knowing if it contained the gunmen. That wasn't enough to go on to put out a vehicle description.

"Dammit to hell!" He reholstered his pistol and looked at his left arm. His jacket sleeve was soaked, and his blood dripped onto the pavement. In the excitement of the moment, he'd been unable to feel anything, but now the pain kicked in with a vengeance. Stone held the injured arm with his other hand and ran back toward the bank.

He rounded the curve just in time to see the ambulance pull away from the curb, its siren screaming.

Two days after the bank shoot-out, he'd walked back into the station, straight into another damn nightmare.

The captain had spotted him instantly and said, "Get in here, McCall. I wanna talk to you."

Same old song, Stone thought wearily, just a different verse. But for once, none of the other cops said a word. They merely stared at him as he made his way toward the inner sanctum. His cohorts' sealed lips should've been his first clue that the hatchet was about to fall. Only he hadn't paid much attention, as he was still weak from the gunshot wound and from losing so much blood. Also, the drugs they had given him had his mind a bit fogged.

But Captain Rutgers's mind wasn't fogged, nor had he danced around the proverbial rosebush. He'd stuck the thorn straight into Stone's unsuspecting flesh.

"This time you've stepped in it way over your head," Rutgers said without even asking him to sit down. Stone sat down anyway, too exhausted to remain standing.

"I suppose you're referring to the bank fiasco."

"What else?"

"Yeah, what else?" Stone muttered. While he'd been recovering in the hospital, he'd assumed he'd be exonerated without Internal Affairs ever sticking their nose in the case. So much for his thoughts on the matter.

"I did my job, Captain," he said, closing the silence.

"No, what you did was shoot an innocent bystander."

"Who was about to get drilled by that gun-wielding robber."

"That's your side of it."

"And that's the right side because that's the truth."

Rutgers moved his mouth around as though he had a wad of snuff in the bottom of his lower lip and was about to spit instead of puffing on the burning cigarette between his fingers. "Not according to IA."

"Screw IA."

"Not this time, McCall. IA returned a finding that you violated departmental policy in firing your weapon."

"Even if I was trying to save a man's life?"

"Goddammit, don't you understand who you iced?"

"Ah, so that's what this is all about. The Whitmores are saber rattling, huh?"

"You could say that." For once Rutgers looked uncomfortable.

"Ah, shit, Captain, don't go soft on me now. Give it to me straight. I'm a big boy; I can take it."

"Can you?"

"Try me."

"Okay, the Whitmores have indeed been saber rattling. Either that rogue cop is dismissed, old man Whitmore said, or the city can expect a federal Section 1983 lawsuit."

"So the city figures the family would collect, which means it's cheaper just to go ahead and fire McCall's butt. Does that about cover it, Captain?"

"That about covers it, I'm afraid."

While it might have been a close call, Stone knew he had made enough enemies within the rank and file that most of the higher-ups wanted him gone. The die had been cast, and there wasn't one thing he could do about it, except get the hell out of Dodge and never look back.

He stood, stared hard at the man he knew had an intense personal dislike of him, reached for his gun and then his badge, and slammed them down on Rutgers's desk. Then, with a crooked smile, he said, "Have a nice life, Captain."

When he'd made that smart-ass statement, Stone had thought he'd be the one who'd have the nice life. Unfortunately that hadn't been the case. He'd found that he'd had to sink deeper into hell before he could begin to climb out.

"*Ex-cop* McCall," he'd said aloud as he drove away from the bank and toward the International House of Pancakes two blocks away. But he'd known he would always think of himself as a cop, even though he was finished in law enforcement. He didn't miss it, especially once he had reached New Mexico and gotten a taste of working as a hand on a cattle ranch.

He smirked now, thinking it bizarre that a fired cop would end up working on a ranch. Well, stranger things had happened, he guessed. In the scheme of things it hadn't meant a tinker's damn how it came about. The fact was it had saved his life.

One morning he'd picked up the *American Statesman*, the first he'd opened in months, and over numerous cups of coffee perused the want ads.

The advertisement for hands on a New Mexico ranch had leapt out at him, and for the first time in weeks he had felt a twitch of excitement, of hope. Then both had died an instantaneous death, especially after he stood, walked to the mirror in the bedroom, and stared at himself.

Sloppy. Overweight. Bloodshot eyes. Those had been just a few of the colorful adjectives that had described him. Hell, who would want to hire a has-been? He'd laughed, but the laughter held no mirth. Maybe a circus, he'd told himself, turning away from the image, sickened.

In that moment Stone had known he had to do something about his lifestyle or he was destined to become a statistic. He couldn't keep drinking instead of eating. He couldn't keep beating up on himself because he was no longer gainfully employed. And he couldn't do without any more sleep.

With those thoughts preying on his mind, he had continued to think about that advertisement. Finally he'd decided, Aw, what the hell. He'd go for it, and if he got turned down, then he'd survive that, too. But then all he'd been doing was just that—surviving. He hadn't been living; he was merely a dead man walking among the living.

He'd called the number, and miraculously he'd been hired. The fact that he could ride—his ex-wife had been an avid horsewoman—and the fact that he'd had no obligations had weighed heavily in his favor.

Once he'd arrived on the ranch, he'd worked as he'd never worked before, even counting the long hours he'd put in as a cop. The weight began to fall off. His skin tanned a golden brown. But more important, he stopped drinking and smoking, hurdles he hadn't thought he'd ever jump.

And he'd been damn proud of himself for that and for the transformation of his body. Too bad he hadn't tried this type of rigorous self-discipline when he'd been on the force. He'd managed to live one day at a time on the ranch, on the open range, and get his mind and body in tiptop condition. At least he could look into the mirror these days and not want to smash it with his fist.

He was damn proud of what he'd accomplished, especially staying off the booze and the cigarettes. But down deep in his soul was a different matter altogether. That part of him hadn't received the same make-over. His soul remained in sad shape.

Before and after he'd left Austin, he hadn't given a rip about anything or anyone, except Sally. She'd been on his mind, though he'd been too crippled mentally and physically to reach out to her. Yet he'd written her numerous letters, only to tear them into tiny pieces.

So when it came to his daughter, he still had some whopping sins to pay for.

How had he let their relationship get so far out of hand? Hell, for the first few years of her life, he'd been a good father. Maybe not an excellent one, but a good one. And through all the horrific pain and despair he'd suffered, he'd never stopped loving her.

Good, bad, or ugly, he was her father, goddammit. The job and the bottle had colored his judgment, and somewhere along the journey in and out of that jungle, he'd convinced himself that she had been better off without him.

He'd never make that mistake again.

# Five

The sunlight streaming through the window of Natalie's office warmed her neckline. She closed her eyes and fantasized that everything was all right, that her insides weren't knotted in turmoil. Last night's confrontation with Fletcher at the dinner party had left her more shaken than she cared to admit.

"Hey, why don't you go home?"

Natalie blinked, then opened her eyes fully as she saw the owner of Miracle Realtors, her boss, Lucy Gentry, standing in the doorway.

Natalie frowned. "Now, why would I want to do that? It's early yet."

"For starters, you look like hammered shit."

Natalie had to smile. If anyone else had talked to her like that, she would've taken offense, especially in her highly emotional state of late. But not so with Lucy, who was more of a friend than a boss.

Lucy had a tiny body and features. However, when she opened her mouth, that doll-like demeanor was quickly dispelled. One realized instantly that underneath the charm was an intelligent and savvy businesswoman who knew how to bring out the best in people. That was one reason her real estate company was getting a name for itself.

Natalie counted her blessings that she'd been given the opportunity to work for Lucy and learn the business from the ground up.

Now, however, business appeared to be the last thing on Lucy's mind. Her face registered concern. "Did you hear what I just said?"

"Of course I heard you," Natalie responded, a pensive look on her face. "Maybe there is something I need to take care of. . . ."

"Anything I can do to help?"

"No, it's something I have to do for myself, but thanks for letting me leave early."

"You don't have to thank me for that. I don't need one of my agents scaring off the paying customers. Get lost for the day, kid."

Natalie pulled up and parked at the Austin Public Library, her mind in disarray as she faced the prospect of beginning the research into Phillip's death. As distasteful as this was to her, she would see this through despite Fletcher's thinking this was a mere whim that would go away. It wouldn't, for she had no intention of backing down.

A short time later she made herself at home, pulling a halfway comfortable chair up to the microfiche projector. The task of wading through all the publicity that had surrounded her husband's death was so overwhelming that her stomach did a flip-flop.

None of this would have been necessary if she hadn't overheard that one conversation between Fletcher and Martha, the one that had set this painful chain of events in motion and changed the way she would look at the Whitmore family for the rest of her life.

Natalie hadn't planned on eavesdropping on her in-laws' conversation, but she couldn't have moved even if she'd wanted to. Her legs had taken on the consistency of Jell-O. What had Martha been talking about? Had the daily paper done another story on Phillip? She had her own copy in her room, but she hadn't read it, nor had she wanted to read it. Following the tragedy, she hadn't been well enough to read. Later she hadn't wanted to know the sensational accounts of what happened. And still didn't.

Didn't the columnist have anything else to write about? How cruel, she cried silently, and how unnecessary to keep harping on Phillip. Even though she hadn't read them, she knew they had already written, rewritten, hashed, and rehashed the tragedy many times. And now they had apparently done it again.

"Because they're a bunch of goddamn idiots, that's why!" Fletcher was saying, his tone filled with venom.

"There's no need to curse." Martha's tone was soft, but her chin wobbled as if she would break into tears at any moment.

"You're damn right there is," Fletcher countered, "especially when this garbage's splattered all over the paper."

Natalie was about to force herself to move, to enter the room, when again Martha's voice stopped her. "Fletcher, do you think we'll ever know what really happened that day? I mean—"

Martha broke off suddenly, and Natalie didn't blame her. From where she was standing, she could see her father-in-law's face, and it had turned brutally harder and colder than usual.

"We *know* what happened that day," he said through clenched teeth. "And don't you ever question that or me again." He shoved back his chair and stood, then gazed down at her for what seemed a long bitter moment, as if trying to compose himself.

Martha began to shake all over, and Natalie had to fight the urge to defend her fragile mother-in-law. But she didn't. No one had crossed Fletcher on that issue. So far.

"I oughta sue that goddamn paper and shut them up once and for all."

"I don't think that's the answer," Martha said in a still wobbly tone. "I want so desperately for us to pick up the pieces of our lives and go on, but we can't seem to do that."

"Maybe there is a way."

Though Fletcher's tone remained harsh, at least some of the venom had disappeared. He seemed limp and drained.

Martha's face brightened. "How?"

"Through Clancy."

"Clancy?" Her features turned into a frown. "You're not making sense."

"Oh, yes, I am. Think about it. Clancy's the only thing we have left of our son. I can't bear the thought of losing—"

"We're not going to lose her," Martha finished for him, a confident smile on her face. "This is her home and always will be."

"I know, which makes her *our* responsibility."

Martha looked confused. "I . . . guess so."

"There's no guessing about it. Even though she's only a baby, it's time we thought about her present as well as her future, like which private school to enroll her in, among other things."

Natalie balled her fist and crammed it against her mouth to keep from gasping aloud and alerting them to her presence.

Fletcher had a faraway look in his eyes. "There's nothing too good for my granddaughter."

"Now, Fletcher, that's going a bit far too fast, don't you think? After all, she has a mother. Natalie's perfectly capable of making the right decisions for *our* granddaughter."

Fletcher snorted. "You don't really believe that, do you?"

"Of course I believe that," Martha snapped, an incredulous look on her face.

"Well, I don't."

"Just what are you saying?" Though Martha's tone was quiet, Natalie heard the steel behind it.

"For chrissake, Martha, have you forgotten where that girl came from?"

" 'That girl,' as you're calling her, is Natalie, our daughter, for God's sake."

"I'm not disputing that."

"Oh, yes, you are. Besides, none of this matters. She's—"

"Oh, but it does matter," Fletcher said, cutting her off. "It matters a whole helluva lot."

"Fletcher, you're talking absolute nonsense. If these articles are going to upset you like this, don't read any more of them."

"What I'm saying here goes much deeper than that goddamn article."

"You're really serious, aren't you?"

"Hell, yes! All I want is what's best for Phillip's daughter." When Martha would've opened her mouth again, he went on, "What if Clancy turns out like Natalie's mother? Stranger things have happened. Have you ever thought about that?"

Martha gasped, then stared at her husband as though he'd taken complete leave of his senses.

Natalie didn't gasp, but she wanted to, only she was too weak to open her mouth. It was as if Fletcher's brutal words had severed an artery and all her blood had seeped from her body.

"I'm right, you know," Fletcher pressed, his features angry. "We can't take that chance. We have to have a hand in Clancy's raising."

"My God," Martha said at last, "why on earth did you ever agree to take Natalie into our home?"

"Because you wanted to so badly. At the time, who could have known that she would marry our oldest son and have a child? Hell, if I'd ever suspected that, Natalie would never have set foot in this house."

Tears trickled down Martha's face. "Oh, God, I had no idea you felt that way, but even at that you were never able to refuse Phillip anything."

"Well, I should've bucked him on this. There's bad genes there. You can't deny that, and it's our job to see that our granddaughter's never exposed to such evil goings-on."

"What you're saying is that Natalie might eventually become like her mother and drag Clancy with her. Why, that's crazy, Fletcher!"

"Crazy or not, that's the way I feel. I won't allow Clancy to become poor white trash. Clancy's a *Whitmore*, and I intend to have a say in her raising, mother or no mother. She's the only thing I have left of my . . . son."

Natalie reeled against the growing impact of Fletcher's vicious words. He might as well have hammered an ice pick into her heart.

*Damn you, Fletcher Whitmore!*

Natalie sat upright, staring at the dark projector screen. She hadn't even turned it on yet, but the memories continued to crowd their way into her mind.

Fletcher had wanted to control her life and Clancy's. No, she corrected herself, that wasn't quite the case. He not only *wanted* to control them, he *was* controlling them.

On the heels of that came another thought, one more jarring and frightening: Whose fault was that? Hers. She had let him get away with it.

Phillip's death, combined with that dreadful conversation, had crippled her emotions to the extent that she had put her life on hold, had lived in a zombielike state, except where Clancy was concerned. Only when she was around her daughter did she come alive.

While her child had not suffered, she had. Natalie could see that now. By refusing to deal with Phillip's death, she had done herself and her daughter a grave injustice. As of now, today, in this library, that would stop. She wouldn't hide from the truth anymore.

No longer was anyone going to make decisions for her or Clancy. She was sure that later, after the feeling of betrayal had subsided, she would be comforted by the fact that Clancy was loved by her grandparents and that they had her best interests at heart.

Now, though, pain and anger blinded her. Clancy was *her* child, and *she* knew what was best for her.

She had to get her head out of the sand and join the land of the living, Natalie told herself, which meant she had to do what no other person in the family was willing to do. She had to consider what the media had questioned and what had been in the back of her mind all along—the ugly truth that Phillip's death might not have been an accident.

She'd brought yesterday's paper with her and now reached for it, reading a lowercase headline of a front-page story:

"The Truth Concerning Texas Senatorial Candidate and Businessman Phillip Whitmore's Death Is Still Unknown"

Natalie cringed inside at the same time she wadded the paper and tossed it into her makeshift file folder.

"Leeches!" she muttered. "Nothing but bloodsucking leeches!"

Suddenly the old fear seemed to reach out and squeeze her heart. She didn't want to be reminded about Phillip's death. She wanted to keep that buried in the closet of her soul. She knew, however, that luxury was no longer possible. Again, she had to face the brutal truth that the newspaper could be right in its innuendos concerning Phillip's death, that there might have been more to it than his having been in the wrong place at the wrong time.

Too, she had to make a life for herself outside this family, more for Clancy's sake than hers. An embittered old man, no matter how much he had done for her, was not going to usurp her position in Clancy's life. His veiled threats at the dinner party were meaningless to her; she would not be put off.

She no longer had an alternative. She had to resolve the past and move forward into the future, no matter how painful or difficult. Natalie knew this newfound determination wouldn't be easy. No matter what her plan of action, the family would fight her. They were convinced Phillip's death had been a tragic accident. She wondered how it was that the entire family were much more intent upon punishing the cop who had accidentally shot her husband than they were on finding the robbers who had initiated the entire incident.

Public pressure and pressure from within the department had forced this cop to resign in disgrace, though again she had shied away from the newspaper accounts of the furor raised over all that. Part of that reluctance had stemmed from her complications with Clancy; both mother and child had almost died. But that was no longer an excuse.

She'd made a life-altering decision. What she had to do next was figure out how to carry it out.

Natalie's stomach continued to churn, and her head as well. She wished she could control her mind; if so, she would never have recalled that horrible conversation. How could Fletcher have faked his love all these years? It had been traumatic enough as a child, worrying whether she was ever accepted or not; then, when she'd come to grips as an adult, feeling she was *really* a Whitmore, this happens.

At age fourteen Natalie had been placed in a church juvenile home, having been sent there after a run-in with the law.

Although Natalie was considered a child, she had the maturity of one much older. She didn't view life through the same rose-colored glasses as most teens did.

She rarely smiled, but when she did, it lighted her entire face. That particular day she'd smiled. Martha Whitmore was taking her to visit the Whitmore ranch.

The Whitmores were large contributors to charity. The church juvenile home was Martha's favorite.

The first time Martha saw her, Natalie had sensed Martha cared. She had seen it in her eyes. Still, Natalie hadn't responded to the pull of Martha's heartstrings. Instead she'd stared at her out of sad eyes, afraid of getting close to others for fear she would lose them just as she had lost her mother.

Eventually Martha, in her sweet way, broke through Natalie's barrier. Natalie told her what happened to her mother and the type of life she had led. When Natalie finally stopped talking, both were crying.

That was why Natalie was both excited and shocked when the Whitmores' limousine parked in front of the colonial home in the Texas hill country. She had never seen a house like that, much less been inside one.

That day marked a new beginning for Natalie. Martha had always yearned for a daughter, and after discussing it with her husband, they had invited Natalie to move in with them. The ranch became her new home.

The Whitmores' three sons reacted differently to Natalie's presence. Phillip, the oldest, while polite, was rarely home; he was either at college or off with friends his own age. Daniel, the middle son, befriended her immediately. Stanley, the youngest, saw her as a threat and disliked her on sight.

During the years that followed, Natalie had the best money could buy. More than that, she learned what it meant to be part of a family, even though she experienced heartaches along the way.

But those heartaches were made bearable by Martha's never-failing love and Daniel's brotherly devotion. He became her shadow. When her favorite pet died, it was Daniel who comforted her. When she had trouble in school, it was Daniel who helped her. And when Stanley purposely hurt her, it was Daniel who defended her.

Yet it was Phillip she ultimately wanted to marry. Natalie had always admired Phillip and yearned for his attention. But it wasn't until after she graduated from college and went to work that he finally noticed she had grown up. Their relationship changed.

On Natalie's twenty-seventh birthday and shortly after Phillip's thirty-seventh, they married, then moved into a newly decorated wing of the house. At first she'd been reluctant to live with his parents, but Phillip had assured her it would be all right, that it was the "Whitmore way."

Two years later Natalie discovered she was pregnant. She

was delighted about the baby. She was also pleased with the success she'd made of her career.

She had gone to work for a real estate firm. Even though she was secure in her marriage and home life, holding on to her independence was extremely important to her.

Phillip had been successful as well. Following two successful terms in the Texas House, then the Texas Senate, he was a viable candidate for a seat in the U.S. Senate. Though Natalie didn't travel the campaign trail with him, she was actively supportive and along with the other family members eagerly awaited the outcome of the election.

Consequently, life was good. Martha continued to rule the household, Fletcher his cattle empire. Phillip had taken over the family's other businesses and kept them profitable.

Daniel was single and taught English at the university. He also lived at the ranch. Only Stanley, who worked on the ranch, had used part of his land to build on. Paula, his wife, refused to live in the big house.

Not so with Natalie. She'd loved being a part of a large, close-knit family, but had been constantly fearful that her good fortune would be snatched from her, and that fear became a brutal reality. . . .

"Ma'am, are you all right?"

Natalie jerked her head up and stared at the gray-haired librarian who was watching her.

"I'm . . . fine," she responded, swallowing around the lump in her throat.

The woman's expression didn't change; it remained troubled. "Are you sure? You haven't even started the projector yet."

Natalie forced a smile at the same time she dabbed at the tears on her cheek. "Yes, I'm sure. Thanks for asking."

"You're welcome." The woman stood there a second longer, then turned and walked off.

Natalie released a pent-up breath, focused her thoughts clearly on the present, and began work in earnest. After what seemed like only a moment, she glanced at her watch and saw that she'd been hunched over the microfiche reader for two hours. No wonder her shoulders and back burned, she thought, moving them up and down to get the circulation active again.

If it were not for the fact that she was sitting in the austere public library, she would have fallen to pieces. The old accounts of Phillip's death were hard to take. She had a few more newspaper articles to read, but she wasn't sure if she could get through them. Her heart had borne enough for one afternoon. Yet she knew she had to see this torture session through to the bitter end.

For all her show of confidence last night when she'd announced her intentions, she had realized this morning that she had no plan of action. Her verbal boasting had been just that and nothing more. She needed facts. That was why she had come to the library determined to read everything related to her husband's death.

SENATORIAL CANDIDATE KILLED BY POLICE IN FOILED
BANK HEIST

That headline was typical of how Phillip's death had been related in gory detail, as if each writer took great joy in reporting the tragic story. Only one writer, a certain Scott Timpson, seemed to be the exception. She sensed that he genuinely felt the pain of it all by the wording of his articles.

But it was the pictures of Phillip lying in a pool of his own blood that had brought on the tears of anger and helplessness. It was also those pictures that drove her to her feet, her chair giving off an agonizing screech.

Enough. She couldn't endure any more. Besides, she had accomplished what she'd set out to do, and that was force herself to find out what had happened that day. So a plainclothes detective had killed her husband. The man's name meant nothing to her, though she was determined that it would mean plenty before she was finished.

She had to leave the premises, get away from those photographs. The cramped microfiche area and the sterile surroundings had begun to grate on her nerves. Suddenly Natalie felt cold.

Only after she walked outside into the arms of the warm sunlight did she realize that never once had she seen a picture of the cop who'd shot Phillip.

Why? she asked herself, uneasy all over again.

# Six

The following morning that question still hovered on the edges of her mind. Natalie checked on Clancy, who was still asleep. When she came back upstairs, after getting a cup of coffee, she'd awaken her daughter and dress her. Today was Clancy's day at the nursery.

With the exception of Josie, Natalie expected to have the breakfast room to herself. This morning, however, she was far from alone. She pulled up short when she walked in and saw Daniel sitting at the glass-topped table with a cup of coffee in his hand.

"You're stirring early, and boy, am I glad to see you. I can really use your help with Fletcher; he intends to fight me every step of the way about looking into Phillip's death."

"Huh? What makes you think Daddy'll listen to me?" Daniel paused, giving her a sardonic grin. "Every time he looks at me, he still sees a long-haired, dirty-toed hippielike person."

"Don't leave out unshaven," Natalie cut in, forcing herself to smile, trying to relieve the pained expression on Daniel's face.

He cocked his head. "Yeah, can't forget that, can we?"

"Surely Fletcher's gotten past all that, now that you're a professor—an endowed chair, no less!"

That pained expression on Daniel's face deepened. "Don't count on it. You know I've always been different, marched to my own drummer. . . . Daddy couldn't accept my rebellion. I guess I embarrassed and shamed him, and he's never gotten over that."

Natalie frowned. "True, but Jeez—you were just a kid. We all did dumb things. Stanley and I certainly weren't perfect."

"Amen, but Stanley never wore long hair and had a hole in his jeans."

"At least you didn't wear an earring."

"God forbid. He would have disowned me for sure."

"Speaking of disowning," Natalie said, smiling, "I thought you were a goner that day you blew into the kitchen with your hair slicked back in a ponytail."

"And the judge, Daddy's best friend, was with him." Daniel rolled his eyes. "That old fart looked like he'd seen an alien. And I swear Daddy would've had a coronary on the spot if you hadn't laughed, jerked my ponytail, and said 'Let's split.'"

Natalie's smile was pensive. "Remember what we did?"

"How could I forget? We got a package of Chesterfields, sneaked out to the woods, and tried to smoke them."

They both laughed out loud, then Natalie sobered. "It's funny now, you jerk, but it wasn't at the time! You'd smoked before, but I hadn't. I thought I'd never stop throwing up."

"Yeah, Mom thought you were having an appendicitis attack and wanted to take you to the hospital. You were positively green."

"Thank God I stopped heaving about that time or I'd have had to 'fess up about what we'd done. I never smoked another cigarette, so I guess you did me a favor."

"I wish smoking had made me sick. Maybe I wouldn't have had to go through hell to kick the habit." He paused again. "What I'd give for those good old days and the fun times we had." Daniel's tone held sadness.

"I sometimes wish for them, too. I think what I miss most are the nights we watched all those horror movies we weren't supposed to watch."

"You used to bloody freak out."

Natalie smiled, then shivered as a silence fell between them. Both straightened noticeably as Fletcher and Martha walked in.

"Good morning," Natalie said, hearing the hesitancy in her voice. But then who wouldn't be hesitant, she asked herself, especially when the eyes turned on her were filled with hostility.

"Morning, all." Fletcher's tone was gruff, and he didn't look at her.

Only Martha's greeting seemed sincere. "Did you and Clancy rest well?"

"Actually, Clancy's still asleep."

Martha smiled over the rim of her cup, then began talking fast as if to cover up the smothering silence that had fallen over the room. "I plan to go into town today and buy Clancy a couple of new outfits."

"Oh, Martha, that's sweet of you. But really, she doesn't need anything else to wear. She outgrows them so fast."

"That doesn't matter."

Recognizing the stubbornness in Martha's tone, Natalie conceded. "All right, if that's what you want to do."

"So, what about you?" Fletcher asked. "What are you going to do today? Sell houses, I hope."

Natalie swallowed the scalding retort that rose to her lips. She would love to lash out at Fletcher, to let him know that she had overheard his and Martha's conversation, to watch his facial expression change to shock. But now was not the time to call his hand. Now was the time to remain true to her mission.

"Of course I plan to sell houses," she said with forced ease, "but that's not all I plan to do, as you well know."

"Then you're still going through with that cockamamie idea of yours?"

"That's right."

"No matter how Martha or I feel about it?"

It took a tremendous effort to maintain her composure under so much fire. "I don't want to hurt either you or Martha. You know that, or you should."

"I . . . none of us want to relive the pain that Phillip's death caused," Martha said in her sweet voice, reaching her hands toward Natalie. "Surely you don't want that, either." Her eyes were pleading.

"You're right, I don't. But I have to do what I think is best for me and Clancy."

"And to hell with everyone else. That's what you're saying, isn't it?" Before she could respond, Fletcher continued, "What the hell good will it do to find that cop? That's what I'd like to know."

"I want to talk to him."

"Pray tell, what for? Anyway, no telling where he is. After his screw-up, he hightailed it out of town in disgrace."

"He insisted one of those holdup men was going to shoot Phillip."

Fletcher snorted. "Just how the hell would you know that? You haven't shown any interest in talking or reading about anything to do with Phillip's death."

"You're right, I haven't. But that's changed now. I went to the library and read every article that was available." She paused. "And if it's the last thing I do, I'm going to find out what *really* happened that day in the bank."

Natalie looked up at Fletcher, who now stood, his stance formidable, like a slab of granite. She took a sip of coffee, trying to shake off a distinct chill.

"Take it easy, Dad," Daniel said, squirming uncomfortably on his chair but trying desperately to play the peacemaker. "Let's not say things here we'll all regret."

"Tell her that, not me."

Martha suddenly began to sob.

"See!" Fletcher bellowed, pointing at his wife. "That's all this kind of talk is good for. For God's sake, Natalie, think about Martha and what this will do to her. Hellfire, she's already had a near breakdown. You want her to have another one?"

"Dad, please calm down," Daniel said. "You know your blood pressure—"

"You let me worry about my goddamn blood pressure. If you ever had any influence with your sister-in-law, then I suggest you put it to good use right now."

Natalie felt her face drain of color as she stared wide-eyed at Daniel. She knew he was caught in the middle.

"So how 'bout it, sis? Will you reconsider? Will you let Phillip rest in peace?"

Natalie soothed her damp palms down her robe at the same time she strove to keep the tremor out of her voice. Daniel's rejection was almost more than she could bear.

"Again, I'm sorry if my intentions hurt you, but it's something I have to do."

"Goddammit!"

She ignored Fletcher's expletive and went on, "And there's something else I have to do, too."

"And what is that?" Daniel asked with unmasked pain in his tone.

Natalie disengaged her hand from Martha's clinging one. "As soon as I can financially swing it, I'm going to get a place of our own."

Although Phillip had left her a substantial life insurance policy, she intended to save that for Clancy's education. As far as cash, there hadn't been much left. His campaign had taken its toll on their bank accounts.

Fletcher stared at her in disbelief, his jaw hanging suspended as if frozen.

Daniel muttered, "Oh, God," and rolled his eyes heavenward.

Martha's sobs grew louder.

"Under the circumstances, I think it would be best," Natalie said, feeling as if a firecracker had just exploded inside her.

She wanted to lean over and empty the contents of her stomach. Instead she stood reed straight and waited for the ax to fall.

"I won't let you take the only thing that's left of my son," Fletcher said in a cold, biting tone.

"Please," Martha said, weeping. "You can't leave. This is your home."

Daniel stood now. "Natalie, have you lost your mind?"

She gave him a sad smile, feeling as if she were on the edge of a crumbling cliff. "No, Danny, I haven't lost my mind. Quite the contrary, in fact. After a year of aimlessness, I've found it again."

"Think about what's at stake here. If nothing else, think of what Mother and Dad have done for you."

She flinched as if Daniel had struck her physically. "I know I owe them my life."

"Well, then, pay us back by stopping this fool notion of yours." Fletcher's forehead was sprinkled with sweat, and his lips were taut.

For a moment Natalie felt her defenses waver. Daniel was right; she did indeed owe them more than she could ever repay, but she owed herself something, too, especially in light of Fletcher's true feelings for her. He had never loved her. She knew that now. And while that truth cut her to the bone, it also gave her the strength she needed to do what she had to do.

Natalie shifted her gaze from Fletcher to Martha. "Since I don't have a place of my own yet, I hope you'll let me stay till I do. Because I'm leaving doesn't mean I've stopped loving you. You're the only real mother I've ever known."

Martha looked at Fletcher with tears in her eyes. Her look met with a stony silence.

"But you should understand that I'm going ahead with my plans," Natalie added. She paused to let those words sink in. Then she turned and walked out of the room, but unfortunately not out of hearing distance.

"What . . . what are we going to do?" Martha wailed.

Natalie stopped and listened.

"Don't you worry," Fletcher said in a terse tone. "I'll take care of Natalie."

Was that a threat? She tasted bile at the back of her throat and walked away.

# Seven

He thrust hard, once, twice, then fell against her chest.

Paula dug her clawlike fingernails into the cheeks of his buttocks. "Get off me, this second."

Stanley raised up enough to look into his wife's pinched face. "What the hell you mean by that?"

"Exactly what I said. All you care about is yourself. You grunt two or three times, then come. You don't give a damn about me."

"So are you saying I'm not satisfying you?"

"That's exactly what I'm saying. I've seen some limp peckers in my day, but yours is—"

Stanley slapped her hard across the face.

She yelped before placing a palm over her smarting cheek. "Why, you . . . you—"

Still straddling her, Stanley lifted his hand again. "I suggest you keep your mouth shut. Besides, I've never had any complaints from anyone else about my pecker."

Paula shoved him off her and scrambled to the side of the bed. "I hate you, Stanley Whitmore!" she flung back over her shoulder.

"Yeah, yeah. So what else is new?"

She faced him. "You don't care about anybody but yourself and never have."

He looked her body up and down, his eyes lingering on the sagging breasts. Repulsed, he shifted his gaze. "At one time I cared, but no longer. You chose the bottle over me, remember? So, you don't have any bellyaching coming."

"Don't you ever hit me again!"

"I'll hit you any time the notion strikes me." He laughed, only it came out a sneer. "And you'll take it 'cause you like living off the fat of the land. Right, baby?"

"You're a sadistic brute."

He laughed again. "And you're a bitch. But that's about to change."

Paula rubbed her still-red cheek, then looked at him through leery eyes. "What does that mean?"

"It means you're going to clean up your act or I'm going to kick your drunken ass out."

"You wouldn't do that. Your daddy would have a conniption fit. You know how he feels about divorce."

"Not if he knew you'd been fucking around."

Her eyes widened with fear. "How'd you—"

"Hey, baby, I know everything that goes on, especially when it's related to what belongs to me. As far as I'm concerned, I don't give a shit who you get off with, but Daddy does."

"So what's your point?"

"My point is that you're going to stop behaving like a drunken slut and . . ." He paused and smiled suddenly, a cold, menacing smile.

"What, dammit?"

"Get pregnant."

"Me, get pregnant?" Her voice was high and shrill. "No way. I don't want a—"

Stanley got up, grabbed her, yanked her off the bed, and pitted them nose to nose. "Yes, you do."

"Stanley, stop it," she whined. "Stop talking crazy like

this. You know we agreed not to have any children. I don't want to be tied down. Besides, I hate kids."

"Well, you're gonna learn to love 'em." He pushed her away.

"What in God's name brought this about?"

"Clancy."

Paula blinked. "Clancy?"

"Yeah, Clancy. You haven't noticed, of course, 'cause you're drunk most of the time, but my old man is totally smitten with that kid, especially since his fair-haired son is pushing up daisies."

"Jeez, Stanley, you shouldn't talk about the dead that way."

"Who gives a shit? When you're dead, you're dead."

Paula didn't respond.

"Anyway, I don't want to take a chance on that brat getting any of my inheritance, like stocks and bonds and cashola."

Paula's eyebrows lifted. "Do you think there's that chance?"

"Ah, now I've got your attention."

"Go on," Paula said tightly.

"Hell, yes, I think there's that chance, although I don't think his holier-than-thou wife'll get a dime, especially after the stunts she pulled."

"Stunts?"

"Yeah. Not only is she planning to snoop into the cause of my brother's death, but she's also planning to haul ass."

"As in moving?"

"You got it."

"You mean Natalie's moving out of the big house?"

"That's what Dad told me."

Paula chewed on her bottom lip while seemingly lost in thought. "So it's safe to say Fletcher's pissed?"

"That's putting it mildly. And because his piss factor is so high, I think it's time to strike."

"I still don't see what good it would do if I got pregnant. Like you said, your old man's smitten with that brat simply because she's part of Phillip."

"Paula, use your brain for something other than banging it against a headboard. With Phillip's brat gone, maybe Daddy would make room for *our* kid."

Stanley spat his deceased brother's name as if he were spitting out a dose of poison. He wouldn't admit it to anyone, but he had always hated Phillip, and now he would make no apologies for his feelings. He had played second banana to his oldest brother all his life, and now he didn't have to. What he did have to do was figure out a way to get into his daddy's good graces and stay there.

At the moment a kid was the only thing he could think of that could elevate him to a higher standing. Hell, stuffy old Daniel wouldn't ever get married; he'd bet on that.

Yet he didn't really want a squalling brat to keep him awake at night any more than Paula did. Besides, Paula would make a terrible mother. But if a brat was what it took to hold to what was rightfully his and gain respect in Fletcher's eyes, then he'd bite the bullet and just hire a nanny.

"Maybe it would do some good, if I had a boy."

He stilled. "What did you say?"

"A boy," Paula repeated impatiently. "The old man would probably do handsprings over a *grandson*. You know how goddamn macho you men are, especially Fletcher. I'm surprised he didn't have Phillip tarred and feathered for producing a girl."

"Funny."

"I didn't mean for it to be. I'm serious."

He reached out suddenly and grabbed a breast.

"Ouch! Why'd you do that?"

"'Cause you gotta understand this isn't a game. If you want to stay Mrs. Stanley Whitmore, then you'd better listen. You stay your ass away from those scumbags you're sleeping with or I'll make you sorry in more ways than one."

Paula pulled back. "You're . . . you're scaring me."

"Good. Now, come on, play the whore with your husband."

"Stanley!" she cried as he sat down, grabbed her by the hair, and smeared her face into his crotch.

* * *

Stone craved a cigarette, but thank God he didn't want any booze. He could thank Sally for that, he thought with a smile, getting up and stretching his back. As he did so, he gazed around his apartment, then frowned.

While not a pigsty, it came close, which was too bad, as his daughter was about to visit him. He ought to be working like hell to clean it.

Ah, he still had plenty of time. Sally wasn't due for a few hours yet. But God, was he ever nervous. The closer the time came for her visit, the more his gut rebelled. Cleaning the apartment might be just the therapy he needed to ward off those nerves.

He grunted suddenly, thinking how ludicrous it was for a grown man who had addled more than one man's brain and had even taken a human life—all in the line of duty, of course—to be afraid of his daughter's impending visit.

Instead he should have nerves of steel from the days he'd stayed by her bedside in the hospital. But once she'd regained consciousness, her mother and stepfather had taken over. Still, Sally had insisted he come every day, and Connie had humored her.

Now, though, Sally was out of the hospital, and he hadn't seen her in a while, though he talked to her every day on the phone. It was yesterday that Sally had asked to visit him at his apartment.

"Daddy, when am I going to see you again?" Her tone was petulant.

"Whenever you want. Or whenever your mother or the doctor or both says it's okay."

"How about this afternoon?"

"This afternoon?" he repeated inanely, while his eyes circled the room that looked liked Beirut. "How 'bout tomorrow instead, sweetheart?"

She giggled. "Is your apartment a mess?"

"Yeah. How'd you guess?"

"It wasn't hard," she said airily.

"Hey, give your old dad a break, will ya?"

"All right," she said, following another giggle. "I'll wait till tomorrow."

"What time you want me to pick you up?"

"Mom said she'd bring me over."

"I'll take you home, then."

"Cool."

That had ended the conversation, and yesterday was now today, and the apartment still looked like hell.

In defense of himself, he'd been working, though not for bucks, Stone reminded himself. But a "real" job was something he wasn't worried about now. He was a man driven to fulfill a promise.

Besides, he'd saved enough money so that on occasion he could eat, pay his rent, and entertain his kid.

In between hospital visits, he'd gone to the newspaper morgue, where he had reread everything about the case, though he'd thought every detail was engraved in his brain. Yet he couldn't be sure because so much of that time his head had been filled with booze.

He'd been right. His long hours at the microfiche had been wasted. He'd come up with zip, except the undiluted fact that the Whitmores' influence had cost him his badge. He had come away with the old resentment and anger roiling inside him. But he hadn't let that anger cause him to self-destruct.

He had vowed to clear his name, which meant he had to find out *why* his probe of the family had proved so damaging. So he'd called a buddy on the force and asked a favor.

He needed Phillip and Natalie Whitmore's dossier, and that buddy had provided it. Natalie was the key he hoped would open the door to the past. He figured that *she* must have known what her husband was involved in, especially if he was the "Whitmore" who had been fingered by the dying employee that day in the warehouse. Perhaps she had not only known but had been in cahoots with him.

That nagging thought drove him to the cluttered desk in

the corner of the room. He picked up the manila folder again, sat down on the creaky chair, and thumbed through it.

Nothing had changed. The information on Natalie Whitmore had been and still was disappointing. Her parents were dead, and the Whitmores had taken her in.

"Lucky you," he mused aloud, though with a smirk on his lips.

Although there was a block of years missing in the report, he couldn't find a smoking gun there or in the here and now, at least nothing that caught his eye.

The fact that she worked for a real estate agency in the vicinity of his apartment, but continued to live at the family ranch and commute, wasn't surprising. What he did find surprising was that she even worked.

But it didn't matter what was on paper. He had to meet her. But how? That was the million-dollar question. Not only did he want to meet her, he wanted to get to know her—up close and personal, her strengths as well as her weaknesses. That was a tall order, but he was up to it. In fact, he was looking damn forward to nailing her hide along with her family's.

Once he made that personal contact, he intended to test *his* reaction as to her involvement in her husband's suspected criminal activities. That would definitely require finesse, more finesse than he currently possessed. But he'd do it. Hell, he'd turn on the charm, become a copycat Tom Cruise if that was what it took.

Stone had a sure thing in his favor. Even if she'd seen him, she wouldn't recognize him now. A year in the New Mexico sun on the back of a horse had changed his appearance drastically, not to mention the rigorous physical training he'd undergone.

Before, he'd had the makings of a paunch around his middle—beer gut, to be more exact. Now he was thin, but with muscles instead of flab. His hair was lighter, longer, and threaded with gray. Even his skin texture had changed; it was deeply tanned and leathery.

Besides his appearance, he had another plus in his corner. The department had never released his picture to the press.

Stone looked at his watch and, noticing the time, cursed. Not only did he have to clean, but he had to go to the grocery store as well.

God forbid. But kids ate a lot, didn't they? Weren't they supposedly human garbage disposals? Well, if Sally wasn't, she needed to be, having lost weight after her accident.

Opting to grocery shop rather than clean, he flipped off the light and sauntered out the door.

A short time later Stone had his basket loaded with both junk and healthy food when he stopped and did a double take.

"Nah," he muttered. "You're seeing things."

But was he? Hell, no. The woman who stood in front of the canned goods was none other than Natalie Whitmore in the flesh.

Talk about the gods smiling down on him! He began to shake all over. He'd never had luck of any kind. He'd never won a door prize, for chrissake! But he'd hit the jackpot today.

Slowly and deliberately he pushed his basket toward her, his tongue clinging to the roof of his mouth. She hadn't seen him, but the toddler occupying the seat in the buggy had.

She pointed at him, then said with a toothy grin, "Man."

Stone smiled to himself, thinking about his own child when she'd been that age. Only Sally hadn't been as pretty as this baby.

Her mother chose that moment to turn the cart, and when she did she rammed straight into his.

"Oops, sorry," she said in an abstracted but husky-toned voice.

He'd seen her only once, that day in the bank. He'd thought she was stunning then, but now she was even lovelier, taking his breath away.

Suddenly their eyes met, and he forgot about her beauty. The incredibly haunted look in those eyes was like a kick in his gut, something he wanted badly to ignore; only he couldn't. Like him, this woman had been to hell and back.

But that didn't mean she wasn't guilty.

Stone cleared his throat. "No need to apologize; it was my fault."

She gave him a tentative smile, then rolled the cart toward the checkout counter. He simply stood there and watched her, unable to say another word.

*Shit!*

# Eight

"Man, huh?"

Natalie grinned at her daughter, whose rosebud-shaped mouth was stretched in an answering grin.

"Looks like I'm going to have to keep a close eye on you, young lady," she added.

Clancy's two top teeth glistened in the sunlight as Natalie lifted her out of the shopping cart into the car seat. "Yeah, already you're making eyes at a man." She tweaked Clancy's nose. "Shame on you. One of the few times we go to the grocery store, and *you* try to pick up a man."

Natalie shook her head, her mind jumping back to the man of the moment. Beyond his bumping into her cart, she didn't know why she'd even given him a thought. But for a second something had clicked, and she'd thought maybe she knew him. On closer observation, however, she'd known better. No one would forget an embattled face like that.

Clancy slapped her hands against the seat and kicked her legs, all the while grinning and pointing toward the store.

"So, he was okay looking—not handsome, mind you. He was much too intense for that."

"Man," Clancy said again as if she knew exactly what and whom Natalie was talking about.

Natalie shook her head in amazement. Sometimes she wondered how she'd borne such an intelligent child. She smiled with pride, remembering the story she'd read Clancy last night about a man—a father, actually—who played ball with his small children. She had emphasized the word "man" rather than "Daddy" because Clancy had no . . .

The smile disappeared, and Natalie climbed quickly into the car and cranked the engine. When she thought about how Clancy had been robbed of the joys of joint parenthood, both anger and pain warred within her. Right now anger was the dominant emotion, which fused her desire not to falter in her mission. Then, as she'd told Lucy, she would live with the outcome, good or bad.

After heading in the direction of Highway 71 out of the Barton Springs area, Natalie tried to relax. But that wasn't possible. Her mind continued to churn, and the long drive didn't help. In fact, it contributed to her discontent. Her only comfort was that she intended to remedy that situation as soon as she could.

Although she hadn't found a place to live near her office as yet, she had gotten a list of day care centers and individuals she planned to interview. After Josie, it would be hard to find someone she thought qualified to look after Clancy.

Natalie fidgeted in the seat, recalling the look on Martha's and Fletcher's faces when she'd delivered her second bombshell, that she intended to move. But she couldn't let that dent her resolve, not after what Fletcher had said about her. *Poor white trash.* God, that hurt. Even now her heart felt as though it would burst under the strain of pain and regret.

She wouldn't think about that now. She couldn't. It only added to her vulnerability.

Besides, she had other things to think about—her strategy. She'd been mulling over the idea of hiring a private detective to locate the cop involved in the shooting.

Having realized she'd slowed to under fifty miles an hour,

Natalie peered into the rearview mirror. Thank goodness, no one was behind her. She lowered her eyes to her daughter, who was gnawing on a toy.

It wasn't often she brought Clancy into the office with her. This particular Saturday morning, however, she'd had an appointment to show another old home in Terry Town. And while on a gorgeous lot, the house itself was in a state of disrepair. Yet she could see the potential, and she guessed her enthusiasm had rubbed off on the clients, because she believed she had a sale even though they hadn't signed on the dotted line.

"Or maybe, sweetheart, they were simply smitten with you," she said to Clancy.

"Mamma."

"Well, keep your fingers crossed that Mamma sells that big old barn."

Speaking of barns jumped Natalie's thoughts to her horse, Magic. This afternoon would be a perfect one to ride her. Again she felt the need to think, to clear the cobwebs from her brain, especially as it was one of those rare summer days when everything was in sync.

She'd like to ask Daniel to go with her, but she figured he wouldn't be available. Daniel often worked on Saturday at the university, playing paper catch-up. And Martha would be at a friend's house, working on either charity functions or a church-related agenda. As far as Fletcher was concerned, she didn't know. He might be at the Whitmore office or with Stanley out on the range.

Even if they were all at home, she doubted she'd be welcomed into the fold. Since she'd announced her plans, and Fletcher hadn't been able to talk her out of them, she'd become the prodigal daughter. Only Daniel had stood by her, and still, at times, she experienced a coolness from him.

"How 'bout you playing with Josie while Mommy takes a ride?" she asked Clancy.

Clancy kicked her chubby legs and grinned.

"I'll take that as a yes." Natalie blew her daughter a kiss. "You're my heart. Did you know that?"

And she was, Natalie thought, fighting off the feeling that without Clancy she would be alone in the world.

She shivered.

"Stop giggling, will ya?"

"Then stop tickling me you-know-where with that piece of straw," Paula Whitmore said, stilling his hand.

Dave Rathman, the ranch foreman, who had worked for the Whitmores for nearly five years, stared down at the woman who lay naked beside him on hay in a back room of the barn. "Hey, I never heard you complain before." He'd been screwing her for three of those five years.

"It's never tickled before," Paula said.

Dave grinned, then inched his oversize belly closer to her side, where he then jammed two fingers into the warmth between her thighs.

"Oh, God, Dave," she panted, bucking against the harsh onslaught even as he surrounded a big brown nipple with his teeth and bit it.

"You like that, huh?"

"Oh . . . yes," she cried, continuing to thrash on the straw. "But I'd rather have the real thing," she added on a guttural note.

"Man alive, you're sure a greedy bitch," he said, watching her thrash through another orgasm. "What's with you and Stanley, anyway? Don't he ever fuck you?"

"Yeah, only his dick's about half the size of yours."

Dave chuckled, feeling his pride and his ego swell. He often wondered why he put up with this drunken bitch, not that he was pure when it came to alcohol himself. Maybe she had the gift that made a fella feel real good about himself. Besides, she was game to try anything, and he liked that in a woman.

But if Stanley ever found out . . .

Dave fell back on his side and stared up at the exposed beams in the barn's high ceiling.

"Will you stop worrying, for chrissake?"

His craggy features took on a mutinous look. "How do you know I'm worrying?"

Paula yanked a piece of straw out of her hair, then rested on a crooked elbow and stared down at him, all the while fondling his flaccid penis.

" 'Cause I've seen that expression on your face a million times since we've been fucking."

"I don't wanna lose this job."

"Get real. That's not going to happen."

"It will if Stanley ever finds out about you and me."

"Well, he hasn't found out yet, has he?"

"No."

"So, see? You're worrying for nothing. Besides, he's got other things on his mind."

Dave cut sunken eyes at her. "Such as?"

"A baby."

Dave lurched to a sitting position and opened his mouth, calling attention to his stained teeth. "What the hell does that mean?"

"He wants me to have a kid."

"You're shittin' me."

"I wish I was."

"I 'spect that notion has something to do with Miz Astorbutt threatening to haul ass."

"Is there anything that goes on around here that you don't know about?"

Dave scratched his balding head. "Nope."

"Well, you're right. Stanley thinks that if we can make a baby, then the old man'll forget about Natalie and Clancy."

"Fat chance."

"Not if we have a son."

Dave snorted.

"You might be right," Paula said. "But if I don't get

pregnant, then Stanley'll have to find another way to put that bitch in her place."

"All I know is that there's been hell to pay since she's announced all her plans 'bout Phillip and moving. In fact, both Stanley and the old man have been walking around with a case of the red-ass. Can't do nothin' to please 'em. Why, I've had to restring that goldarn fence in the south pasture three times already."

"Well, I'd say you're getting off light. Now me—I'm the one who's going to catch hell, having my stomach swell and all."

"Not to mention puking your guts up every morning."

Paula gave him an incredulous look. "How would you know about that?"

"I ain't stupid, you know. Besides, I had a kid once. But when my old lady lit a shuck, she took the brat with her."

Paula was quiet for a moment, then said, "Well, we won't let anything mess up our playhouse."

"That's where you're wrong. Your pussy or anyone else's ain't worth this job."

And it wasn't. A blast of dynamite couldn't drive him away from this ranch. He liked working outdoors. He never wanted to be trapped indoors ever again. Prison had taught him that. No, he had a plum job—three squares a day, a place to sleep, good wages, and even better wages when he did special favors for Mr. Fletcher.

And he got along well with everyone, except Natalie Whitmore. Why, that bitch had not only her nose in the air, but her tits as well. She needed to get knocked off that pedestal, and he'd sure like to be the one to do it, only she wouldn't give him the time of day.

He'd sidled up to her six months after Phillip had bought that bullet, thinking she might need a little tender loving care.

She'd looked at him like he smelled of hog shit, then said, "You stay away from me, or I promise you'll get fired."

He'd had to quell the urge to slam her against the wall and fuck her into tomorrow, but he'd backed off, knowing that she had the power, through old man Whitmore, to carry out her threat. But he'd never forgotten or forgiven her for making him feel like a fool.

"Dave," Paula said in a cajoling tone, "I want a little more for the road. So how 'bout it?"

"Yeah, why not," he said in a distracted tone, until she placed her mouth on him. Groaning, he rolled her onto her back, then mounted her.

Then he heard the noise.

"Did you hear that?"

"No." Her whisper turned into a groan. "You're just hearing things. Everyone's gone."

He began to move, then suddenly felt a tingle down his spine. He stopped midthrust and swung around. His heart plummeted to his toes.

"Dave, don't stop," Paula pleaded, her eyes still closed.

"Jesus Christ!"

Paula's eyes opened, then she yelped.

Natalie Whitmore stood in the doorway, staring at them with a horrified look on her face and her hand over her mouth.

"Oh . . . my God . . . oh . . . my God," she choked as she backed away.

"Don't you dare run off!" Dave yelled. "I can explain this!"

Natalie turned and bolted.

For a moment neither Dave nor Paula said a word. Dave fought the urge to bolt after her, while rage built inside him. But what could he say?

"What . . . what if she tattles?" Paula sniveled, her eyes wide and frightened.

"She won't or I'll—" He broke off, stopping just short of adding that he'd kill her.

"You'll what?" Paula pressed.

"Just shut the fuck up, will ya? I gotta think."

# Nine

Stone dragged the hot sultry air through his lungs as he unlatched the stand on his bicycle. It was now or never, he thought as he watched Natalie Whitmore, with daughter in tow, pedaling a bicycle a few yards in front of him.

For several days he'd been playing detective again, and he hated to admit it but it felt damn good. Or maybe it was the person he was following who had kicked his adrenaline into jump start. Since he'd decided to make the Whitmore widow the focal point of his investigation, at least for the moment, he'd been tailing her.

On this particular day he had waited outside her office until she'd shown up. Afterward he'd followed her to show two houses. At two o'clock she had obviously decided to call it a day because she'd left the building, gone to a day care center, picked up her child, and headed for the park.

Now, as Stone followed her on his rented bicycle, he forced himself to maintain a discreet distance behind while he plotted what he would say to her. No words came to mind. What *did* come to mind was how great her statuesque body looked in the pair of tight-fitting jeans and yellow T-shirt. The breeze had tossed her curls until they were in total disarray, adding to her attractiveness.

And the baby was nothing short of perfection, with rosy cheeks that matched her pink romper suit. Together they made a striking pair. Stone knew he wasn't alone in his opinion, as he saw others in the park stare at them.

An expletive split his lips. He had botched their first encounter, and he damn well didn't want to do a repeat performance. Yet there was something about this woman that set him on edge. Maybe it was that cool "hands off" aura about her. Even though he couldn't quite tag the source of his trepidation, it was there nonetheless, and it pissed him off.

But as the old saying went, he might as well take the bull by the horns. . . . Stone upped his speed and within minutes deliberately crossed the path in front of her.

She put on her brakes and glared at him. Stone prepared himself to take the brunt of what he figured would be a tongue-lashing. Only that didn't happen.

Instead, her eyes widened with apparent recognition. "Aren't you—"

"Yep," Stone said with what he hoped was a disarming grin. "I am."

"Do you make it a habit of bumping into people?"

"Actually, I'm very selective."

This time his direct answer appeared to take her by surprise, and she seemed at a sudden loss for words. Not so with the child, whose name he knew was Clancy.

"Man," she said.

"Hiya, kiddo." Stone switched his gaze from mother to child, only to feel a sharp stab in his gut. Again Clancy reminded him of Sally when she was a baby, at a time when he'd been too busy to spend quality time with her. He wished he could . . . Hell, he couldn't go back. He could only go forward.

Jerking himself out of his thoughts, he continued to stare at the baby. The tiny pink bow that appeared to be taped to her curls held him captive. He felt his smile stretch into a grin.

"Well, at least you're honest," Natalie said in a voice that sounded to Stone like pure southern belle.

"Did you get all your groceries?" he asked innocently.

While she smiled in return, it lacked warmth. At least it was a smile, though, Stone thought, fearing that she'd simply tell him to take a hike and be done with it. "Yes, how about you?"

"Sure did, though I have to say, I'd rather be drawn and quartered than go in one of those places."

"Me too. But they're necessary evils."

"Especially if you have a teenage daughter who eats you out of house and home." He thought if he threw in the tidbit about his having a daughter, then she might not be so leery or likely to bolt.

"So I've heard from some of my friends," she said, that coolness back in her tone.

He gave her what he hoped was another disarming grin. "Mind if I tag along with the two of you for a while?"

She didn't budge. Instead she asked bluntly, "Why *are* you following us, Mr.—?"

He forced himself not to so much as blink. "McCall. Michael McCall," Stone lied. "And yours?"

She hesitated, looking around as if to make sure there were safety in numbers. And on this day, the park was indeed crawling with walkers, joggers, and bike riders.

"Natalie Whitmore, and this is my daughter, Clancy."

"Pleased to meet you both."

"So, again, why are you—"

"I know, following you," he said, interrupting her. "It's simple; you're an attractive woman, and your kid's a beauty."

"Thank you," she said with a cool edge to her tone.

That tone told Stone that she was uncomfortable with being "hit on" and that her politeness would stretch only so far. He didn't have any more time to dally.

"I think Clancy's ready to go," he said in an unruffled

tone, then winked at the child, who was busy kicking the underneath part of her mother's seat.

"Okay, okay, Clance. Mommy's going."

Although she didn't invite Stone to ride with her, she didn't protest when he maneuvered his bike beside her, and they began to pedal down the asphalt trail that was shaded by oak trees.

They rode in silence for a while, then Stone asked casually, "Do you work?"

"Yes, I'm a real estate agent."

He feigned surprise. "Mmm, that's interesting. I would've never picked you for that."

She ignored that. "What about you?"

Careful, McCall. "Right now I'm between jobs. I was working on a ranch in New Mexico, but when my daughter was seriously injured in an automobile accident, I came back here."

"Is she all right? Your daughter, I mean?"

"Yeah. She's almost back to her old self—mouthy and bossing old Dad around."

Another fleeting smile touched her mouth. "That's good. If anything happened to Clancy—" She broke off.

"I know. For a few days there I thought I'd go berserk."

"I'm sure your wife did go berserk."

"Ex-wife. But, yes, she did."

They were silent for a moment.

"So is there a Mr. Whitmore?" he questioned again with smooth innocence. "I notice you're not wearing a ring."

She stopped suddenly as if out of breath, then faced him. "I'm a widow."

This time the silence was awkward.

"I'm sorry."

"Me too."

"Mommy!" Clancy cried, rocking back and forth. "Go!"

Natalie twisted around and laughed. "You need to learn some patience, my darling."

Stone laughed and flicked the baby on her nose. "I'm with you, kiddo."

Clancy pointed at him and grinned. "Man."

"I don't know what I'm going to do with her," Natalie said, shaking her head and smiling.

Relief shot through Stone as he sensed the atmosphere had changed from one of open mistrust to guarded trust. They rode for a stretch, then Natalie stopped and looked at her watch.

"It's getting late. I have to go."

Their eyes met for a moment. "Would you have dinner with me?"

It was obvious she was taken aback. First her face turned white, then red, then she shook her head. "No, no, I'm sorry, I can't. But thanks anyway."

Before he could open his mouth and argue, she rode off.

Again he stood there and watched another opportunity go down the toilet. "Dammit!"

Thirty minutes later when he walked into his apartment, Stone was still steamed. He paused in the middle of the room and fought off the urge to bang his fist into the thin wall. Another chance blown. How could he have let her get away a second time? Man, had he ever lost his touch. To make a bad situation worse, he remained convinced he needed Natalie Whitmore if his plan was to work. Establishing any kind of relationship with her was turning out to be more difficult than he'd first thought.

Hell, he thought, smirking. Wasn't he being just a little unrealistic to think that she'd pour out her heart and soul to a stranger? Perhaps he should pursue her from a totally different angle?

He shut down that thought even as he broke into a cold sweat. No way was he going to fall into that gar hole. Granted, she was a good-looking woman with a dynamite body. But he was interested in her only as a means to an end. Nothing more. Nothing less. Absolutely no hanky-panky.

Suddenly the phone rang. He tried to ignore it. Only when it persisted did he walk over, lift the receiver, and growl, "McCall."

"Whoa! Maybe I should call back another time."

Stone recognized the voice immediately and grinned. "Why, Larry Meadows, you old sonuvagun."

Larry chuckled. "What happened, McCall, did I catch you with your drawers down?"

"Go to hell."

Larry's chuckle burgeoned into laughter. "Mmm, still the same old McCall. I thought by now an enema might've removed that burr from your ass."

"I can see that working as a bigtime insurance guy sure hasn't cleaned up your toilet mouth."

They both laughed.

"To what do I owe the honor of this call?" Stone asked.

"I heard you were back in town."

"You heard right."

"But for how long?"

"For good."

"Look, I just heard about Sally." Larry paused. "Is she going to be all right?"

"Yeah, she's doing good. Thanks for asking."

"That's not the only reason I called."

"Oh?"

"Would you by chance want to work for me? I know you turned me down once already, but—"

"Doing what?" Stone cut in, not bothering to mask his eagerness.

"Same as before."

"Which was?"

"Working as a part-time investigator. Hell, McCall, the company's grown by such leaps and bounds that we could sure use you."

"Me and my bad-ass personality, huh?"

"The whole package, down to your ugly mug."

Stone chuckled. "All right. I'll sure as hell listen. Besides, I could use the dough."

"Figured you could." Larry paused again. "You don't have to level with me if you don't want to. But I didn't think you'd ever come back to this town to stay."

"I'm going to clear my name, Larry. Or at least make a stab at it."

"It's about goddamn time."

"After Sally's accident, I felt I didn't have a choice. Besides, I'm tired of running."

"Then you're going to find this very interesting."

"What?"

"Since you've been riding the ranges, Texas Aero Industries has become one of our clients."

Stone's Adam's apple gave a convulsive jump. "Is that for real?"

"Swear it is."

"Can we talk tomorrow?"

Larry laughed. "It's your call, my man."

Once a time and place was agreed on, Stone hung up. While that phone call had certainly improved his mood, he was a long way from feeling jubilant. He couldn't get over how he'd screwed up when it came to Natalie Whitmore.

Maybe he should call and see if Sally wanted to come over. She'd cheer him. The day she'd visited had been one of the best of his life. They had talked, then gone to a movie, where they shared laughter, popcorn, and Coke.

He looked around the apartment and realized that was not a good idea. It was messier now than it had been the day she'd come over. Even if he cleaned it up, it wouldn't make that much difference.

The first words out of her mouth had been, "Daddy, for heaven's sake, can't you afford a better place than this dump?"

He could, only he was too preoccupied to make another move. But maybe he should, and while he was at it maybe he should—"You idiot, McCall!" he said out loud. "Why, that's your answer!"

\* \* \*

Natalie wanted to rub her eyes; they felt as if tiny shards of glass were in them. Yet she didn't touch them because she didn't want to smear her makeup. Paperwork. She stared down at the mess on her desk and wondered if she'd ever get through it all.

Concentrate, she told herself. But her mind hadn't been on her work lately. She couldn't seem to get the scene in the barn between Dave and Paula off her mind. She had tried to block it out for days, but with no luck.

When she'd left the barn and run to her room, she'd been both out of breath and sick to her stomach. The sight had been repulsive, disgusting, and shocking.

After she had calmed down, she'd told herself that Daniel would know what to do. But since Daniel wasn't home, she had left Clancy with Josie and driven back to the office, where she'd literally bumped into Lucy.

"Hey, honey, what's wrong?" Lucy had demanded after placing both hands on Natalie's shoulders to steady her. "You look like the bugger bear's after you."

Natalie took a deep, shaky breath. "I'm all right. Or at least I will be."

"Couldn't prove it by me. Want something to drink?"

Natalie shook her head.

"Come on, let's go to the bar. I've got some white wine."

After Lucy had poured two glasses half full, she plopped down on a stool and said, "Okay, let's have it. Did the old man say something that set you off?"

"No, this time it wasn't Fletcher."

"Then who the hell was it? Don't make me pull this out of you, okay?"

Natalie took a sip of the wine, then began to talk. When she finished, Lucy was laughing.

"It's not funny." Natalie's tone was huffy.

"I know, but I can just see the two of them getting it on in that hay."

Natalie's mouth hinted at a smile. "No, you can't. It's something you'd have to see to believe."

"I doubt that. I've met that creepy foreman as well as Paula dear. I can just betcha that while he was pounding her his fat gut was jiggling and her legs were flailing in the air like a crab's. Right?"

Natalie rolled her eyes. "Did I ever tell you that you have a way with words?"

Lucy smiled, then shrugged. "So what are you going to do?"

"I don't know. I'll probably tell Daniel, then let him decide if Fletcher should know."

"Sounds like you oughta hurry up and get out of there."

"You're right, I should."

Yet she hadn't. And now those emotions she'd felt at the scene paled in comparison with the overriding fear that she felt when she thought about the way Dave had looked at her. His eyes had been filled with venomous hatred, and she knew that he'd do whatever it took to keep his job. If Fletcher had any idea such shenanigans were going on, he'd fire Dave on the spot. Of course Dave would blame her.

She couldn't forget about Paula, either. Her eyes had held their own venom.

As Lucy had said, she should move out of the house. Instead she had become a master in the art of procrastination, not having found a full-time baby-sitter for Clancy or hired a private detective. What was holding her back? Fear of the unknown or fear of losing the family's protection she had reveled in for so many years?

She hated to admit it, but the answer was yes to both questions.

"Hope I'm not interrupting anything."

At the sound of the unexpected voice, Natalie jerked her head up, then almost bit her tongue. "You!" she said, her eyes connecting with those of Michael McCall, whose well-toned frame lounged against the door of her office as if he were perfectly at home.

Since the incident in the park, she had put this man on the back burner of her mind, certain she wouldn't see him again. Now . . .

"You don't look or sound pleased to see me," he said as if he could read her mind.

"What do you want?" she asked in an exasperated tone.

"Now, is that any way to talk to a prospective client?"

Natalie felt an unpleasant sensation in her stomach, though she tried to ignore it as well as *him*. Both proved impossible. He looked as though he'd just gotten out of the shower, with his damp and disheveled hair. Or maybe he hadn't bothered to comb it.

He was dressed in a blue shirt, jeans, and highly polished boots. The open neck allowed her to see a shadow of hairs. From where she stood, the smell of his cologne was faint but tantalizing. She wanted to shift her gaze from the blatant sexual aura he brought to the office, but she wasn't about to give him the satisfaction of knowing that he had rattled her.

"Are you referring to yourself?" she asked when the silence became untenable.

"Sure am."

"Just what makes you a prospective client?"

He looked at her another long moment. "I'm in the market for a town house."

# Ten

His fly was open.

If that wasn't repulsive enough, the earring in his right ear definitely nailed him as an unsuitable candidate before he ever said a word.

Repulsed, she turned her gaze off the latest private detective who now sat in her office, asking herself how she had gotten into this situation. The minute he'd plopped down on the chair in front of her, she'd noticed the open zipper, though she'd kept her eyes off it.

"So do we have a deal?"

Mike Sutton's question forced her to face him again, and if anything, he was more repulsive than ever. Some women, though, would probably think of him as good-looking. He had longish black hair and a nice build. But neither of those impressed Natalie. Even though his clothes were clean, he looked as if he needed a good scrubbing. She shivered inwardly.

"I'll have to let you know, Mr. Sutton. You're one of several private detectives I've interviewed."

"Mmm," he said, scratching his chin. "That's too bad. I

know I can do the job for you. What if I come off the fee I quoted you? Would that make you hire me on the spot?"

Not in this lifetime, Natalie thought. "No, I'm sorry." She smiled with no warmth. "This is something I'm not prepared to rush into." She stood but didn't hold out her hand. She couldn't bear the thought of touching this man.

He followed suit, though with a scowl on his face. "I hope I haven't wasted my time."

"I hope so, too, Mr. Sutton."

He stared at her a long moment, then shuffled out the door.

When it closed behind him, Natalie sank back onto her chair and, gritting her teeth, stared at the list of names in front of her.

Lyle Hamilton, PI

Cameron Hemphill, PI

Mitch Inland, PI

Mike Sutton, PI

Duds. All of them were duds, or at least that was how she'd perceived them. In between showing homes, she had interviewed two yesterday morning. She'd added two more today.

After forcing herself to read and familiarize herself with the details surrounding the shoot-out in the bank, which had been her first priority, she had moved to the next one—finding a competent private detective, only to find that good private detectives were hard to come by.

She had even asked Lucy if she knew one. Natalie had to smile again at the strange look and blunt comment she'd received.

"Don't have a clue, honey. Why, I wouldn't know a PI if he walked up and bit me on the bottom."

"Hey, I'm serious about this."

Lucy's grin disappeared. "You are, aren't you? So, you want to tell me what's buzzing around in that head of yours? Besides real estate business, that is."

Natalie flushed. "Sorry, I've been distracted."

"Whoa. Don't get me wrong. I wasn't asking for an apology. You're more than doing your job, but I still sense your preoccupation."

Natalie gave her the gist of what had taken place at that recent family dinner.

Lucy's eyes widened. "You're shittin' me?"

"No, I'm dead serious."

Lucy fell onto the chair in front of Natalie's desk, her eyes filled with concern. "I think you are at that."

"I know it sounds crazy and probably is. But I have to know once and for all the circumstances surrounding Phillip's death."

"Then what?" Lucy's tone was suspicious.

"Lay it to rest and go on with my life."

"If I thought you meant that, I'd stand up and sing the Hallelujah Chorus."

Natalie picked up her pen as if to throw it at her friend.

Lucy dodged it with a laugh. "I mean every word of that."

"I know you do. The past sixteen months have been a nightmare of my own making. I've felt like I've been walking around in a cold mist, unable to find my way in or out."

"So what jerked a knot in your butt?"

"Two things: another newspaper article and something Fletcher said that I overheard, something to do with Clancy and me."

"Well, I can't say that surprises me. Fletcher Whitmore is known for his ability to twist and mold people into what he wants them to be."

"At one time I wouldn't have agreed with you. Only—" Natalie paused.

"Only what?"

"Nothing," Natalie said, averting her gaze.

Lucy held up her hands. "Hey, I'd like to defend him because he's done a lot of good for this city. But he's a dominating, pushy old man who doesn't allow anyone to get in his way. You know that, whether you'll admit it or not."

"Oh, I admit it," Natalie responded softly, thinking again of Fletcher's attack on her and how raw and vulnerable she felt as a result of it. She loved her family despite their short-comings, but she wasn't about to crumble in her resolve. It grieved her to think that the underpinnings of that longtime love and security were in jeopardy.

"So back to the nitty-gritty," Lucy said, breaking the small silence. "You think a PI's the way to go?"

"You have any better suggestions for tracking down an ex-cop who seems to have disappeared from the face of the earth?"

Lucy played with the gold chain around her neck and pursed her lips. "Nope, guess not. But I'd be careful."

"Why?"

"Jeez, Nat, didn't you hear a word I said?"

Natalie frowned. "I don't follow you."

"That's the problem. Think. Fletcher has so many people in this town in his pocket that he's bound to find out."

"So?"

"So, he might try to stop you."

"Are you saying that Fletcher has the power to actually thwart my plans to that degree?"

Lucy stood. "Honey, I'm not saying another thing! After all, this is your gig. But you'd best be prepared for anything, and get your guns loaded."

Hopefully that was what she was doing now, Natalie told herself as Lucy's last statement rattled around inside her head. She was trying to "load her guns," but so far she'd had no luck.

Pausing in her thoughts, Natalie massaged her temples, then reached for the phone directory and turned to the Yellow Pages, only to slam it shut.

The thought of interviewing another private investigator turned her stomach; *they* turned her stomach. Oh, they had all been polite enough, but there had been something about each one that had made her uneasy.

Maybe it had been the way they'd looked at her. Or maybe it had been the way they had probed, had expected her to open up and tell them everything, which she hadn't been prepared to do yet.

If not, though, how did she expect to get the job done? Initially she'd planned to ask Daniel for help. But the next morning after the dinner fiasco, when she'd run into him downstairs in the kitchen and he'd pledged his support, she'd sensed that support was tepid at best.

She'd struggled against discouragement and forged ahead with the private detectives on her own. And struck out. But she wouldn't quit.

No one was going to thwart her now.

The meeting adjourned, and Lucy followed Natalie into her office.

"Congratulations again, sweetie," Lucy said, resting on the edge of Natalie's desk, then kicking off her shoes.

"Thanks, Luce. I'm still in a state of shock."

"Don't be. You earned it. You've been working your butt off lately."

"True," Natalie said, "but still I never thought I'd done that well."

"Just keep up the good work, you hear?"

"I plan to, for more reasons than one."

They were quiet for a moment, then Lucy said, "God, my feet hurt."

"It's my head that hurts," Natalie mumbled, and rubbed her temple.

"I know you're happy about being named Sales Producer of the Month, but you still have something on your mind that usurps part of the joy. Right?"

Natalie's smile was forlorn. "Lots of things, actually."

"One of them wouldn't have anything to do with that man who showed up a couple of days ago?"

"What makes you ask that?" Natalie said in what she hoped was a bland tone.

"Ah, pooh, you can't fool me. I saw the look on your face when the two of you walked out together."

Natalie averted her gaze. "You're just imagining things. It was strictly business. I showed him several town houses, one of which he leased. End of story."

"Whatever you say." Lucy slid off the desk, leaned over, and swept up her shoes. But when she reached the door, she turned and grinned. "Too bad about that. I thought he was kinda cute. You know, a real 'man's man.' "

Natalie flushed.

"Ah-hah, gotcha! You thought so, too."

"I did not," Natalie countered sweetly, turning on her brightest, falsest smile.

When Lucy continued to look at her with that superior grin, Natalie picked up a paperweight on her desk and slung her arm backward.

"Okay, okay, I'm going. No need to get violent just because I suggested you might be interested in a man." She stared at the ceiling while her grin widened. "God forbid that should ever happen."

"Lucy!"

"I'm going. I'm going."

Once the door slammed behind her, Natalie sank on her chair and placed her hands over her scalding cheeks. She hadn't lied to Lucy, but she hadn't told her the entire truth, either. She had indeed shown Michael McCall several town houses, and he had settled on one to lease.

What she hadn't told Lucy was that she had agreed to go to dinner with him.

"Grrrrh!" Natalie cried aloud, furious with herself.

After turning him down flat in the park, she had let him talk her into going this time. No, she corrected mentally. That wasn't a fair assessment, because she could have remained firm. He hadn't held a gun to her head. What he'd done was catch her off guard again. This time it had worked because she hadn't seen the invitation coming.

They had just looked at the last town houses in the Barton Springs area and had pulled back into the office parking lot, where he'd sat, stationary and silent. Suddenly uncomfortable in the close confines of the car, especially as his cologne once more stirred her senses, she'd shifted sideways and studied his profile. She had to do something, she'd told herself, fighting off a smothering feeling that she'd often felt as a child.

Some women might put him into the clichéd category of tall, dark, and handsome, she'd thought. The tall and dark definitely fit him, but the handsome did not. Yet there was something about his uneven features that commanded attention. Or maybe it was the hardness about him, his hard-boiled demeanor, that made her far too curious. Or maybe it was that disarming grin that changed everything about him when he chose to use it, such as when he'd turned unexpectedly and said, "Well?"

"Well, what?" she managed to ask.

"Do I pass muster?"

"I don't know what you're talking about."

He laughed. "Oh, you know all right. But if you don't want to say, that's fine, too."

"Thank you."

She knew her sarcasm wasn't lost on him, though it seemed to roll off him like water off a duck's back. His lips twitched. "You're welcome."

"Look, I appreciate your business, but I have other clients to—"

"Have dinner with me."

Their gazes locked.

"I—"

"Please."

Panic swept over her, and she opened her mouth to answer but found her tongue had turned to chalk.

"I know this Chinese place close by that has great food. Surely you like Chinese."

Natalie raked her fingernails through her hair. "You just don't give up, do you?"

"Nope. So just say yes and be done with it."

"If I say yes, then what?"

He gave her a curious look. "You won't be sorry, I can tell you that."

Only she was sorry, and the dinner date was still two days away. Plenty of time to cancel, she told herself. She didn't need or want a man to further complicate her life. Since Phillip's death, she hadn't been with a man. She wasn't interested in another relationship, especially not at this point in her life, not when she was trying to find the truth about his death.

Besides, she hadn't found a man who measured up to Phillip, certainly not someone like Michael McCall. Phillip had been polished; Michael was rough.

So what was there about that man who wore boots and jeans with such ease that set her teeth on edge and attracted her at the same time?

That was the question that frightened her the most. In light of that, she wouldn't keep the date. Again, no one was holding a gun to her head. For a moment her stomach uncoiled and her pulse rate settled. Then reality returned with a vengeance. Something told her that even if she broke the date, she wouldn't be rid of Michael McCall.

Why? she wondered. Why had he bumped her cart in the grocery store, then later followed her to the park? And why had he chosen the real estate agency where she worked? All coincidental? Or a quirk of fate? She didn't think so. Something wasn't right.

"Grrrrh!" she said again.

Dear God, what a mess. What a miserable, infuriating mess.

# Eleven

Lonely.

That was the word that jumped to mind after Natalie entered the Chinese restaurant and saw Michael McCall. And angry, too, she thought. For an instant she asked herself if she'd lost her mind for actually showing up to meet him for dinner.

He had called her and told her he'd pick her up. She'd said no, that the restaurant was only a block from her office and she'd meet him.

Why on earth was she here? Dear Lord, he could be a pervert, or worse. After all, she knew nothing about him. Since he hadn't seen her, maybe now was the time to call a halt to this nonsense and bolt. She didn't need to be around someone who was as badly scarred as she was, someone who'd been through combat experience. She wasn't referring to the military, either.

It wasn't as if she were attracted to him, she assured herself, despite the fact that she noticed how great he looked in his usual attire of jeans, shirt, and boots.

But she didn't bolt, deciding the loneliness took precedent over the anger, which somehow made him safe. He actually looked like someone who needed desperately to be hugged.

Yet she sensed that if anyone tried to get close to him, he'd rebuff them.

He turned then and saw her. Natalie still didn't move, but for a different reason. The difference in his expression a second ago and now was staggering. His face, with its square-jaw cragginess, had looked like a thundercloud. Now that cloud had passed, and that same face was filled with sunshine.

He smiled.

Natalie dragged her eyes away from that smiling mouth and swallowed, determined to think of him as a client and this a business dinner—nothing more, nothing less.

"Hi," he said, getting up and pulling out the chair for her. "I'd about given you up."

"Sorry I'm late, but I had to finish some paperwork."

"That's all right. I have the patience of Job."

Wrong. There was nothing patient about this man. She voiced that thought. "Somehow I don't believe that."

He raised his eyebrows in a mocking manner just as a waitress walked up to their table. "Can I get you something to drink, ma'am?"

"Coffee, please."

"And I'll have a refill," he said.

Once the waitress had shuffled off, a waiting, uneasy silence fell between them.

He lifted the coffee cup to his lips and stared at her over the rim. The glacial purity of his green eyes seemed to see through her.

Natalie shifted on her chair, wondering again what had ever possessed her to keep this date. Only after the waitress reappeared with the coffeepot, then took their orders, did the silence end.

"You can relax, you know?" His tone was warm with humor.

"What makes you think I'm not?" she responded, resenting his familiarity.

He set down his coffee cup, but his gaze was as piercing as ever. "So are you?"

She drew a trembling breath. "Of course."

"Well, you should be, because I'm harmless."

Her smile was false. "Really?"

"Scout's honor," he said with a chuckle.

She knew he was trying his best to put her at ease. That was why she played along with this nonsensical small talk. Besides, she was behaving like a virgin on her wedding night, for heaven's sake.

"Something tells me you weren't ever a Scout."

His grin was sheepish. "You're right, I wasn't."

"So how do I know you're harmless?" She asked that question half in jest and half in truth.

"Well, for starters, you can rest assured I don't bite."

She took a drink of her coffee, then said, "I've heard that before."

"I'm sure you've heard this before, too."

"And what is that?"

"I have no intention of jumping your bones."

Her face turned red at the same time she gave him an incredulous look. "I didn't—"

"Yes, you did."

Her response was to glare at him, which wasted good energy because he added, "You've been sitting there as tense as a startled deer ready to bolt."

She manufactured a brave smile, determined this smart-ass wasn't going to get the upper hand. "Are you always so blunt?"

"I don't believe in pussyfooting around. I believe in cutting to the chase."

"So is that what we're doing—cutting to the chase?"

"Yes."

"So why did you ask me out?"

"So why did you come?"

Natalie bristled, feeling as if he were getting the upper hand again. She spoke sharply to mask her alarm. "To celebrate our deal, of course."

He leaned toward her, and when he spoke his voice was

low and a trifle husky. "I asked you out because you're an attractive woman, just like I told you that day in the park."

She shifted her gaze, uncomfortable with his words and with him in general. Again she questioned her sanity in even being here.

"You haven't gone out with a man since your husband died."

It wasn't a question, but a statement of fact. Natalie's head swung back around, and for a moment she showed her fangs. *"That's* none of your business."

"You're right, it isn't."

They were silent for a moment, while they sipped their coffee.

"Is it that obvious?" She heard the tremulous edge to her voice and was mortified, first, that she had let him get this far with his personal line of questioning, and second, that she had answered him.

"Yes," he said in his blunt fashion, though his tone was soft.

She looked at him quickly, then away. This is crazy! she told herself.

The waitress appeared with their food, and Natalie felt herself wilt inside with relief. Although she wasn't hungry, she ate as though she were.

She finished before he did and looked around. There were other customers in this main dining room, which was decorated in typical Chinese decor, with red the dominant color. But there were several other rooms with customers in them as well. She could understand the restaurant's popularity; the food had been delicious.

"So what's the verdict?"

She faced him. "Excuse me?"

"The food. How'd you like it? Did I do good?"

Her laughter was full throated and warm as in her relief to be back on solid ground. "You did great, actually."

"Good. So how's Clancy?"

Natalie flashed him a brilliant smile. "She's as impish as ever."

"She's a doll, is what she is."

"Even though she calls you 'man.'"

His lips twitched. "I've been called worse, that's for sure."

Her own lips twitched. "So how about your daughter? What's her name?"

"Sally. If it hadn't been for her, I wouldn't have been in the market for a condo."

"Well, then, I guess I have Sally to thank for the deal."

His eyes turned dark, holding her gaze. "Maybe you'll get that chance."

It took a tremendous effort for Natalie to remove her gaze, but she did, determined that she was not going to let this man get under her skin, not going to fall susceptible to his offbeat brand of charm. Despite what he'd said earlier about being harmless, she didn't believe it for a minute. And as far as meeting his daughter, he could forget that. It wasn't going to happen. She didn't intend to see him again.

"Sally's one of the reasons I came back here," he said, breaking the short silence.

"How's she doing since the accident?"

"Making progress every day. The doctor's prognosis is that she'll suffer no lasting effects."

"That's a miracle."

"You're telling me, especially since I have a lot of wrongs to right when it comes to that kid."

Though she was curious as to what he was talking about, she didn't probe. Because of her own sordid past, she respected his right to privacy.

So she was shocked when he said, "How about some more coffee? Or maybe a bottle of champagne?"

"Champagne?"

"Yeah. I've become gainfully employed again."

"Well, congratulations."

"Thanks. An old buddy called and asked if I'd help him out part-time in his insurance company as a fraud investigator."

"And you obviously have the expertise to do that?"

"Enough," he said, removing his gaze.

She was quick to note that he also didn't want to talk about himself, which was fine with her. The less she knew about him, the better. Still, she heard herself asking, "Do you think you'll miss ranch life?"

The muscles along his jaw bunched into knots. "In the worst way."

"At least you'll be out in the field and not cooped up in an office."

"That's the job's only saving grace."

"You'll survive."

He smiled and his eyes darkened. "I'll remember that."

"I really need to go," she said, peering at her watch.

He looked at her. "So soon?"

"Yes." She expelled a breath.

"Let's get out of here, then."


He stared at the back of the man pulling out the chair for Natalie.

"Daniel, honey, what's wrong?"

Daniel blinked and forced his attention back on Megan Foster, the woman he'd been seeing off and on for over a year now.

"Surely it isn't the Chinese food?" she asked with a teasing smile, reaching over and placing her hand on his.

"No, actually it was quite delicious."

He forced himself to make small talk, when in fact he'd rather be anywhere but here. It wasn't Megan's fault, either. He cared about her, but he wasn't in love with her, which he feared would soon turn into a major problem. Like now.

"Daniel?"

"Mmm?"

"What's wrong? I know something's bothering you."

He made himself smile. "Now, just how would you know that?"

"For starters, I share your bed."

"And that makes you clairvoyant?"

She looked suddenly uneasy. "No, but because of that, you learn things about your lover that you wouldn't otherwise know."

"It's business."

"University business?" she pressed.

"Yeah, university business."

She sighed and pulled her hand back. "Sometimes, Daniel Whitmore, I wonder why I put up with you."

"If it makes you unhappy, then don't."

Tears flooded her eyes. "You wouldn't give a damn, would you?"

"Look, Meg," he said, putting down his napkin, "now's not the time to go into all this. I've never lied to you about my feelings——" He broke off and stared toward the back of the restaurant, a look of surprise altering his features.

"Daniel, are you all right?"

He heard the change in Meg's tone and hastened to reassure her. "Of course."

"Then what's the matter?"

"Nothing, really. It just hit me again that my brother's dead and my sister-in-law's sitting over there with another man. It's just a shock, that's all."

When they reached the parking lot and his car, Stone insisted on driving her back to her car. Natalie didn't argue. Once back at the office, Natalie stood beside her own car and looked up at him.

"Thanks for dinner, Michael," she said in a voice that sounded tightly coiled even to her own ears.

"You're welcome."

He stepped closer. In the moonlight she could see the expression on his face, and even before he spoke, it frightened her. "Can I see you again?"

She licked her lips. "No, I don't think that would——"

"I do." His mouth was taut, and he spoke in a harsh whisper.

She opened her mouth, and that was when it happened, out of the blue, so fast that she was unprepared for it and couldn't have stopped it even if she'd wanted to.

In a fluid move, he placed his hand around her neck, bent, and crushed his mouth against hers. At first she was too dumbfounded to respond. But then his tongue, hot, moist, and hungry, teased her lips apart. She clung to his wide shoulders in order to keep her rubbery legs from giving way.

Finally he pulled back, then said in a strained voice, "Jesus, I didn't mean for that to happen."

"Like hell you didn't!"

"Natalie—"

She didn't wait to hear any more. She jerked open her car door, got inside, and drove off. But she couldn't leave behind the smell and touch of Michael McCall.

"Was he a client?"

Natalie's heart almost leapt out of her throat. She had just walked in the door of the ranch house and was on her way upstairs. Now she swung around and stared in the direction of the voice. Daniel stood in the doorway of the parlor.

Natalie's hand flew to her chest. "God, you nearly scared me out of my wits."

"Sorry, didn't mean to."

"What are you doing still up?" she asked inanely, her heart continuing to beat hard, her lips still tingling.

Daniel gave her a strange look. "It's only a little after ten."

"Oh," she responded, feeling foolish.

"Want to join me for a nightcap?"

"Thanks, but not tonight. I'm pooped."

"Please."

She mustered a weak smile. "Oh, all right."

Once they were seated on the couch, Daniel sipped on a martini, while she drank a Coke with a twist of lemon.

"So was he a client?"

She gave a start, remembering now the question with which he'd greeted her. "Who?"

"Oh, come off it, sis. You know exactly who I'm talking about."

"Look, Danny, I'm tired. If you have something to say, then spit it out. You never were good at games."

He regarded her through narrowed eyes. "Okay, I saw you in the Chinese restaurant."

"Were you spying on me?" She struggled to keep her voice steady.

"Oh, for chrissake! Of course I wasn't spying on you. Meg and I were having dinner."

"Then why didn't you come to our table?"

"I guess I was too stunned to make polite conversation."

"Why?"

"Because I didn't know . . ." He paused and cleared his throat.

"Go on. You thought what?"

"That you might be having a dinner date."

"And would that have been so terrible?"

"No, except I don't want to see you get hurt."

"Are you sure it's not the family you're thinking about?"

He flushed, then his tone turned defensive. "Well, I don't think Dad would approve."

"No, I'm sure he wouldn't," she said, trying to conceal her anger.

"But then you obviously don't care what he thinks or the rest of us, either, for that matter."

"Look, if you asked me in here to pick a fight, I'm not in the mood. I'm going to bed." She stood.

He followed suit. "Wait. I didn't mean to upset you."

"Then what did you mean?"

He played with his necktie in a nervous gesture. "I meant what I said earlier. I just don't want to see you get hurt."

"Danny, sweet Danny," she whispered, reaching over and pecking him on the cheek. "Thanks for caring, but I'm a big girl now and I can take care of myself."

"I know, but humor me anyway. I'd still like to know who you were with."

"A client. We closed a deal today on a town house, and he asked me out to dinner." She forced a smile. "It was no big deal and won't happen again."

"I know you better than perhaps you know yourself," Daniel said. "And I don't think you're ready for another relationship."

"You're right, I'm not." She gave him another kiss on the cheek. "Good night, dear brother."

Only after she'd reached her room and sunk onto the bed did an ugly truth hit her. The man she had said was only a client had done something Phillip had never been able to do.

*With one kiss, he'd made her wet and left her aching for more.*

# *Twelve*

"Is it okay?"

"Yeah, it'll do," Stone said, then smiled at his new boss, Larry Meadows.

"Gosh, don't go getting all choked up, old buddy. If you knew what I had to go through to get you this office with a window, you'd gladly kiss my ass."

"Kick it, is more like it." Stone's smile widened into a grin as he slapped his friend on the shoulder. He was a genuinely nice man, too nice to have ever been a cop. He finally realized that was why Larry had called it quits. He seemed a better man for having done so, too. He no longer had that thin, gaunt look about him.

"Well, you know how it is with me," Stone said, ending the short silence. "Give me the wide-open spaces. I swore off these cubbyholes when I left the department."

Larry chuckled. "In other words, you'd just as soon someone grab you up by the short and curlies and hold you a foot off the ground."

"You got it."

"Then rest easy, 'cause you won't be in here much at all. You'll be in the field chasing down insurance criminals."

"I can handle that."

"Better than anyone I know," Larry said. "It takes someone meaner than a junkyard dog, who goes for the jugular, to do this type of work."

"It's nice to know you have such a high opinion of me."

Larry's dark eyebrows shot up. "Well, it's the truth, isn't it?"

"Yep, guess it is, at that."

"Not really. I'm just giving you a hard time. Maybe I'm just envious that you look so goddamn fit."

"Yeah, right."

Larry chuckled again. "I'm serious. Hell, if it hadn't been for your ugly mug, I wouldn't have known you."

"Thanks, but on the inside nothing's changed. You're right, I'm still meaner than that junkyard dog you mentioned."

"You know why I think Rutgers had it in for you?"

"For one thing, he just wasn't an effective supervisor," Stone said. "In my opinion, he couldn't supervise a good bowel movement."

"I agree, but I think he was afraid of you."

"You weren't around by that time, man. He was always busting my chops."

Larry shook his head. "Just think about that a minute. You never failed to call his bluff on something you felt wasn't right, and he didn't like being crossed. You were a rebel who might just do something that could cost him his almighty pension."

"Rutgers can rot in hell for all I care," Stone added, his features darkening. "But I'll sure enjoy rubbing that prick's nose in it once I've cleared myself of all this."

Larry slapped him on the back. "Now that's the kind of attitude I like. I'm truly glad you've stopped running."

"Like I told you on the phone, those days are over, Larry. And it's not just because of Sally, either. It's for myself; I spent too many years in that department to roll over for Rutgers. I'm tired."

"So let's get down to business, then. Park your butt behind

your new desk. I know Texas Aero's an itch you've been dying to scratch."

"That's putting it mildly," Stone responded, feeling his pulse accelerate. "I want to know everything about the company and its management, every time those bastards flush the toilet, if possible."

"I'm not so sure we can supply their bathroom habits," Larry said, "but we sure as hell can supply you with information about what looks and smells like a bogus claim. They say the warehouse was broken into and hundreds of thousands of dollars in airplane parts were stolen. We don't think this one's a righteous burglary—it's all in the claim file here. The last thing National American wants to do is pay this claim— unless it's legit, of course. That's where you, the fraud investigator, come in."

Stone rubbed his chin. That was the break he'd been waiting for. "Has someone already been assigned the case?"

"Yes."

His excitement waned. "Well, hell."

Larry grinned. "Patience. You didn't let me finish. I took the other guy off this case and put him on another one. The boss even cleared it, so Texas Aero's your baby, and your baby's got the colic. It's up to you to nurse it back to health."

"Thanks, Larry. You don't know how much I needed a friend about now."

"No thanks necessary. You've covered my ass too many times for that." Meadows looked down at the floor a moment, then added, "So after a short training session this morning, I suggest you take the file home and go over it, see if you smell the same stench we do. Since we've taken on the company as a client, we hear rumors they're in trouble with the government."

"If the feds are involved, their goose just might already be cooked."

"I doubt that. From what we've gathered, this bunch is slick and professional. Let's just hope they're not slick enough to milk us out of any dough."

"Other than the fact that the Whitmores leased them the building, I haven't found another link," Stone said, staring at the bare walls of his office.

"Fill me in," Larry said. "I know about the murder at the warehouse, of course, the one that eventually cost you your job. But I don't know the particulars."

Stone told him about the man who was shot, muttering the name "Whitmore" just before he died.

"So the logical conclusion would be that he was saying either the Whitmores were involved or one of them actually pulled the trigger."

"I doubt it was the latter." Stone made a face. "You know how those people are. They only sin behind closed doors."

Larry laughed out loud. "I guess that's as good a way of putting it as any."

"I wanted to check the family out, especially after Phillip Whitmore's death—nothing about that whole death was an accident, and I wanted to see how they were involved. Anyway, Rutgers suddenly started shaking like a dog crapping peach seeds. After I shot Phillip, he and old man Whitmore went after my balls."

"And got them."

"Almost got them," Stone corrected.

"Because of the circumstances surrounding the dying man, you feel Texas Aero and the Whitmores are somehow involved?"

Stone felt that same dull ache he always got whenever he knew something in his gut but couldn't prove it. "Oh, yeah. They're knee deep in this mess, and when I get enough evidence together, it'll be my turn to yank some nuts."

Larry laughed. "I'd hate to be in old man Whitmore's shoes, with you hot on his tail."

"First I've got to nail the powers-that-be at Texas Aero. You by any chance know anything else about them? I figure since you're insuring them now, you might be privy to their business in general."

"All we know is that they have in fact branched out. The

company owns lots of other industrial rental property and a couple of hardware stores. We're insuring a Thoroughbred racehorse farm in Kentucky for them, too. I understand they own controlling stock in some banks, though someone else has that coverage. We don't.''

''Mmm, sounds like they're setting the world on fire financially.''

''Yep, it looks that way. But if they are indeed trying to shaft us on this claim, we'll bring 'em to their knees.''

''Let's hope you're right.''

''So do you have any other leads?'' Larry asked.

''Sort of,'' Stone hedged, not yet ready to discuss Natalie Whitmore.

As if he picked up on Stone's reluctance to discuss that, Larry said, ''Okay, how 'bout we get down to the nitty-gritty of fraud investigation? It won't take you long to learn the ropes. It's mostly common sense and a healthy sense of skepticism.''

Stone smirked. ''I can handle that.''

Two hours later the training session was over and Stone was alone in his cubbyhole. He ought to fix it up, he told himself, only he knew he wouldn't. Hell, he'd never even hung one picture in his office at police headquarters. Besides, he'd rarely be here, so what was the point? If he put his stamp on anything, it would be the condo he'd leased.

He groaned suddenly and leaned back on his chair. Every time he thought of that condo, he thought of Natalie Whitmore. *Liar.* He thought of her regardless—all the time, in fact.

He still couldn't believe he'd kissed her. He'd allowed himself to go tree-swinging, apeshit insane!

The last thing Stone had meant to do was touch her, for God's sake! And to kiss her . . . well, that was the height of insanity. But it had just happened, one of those crazy things that was unplanned and unrehearsed—another of life's little surprises.

Who was he trying to kid? Nothing excused what he'd

done. It could definitely put a kink in his plan to get close to Natalie Whitmore.

Oh, he'd gotten close all right—too goddamn close, which was a rarity for him. Stone had thought that his heart was frozen and would never thaw. Because of that, he saw no reason to keep up his guard. He had grown accustomed to feeling nothing, except where Sally was concerned.

Had he been wrong. Even now he could still feel Natalie's lips under his: cool and moist at first, only to feel them turn sweet and enticing, as though he'd just bitten into a ripe, succulent peach. He felt a curious, alien feeling race through him—the same feeling he'd had when he first saw her at the bank that fateful day.

Yeah, his body had betrayed him, sinking a dagger into his unguarded back. It wouldn't happen again; he'd make sure there were no more hot, unexpected stabs between his ribs, *if* he ever saw her again.

Fury at himself suddenly swept from his belly up to his throat and lodged there like a rock. He'd find a way to get back into her good graces; he had no choice. Hell, it wasn't as if he cared about her or that she was anything special. He didn't and she wasn't. Granted, she was a looker, even had great legs and breasts. But so did a lot of women. He guessed he was hornier than he'd thought. That was it in a nutshell. Next time their meeting would be all business.

He just wished he believed that.

"What do you want?"

Stone jumped, swung around, and faced a greasy-headed man who was in the process of fingering a pimple on the side of his nose.

When Stone left the office for the day, he had planned on going straight home. Instead he'd found himself driving toward the warehouse. Once he'd reached the location, he'd pulled against the curb, gotten out of his car, and walked inside the gate. Thinking that the place looked deserted, he had tramped through the high grass to a window.

Now, facing this man, he knew better; it wasn't deserted. Still, it was nothing like the hub of activity that it had been during his prior investigation.

"I'm interested in applying for a job," Stone said off the top of his head.

"Peeping in windows is a funny way of going about that, mister." The man paused. "I'd say you was asking for trouble."

"Do they still manufacture airplane parts here?"

"Nope."

"Then what *do* they do here?"

"Nothing now."

"So why are you here?"

The man continued to pick at the pimple. "That ain't none of your business."

Stone almost gave a cop response, remembering just in time. "Hey, I'm sorry. You're right. It's just that I could use a job. Did they move?"

"Yep. About a month ago. Took 'em all one Thursday and Friday to get it all out, too."

Stone thought back over the claim file, which stated that Texas Aero had left hundreds of thousands of dollars' worth of spare parts in the warehouse, with plans to pick them up the following Monday. They claimed the burglary happened over the weekend.

"Wasn't nothing left in there over the weekend?" Stone asked.

"Bunch of trash and empty boxes. I worked all that Saturday and Sunday just to get a head start on this mess. They just hired me to clean up around here, that's all. I do a little nightwatching, but mostly I push this broom and carry out all the junk. It's a big place, but I've about got it clean again. Beats sittin' at home drawing unemployment."

"So when they left that Friday, the whole building was empty?"

"Didn't I just tell you that? All was left was trash, like I said." The man stopped worrying his nose long enough to take a good look at Stone. "You ain't really here for a job, are you?"

"No, not really."

"You look more like a cop to me," the old man said.

"You're a pretty fair judge of people. What's your name?" Stone asked, then wrote down the old man's name and address.

"Well, I sure ain't doing nothing wrong. I've been hired to clean up around here, that's all," the man stressed.

"Who hired you?"

"I got this job through the employment commission. They sent me over to the Whitmore Holdings office. I guess they must own the building."

Stone believed him. Anyway, it didn't matter. He was wasting valuable time talking to this old fart. The factory had obviously relocated. When he got home he'd check the address in the folder, then visit their new location another day.

Right now he had something more pressing to take care of, something that had just occurred to him.

"Thanks anyway," Stone said to the man, noticing that he was once again digging at the pimple.

Stomach juices rushed up the back of Stone's throat, and he had to swallow hard to get them back down.

# Thirteen

Her head ached as though someone were pushing thumbtacks inside it. Too many questions with no answers. Too many problems with no solutions—the pain of Fletcher's betrayal, Daniel's overprotectiveness, and Michael McCall—to name a few.

"Don't think about *him*."

Muttering aloud did little to steer Natalie's mind away from the man or the heated kiss they had exchanged—a knee-jerk kiss that had meant nothing, she reminded herself.

*Liar*. It had meant something or she would be able to put it out of her mind. After all, it had been two days now and here she was still replaying it over and over. The fact that she'd returned the kiss was the underpinning of her discontent. Actually, she was horrified by her behavior.

Her tongue circled her lips, which instantly reminded her of how *his* tongue had done that very same thing before it had plunged inside her mouth. It was as if her system had been electrically wired, then shocked.

Natalie lunged out of her chair and made her way into the tiny kitchen in the rear of the office. She'd put the coffee on to drip earlier, having arrived at work before seven o'clock.

She reached for a cup and poured it full, though it was with palsylike hands. Even though the warmth seemed to settle her jagged nerves, it did nothing to temper thoughts of Michael McCall.

While her mind seemed hell-bent on resisting him, her emotions were not so controllable. Even now another flush of adrenaline invaded her lower limbs, and the memory of how her body had responded to him was hard to forget.

She'd never reacted that irrationally or boldly with any man, not even Phillip. Blood rushed into her cheeks and her hand shook. She put the cup on the table, anticipating that soon the dark liquid would splatter on her suit.

Her only consolation was that she wouldn't allow him to touch her again. With that thought utmost in her mind, Natalie made her way back to her desk, sat down, opened the thick folder, and began reading in preparation for her upcoming meeting.

Her gaze, however, kept shifting to another folder that contained photocopies of some of the articles she'd read at the library. Just last evening she'd studied them again until her stomach knotted so that she couldn't eat or drink anything without feeling nauseated. Still, nothing had clicked.

This morning was no different. Not only had she reviewed the articles, she'd gone even further before she'd arrived at the office. She'd looked back through the boxes of Phillip's personal papers that she kept in the bottom of his closet. Again she'd come away with nothing concrete to support her instinct that he'd been a victim of foul play.

Natalie stared into space. So was she creating a crisis where there wasn't one? Was it guilt that made her continue down this treacherous road? Sure, guilt played a part; she would admit that. Phillip's strange behavior and mysterious phone calls prior to his death weighed heavily on her mind and heart. If only she'd forced him to confide in her. But how did one force another to do something against their will?

Still, the end result might have been different had she not wallowed in self-pity for over a year. The trail wouldn't be so cold. Hindsight was a wonderful thing, she told herself, only it wouldn't get the job done.

She felt the urge to give in to the tears of frustration that burned the backs of her eyelids, but she didn't. She couldn't afford that luxury. She had to be strong, something she hadn't been since Phillip's death.

Natalie shuddered, thinking about the tasks ahead of her. She still hadn't summoned the courage to interview any more private detectives, but she knew she couldn't put that off much longer. She balked at recounting anything personal to anyone, with the exception of Michael McCall, that was.

She shook her head, then peered at her watch. In thirty minutes she had an appointment at police headquarters with the captain who'd spearheaded the investigation into Phillip's death. That was where all her efforts and thoughts should be channeled, not on Michael McCall.

*That* encounter had been a onetime screw-up that wouldn't be repeated.

He hacked into a plain white handkerchief, then blew his nose.

Repulsed, Natalie turned away and pretended to look around the office of Captain Bill Rutgers. It was as cold and austere as the man himself.

"Sorry, but I've had this bug for several days now and can't seem to get rid of it."

"I understand," she responded with uncomfortable politeness. Only she didn't understand. There was something about this man besides his icy demeanor and uncouth behavior that made her wary.

Rutgers sat down behind his desk and leaned forward. "I have to say I was surprised when you asked to see me."

"I'm sure you were."

His expression was stoic. "So what can I do for you?"

Two could play this game. Her expression matched his. "I want you to reopen my husband's case."

Suddenly his eyes bulged, and she almost smiled, confident she'd struck a nerve.

"Now, why would *I* want to do a thing like that?" he asked.

"I'm not satisfied with the results of the investigation, that's why."

Rutgers looked at her with an air of dismissal. "Oh, really? That's too bad, because the department is. My men did an outstanding job."

"What about the cop who shot him?" she asked, her anger building at his condescending attitude.

He fingered the scar on his right temple, then said in a blatantly hedging tone, "What about him?"

"Apparently he didn't do a good job or he wouldn't have gotten fired."

Rutgers's face went blank. "I'm not at liberty to discuss that."

"Why not?"

"Look, ma'am, I suggest you draw your own conclusions. The man was investigated several times by IAD. He shot your husband. He's no longer a cop."

"But you're saying he wasn't dismissed because of his part in my husband's death?"

"I've said all I'm going to say in the matter of that particular officer, except—"

"Except what?"

"I don't really know what's behind the inquisition, but if you're planning on investigating him, I'd mind my *p*'s and *q*'s. And I'd be damned careful about who I trusted."

She pushed that disturbing thought aside for the moment. "I don't believe my husband's death was an accident."

"What you think and what you can prove are two different things."

"I know for a fact that he was disturbed about something, and I think that 'something' resulted in his death."

Rutgers reached for a cigarette and lit it. "Don't mind if I smoke, do you?"

She did, but she knew that if she said yes, she'd further

antagonize him. She knew he already looked on her as a woman who was suffering from PMS. She'd like nothing better than to slap his smug face.

"Does Fletcher know you're here?" he asked, through a haze of blue gray smoke.

Her eyes flashed. "What difference does that make?"

"None, except I figure he wouldn't cotton to you stirring up all that grief again, especially when he was satisfied with the police report."

"Well, I'm not."

Rutgers's mouth tightened. "That's too bad, because I'm not about to reopen a case just on your whim. I'd need hard evidence to do that."

"If I got you that hard evidence, would you do it?"

"Look, Mrs. Whitmore, I—"

"Don't patronize me, Captain. I think there was foul play involved, and I intend to prove it."

"Why are you just now coming forward with this request?"

"Because I can't live with myself any longer."

He seemed taken aback by that statement. "You feel that strongly, then?"

"Yes, I do. So can I count on your cooperation?"

He stood and stared at her through eyes devoid of passion. "My advice to you, Mrs. Whitmore, would be to just let the dead rest in peace."

"I need your help, Captain, not a lecture." The taste of rubber was so strong in her mouth that she thought she'd gag.

"Sorry, ma'am."

"I'm sure you are."

The thick sarcasm in her tone wasn't lost on him. His veined nose turned almost purple, and he opened his mouth to speak.

But it was too late. Natalie ignored him, walked to the door, and slammed it behind her.

"Shit," Rutgers spat, then walked to the window, his thoughts splintering in a million different directions. That was all he needed, to have that Whitmore woman breathing down his neck.

Reopen the case, his ass.

Someone would have to hold a gun to his head and he'd have to know that they had the guts to pull it to make him even think about that. And the only person he knew with that kind of balls was Stone McCall.

A thin, irritating line of sweat rolled down his face as something clicked in his mind. Surely that bastard wasn't back in town. No way. This visit from the Whitmore woman and McCall didn't have any connection. So what did it mean?

"Shit, shit, shit," Rutgers spat out loud.

He was about to retire. Three more months before he'd be out of this stink-hole for good. The last thing he wanted to do before he left office was to reopen a case that had been too hot to handle in the first place. He'd been lucky to have come out of it with only minor scratches.

Now that arrogant broad waltzes into his office and drops her bombshell. Well, that was too damn bad. She wasn't about to fuck up his last days on the job.

He lifted the phone and punched out a number. Following a few moments of silence, he said in a clipped tone, "Rutgers here. I thought you'd like to know that Natalie Whitmore just left my office."

He held the receiver away from his ear until the swearing on the other end stopped.

"Look, I gotta go. Just thought you'd like to know."

When he replaced the receiver, Rutgers reached for another cigarette, sat back on his chair, French inhaled, then smiled. His problem had just disappeared.

With that one phone call, he had fixed little Miss Tight-ass.


"If you don't calm down, you're going to have a stroke."

Fletcher swung around and glared at his attorney, Ben Byers. "Hell, you ought to be the one who's about to have the stroke! After all, that's what you're getting paid for."

"Now, Dad," Daniel said, "don't you think you're being a tad unreasonable?"

Stanley, who stood to the side of his brother's chair, gave him a steely look. "Well, I sure as hell don't. But then you always did take up for her." A smirk crossed his face as he looked Daniel up and down. "Hell, if I didn't know better, I'd think you had the hots for her—"

Daniel leapt out of the chair, grabbed Stanley's shirt, and pushed him against the nearest wall. "You ever say anything like that again, I'll—"

"Enough!" Fletcher bellowed. "Both of you stop behaving like assholes and sit down."

"Yes, please," the attorney pleaded in his soft-spoken voice while he wiped the perspiration off his forehead with an unsteady hand.

Daniel let Stanley go, and both sat down. Fletcher stared at them for a long moment, then said, "The purpose of this meeting is to discuss how we can stop Natalie from going any further with her asinine plan. Instead, I'm having to referee the two of you. Jesus Christ!"

"Sorry, Daddy," Stanley muttered, not looking at Daniel. "Maybe if you cut her out of the will . . ." He let his voice drift into nothingness.

"You'd like that, wouldn't you?" Daniel said to his brother. "Then your share would be more."

Fletcher glared at them again, then faced Ben. "What's your read on this?"

"Well, you could always threaten to sue."

Fletcher shoved his Stetson back and massaged his forehead. "There's got to be another way."

"Well, then, maybe Stanley has the right idea," Ben added. "Threaten to cut Clancy out of your will."

Fletcher didn't say anything. He hunched his shoulders as if totally defeated.

"Dad, let me have another crack at her," Daniel said. "So far all she's done is approach Rutgers, and since he flatly refused to cooperate, maybe she's changed her mind."

"Maybe," Fletcher said. "But if she moves out, then we won't know what she's up to for sure."

"I have hopes that I can change her mind about that as well. To my knowledge, she hasn't even found a place to move to yet."

"If anyone can change her mind," Stanley said, "it'd be you, brother dear. She hates my guts."

Fletcher's eyes darted from Daniel to Stanley. "I don't know why I even bothered to seek advice from either of you." He paused, a bitter expression on his face. "You're too busy bickering among yourselves."

"Fletcher, I—" Ben began, his face red as if he'd rather be anywhere else but caught in the middle of this family squabble.

Fletcher held up his hand. "Forget it, Ben."

"I don't think—"

The old man's rude gesture cut him off. "I can see this meeting is a waste of time." He stomped toward the door, where he turned around. "Besides, the only son I could count on is dead."

# *Fourteen*

A vase full of red roses adorned the top of her desk. Natalie did a double take, but they were no figment of her imagination. They were breathtakingly real. She took a tentative step farther into her office, still not believing what she saw.

Where had they come from? Daniel, she thought with a warm glow. Or maybe Martha. Perhaps the flowers were a peace offering for the cold shoulder they had been giving her of late. She buried her head in their foliage and inhaled their sweet scent into her lungs.

"My, my, is something going on I don't know about?"

Natalie turned slightly and grinned at Lucy, who stood in the doorway. "Not to my knowledge," she responded. "I haven't looked at the card. I've been too busy enjoying them."

Lucy whistled. "They're gorgeous and cost a pretty penny, too."

"I know." Natalie reached for the card and opened it. She read the words and felt the color drain from her face.

I want to see you again.

\* \* \*

"Hey, are you all right?" Lucy asked, rushing to Natalie's side.

Natalie eased onto her chair and fought off a bout of dizziness. "I'm . . . fine."

"Yeah, and I'm going to marry Richard Gere tomorrow, too."

Natalie couldn't help but smile now that the shock was beginning to wear off. "They're from a client."

"Ah, but not just any client, I'll bet. They're from Michael McCall, right?"

"Right," Natalie said in a weak tone. A side of her told her she shouldn't have been surprised. Yet another side told her that the roses were totally out of character for him.

What did he want from her? More important, what did she want from him?

"Is he by any chance coming on to you?"

Natalie shook her head and watched as Lucy walked deeper into the room.

"I think he is. But the important thing is, do you want him to be interested?"

"Yes and no."

Lucy threw up her hands. "I give up. Either you like the guy or you don't."

"It's not that simple, or at least it isn't for me."

Lucy dipped her head, smelled the roses, then looked up. "If a man sent me a dozen long-stem red roses, I'd be jumping through hoops."

Natalie laughed. "You're impossible. And if you don't hurry up and get out of here, I'm not going to make my first appointment."

"Okay, I'm going." Lucy's face sobered. "I just want you to be happy, you know. And since Phillip's death, you've been anything but that."

"I'm still not ready for a relationship."

"Hells bells, honey, who said anything about a relationship? I'm talking about sex." She grinned. "You know, the thing that two people do together when—"

"Lucy!"

"Okay, I'll shut up, but if this man turns you on, then go for it."

"One of these days," Natalie said to Lucy's retreating back, "I'm going to make you pay for your sins."

Lucy merely shook her head as she dashed out the door and shut it behind her.

A few minutes later Natalie had her briefcase and shoulder bag and was about to walk out the door when her phone rang. Dropping her purse, she lifted the receiver and said, "Miracle Realty, Natalie."

"Do you like the roses?"

Her heart suddenly lodged in her throat, and she thought for a minute she wouldn't be able to say anything. She swallowed hard. "Yes, they're lovely."

"Good."

Silence.

"I meant what I said. I want to see you again."

"Michael, I don't think—"

"I'm taking my daughter to the park Saturday for a picnic. I'd like for you and Clancy to come, too."

His features swam before her eyes, and Natalie expelled her breath in a rush. "I don't know if—"

"Please."

It was that low, husky tone spoken through lips that had devoured hers, leaving her wanting more, that was her undoing. "All right," she said, noticing that her palms were damp. She smoothed them down the side of her skirt.

"How 'bout we meet by the pavilion at ten o'clock?"

"Fine."

There was another brief silence, then he said, "Natalie—"

"Look, I have to go."

She heard his deep sigh through the phone line. "See you Saturday."

Natalie stood still, her mind twisting like a whirlwind. So much for all that psychological nonsense about not seeing him again.

* * *

No rain was in sight. The sky was filled with stars on this summer evening.

Natalie was glad, for the family was in the midst of celebrating Fletcher's seventieth birthday. The select group of guests was made up of both employees and friends. They had enjoyed a scrumptious dinner around the huge dining room table before adjourning to the living room for drinks.

Natalie had even bought a new dress for the occasion and felt she could hold her own among the other women present. She had brought Clancy to the party for about thirty minutes and had just moments before tucked her into bed.

Once she'd made her way back downstairs, she had walked through the French doors onto the deck, where she now looked over the lighted grounds. She wouldn't be enjoying this lovely sight much longer, which made her sad.

The breeze was gentle but sultry. Still, she shivered while groping to come to terms with another feeling besides sadness. Fear. She feared leaving the only real home she'd ever known. Even though she'd procrastinated moving, she fully intended to do so, but the prospect scared her to death.

The family had treated her with respect in front of their guests, but she had seen Fletcher's brooding gaze follow her. In these moments it would hit her again how Fletcher felt about her. She wanted to crawl in a dark corner and whimper. His cruel words had broken her heart. Yet without Fletcher and Martha, she might still be—

Shivering again, she broke off that thought. To relive her past would only undermine her confidence and her newfound determination in herself.

"If I was a gentleman, I'd offer you my coat."

Natalie cringed, having recognized the voice. She turned and stared into Dave Rathman's eyes at the same time the image of him and Paula in the barn sprang to mind.

"But then we both know I'm no gentleman, don't we?" His face was contorted into a nasty expression of mockery.

"What do you want?" Natalie snapped, ignoring his question.

"I figure it's what you want that counts."

"I don't know what you're talking about."

"Ah, come on now, Miz Whitmore, don't play the dumb broad routine with me. It won't work."

"Leave me alone," she said, biting down on her lower lip.

He stepped forward, a menacing look replacing the mockery. "What will it take for you to keep those lips of yours sealed about me and Paula? I don't want no trouble, you hear, especially since she's the one who started all that."

Natalie smelled the booze mixed with garlic on his breath. She almost gagged. Instead she stepped back. "Get away from me!"

"Only if you promise to keep your mouth shut."

She stiffened. "And if I don't?"

"I reckon someone just might get hurt."

Her expression turned glacial. "You don't scare me."

Only he did. It took all the effort she could muster to hold her head high and skirt past him, straight into Daniel.

"Whoa," he said, smiling. "What's your hurry? I was about to come looking for you."

She clung to his arm and answered his smile more brightly than normal. "I was just enjoying some of the cool air."

"Who were you talking to?"

"Dave."

Daniel made a face but didn't say anything. She had never told him about Dave and Paula. Now was her chance. For a moment she was tempted to blurt out the disgusting facts, only something held her back. Maybe it was the place and the timing—too many people around. She certainly didn't want to think that she'd given any credence to Dave's veiled threat.

"How 'bout another drink? As you can see, all the guests have gone."

Natalie hadn't noticed, but now as her gaze roamed the room, she saw only the family was present.

"You outdid yourself, Martha," Fletcher was saying, giving his wife an indulgent smile.

Stanley lifted his glass. "I second that, Mamma."

"Me too," Daniel chimed in.

Natalie smiled. "Make that four."

Martha beamed, which added to her soft loveliness.

Paula was the only one who remained silent, taking the toast as another opportunity to gulp more Scotch.

Natalie walked over and kissed Martha on the cheek. While Martha didn't flinch outwardly, Natalie sensed her mother-in-law's coolness. No doubt Martha was still miffed at her. The sadness inside Natalie burgeoned into a dull ache. She couldn't bear to lose her family. Yet she couldn't bear to lose her own identity, either.

She sat on the couch beside her mother-in-law, feeling Fletcher's eyes on her now.

"You look lovely, my dear."

"Thanks," Natalie muttered, uncomfortable with Fletcher having singled her out. She was sure he had an ulterior motive, for in his eyes she knew she was anything but lovely.

"Phillip would've thought so, too," Fletcher added.

The room plunged into silence. It was as if everyone were struck speechless by Fletcher's remark.

He did that on purpose, Natalie thought, fury building inside her. He wanted to reinforce the brutal fact that even though Phillip was dead, he would never be forgotten or replaced. How had she been so blind all those years to the "real" Fletcher? Was it because she'd never crossed him in the past?

"But what Phillip wouldn't have liked is you snooping where you shouldn't."

Another silence.

"Daddy," Daniel said, "this is your birthday, for heaven's sake. Don't start anything."

Natalie set her jaw and her eyes flashed. "Are you by chance referring to my visit to the police station?"

"Yes."

"How did you know about that?"

Fletcher snorted. "I have my sources."

"Spies, don't you mean?"

"Whatever you want to call them," Fletcher said in a biting tone.

"You were warned, Fletcher. I'm not doing anything behind your back."

"Except sticking a goddamn knife in it."

"Fletcher!" Martha cried, her eyes going from one to the other.

"My son's death was an accident. Rutgers thinks so, and so do I."

"Well, I don't," Natalie said just as Daniel placed an arm around her shoulder.

"Jesus, why are you doing this?" Fletcher demanded, his bushy eyebrows drawn together in a harsh frown.

"Why don't you want to know the truth once and for all?"

The room became quiet. Fletcher's mouth moved several times, but no words came out. He tried again, with the same result. Finally he put his hand to his forehead and made one last attempt at answering her. "Because down deep, I don't want to know, dammit. I want to always think of Phillip as I do right this minute. Can you understand that?"

"Believe me, I don't want to bring unnecessary pain to you or Martha."

"You couldn't prove that by me. How the hell do you think I felt when Rutgers called me?"

A slow burn was building inside Natalie. Damn that captain. But she'd keep her cool under fire if it killed her. She must not forget that Fletcher's strength came from others' weaknesses.

Natalie took a deep breath and straightened her spine. "No matter what you say or do, I'm going to see this through. You might as well accept that."

"I guess you're still planning to move as well."

"Yes."

"Oh, Natalie," Martha whispered in a pleading voice, "please reconsider. I can't stand the thought of you taking Clancy away from us."

"Martha, that's not my intention at all, and you know it. You'll be able to see Clancy anytime you want."

"Still, it won't be the same."

Natalie's eyes were dark with sorrow, as she was tempted to blurt out that no, it wouldn't be the same, because Clancy was *hers* to rear as *she* saw fit.

Now, though, she just wanted to be by herself. She was tired and her head pounded. More than anything, she had been drawn and quartered enough for one night.

Rising to her feet, she put on a brave front and said, "I'm going to bed. Good night."

She was in her room, leaning against the door for much needed support, before it dawned on her that no one had even bothered to respond.

The next three days passed in a blur. Natalie worked long hours, so as not to think about the nightmare her life had become. She had looked for an affordable place for her and Clancy to live, but so far she'd hadn't found anything suitable. Besides, she wouldn't make a final decision on a home until Daniel had seen it. Thank God for him.

The morning following the dinner party, he'd met her in the kitchen and hugged her.

"I don't agree with what you're doing, but I'll never stop being your big brother," he'd said.

She knew he'd meant it, and that was what kept her going.

Now, as she looked over at Clancy, who was sitting in the middle of the floor in her office, she smiled with relief. Clancy had suffered from an ear infection the last two nights. After her two o'clock appointment, Natalie had gone to the ranch and picked up her daughter and brought her back into town for a doctor's appointment.

Once they had left the pediatrician's office, armed with medication samples, Natalie had stopped by the office to get some files, as she feared she might not return to work for a couple of days. If Clancy's condition worsened, she wouldn't leave her.

She just hoped she'd be well by Saturday to enjoy the picnic with Michael McCall. Feeling her heart begin to pound a little more than usual, Natalie lifted Clancy in her arms and whispered, "Your mommy's a fool."

Clancy grinned and pressed her palm into Natalie's nose just as the phone rang.

After balancing the baby on one hip, she reached for it, thinking it was probably Michael confirming their outing.

"Hello," she said in what she hoped was a cool tone.

"Natalie Whitmore?"

The voice was unfamiliar. "Yes?" she said hesitantly.

"Back off the investigation, you hear?"

"Who is this?"

"Do as I say, and you won't get hurt!"

"Who is this?" Natalie cried.

Click.

Panic squeezed Natalie's heart, and she opened her mouth to scream, only her throat was paralyzed.

The upscale, downtown Austin club was filled to capacity on that Wednesday evening. A live band struck up a Whitney Houston tune, which sent several couples onto the mirrored dance floor.

The two men in a private room at the rear of the club, however, were oblivious of the goings-on beyond the heavy door. Lewis, the shorter of the two, puffed on his pipe as he stood by the window and gazed onto a deserted street.

Ralph, the other man, who was tall, with dark hair and a heavy beard that served to hide his pockmarked face, sat on a chair, his long legs sprawled in front of him.

"Hell, Lewis, you're making me nervous. Why don't you sit down? You've been either pacing or standing at that window for the past thirty minutes."

Lewis swung around and glared at his companion. "Good, I hope I'm making you nervous. Misery loves company."

"Who says I'm miserable?"

Lewis ran a hand over the back of his neck, sending the

lacquered blond hair at his collar straight out. "Okay, so miserable's not the right word. I probably should've said scared."

Ralph grunted and dug in his beard as if he had lice. "Simmer down, for God's sake. You don't even know what's going on yet. This just might be a socially called meeting."

"Yeah, right. And I'm going to win the lottery tomorrow."

"Well, I will concede that he wouldn't have ordered us here unless something was brewing."

Lewis tamped the tobacco farther down in the huge pipe bowl, then said, "Oh, something's brewing all right. And I suspect we're not going to like its odor, either."

"We'll just have to wait and see, I guess." Ralph massaged his beard this time while staring off into space, narrowing his beady eyes.

"This is the first time I recall him being late to any of our meetings," Lewis whined, crossing to the table and sitting down.

"You know how he is. He's got his fingers in too many pies to suit me."

Lewis puffed harder on his pipe. "Yeah, I'm beginning to believe you're right."

A cloud of smoke filled the room, which caused Ralph to cough. "Dammit, take it easy, will you? I feel like you're going to suck me and everything else in this room inside that monstrosity attached to your lip."

The blond made a face. "Are you saying you don't like the smell?"

"Not in goddamn lethal doses."

Lewis went right on puffing.

"Jesus," Ralph said, "I'm going outside and get some fresh air."

He made it to the door just as it opened. He backed up and let the third man in. The newcomer stared at Lewis and Ralph, his eyes cold and hard.

"We've got trouble, gentlemen," he said without preamble. "So I suggest we all sit down."

Lewis's face lost all its color; he looked as though he'd been gutted. "You . . . said you'd take care of everything." The last word was spoken in a shrill tone.

"Stop squealing like a stuck pig and just sit down." The voice was frigid now.

After all three were seated, the newcomer continued, "Natalie Whitmore's starting to get nosy and ask questions."

"Where'd you hear that?" Ralph asked. "That's all we need."

"One of my contacts saw her talking to that detective captain in the police station. Why else would she be there?"

Lewis didn't say anything. He simply began to shake all over.

"So what do you gentlemen suggest we do?"

"You're the one in charge," Ralph said. "What do *you* propose we do?"

"Shut her up, would be my suggestion."

"You mean as in waste her?" Lewis's voice remained in the high range.

"If that's what it takes," the man said.

"It's your call, then," Ralph said, turning to Lewis as if to confirm that statement. "I sure as hell don't want to go to the pen."

Lewis's mouth opened and closed like a guppy's.

The man stood, his eyes flickering over them. "All right then, gentlemen, I'll do whatever it takes."

# *Fifteen*

Ben Byers drew his birdlike features into a frown. "Now, Martha, what on earth makes you think such a thing?"

"I guess I'm just plain scared to death, Ben."

"But why? Has Natalie said outright that she wouldn't let you see Clancy?"

Martha's soft voice grew softer. "No, she never said that."

"So again, why are you worrying about something that's not going to happen?"

"I simply can't face the fact that she's going to take Clancy and move out of the house." Martha's lower lip trembled.

Ben didn't respond for a moment. Instead he walked to the window in his opulent, high-rise office that overlooked the State Capitol building in downtown Austin and peered out as if deep in thought.

"I guess I've become a little paranoid," Martha said, clearing her throat. "Suddenly I feel foolish, wasting your time like this."

The Whitmore attorney swung around. "That's rubbish. You're not wasting my time. And even if you were, I'd consider it an honor."

Martha smiled her sweet smile. "Always a gentleman, but I do appreciate your humoring an old woman."

"Look," Ben said, walking back to the leather couch where Martha sat and easing down beside her. "Has Natalie made any visible signs of moving out?"

"Not yet, but I know that she will."

"Then you and Fletcher will just have to adjust. The Natalie I know wouldn't think of depriving you and Fletcher of seeing that baby."

Martha let out a slow breath. "I pray you're right."

"What's really at the bottom of this visit, Martha? Is it Fletcher?"

"Yes, it is," she answered without flinching. "He thinks that . . . that Clancy is his to control, to raise, just because she's part of Phillip."

"Ah, now we're getting down to the nitty-gritty. When Natalie announced that she wanted to probe into the circumstances surrounding Phillip's death and move out of the house, I suspected Fletcher would get his ire up."

"That's putting it mildly."

"Well, he'll settle down, believe me, as soon as he realizes Natalie's not going to deprive you of seeing Clancy. I also feel nothing's going to come of her so-called investigation, either."

"Oh, Ben, for Fletcher's sake I pray that you're right about that, too."

"What about you, Martha?" he asked, his tone gentle. "How do you feel? You're the one who pulled that girl out of the sewer."

Martha's brown eyes clouded. "Well, I have to admit that it never crossed my mind that she'd ever leave the ranch. I envisioned us always being a family."

"I'm sure it never crossed your mind that she might marry again someday, either."

Martha paled, then she gave him a grim smile. "No, it didn't, which isn't very intuitive of me."

"We all have our moments." Ben's tone was indulgent.

"The thought of her marrying again . . . well, that's repugnant to both Fletcher and me. In fact, I can't bear to think about it. I do believe that would hit him harder than any of this other mess she's stirred up."

"I wish I could be of more help, Martha, but in all honesty, while I don't agree with what she's doing about Phillip, she does have the right to a life of her own."

"Without everyone thinking she's the Wicked Witch of the West." Martha made an attempt to smile. "Is that what you're saying?"

"Yes, I guess I am. I've known Natalie since the day you brought her to the ranch. And to my way of thinking, there's not a mean-spirited bone in her body, despite the hell she's been through. I credit that to you, Martha. And I know that Natalie does, too. She's not about to stab you in the back."

"I want more than anything to believe that. It's just that all this has come as such a shock, and I'm scared. I'm . . . none of us are over the fact that we've lost Phillip, and to have all that pain dredged up again is almost more than I can stand."

Ben reached over and patted Martha's hand. "I know, my dear. Somehow, though, I think everything will work out simply because you did such a fine job of rearing Natalie."

"I'll try and cling to that hope. What I regret is that she must still be fighting more demons of her own than I ever imagined."

"Of course she is. Why, that girl's been through more hell in her thirty-one years than anyone else I know or have ever known."

Martha looked bleak. "And I'm sure there are probably scars so deep that neither I or anyone else could ever erase them."

"Add Phillip's death to that, and it compounds the situation."

"For all of us," Martha said, toying with her lower lip. "But you know I love Natalie as if she were my own flesh and blood, but I love Fletcher and my boys, too. . . ." Her voice faded.

"You don't have to explain to me, Martha. I know where you're coming from, and my heart goes out to all of you. But my suggestion is that you wait and see what happens with Natalie. She could change her mind about one or the other or both."

"I doubt that. If there's one thing about Natalie that I've not been able to temper, it's her stubbornness, or maybe hardheadedness is a better word."

Ben smiled. "That's not a bad thing, you know."

"It is if your husband has the same flaw."

Martha stood and Ben followed suit. She held out her hand. "Thanks for listening. I do feel better."

"I'm sorry I couldn't offer you a solution, but at the moment, there doesn't seem to be one."

"No, because I'm torn between Natalie and my husband."

Ben leaned over and kissed her on the cheek. "Feel free to come here anytime you want to talk. My door's always open."

Martha nodded, withdrew her hand, and walked out, trying to pretend the heavy weight no longer lay on her heart.

"Is this the best you can do?"

Natalie balled her fingers into a fist and quelled the urge to strike the big, beefy man in front of her. In addition to his size, the Lord somehow failed to whip all his facial ingredients together. None of them were in sync, which made him downright ugly.

His features, however, didn't have her in a tizzy, but his sharp tongue and quarrelsome personality did. It had been a long day, and she'd about had it.

"Look, Mr. Peterson, I've shown you four houses, four of my *best* and most expensive ones. Surely there's something you like about one of them?"

Jack Peterson stared at her as if she didn't have good sense. Again Natalie fought the urge to knock that condescending look off his face. But he was the customer, and Lucy had taught her that when one dealt with the public, the customer was always in the right. Still, if this fellow didn't back off, that hard-and-fast rule was about to change. She was close to telling the jerk to take a hike.

"What else you got in that book?" Peterson demanded, leaning toward her, his breath smelling as though someone had crawled in his mouth and died.

Natalie cringed inwardly and would've liked to put distance between them, only she didn't have any place to go. They were in the close confines of her car. What she did do was slam the book shut and glare at him.

"Now why'd you do that?" he asked, his tone hard. "I'm not through looking."

"Only I am," she said with as much politeness as she could muster. "At the moment, I don't have another house in mind that I think would come anywhere near your stringent requirements. But," she added with forced brightness, "tomorrow's another day."

He scooted back to his seat, and after mumbling under his breath what Natalie was sure were obscenities, he said aloud, "What time in the morning?"

"I'll have to consult with my boss. Perhaps she'll be available, as I already have another appointment." Before he could open his mouth and take issue with her dismissal of him, she added, "Lucy has several listings that are hers exclusively. Now, if you don't mind, I'll drop you off at your car."

Fifteen minutes later found Natalie free of her mouthy client and on her way back to the office. She should have felt relief at finally being alone for the first time the entire day. She had been going at a hectic pace from the instant she had arrived at the office.

Yet she knew her irritability, her edginess, didn't stem merely from the unpleasant client, although he'd been one of the worst she'd encountered. Her problems resulted from that phone call she'd received.

*Back off the investigation or you'll be sorry.* Maybe those weren't the exact words the person had used, but they were close enough that chill bumps again covered Natalie's skin.

Her knee-jerk reaction was to blame Fletcher for the threat. She'd almost confronted him outright, but then she'd calmed herself, having reached the rational conclusion that it hadn't been Fletcher.

But what if he had? she asked herself, her fear burgeoning. What if he hadn't meant to harm her and Clancy but had used the threat as a scare tactic?

If not Fletcher, who? Dave? Paula? Or both?

Granted, she had caught them in a compromising position, but why would it be to their advantage to threaten her concerning the investigation?

When she had first told the family about her intentions, Sam Coolidge, the Whitmore business manager, had been present, as well as Ben Byers, the attorney. She couldn't forget about Daniel and Stanley; they had been there, too. Neither of them were suspects. Daniel wouldn't harm a hair on her head, and Stanley . . . well, he didn't like her, but he seemed to care more about getting her out of the house than stopping the investigation.

Maybe the culprit was someone she didn't even know. After all, she'd gone to Rutgers at police headquarters and laid her cards on the table. Maybe that had ruffled the feathers of someone she wasn't even aware of.

Whoever was behind it, she wasn't taking it lightly. At the same time, however, she wasn't going to let that threat stop her. Someone, somewhere, had something to hide. If she played it smart and bided her time, she would find that someone.

Feeling somewhat calmer, Natalie turned into the office parking lot, killed the engine, and was about to get out when her hand froze on the door handle.

What was *he* doing here?

While she grappled to ignore the heat that rushed through her, Michael McCall got out of his car, strode over to hers, and tapped on the window.

She let it down, ridiculing herself first for acknowledging his presence and second for registering any reaction to him.

"Hi," he said, staring down into her upturned face.

His simple greeting completely disarmed her. With her heart in her throat, she said, "Hello."

"Bad day?"

His question was as blunt as his eyes, which roamed over her. When they lingered on her lips, the heat that had surged through her a moment ago pooled in her lower stomach, which frightened her more than it excited her. Nevertheless, she couldn't find the words to tell him to go away.

"Yes, as a matter of fact, it was."

"I figured as much."

"How can you tell? Do I look that frazzled?"

"No, actually you look lovely. As always."

It took a tremendous effort not to react to his huskily spoken words, but she forced herself not to. The sexual attraction that had been there from the beginning was still there and couldn't be ignored.

"Let me buy you a cup of coffee," he said at last. "It's guaranteed to make you feel better."

"Oh, no, I don't think—"

"Ah, one cup. Come on, you can handle that." His chuckle was full throated and warm. "It'll do you good."

"You're persistent."

"Think so?"

"Stubborn, actually."

"I call it determination."

That brought on a weak smile. "Okay, you win. One cup."

The coffee bar he took her to was quiet, for which she was thankful, as her nerves were frayed. She shouldn't have come, but since she had, she thought it best not to ask herself why.

Once they were seated and the order given for two cups of black coffee, he faced her. She wondered why she'd never before noticed how thick his eyelashes were. Flushing, she turned away.

"So tell me what made your day so bad."

"I don't think you really want to know."

"Sure I do," he said in his slow drawl, staring at her with a focus that further unnerved her.

Reluctantly she told him only about Jack Peterson. By the time she was finished, she was actually smiling.

"See, I told you this was a good idea."

"How's that?"

"Well, you're smiling now, where before you looked like you could have bitten a ten-penny nail in two."

"Actually, I could've bitten him."

"Only you were afraid you'd get something contagious, right?" His lips twitched.

She made a face.

"Hell, just blow him off. In every crowd there has to be one potbellied asshole."

Natalie looked dumbfounded. "How did you know he had a potbelly?"

"Lucky guess. But I was right, huh?"

She laughed, and for a moment their eyes met. The tension hadn't gone away. It was just on hold, while a waiting, uneasy silence fell between them.

"So how's your new job?" she asked, desperation spurring the question.

He shrugged. "Don't know. Haven't really started yet."

She sensed his reluctance—or was it annoyance?—at having her invade his private space. Apparently he could probe, but he didn't like *being* probed.

The waitress appeared with their coffee. They each sipped for a moment, then Natalie set down her cup, removed her gaze, and gnawed at her lower lip.

"There's something else bothering you, isn't there?"

She swung her head around, her eyes wide.

He shrugged. "Just chalk my insight up to a great gut instinct."

In spite of herself, she smiled again. If nothing else, this man was as incorrigible as he was charming.

"I do have lots on my mind," she said, her tone hesitant.

"Want to talk about it?"

"No."

"What do you want to talk about, then?"

Natalie didn't respond.

He looked at her for a long moment, then sighed. "You're a hard nut to crack, Natalie Whitmore." He paused. "But then you tried to tell me that this wasn't a good idea, and like you said, I'm too stubborn for my own good."

"You said it; I didn't." She avoided his gaze, afraid he would see something in her eyes she didn't want him to see.

"Come on, let's get out of here." A slight edge had crept into his voice.

A stony silence fell between them on the way back to the office. Still, Natalie was very much aware of him. Stealing a look at his stiff profile, she knew he was not happy, probably royally pissed, but she couldn't help it. That was his problem, not hers. He should never have intruded where he wasn't wanted. Only that wasn't so, and she knew it. He was wanted, and that was the problem.

While fighting it, she found herself fascinated by this man. There was something volatile about him, as though he enjoyed living on an explosive edge.

But to try to take on a man like Michael McCall, who was so different from Phillip, would be suicidal, not to mention the fact that she felt she was doing something she shouldn't. In her mind she was still Mrs. Phillip Whitmore.

He braked the car, and instead of his cutting off the engine, she felt him turn and look at her. Finally Natalie reached for the handle and lifted it.

"Wait a sec." His voice was like gravel as he laid his hand on her bare arm.

The bottom fell out of her stomach, as though she'd hit a bump in the road while going too fast. She looked down at his hand and noticed the tiny scars buried in the hair on his knuckles. She fought the urge to cover that hand with hers.

"Natalie?"

"What?" she whispered, finally looking at him, which she

later realized was a big mistake. Their eyes connected. The pulse in her throat fluttered as he leaned toward her.

"Don't, please," she said with a tremor. "You're . . . moving too fast."

"I know, but I can't slow down."

Roughly, he clasped her behind the neck and pulled her toward him. His lips, when they touched hers, were hot, wet, and demanding. And even though she longed to push him away, she couldn't. Like the last time he'd kissed her, sensations that she'd never felt before spiraled through her. She felt them clear down to the soles of her feet.

She knew he felt the same way, for when he released her, his face was stark white.

"I had no intention of kissing you again," he said in a shaky voice.

"And I had no intention of letting you."

"So where do we go from here?" he asked, his warm breath fanning her cheek.

Natalie's heart thumped in her throat even as she heard herself say, "I still have the picnic on my calendar."

# Sixteen

Stone drove at a snail's pace. While he didn't want to be seen cruising by the newly located Texas Aero warehouse and raise suspicion, he sure as hell wanted to know where it was and to look it over.

Too bad there wasn't much to see. It looked like the premises the company had vacated, except this building appeared in better condition. Also, there was a high fence surrounding the area and a guard on duty at the gate. Cars and trucks littered the parking lot, which proved that the business was an around-the-clock operation.

He pulled next to the curb while the car's engine idled. He fought the temptation to try to get inside, but time was against him. He had to get back to the office and work on a jewelry fraud case he'd been assigned, then meet with Larry.

Twenty minutes later Stone walked into a deserted insurance building. He peered at his watch and noticed that it was barely seven-thirty.

God, but he was tired. If he stopped long enough to take his pulse, he'd probably find he didn't have one. Sleep had been hard to come by, and he knew he looked like shit. But what the hell, he thought, making his way onto the elevator. He wasn't trying to impress anyone.

*Liar.*

He cursed, hating it when his conscience talked back to him. One thing he'd always prided himself on was *not* having a conscience. Lately, though, since he'd set his life on a new path, he seemed to have developed one.

And it had been squawking at him about his liaison with Natalie Whitmore, which was the reason for his loss of sleep. Trying his best to put her out of his mind, Stone stalked into his office and switched on the lights.

He blinked against the glare, or was it the fact that he still couldn't believe he actually had a classy office? He leaned against the jamb while his eyes wandered over the premises. The walls remained bare, but what the hell? The furniture was nice, even plush. He had a desk that wasn't scarred and a chair that didn't squeak.

A smirk relaxed his lips as he plopped down on that chair. Hell, maybe he was moving up in this old world, he told himself, only he knew better. Until he cleared his name, he wouldn't be worth a damn to himself or Sally, who was the only one he cared about.

*Liar.*

Again his conscience interfered, twisting his thoughts back to Natalie Whitmore.

"Shit," Stone muttered, crossing his hands behind his head and staring at the ceiling.

Like he'd told her, he hadn't planned on kissing her again. Hell, he hadn't planned on *touching* her again. Now he was guilty of both, which was one of the most asinine stunts he'd ever pulled. The last thing he wanted was to get emotionally involved with the woman he intended to use and who might even be involved in conspiracy and murder.

Because of that asinine behavior, he had jeopardized his entire plan. At some point he had to tell her who he was. If he'd been all business up front, then maybe he wouldn't have this problem with his out-of-control libido.

Now he was caught in a trap of his own making, aching to taste not only her lips, but the rest of her as well. Christ! How could he have been so stupid as to cross that line?

"Hey, man, you look like you've been in a pissing contest and lost."

Stone gripped the arms on his chair, then pivoted. Larry stood in the doorway. He forced a smile and a lightness in his voice that he didn't feel. "You could say that." Then, changing the subject asked, "What brings you here so early? I envisioned getting all this work done before anyone showed up."

"Bullshit."

"Wipe that shit-eatin' grin off your face and come on in."

Larry laughed outright, sauntered to the nearest chair, and eased onto it.

"I think I uncovered something you'll be happy about," Stone said without preamble.

"Oh?"

Stone gave his new boss a smug grin. "Before I tell you, I want you to promise I'll get a raise."

"Go to hell."

"Somehow, I thought you'd say that."

"What you got?" Larry asked, pulling on one of his cauli-flower ears.

"I dropped by both the old and new locations of Texas Aero."

Larry looked perplexed. "Why the old one?"

"Like an idiot, I didn't know they'd moved, and you didn't tell me."

"You had the file with you."

"I know, but I didn't think to look. Anyway, I got out and was walking around until an old fart stopped me."

"Just get to the point."

"The point is that no parts were left in the warehouse."

Larry straightened on his chair. "Who said?"

"This old pimple-gouging janitor. He told me when they moved out of the place, they took everything with them."

"You believe him?" Larry asked.

"Yep."

"Which means that even if someone did break in, which I doubt, nothing was taken because nothing was there."

"Right."

"So the bastards *are* trying to dig in the company's hip pocket."

"Looks like that to me," Stone said, his lips thin.

"Good job, my friend. Thanks to you, we have grounds to deny the claim."

"You mean it's that simple?"

"Oh, we're not going to push it or even make a big deal out of it, but we're sure as hell not going to settle, either." Larry leaned over and placed something on Stone's desk. "Take a look-see. Turn about's fair play."

Stone frowned as he picked up the sheet. "What's this?"

"Several prospectuses on other companies in competition with Texas Aero. Also, here's their prospectus as well. I picked it up from my stockbroker."

"Ah, stockbroker. So that's how rich insurance executives live, huh?"

"Fuck you."

Stone grinned.

"Read the paper," Larry said in a quarrelsome tone.

Stone did as he was told, and by the time he was finished, the blood in his veins was tingling. He looked up at Larry. "This is worth its weight in gold."

"I figured you might think so."

"Hell," Stone said, rocking back on his chair, "compared to other manufacturers in the spare parts business, Texas Aero's profit margin is substantially higher."

"Which means there's something rotten in Denmark." Larry rose suddenly and walked to the door.

"Which is what I've thought all along," Stone said to his boss's back.

Larry turned. "Now, all you've got to do is prove it."

Stone's features hardened. "I will; believe me, I will."

Larry closed the door behind him, but Stone was barely aware that he was alone. His thoughts were focused on one thing—retribution.

"Are you Mommy's sweetie?"

Clancy squirmed, then squealed as Natalie continued to bounce her on the end of her foot. "Ride 'em, horsey!"

Clancy's squeal grew louder.

"Lord a-mercy, what's going on out here?"

Natalie swung around. "Oh, hi, Danny."

She had brought Clancy to the pool with her, and while she had lapped the pool, she'd put Clancy in her automatic swing. Now she and the child were playing.

Daniel tousled Clancy's curls, then eased down on the chaise longue near Natalie. "How come you're home early?"

"Since it's Wednesday, hump day, I decided to give myself a break. Treat myself, if you will. And Clancy."

"Well, I'll be damned. The machine can run down."

Natalie flushed. "That's not nice."

"What?" Daniel feigned innocence.

"I'm no machine," she said with hurt in her voice, "and you know it."

"Couldn't have proved it by me," Daniel responded in an unruffled tone.

Natalie held her tongue. She didn't want to argue with her brother. She hadn't seen him in a few days, and she'd missed him.

As if he'd read her thoughts, Daniel asked, "How 'bout going for a ride? It's a lovely evening."

Natalie brightened. "That sounds great. I'm sure Magic would appreciate being ridden, as I haven't been on her lately."

"I'll see that the horses are saddled while you take Clance in to Josie."

They met later at the stables. Natalie looked for Dave, but he was nowhere around. Thank goodness, she thought, as he was the last person she wanted to see.

"Ready?"

Natalie shook herself, then returned Daniel's smile. "Yep."

They rode in silence to the top of their favorite hill, where they had spent many hours talking and laughing. But there was no laughter between them now, and that fact saddened Natalie.

Once they brought the horses to a stop, she faced her brother. "You're not happy with me, either, are you?"

He shrugged, a weak smile coming to his face. "Oh, well. At least I'm not going to pull your doll's head off again."

She giggled, pointing her finger at him. "I'd forgotten all about that, Daniel Whitmore! That was my favorite doll, and I cried for days over it. I can't even remember now what you were mad at me about."

"I don't know, either, but whatever it was, I must have been pissed. I didn't mean anything by it. Cut me some slack, Nat; I was a kid, remember?"

"Yeah, but that's gross. I mean, you pulled the poor thing's *head* off, for heaven's sakes!"

He threw his hands in the air. "Okay, okay. I'm sorry I brought it up, and I promise I'll never pull another doll's head off as long as I live."

"Okay, but back to the subject at hand, which is: you're still not happy with me."

"What makes you think that? . . ."

"Come on, Danny, it's me you're talking to. I know you like a book."

He sighed, then cocked his head so as to look her straight in the eye. "That's not the point. What *is* the point is that not only have you turned all our lives upside down, but—" He broke off and shifted his gaze.

"Go on," Natalie pressed.

He faced her again. "I can't pinpoint it, only there's that haunted look in your eyes, the same look you had for so long after Phillip died."

Natalie didn't say anything.

"Are you having second thoughts about probing into Phillip's death?"

"No, Danny, I'm not. That's something I have to do. For me."

"So then, are you having second thoughts about moving out of the house?"

"The answer is no to that, too. However, I'm in no hurry. I haven't found a place I like as yet or can afford."

"Does that mean there's a chance I can talk you into changing your mind and staying here permanently?"

She shook her head.

"Then what the hell's going on? I know something's wrong."

"The other day I received a threatening phone call," she blurted out.

Daniel's mouth gaped two inches. "What?"

"It's true." Feeling her lower lip begin to tremble, she bit down on it.

"But . . . who . . .?" Again he broke off, as if grappling to come to terms with what she'd told him.

"That's exactly what I'd like to know."

"Was it a man?"

"Yes."

"Tell me exactly what he said."

Once she'd repeated the terse conversation, Daniel cursed. "Why didn't you come to me immediately?"

"What would you have done?"

Her question seemed to stop him cold for a moment. Then he said, "Well, for one thing, I would've suggested we get your phone tapped in case this nut tries something like that again."

"I know," she whispered, reaching over and squeezing his hand. "But it shook me up so that I was numb for a while. Then I got mad, then frightened because I thought it might've been Fletcher."

"Dad! Why, that's crazy."

"That's what I hoped you'd say, knowing in my heart that it wasn't him. But who *was* it? Someone called me."

"I haven't the foggiest idea, but don't you worry about it. First, I think it's an empty threat, and second, I'll see what I can find out."

"There's a possibility it might've been Dave."

This time Daniel looked stupefied. "Dave? Why on earth—"

"Because I caught him in the barn with Paula."

Daniel didn't so much as flinch. "I know about that, I'm sorry to say."

"Does Fletcher?"

"If he does, he hasn't said anything to me."

"What about Stanley? Does he know?"

"I'm not sure about that, either."

"Well, that episode in the barn probably has nothing to do with the threatening call. It's just that I'm grasping for an answer."

Again Daniel was quiet.

"So what's your read on this mess?"

"Is there anything else you haven't told me?"

She almost said yes, thinking about Michael McCall, only she didn't. As much as she trusted and confided in Daniel, her unsettling relationship with that man was something she couldn't share, maybe because she didn't understand it herself.

Where he was concerned, nothing made any sense, except her responses to his kisses. He knew how to use his lips and tongue to full advantage. Even now, just thinking about his hot lips on hers turned her breathing shallow and her skin moist.

"Natalie?"

She jerked herself back to the moment at hand and gave Daniel a lame smile. "Sorry. And no, there's nothing else."

He reached out and caressed one side of her cheek. "Don't you worry about all this, you hear?"

She trapped his palm against her cheek. "Oh, Danny, I don't know what I'd do without you."

"Same here," he said in a gruff voice, followed by a silence.

Then he grinned and, nudging his stallion, took off. "Come on, I'll race you!"

"Hey, don't—" Natalie's words were cut short when her mount balked.

"Last one back has to buy dinner!" Daniel called over his shoulder.

"That's not fair, Danny!" she cried, galloping into his dust.

# Seventeen

Captain Bill Rutgers held the phone away from his ear. It didn't solve his problem. He could still hear his brother-in-law's whiny voice. "Dammit, Bill, are you listening?"

"Yeah, I'm listening."

"So when are you going to pay me back the money?"

"When I get it, damn you!"

With that Rutgers slammed down the receiver, then stomped to the window in his office and peered outside into the blinding sunlight. He rubbed his wet forehead, hoping to regroup, recover from that rear attack. Everybody wanted a piece of him, only there just wasn't enough to go around.

He tightened his necktie in another nervous gesture. The financial predicament he was in was his wife's fault. Hell, she just had to have the house redone, knowing their savings wouldn't near cover what she wanted. So in a weak moment he'd let her talk him into borrowing from her brother, which turned out to be a big mistake.

He never did like the fucker, anyway. So maybe his wife could pay her own brother back. Maybe she'd just have to get off her butt and go to work. Rutgers smiled. Not a bad idea, considering he worked his butt off daily, got kicked in the nuts by his superiors daily, just so Marion could hobnob with her rich-bitch friends.

At first he didn't hear the knock, so lost was he in his miserable thoughts. But when it became louder, Rutgers whipped around, a scowl on his face.

Detective Andrew Logan stood outside the glass door.

Rutgers beckoned him in. "This had better be good, Logan, 'cause I'm in a pissy mood."

Logan shifted from one foot to the other, though he didn't back down; Rutgers had to hand that to him. But then Logan had been on the force for a number of years and had endured his many mood swings.

"You'll never guess who's back in town, Captain." Logan was a large man with a high voice.

"Suppose you just tell me," Rutgers said, sarcasm thick in his voice. "I'm not into playing guessing games."

"Sorry, sir."

"So who's back in town?" Rutgers asked in a tired tone.

"Stone McCall."

Dammit, another dose of McCall was the last thing he needed.

"You all right, sir?"

"Shit, yes, I'm all right." Rutgers wiped his moist upper lip with the back of his hand. "Did you see him with your own eyes?"

"Yes, sir. I was at my sister's house this week, and he was moving into the condo three doors down from hers."

"You're positive? You could've been mistaken, you know."

"I'm positive." Logan's tone was firm. "At first, though, I wasn't; I'll admit that. He's changed. Lost a lot of weight, which makes him look younger, but still, I'd know him anywhere. Only thing, I didn't think McCall would have the balls to show his face in this town again."

"Me either," Rutgers muttered after taking a deep breath to try to conquer his nausea. "Thanks, Logan. Now, go on, get outta here."

What the hell was McCall doing back? If McCall found out that he, Rutgers, had pushed IAD . . .

Hell, he couldn't think about that now. Pension or not, he was beginning to hate his job.

He had a call to make. Now. Rutgers placed his hand on the receiver, just as it buzzed.

"Yeah?" he growled, then listened. "Tell him I'll be right there."

The chief wanted him in her office ASAP. The timing couldn't have been worse. Rutgers slammed his office door behind him and marched down the hall, the glands in his neck feeling as if they were about to explode.

"I was afraid you would change your mind."

Natalie stared at him, then looked away. The day was perfect for a picnic, even though she suspected the heat and humidity would be a problem. The sun was like a ball of fire in the blue sky, already warming their skin.

Declining his invitation to pick them up, Natalie and Clancy had met Michael McCall and his daughter, Sally, in the park.

Clancy had taken to Sally immediately, for which Natalie was thrilled. But then she, too, had bonded with the doe-eyed teenager, who reminded her of herself when she was that age.

Beyond the beauty of Sally's eyes, Natalie saw a sad, haunted look that she hoped would disappear now that the girl had her daddy back in her life.

They had just consumed a huge lunch of sandwiches, fried chicken, potato salad, and fried peach pies. The children were off to their left, playing with a ball and having a good time.

"I thought about not coming, all right," she finally said into the growing silence.

"That doesn't surprise me. But I'm glad you came."

Natalie looked away again, her emotions in an upheaval. But then they always were when she was around this man. He moved, which drew her gaze back to him. He was standing and had propped his foot on the bench next to where she sat.

He had on shorts and a green shirt that matched his eyes.

He looked a little pale, and as always, he needed a haircut. That longish hair didn't bother her. Somehow it fit him, added to the dangerous aura that surrounded him.

"Have you moved into your condo yet?" she asked to counteract the probing eyes that peered down at her.

"As a matter of fact, I have; I finished that task last night."

"Last night. Why, you must be exhausted."

He gave her a twisted smile. "Hardly. I can almost get all my worldly possessions in the palm of one hand."

"You're kidding, surely?"

"Nope. However, now that Sally's going to be spending a lot of time with me, or at least I hope she is, I figure I'll have to go shopping."

Natalie smiled. "I'm sure she'll lend you a hand."

"Only if I come through with the bunk beds she's been begging for."

"Oh, Lord." Natalie laughed. "I've always considered those the most uncomfortable beds made."

"Hey, according to my kid, they're cool."

"Speaking of kids, your daughter's a gem."

"Thanks." He grinned. "I think so, too, but then, she's mine."

"Is she still all right? I mean—"

"So far so good. The doctor says she has no permanent damage and continues to give her a clean bill of health."

"Well, she certainly looks good and has enough energy for two people. Just look at the way she chases after Clancy." Natalie smiled as she watched the teenager and the toddler chase the ball. "Too bad I can't hire her to baby-sit Clance."

"Yeah, too bad, 'cause that means I'd get to see more of you."

They fell into an awkward silence while they stared at each other.

After a moment, he leaned forward and said in a low, charged tone, "How does it feel to know that you've got me over a barrel, to know that I want you so much that I'm prepared to make a fool of myself."

"Michael, don't . . ."

She had only to move ever so slightly, and she could touch his mouth. And she wanted to. Oh, God, she wanted to. But she didn't. Instead she licked her dry lips and ran a nervous hand behind her neck.

He straightened suddenly and tossed the empty Coke can in the trash bin a few yards away. He had an indolent, confident presence that couldn't be overlooked. And when he shoved a hand down in the pocket of his running shorts, her eyes were drawn to his flat stomach. She ached to look lower, knowing what she would see if she did. She tried to refocus her gaze, only she couldn't. The knit material did little to hide his arousal.

"Natalie?" Her name was spoken in a half whisper.

"What?"

"You know what, don't you?"

She swallowed but didn't answer, hating the fact that he knew exactly how she was feeling.

"I want to kiss you so bad that I'm hurting."

"Please," she whispered as she glanced toward the children.

He took a deep breath, then pulled back. "Okay, I'll behave."

"Spoken like a true gentleman," she responded, forcing a lightness into her tone that she wasn't feeling.

"But one in great pain."

She flushed. "I thought you said you'd behave."

"I'm trying, dammit, I'm trying." He leaned closer again. "But you gotta know that when you're around, you suck all the resistance out of me."

She made a helpless gesture with her hands, and her cheeks turned red, knowing that she was treading in water way over her head.

"So, are you feeling better?" he asked, adeptly changing the subject.

Relieved, she said, "I didn't know I'd been feeling bad."

"Well, maybe that wasn't quite the correct term. Maybe upset's the word."

Natalie's cheeks lost their color. "I suppose you're referring to the day we had coffee?"

"Right. You were upset about something. Has that 'something' been taken care of?"

She sighed. "No, actually it hasn't."

"I'm still willing to listen."

"You don't by any chance know of a good private detective, do you?"

She knew she'd shocked him. His eyes narrowed, as had his lips before he'd snapped them shut.

"Are you surprised?" she asked.

"Are you *serious*?"

"Absolutely."

"I don't get it. Why would you want a private detective?"

Natalie hesitated, but only for a second. "I want to know *all* the facts surrounding my husband's death."

He blew air out of his lungs, then was quiet for a moment, as if he were digesting what she'd told him. Then he finally asked, "And you think a PI can do that?"

"Actually, I want the PI to find the cop who *shot* my husband."

Stone's jaw dropped, and he could only stare at her, feeling as if he'd been sucker-punched in the gut. Only by sheer force of will did he remain upright. Before he could respond, however, Clancy let out a piercing scream.

"What the hell?" Stone began as they both jumped up and ran toward the children.

Clancy was jumping up and down while Sally looked frantic. "Daddy, she got into an ant bed!" Sally wailed.

"It's going to be all right, sweetheart," Stone said, lifting the baby before Natalie could. "I've got something that'll make the baby feel better."

"Want me to take her?" Natalie asked, following behind as if in shock that Clancy had let him pick her up.

"No, she's fine, or soon will be."

Ten minutes later Clancy was indeed fine. She had stopped crying and was laughing at Sally.

Natalie laughed herself, then got up from the bench. "The little minx. She scared me out of my wits, but now that I'm up, I might as well change her diaper. I know she's wet."

Stone handed the child to Natalie.

"You mean you aren't willing to change her, too?"

He cleared his throat. "Naw, I think I'll sit this one out."

"Chicken."

He grinned, only that grin was short-lived as he watched her stand and proceed to take care of the task.

He wanted just to concentrate on her tight ass and seemingly endless legs that were his for the viewing, since she was wearing cut-offs and a T-shirt, which left him privy to her other assets as well—high, firm breasts, slender waist, and flat stomach. And he couldn't forget about that lower, pillowy lip that drove his lust to new heights.

No doubt about it, whenever she walked she had the power to break necks and dislodge vertebrae—especially his.

Right now he couldn't appreciate those attributes, not when his brain was going crazy inside his skull. First, he couldn't believe she had said *she* wanted an investigation into her husband's death. Second, he couldn't believe that she wanted to find *him*, for chrissake!

Cold sweat broke out on his skin. Hell, he'd been afraid he would end up with his nuts in a grinder, and sure enough he had. The question was how to handle this sudden turn of events.

Brooding, Stone watched while she placed a blanket on the soft grass, then laid Clancy on it while Sally knelt beside her. He felt something stir inside, a warm sensation, something that had nothing to do with sex and sent his heart bolting to his throat.

He turned away, striving to get control of himself. A few minutes later Natalie plopped down on the bench across from him, the smile gone from her face. He knew she was thinking about the conversation they had started before Clancy squealed.

He forced himself to say, "You want to tell me about what happened to your husband?"

She licked her lips again, leaving them dewy and begging to be kissed, which was again what he longed to do. *Stop it, McCall!*

"It's not a pretty story," she was saying.

"I didn't figure it was."

She told him then, in a halting voice, what had happened that day in the bank.

He reached out and covered her hand, trying to ignore the fact that they both trembled. "So what you're saying is that you think your husband was in some kind of trouble?"

"Oh, he was definitely in trouble all right, only I don't know to what extent. He wouldn't confide in me."

"But he was going to confide in his attorney?"

"Yes, only he . . . he never got the chance."

She withdrew her hand and focused her attention on the children, who were still playing with the ball. Stone stared at her, his mind still in a turmoil. If she wanted an investigation, then was it possible that she wasn't in cahoots with her husband? Or was this one helluva good acting job?

Whatever the case, it was too late for him to back out now. He intended to see his mission through. And this woman, who sent a hot stab to his sternum every time he so much as looked at her, remained suspect in his eyes despite her show of innocence.

"So have you talked to anyone else about this?"

"My family knows, of course. And I've interviewed several private detectives."

"Have you hired one?"

"No. I haven't found any I feel I can trust."

"I'm not surprised. They're usually a bunch of scumbags."

"Unfortunately, I agree. Anyway, I also spoke to Captain Rutgers at the police department."

Great, Stone thought, a chill going through him. "And what did he say?" His tone was terse.

She gave him an odd look, then said, "He acted like I was suffering from PMS, which means he dismissed me and my request."

Stone's gut reaction was to smile without humor. That sounded just like the asshole.

"How much did you know about your husband's business dealings?" he asked suddenly.

"Not much, I'm afraid. You see, he ran the family businesses and I wasn't encouraged to interfere."

"Forget about hiring a private detective."

She blinked. "What did you say?"

"You heard me."

"Okay, but why should I do that?"

"I think I can help you, that's why."

She drew back, a suspicious look on her face. "How?"

He didn't respond. He couldn't. His mouth was suddenly devoid of saliva.

"Just who are you, anyway?"

He heard the sudden alarm in her voice but tried to ignore it. "My name is Michael *Stone* McCall; I'm the cop who killed your husband."

# Eighteen

Natalie sucked in her breath and stared at him while emotions ranging from fury, to shock, to hurt, to mistrust charged through her.

Fury won. "How dare you!" she cried, backing away, afraid that if she stayed close, she might attack him physically, even go so far as to claw his eyes out. Her heart was pounding so hard, she could feel it throughout her body.

"Natalie—"

"No!" She stopped up her ears, then she turned toward the children to make certain they were still playing and not aware of what was going on between the two adults.

When she faced Stone again, their eyes collided.

"Look, I know what you're thinking, but—" His voice sounded hoarse, as though he had a sore throat.

"You don't have any idea what I'm thinking!" she lashed back.

"Believe me, I do." His tone had changed; it was now persuasive and soft as silk.

It fell on deaf ears as Natalie laughed, though there was no mirth in her laughter. She was perilously close to tears, but she'd die before he saw that weakness. "Oh, that's good," she ridiculed. "That's really good. I can't tell you how that admission restores my faith in you."

Stone seemed almost to choke on an expletive that ripped through his lips. "I know I deserve a kick in the balls for not telling you up front who I was, but I had my reasons. And if you'll just let me explain—"

"I don't want to hear another word you have to say, damn you!" Natalie dragged air through her burning lungs. "Everything connected with us has been a sham, starting with that run-in in the grocery store, right?"

"Yes, but—"

"No! Don't you dare try to gloss over that. Anyway, it's *my* turn to set the record straight. You know what? I think you're a 'dirty' cop who shot my husband on purpose."

Stone's eyes narrowed, and his features took on the hardness of ice. "That's bullshit! I was a *victim* in that bloody nightmare. And your husband's death was an accident."

"If you're so innocent, then why the duplicity?" She spat the words at him, then gave another mirthless laugh. "But I know the answer to that. You think my husband was involved in something illegal and that I was part of it, too."

She paused, then went on, her voice thick with anger. "Only the lowest of scum would pull a trick like that."

His features turned icier, and for a moment she actually feared he might strike her. Again, what did she really know about this man? Nothing, except what it felt like to have his lips on hers. . . . Oh, God, what had happened to her?

Natalie turned away, unable to bear looking at him, even though she noticed that his features no longer looked cold, but rather pinched and drawn. In fact, he looked as sick as she felt, which somewhat assured her that after watching the way he'd coddled Clancy when the ants had stung her, she knew he'd never hurt her physically.

But emotionally, he had mangled her heart. And mentally, he'd made a fool out of her. She could never forgive him for either.

"Natalie, please, just listen for a minute." He was pleading in a voice that sounded like rough gravel. "I think we ought to work together and try to find out what really happened that day in the bank."

"*What?*"

"It makes perfect sense, if you'll just think about it. That day changed both our lives, and we have a right—"

"Stop it! I don't want to hear another word."

"Yes, you do! You want to hear the truth, don't you?"

"Yes! But you wouldn't know the truth if it slapped you in the face." Her voice was shrill. "Besides, how do I know it wasn't you who called and threatened me?"

Before she realized his intentions, he reached out and grabbed her.

"Threatened you? What the hell's that all about?"

The muscles in her arm turned rigid under his touch. She sucked in her breath again and held it; they stared at each other.

The silence built.

"Let go of me."

Her eyes stabbed with contempt while his forehead beaded with sweat, and his lips turned ashen. She could hear the sound of his harsh, erratic breathing. The look on his face formed a cold kernel of fear in the pit of her stomach.

He let go just as quickly as he'd grabbed her. "Jesus! Do you really think I'd hurt you?"

She rubbed her arm. "I don't know what you'd do. Remember, I don't know you."

"Well, if you'll just stop and think rationally for a moment, what possible reason would I have had for threatening you? None, goddammit, and you know that."

"You lied to me. You *used* me."

"Only because I'm desperate to clear my name."

Words couldn't penetrate the armor around this man. God, didn't he have a conscience?

"And I intend to do just that," he went on, "with or without your help. And if you and your husband are innocent, then I'll clear you as well."

She felt a shiver roll down her spine. "I'm taking my daughter and we're leaving."

"Natalie, please—"

Her glacial expression stopped him. She stared at him with eyes devoid of mercy. "I don't want anything else to do with you. Do you understand that? As far as I'm concerned, you can rot in hell!"


Stone stopped pacing the floor in his new condo and kneaded the back of his neck. Hell, he was cracking up, and there didn't seem to be a damn thing he could do to prevent it because he'd fucked up.

Oh, he could gloss over the truth with another verb, one much less colorful, but even three days after the fact, he couldn't think of any more appropriate.

He should have used finesse, or at least attempted to use some. But hell, what had he done? He'd told her who he was bluntly and brutally, as if by doing so, he could absolve his own warring conscience.

Yet he'd made a promise to himself for Sally's sake that lies and betrayal would no longer be part of his life. Still, the contempt he'd seen in Natalie's eyes had been almost palpable, and even now he tasted it.

"Shit!" He began pacing again.

He shouldn't have been surprised at her reaction, he told himself, but it stung nonetheless, especially as he wasn't certain *she* was lily white herself. Possibly she had something to hide or she wouldn't have become so defensive.

What stuck in his craw more than anything was the unsuspected weakness in himself. It hadn't been in his plans for her to get under his skin the way she had. Since his divorce, there had been countless women in his life; they had come and gone like a revolving door. None had meant anything, but then none had been in a class with Natalie Whitmore.

That didn't mean she didn't have her own secrets to hide. He damn well knew she had her own agenda, which brought to mind the threatening phone call she'd mentioned. He wasn't surprised that something like that had happened. After all the ruckus she'd raised, anyone, including her family, Texas Aero, and Rutgers, could have a vested interested in keeping her quiet.

The thought of anyone actually hurting her heightened his barely controlled rage. Just give him five minutes with the bastard responsible for that threat and he'd squeeze his balls until he was neutered.

Since he didn't know, he had to concentrate on the moment. So what next? Stone asked himself. The one person he knew could help him get to the truth had told him in a ladylike way to go fuck himself.

He heard the sudden slam of a car door and strode to the window, where he watched his daughter get out of a Buick. He had almost forgotten he'd called Sally and asked her to spend the night. He'd been so tired of his own company and his own miserable thoughts that he'd needed relief.

What better tonic than being with his daughter? But he hadn't expected her this early. While he had no problem with the time element, other than the fact that he was an emotional wreck, he did have a problem with his ex-wife getting out of the car and accompanying Sally to the door.

"Wonderful," he muttered, taking a bitter moment to compose himself.

Seconds later he opened the front door and walked out into the late afternoon sunlight.

"Hi, Daddy," Sally cried, and launched herself into his arms. He hugged her while he looked over her shoulder at his ex-wife.

Connie McCall Newcomb stared back at him with a slight smirk on her too red lips, lips that seemed to enhance the fact that her hair needed another bleach job. The black roots, next to her scalp, looked like dirt. In addition, she had gained more weight than her frame could carry. He thought of Natalie's perfectly proportioned body and cursed silently.

"Hello, Stone," she finally said.

"Connie."

"Mom wants to talk to you," Sally butted in, her eyes flickering between them. "Alone."

Stone drew back and peered into his daughter's upturned face. "Okay. So why don't you go on inside? I'll be along shortly."

She turned back to Connie. "Mom, don't keep him too long, okay?"

Connie actually smiled, which Stone thought for a second might break her face. "I won't."

Once Sally had vanished inside the condo, Stone turned back to his ex-wife, but he didn't say anything. This was her party.

"I guess I might as well get to the point."

"Reckon so," he drawled.

"Look, I just want to know what your intentions are."

He raised an eyebrow. "My intentions?"

"Don't play dumb with me." Her lips tightened. "I want to know when you're going to haul ass again and leave Sally flapping in the wind."

He held on to his patience by a hair. "People in hell want ice water, too."

Connie's face turned red, then white. "You bastard. You owe me an explanation."

"Look, I don't owe you a thing, not even the goddamn time of day. But because of Sally, I'm going to be civil and answer your question. I'm not leaving. I'm here to stay, so you might as well get used to me being part of Sally's life. I thought you understood that from the start."

"I figure Sally's not the real reason you came back, so why don't you dispense with the fatherhood bit and tell the truth."

"Again, I don't owe you the truth or anything else. I don't give a shit. But you're right. I came back to clear my name of the charges leveled against me that cost me my badge."

Connie drew back as if he'd slapped her. "You mean you're going to dredge all that mess back out into the open?"

"That 'mess,' as you call it, cost me over a year of my life."

"What about Sally?"

"That's partly why I'm doing it."

"Yeah, right," she spat, "so her friends can tease her again about her daddy being a 'dirty cop'?"

This was just another romp through the garbage dump, and he'd let himself walk right into it.

"You'll be sorry, you know," she added before he had time to respond.

"Is that a threat?"

She laughed a bitter laugh. "Hardly. It's just the truth, only you're too blind to see it. But then that's always been your problem. It's your way or no way."

Stone's eyes roamed over her until his insolent gaze got the reaction he wanted. She flushed and gnawed on her lower lip as if she realized she might have gone too far. "You've had your say, now I'll have mine. Get out of my life and stay out. You're not wanted."

With that Stone turned and stomped back into the condo, where Sally looked up at him from the middle of the living room floor, her brown eyes troubled.

"Daddy, what were you and Mom arguing about?" she asked.

"You."

"I thought so."

Stone walked over and tweaked her chin, then grinned. "It's okay, though. I won."

She punched him in the ribs, then matched his grin. "You're bad." Then her face sobered. "But you didn't win with Natalie the other day, did you?" She paused. "I mean, you two were arguing, too, weren't you?"

"I guess you could call it that," he said, refusing to lie to her.

"I thought so. I couldn't hear what y'all were saying, but she looked like Mom used to when you'd done something to make her real mad and she'd chew you out."

Sally's voice sounded both shaky and forlorn, and Stone swallowed a curse while his insides knotted.

"I'm not going to lie to you, sweetheart. I walked into a briar patch and the thorns are still sticking in me."

Sally gave him a strange look that told him she didn't know whether to laugh or cry.

"Hey, it's okay. I'll eventually pull 'em out."

"Oh, Daddy." Sally's mouth dipped at the corners. "I'm serious. I like Natalie and Clancy, and I thought you did, too."

Stone draped his arms around her shoulders. "I do, but there's some things we disagree on. Anyway, you don't worry your pretty head about it."

She stood on her tiptoes and kissed him on his bristled cheek.

He held her close for a moment. "Everything's going to be all right, sweetheart."

Too bad he didn't believe that.

# Nineteen

Natalie heard Lucy yapping on the tiny cellular phone in the living room of the empty town house, but she couldn't hear what was being said, nor did she care.

Her mind, as she stood peering out the glassed-in breakfast nook, wasn't on Lucy and business. It was on finding a suitable place for her and Clancy to live.

For the past week she had been living on nothing but adrenaline, and although she had done her best to carry on as normal, the jagged edges were beginning to show.

Actually, Natalie was inconsolable, except during the hours she spent with Clancy. No matter how wired she felt at the end of the day, she could hold her precious child, nuzzle her sweet-smelling neck, read to her, talk to her, listen to her say "Mamma" a million times, and the pressure would drain from her body.

Unfortunately, that euphoric feeling was a fleeting gift. Once she put Clancy to bed and joined the family for dinner, the pressure would start to rebuild.

Even though the family was outwardly civil, the relationship with Fletcher and Martha was not the same. It seemed to further erode every day, despite the fact that she continued to be a part of the household. Natalie felt like an outcast, something she had sworn she would never feel again.

But it was the shock of Stone McCall's duplicity that had knocked the wind from her. She hated to admit it, but she hadn't yet recovered. She'd been so susceptible to his brand of hard-nosed charisma and charm. It galled her that she felt a stronger physical attraction to Stone than she ever had to her husband.

Looking back, she knew that she had adored Phillip more than she had loved him passionately. Before their marriage he had put her on a pedestal, and she had let him. Afterward she had put him on one as well. It was as if they had gone to great lengths to shield each other from reality. She had always thought of him as her hero, her knight in shining armor.

Tears glazed Natalie's eyes, and for a moment she was tempted to give in to them. She refused. After she had come to live with the Whitmores, she had promised herself no more tears, either for self-indulgence or to win a point. Before that, her life had been filled with both open and silent tears. Only when she lost Phillip had she broken that promise.

Stone McCall wasn't worth her tears. He wasn't even worth her thoughts. So why couldn't she forget him and go on about her business? Was it because there was the possibility that he just might be innocent? If that was true, he would definitely be an ally.

But she didn't like the way he made her feel. He had stroked her womanhood and her ego in just the right way, forcing her to remember what it was like to be a woman, to enjoy having a man around for companionship and for sex.

Sex. Was that what this was all about with Stone? She couldn't control her memories of the warmth of his hungry mouth on hers. At unexpected times throughout the day and night, thoughts of his tongue pressing its way between her teeth, and the throbbing heat of his arousal combined with her own, sent her out of the bed and into Clancy's room as if the devil were chasing her.

She hoped that in time those agonizing memories would fade. Meanwhile, how was she going to cope with them? She couldn't ignore the fact that Stone McCall, the man who had killed her husband, was trying to prove his *innocence* while she was trying to prove his *guilt*.

Natalie wondered if she would ever feel peace again, if the constant gnawing inside her would ever subside.

"Well, is this the one or not?"

Natalie whirled and gave Lucy a bright grin.

Her boss seemed taken aback. "Geez, what did I do to earn that? Hell, I haven't even seen you *smile* for a week now."

Natalie shrugged. "You just rescued me from my dreary thoughts, so I thought you should be rewarded."

"What's going on, my friend? And don't you dare say 'Not anything' because I know better."

"I wasn't going to deny it," Natalie said in a soft, troubled tone.

"Do I hear you saying that things are in the toilet and you need cheering up?"

"I guess that pretty well sums it up."

"So let's have a heart-to-heart, shall we?"

Natalie looked around. "Here?"

"Why not? I need to sit down. My feet are killing me." Lucy nodded toward the deck. "Let's go outside and park on the deck benches. It's a lovely afternoon; a little sunshine won't hurt us."

"You sure you have time?" Natalie smiled. "I know you came only because I threatened you."

"Yeah, right, but now that I'm here, nothing less than an earthquake is going to make me leave until I know what has you so upset."

Once they were seated outside, Lucy continued, "Is it safe to assume that your long face has to do with your family acting like asses or with Michael McCall?" She paused and gave Natalie a pointed look. "So which is it?"

"His real name is Stone McCall."

At first Lucy appeared confused, then it was as though a light clicked on inside her head. "You mean, he's . . . he's—" She broke off and took a deep gulp.

"That's right," Natalie said with no emotion. "He's the cop who killed Phillip."

"How on earth did the two of you—" Again Lucy broke off, obviously too shocked to continue.

"That's what I've been asking myself," Natalie said. "How could I have not known? But in defense of myself, I never saw the man. I was in such a stupor after Phillip died, and having Clancy to care for—well, I just never made the effort to concentrate on the cop himself. Besides, the paper never printed his picture. I'm sure the powers-that-be stopped that."

"But they kicked him off the force, right?"

"Right."

"There had to be a reason he got booted."

"I suspect Fletcher had a hand in that."

"So does Fletcher know?"

"That I've been seeing . . . Stone?"

"Yes."

"God, I hope not, though Daniel saw us together at a Chinese restaurant and asked me who he was. I told him that 'Michael' was just a client."

"So apparently he didn't recognize him, either."

"Oh, I'm sure he didn't."

Lucy made a face. "Wonder why not?"

"Probably because Daniel never saw him, either. You know how he is."

"Yeah, kinda lunchy."

"Lucy!"

Lucy grinned. "Well, you know what I mean. Maybe kooky's a better word."

"Much better."

"Anyway, I'm sure you're right. If Daniel had recognized him, the shit would've already hit the fan, if not from Danny boy, then from some other member of the family."

"My thoughts exactly," Natalie said in a faraway voice.

"So, back to McCall. I don't get it. Why did he dupe you? Hell, why would he want to have anything to do with you or any of your family, for that matter? From what I've seen of him, he appears to have all his oars in the water."

Natalie almost smiled. "Oh, he has his oars in the water all right. He set out to meet me, then use me to help clear his name."

"What could knowing *you* do to clear his name?"

"Obviously he feels the Whitmores are up to no good, and I was the easiest Whitmore for him to get close to."

"Man alive, what a friggin' mess."

Natalie went on to tell her the gist of her and Stone's verbal battle at the park.

"Do you think he's telling the truth?"

"Oh, Luce, even if he is, I don't think I should have anything to do with him."

Lucy pinched her nose. "Are you sure?"

"No!" Natalie cried, getting up and walking to the edge of the deck. Finally she turned around, agony registered on her face. "I've even thought about turning the tables on him."

"You mean using him just as he planned to use you?"

"Exactly."

"Sounds good to me, only that might be dangerous, *if* he truly was a dirty cop."

"I know. That's what's stopping me."

"Are you sure that's the only thing?"

Natalie's chin jutted, but when she spoke her tone was even. "I don't know what you're talking about."

"Sure you do."

This time Natalie felt her face turn red, and she looked away.

Lucy sighed. "Look, I'm not asking for anything you're not prepared to tell me. It's obvious that this guy got under your skin in some way, which I thought was grand. But now that we know who he is, I guess it's best if you don't dwell on what might have been."

"I despise him." Natalie didn't bother to mask the venom in her tone.

Lucy cleared her throat and asked, "So are you going to continue with the investigation on your own?"

"If anything, I'm even more determined."

"It's back to hiring a private dick, huh?"

"I guess. At the moment, I'm so confused I don't know what I'm going to do." Natalie balled her hand into a fist. "Except quit, that is. That's one thing I'm *not* going to do."

"Well, whether you like it or not, you and Mr. Stone McCall might be stepping on each other's toes."

"I'm sure of that, but I'll just have to cross that bridge when I come to it."

There was a short silence.

"So are you really interested in buying this town house?" Lucy asked, changing the subject.

Natalie released her pent-up breath. "Yes, I think I am, but as you can see, it needs a lot of work before I'd ever consider moving in."

"Is that going to be a problem?" Lucy asked. "Financially, I mean?"

"No, not if a couple of those sales come through that I'm expecting."

"I can always help, you know."

"I know, and I appreciate it, believe me. But before I make any firm decision, I want to bring Danny to look at it." Natalie's gaze clouded. "I'd love to bring Martha, too, but—" Her voice choked.

"Come on, kiddo, let's go have a martini lunch. These heart-to-hearts are getting worse than barium enemas."

Natalie walked over and gave Lucy a hug. "Forget the martinis. After your sassy mouth, who needs them?"

Later, Natalie almost regretted not having taken Lucy up on the martini lunch, for when she let herself in the ranch house, Paula was stumbling down the stairs.

When she saw Natalie, she stopped but clung to the banister. "Well, well, if it isn't my dear sister-in-law."

"Hello, Paula," Natalie said with as much civility as she could muster.

Paula's grin was bitter. "Always the perfect lady. Only we both know that's not so, don't we?"

"I don't intend to get into a cat fight with you, Paula."

"In that case, why don't you get the hell out of this house like you said you were going to? After what you've done, no one wants you here."

Natalie was tempted to lash back, to defend herself once again. Then she thought, To hell with it. She didn't owe this drunken, miserable person an explanation. She didn't owe her a thing.

"Go home, Paula, and sleep it off."

With that, Natalie walked past her up the stairs.

Paula's crackling laugh followed her. "You may run, sweetie, but you can't hide. We're all watching you."

Natalie felt shaken, even though she wanted to deny it. And it wasn't all because of Paula, either. She was more of a menace than a threat. But Stone—he was both.

As feared, the second she crawled into bed that evening and closed her eyes, his face filled her vision. She sat upright while frightening questions circled her brain.

Could she trust him? *Dared* she trust him?

# Twenty

Stone's eyes felt as if someone had tossed a cup of sand in them, which usually happened when one hadn't slept in several nights.

He rubbed them, then muttered "Damn" when they burned even more. It was imperative that his mind be as sharp as possible. A strong cup of fresh coffee sounded mighty good. It would jolt his sluggish mind and body. Too bad it wasn't accessible.

He took the remaining sip of the old coffee and almost gagged. The stuff tasted like Louisiana stump water. It had lost its punch hours ago. But the noise hadn't. Planes taking off from the Dallas/Fort Worth Airport whizzed above his head.

He had made arrangements through a friend of a friend to talk to an assistant head mechanic for one of the major airlines and was looking forward to that meeting. If it proved successful, he would've made a significant breakthrough in the investigation.

Since studying in detail the Texas Aero Industries profit and loss statement that Larry had given him, Stone had gotten a tightness in his gut that had finally pole-vaulted him into action. Now, as he was ready to get out of his car, Stone peered into the rearview mirror and winced. Not only did he feel like hell, he looked like hell. Again, what could he expect? He smiled ruefully. His condo hadn't fared any better. It could've easily been mistaken for Beirut, even though it had appeared pristine after Sally had left.

"Promise me, Daddy," she'd said, placing her hands on her hips and pointing her finger at him, "that you won't trash this place out like you did your old apartment."

"Mmm, now that's asking a lot, kiddo. You know how your old man is."

She rolled her eyes. "That's why I just said what I did. It's not cool to be a pig, Daddy."

He gave her a swat on the butt. "Not cool, huh? Well, I guess I'd better go find a building and jump off it."

"Daddy! You're impossible. Anyway, you said I could bring some friends over for a slumber party, and if—"

"Did I say that?" This time Stone rolled his eyes. "Lord, I must've taken leave of my senses, *if* I said that. I'm not sure I'm up to a bunch of wormy teenagers—"

Sally giggled, reached for a pillow off the couch, and threw it at him. "You're awful. Besides, my friends aren't wormy, but even if they were, I'd be embarrassed for them to come here, *if* it's a wreck."

"I promise I'll do my best not to embarrass you."

Now, as he rehashed that conversation, Stone experienced a pang of guilt. If Sally were to arrive on his doorstep, she'd have a conniption fit. It wasn't that he didn't like his new pad—he did. And it wasn't that he didn't have good intentions of keeping it neat—he did. Only that wasn't top priority, and maybe he was just a slob by nature. Still, he owed it to Sally to try harder. On her limited designing expertise and his limited pocketbook, she had done her best to make it homey.

Oh, well, hell, tomorrow was another day. Maybe he'd clean it then. But then maybe he'd do a lot of things tomorrow, like get the guts to approach Natalie again and try to work a deal with her. Fat chance, he told himself.

The sorry truth was he wanted to see her, which was all the more reason to shitcan the idea. He certainly hadn't found a way to convince her to change her mind. Even if she let him near her, he wasn't about to grovel. On second thought, maybe he would. He wanted to know what she knew—he wanted her, period, goddammit. He wanted to see what smoldered under those banked fires. Hell, what man wouldn't?

Stone cursed, then squirmed on the seat, feeling as if his libido were in a perpetual state of readiness, which was damned uncomfortable. He had no one to blame but himself. Even though he no longer toted a badge, the rules still applied: Never get personally involved with a witness or a suspect. At this stage of the investigation, Natalie Whitmore was both.

Pissed at himself for thinking about Natalie Whitmore when his mind should be on the business at hand, Stone swallowed another curse, gazed into the mirror again, raked his hands through his disheveled hair, and opened the door.

Once he'd made his way to the area that said AIRLINE PERSONNEL ONLY, he had to pull the guest badge that he'd been issued to be allowed any farther.

Soon, however, he found himself in one of the hangars, where for a moment he stood in awe, peering up into the belly of an American Airlines 747.

"Un-fuckin'-believable," he murmured, wondering how anyone worked on those big sonuvabitches. Even more mind-boggling was that they ever got off the ground.

"Mr. McCall?"

Stone's gaze swung to the large man who stood in front of him, wiping his hands on a rag. He was not only big but burly, with a thicket of black hair and a wad of tobacco lodged in his cheek.

"Right," Stone said, sticking out his hand but wishing he didn't have to.

"Colby Conner, the AP mechanic."

The man grinned, and when he did, Stone saw that his teeth were stained a dark brown. First the janitor with the festered pimple, now this fellow with black teeth.

"Hope you won't mind if I don't return your handshake," Conner said. "I don't think you wanna handful of grease."

Stone shook his head. "Nope, I believe I'll pass."

"So what can I do for you?" Conner asked, casting an eye at one of the men to his left who appeared to be loafing.

Surprisingly, it was much quieter in the massive hangar than Stone thought it would be. He didn't have to yell to be heard. "I understand you get some of your parts from a subcontractor—Texas Aero."

"Yeah. Matter of fact, our landing gear components, brakes, and hydraulic tubing come from them."

"And are you pleased with the product?"

"Nope."

Stone perked up. "Mind telling me why?"

"Nope." Conner shifted the wad around to the other side of his mouth. "They're a pile of crap, that's why."

Stone could barely control his mounting excitement. If he'd written the script himself, it couldn't be rolling off any better. "Pile of crap, huh? In what way?"

"They don't hold up. They crack, break, split—you name it. In a nutshell, we've had bloody hell with both the parts and the company."

"So why are you still doing business with them?"

"We won't be after this contract runs out. It only has a few months left to go."

"So what you're saying is they deal in after-market replacement parts that aren't built to original factory specifications?"

"Off the record, that's exactly what I'm saying. If I had my way, I'd tell them to take a flying fuck into the next century and take their parts with them."

Stone grinned. "I hear you."

"Say, are you one of them government agents?"

"No, but I do have an interest in what the company's doing."

"Well, to my knowledge the defense department ain't been able to nail their hides to the wall."

"So you've talked to them as well?"

"Yep, several times."

"I guess, then, you have to check the parts ever so carefully before you put them on the planes, for fear of failure in the air?"

"You got it. Between you and me, I don't want the Man at the pearly gates tapping me on the shoulder and saying I was responsible for innocent people dying. No siree, not this fellow."

Grease or no grease, Stone shot out his hand again. "Thanks, Mr. Conner. You've made my day."

Conner grinned but still refused Stone's hand. "Suppose you make *my* day by putting those bastards outta business."

"I'm going to try my damnedest to do just that. Thanks for your time, you hear?" Stone paused, then added with a grin, "If you beat me to those pearly gates, put in a good word for me, will ya?"

Conner spat a wad of brown juice on the floor and wiped his mouth with the back of his hand, leaving a dark smear behind. "Will do."

Stone nodded, then hurried out of there, his stomach doing another one of its somersaults. By the time he got back in his car, his excitement was almost out of control.

"Daddy, do you have a sec?"

Fletcher peered over his bifocals at Stanley, who stood in the doorway. "Is it important?"

Stanley tightened his lips. "It's about the cattle and the fencing."

"All right, come on in."

For a moment Stanley was tempted to turn around and stomp out of the room, but not before telling his daddy to go to hell. The main problem with that scenario was that he'd never make it to the foyer before Fletcher Whitmore would be on him like a prizefighter on his opponent's ass.

Even though all his kids were grown, they had never gotten away with smart-mouthing Fletcher. The only person who came close to that was his mother, and even she had to use finesse. Yeah, his daddy could be a bastard when he wanted to, which was most of the time, as far as Stanley was concerned.

Yet he knew where his bread was buttered, and if he crossed the old man too much or too often, he'd pay for it through his pocketbook, and he didn't intend to let that happen. The way he figured it, the old man owed him. Big-time.

"So what's so urgent that it couldn't wait?" Fletcher demanded into the lengthening silence.

Stanley moved his wiry frame toward one of two chairs in front of the massive desk Fletcher sat behind, as though he were lord and master over all.

"What the hell's wrong with you?" Fletcher blurted out. "I thought you wanted to talk. You're acting like you swallowed your goddamn tongue."

Stanley flushed. "Sorry. It's just that I've got a lot on my mind."

"Well, so do I, so what's the problem?"

"First off, old man Rafferty is about to have a coronary because the south herd keeps going through the fence and grazing on his land."

"So?"

"So we're going to have to replace a lot of fencing or get our asses sued."

A scowl deformed Fletcher's features. "How much is the fencing going to cost?"

"A lot. That's why I wanted to talk it over with you before I gave Dave the go-ahead."

"Do we have any choice?"

"None, unless we buy Rafferty out."

Fletcher leaned back on his chair and snorted. "Forget that. That old codger loves being a thorn in my ass and wouldn't sell out if I offered him a million dollars."

"You're right. He's a pain in the ass."

"Fix the fence."

"Also, I have the latest market prices on the cattle. You're not going to like this, either, but they're down."

"That's no surprise to me," Fletcher said. "You think I

don't read the daily quotes? Leave 'em and I'll look 'em over."

Stanley was so stunned to get off without a lecture on how he was *not* running the ranch right that he actually had a spring to his step as he headed for the door.

"Oh, before you go, there's something I want to talk to you about."

Stanley stopped midstride and turned around. "What?"

"You know that north acreage?"

"Of course I know it; you promised it to Paula and me."

"Well, I've changed my mind. We'll work something else out for the two of you."

"What if I don't want to work something else out?"

"I've made up my mind," Fletcher said in a cold tone.

"I'd like for you to unmake it. You see, Paula and I are trying to have a baby. I thought that land could be for my son."

Stanley knew he was pushing his luck, but dammit, Fletcher had promised him that piece of land. And he wanted it because it had a ton of minerals on it that were worth a fortune. And Daniel didn't give a damn about land or money. All he cared about were goddamn books.

"I'm going to offer the land to Natalie."

Stanley felt his face drain of color, and he splattered his hand against the wall to keep his knees from sagging. "But why? I mean—"

"It's a bribe, if you will. I want to put a stop to her nonsense before she takes it any farther. So far, she doesn't seem to have done any harm."

"What makes you think dangling that land in front of her will make her change her mind?"

"Money. It talks. I'll set it up in a trust for Clancy, which means that she'll never have to worry about anything."

Stanley had wanted to strike his father on many occasions, but never more than he did at this moment.

"She's poor white trash, and she doesn't deserve—"

"I'd be careful if I were you," Fletcher interrupted in a

cutting tone. "Your wife doesn't exactly have a family she can be proud of."

"Still, she's—"

"Enough!" Fletcher bellowed. "I'll decides who deserves what in this household. Understood? And I'll do whatever it takes to keep her from dredging up the past and tarnishing the Whitmore name."

"But what about me? And my children? I just told you Paula and I were—"

"I heard what you told me, but that doesn't change my mind."

"Dammit, Daddy!"

Fletcher continued as though he hadn't heard the outburst. "You're a good son, Stanley, and loyal, but there's some things a man has to do that maybe he doesn't like."

"What if Natalie doesn't take your bribe?"

"She will."

Without saying another word, Stanley strode out the door. *We'll see about that, old man!*

# Twenty-one

"Up you go!"

Clancy squealed as Daniel tossed her up out of the water, then back down, waist deep.

"Lord, sweetie, you're going to raise the dead if you don't stop that squealing." Natalie reached for her daughter, then watched as Daniel swam to the steps and got out of the pool.

The day was a scorcher and the water so warm that it might as well have been mechanically heated. Daniel had asked her if she and Clancy would like to join him for a swim, and Natalie had jumped at the chance, partly because she needed an outlet for her nervous energy. She also wanted to be with Daniel. She hadn't seen much of him lately; consequently she hadn't had a chance to mention the condo she'd found.

After they had been swimming for a while, she'd finally told him, and though she could tell he hadn't been jubilant, he had expressed a desire to see it.

Again Natalie wished she could invite Martha, who was now sitting on a chaise by the pool, watching Clancy with a loving smile and knitting at the same time. But again, the subject of her moving was so touchy, Natalie didn't dare risk broaching it.

"Sis, I gotta go," Daniel was saying while slipping a shirt over his head.

She frowned. "To the university?"

"As always."

"Well, you're certainly a party pooper."

"I know, but I'll see you later."

After he'd kissed his mother and walked out, Martha turned to Natalie and asked, "Do you think Clancy's getting too much sun?"

"Probably." Natalie brushed the wet curls aside on Clancy's forehead and kissed a cheek.

"Want me to take her and let you swim a little longer?"

"Would you? I'd love that. Come on, sweetie, let's go to Grandma."

Although Clancy's rosebud mouth quivered when Natalie took her out of the water, her unhappiness soon vanished as Martha, took her, then put her down on the grass near the old but friendly dog, Mert.

Martha chuckled, then turned back to Natalie. "As soon as she plays with the dog a sec, I'll take her in and bathe her."

"Thanks a million."

Martha's features turned pensive. "You should think about all these amenities you'll be giving up when you move out."

The smile fled Natalie's face, and a lump suddenly lodged in her throat. She cleared it before she could say anything. "You're the amenity I'm going to miss." She couldn't bring herself to include Fletcher; she'd choke on the words. He had wounded her so deeply, she didn't know when, if ever, she could forgive him. Yet she didn't want to punish Martha because of Fletcher's feelings toward her.

"Then don't move; stay here."

"I can't," Natalie said in a tight voice.

Martha stared at her, looking as if she might burst into tears, then turned, lifted Clancy, and walked off.

For the next twenty minutes Natalie lapped the pool too many times to count. When she finally paused to catch her breath, she looked up and saw Josie walking toward her with the cordless phone.

"Honey chile, it's for you."

The last thing she wanted to do was talk on the phone, to anyone, but she couldn't very well vent her frustration on Josie. "Thanks," she said, and took the receiver from the grinning housekeeper.

"Hello," she said after grabbing her towel and mopping her face.

"Natalie."

Her hand froze on the phone while her heart felt as if it had received an electric jolt. She would recognize that gruff, sexy voice anywhere, not because she'd heard it all that much, but because it seemed to be seared on her brain, just like his image. *Damn!* She didn't need this, not when her emotions were already in such a fragile state.

"What do you want?" The coldness in her voice should've been a dead giveaway that she didn't want to talk to him, only he seemed oblivious of that as well.

"If I told you, you'd slam the receiver down in my ear."

Her heart constricted again. "What if I slam it down anyway?"

"I wish you wouldn't."

Natalie took a deep breath and tried to ignore the forlorn yet sexy undertone in his voice. Then anger took over. Who did he think he was, for god's sake? He had killed her husband and made no apologies for it.

"Look, this is not a good time for me."

"When is a good time?" he pressed. "We need to talk."

"I'm swimming." She hadn't meant to say that; it just slipped through her lips.

"Alone?"

She gripped the receiver still tighter. "Yes."

"That's too bad."

"I know what you're doing, and it won't work."

A deep sigh filtered through the line. "Okay, I'll admit I'm trying to appeal to your base needs, but time is critical here.

And by us not working together, we're wasting it." He paused. "Remember, it was *you* who wanted to find me."

Natalie didn't respond; she was too busy trying to keep her teeth from chattering. She doubted that problem stemmed from the temperature. She didn't want to react to this man in any way, only she couldn't help it. It was apparent that all she had to do was hear his voice and her body went haywire.

She wanted to die of shame, and she wanted to lash out at him for his cunning attempt to manipulate her. How dared he act as if nothing were amiss, as if he hadn't come on to her under false pretenses? God, to think she had let her husband's killer touch her, kiss her, *make her want him*.

"Stay away from me," she said at last, panicked that the fire he'd started inside her was once again smoldering.

"For now. But just so you'll know, you can't avoid me forever. And are you sure you want to?"

Natalie wanted to scream just as the dial tone sounded in her ear. She punched the off button, then fought the urge to throw the phone across the yard.

Why didn't he leave her alone? She shouldn't want to have anything to do with him. But she did, and that was why she was having a hard time reconciling her own duplicity within herself.

Feeling the urgent need to swim again, Natalie placed the phone on the nearest chair, then turned back to the water. Then she saw Stanley saunter up to the table across the pool.

"Wonderful," Natalie muttered under her breath. Stanley's unexpected appearance was the last thing she needed after Stone's call.

"Well, well, look who's here."

"You'll be glad to know that I'm about to leave," she retorted.

"Hey, not on my account, I hope."

Stanley's voice was congenial enough, but Natalie knew better. His eyes were narrowed and filled with suppressed hostility. She decided in that moment that Stanley actually hated her. Shivering, she turned away from the pool and reached for her towel, conscious of his eyes monitoring her every move.

"No, on my account, actually. I'm tired."

"Stay a moment, all right? I want to talk to you."

Natalie paused. "What could we possibly have to talk about?"

When she made no effort to walk to where he was, he came to her side of the pool and plopped down on the deck chair nearest her. "Are you still planning to haul ass?"

"That's none of your business," she said, ignoring his crude choice of words.

He smirked. "I'm making it my business because you've never really belonged here."

Ah, so he was taking off the padded gloves and using his fists. Fine. If that was what he wanted, then she'd oblige him. Two could play this game, and at the moment she'd love to watch him squirm.

"I'd say you seem to have that same problem."

His features turned deathly white, and for a moment Natalie thought he might strike her. Maybe he should have, she told herself, hating herself for stooping to his level. He wasn't Fletcher's favorite son, and everyone in the family knew it. Still, to have it pointed out by someone he despised was a low blow. It would serve only to fuel his hatred of her.

"You think you've got it made, don't you?" He bore down on her, his face pinched in a sneer.

She pulled back, but not before smelling booze on his breath. She should've guessed that he was well on his way to being drunk, if he wasn't already there. "Get out of my way, Stanley. I'm going inside."

He grabbed her arm and spun her around. "If Fletcher makes you an offer, you'd best turn it down."

Natalie jerked her arm back. "I don't know what you're talking about."

"You will, and you'd best do like I told you."

"That sounds very much like a threat to me."

Stanley leaned back to glare into her face, his own contorted. "That's exactly what it is."

"You don't scare me," she said with confidence, though her heart raced.

Stanley trailed the back of his hand down one side of her cheek, then said in a low tone, "I'd rethink that, if I were you, sister dear."

Natalie saw red and jabbed a finger in his chest. "Back off, Stanley! Besides, looks to me like you'd best tidy things in your own backyard before you mess in mine."

"What the hell does that mean?"

"I suggest you ask your wife and Dave that."

His mouth worked as if he were about to choke on something caught in his throat. "Why, you little bitch—"

"Save it, Stanley," she spat, then turned and, forcing herself not to run, walked toward the house.

First Stone, then Stanley. What had she done to deserve such punishment in one day?

Stone strode into police headquarters as if he owned the place, noticing that nothing had changed. It was still the same depressing place it had always been, but even more so since his resentment and bad memories instantly reared their ugly heads. He was tempted to turn around and get the hell out of there. He shouldn't have come in the first place.

But since he'd called Natalie, he'd been wired just as he used to be when he drank. Only he'd been cold sober when he'd called her and was cold sober now, standing where he swore he'd never stand again. He knew why he was here, and it wasn't necessary or legit, but then he didn't give a damn about either.

He was supposed to have met with one of the Defense Department officials who had investigated Texas Aero Industries, but when that interview had fallen through, his frustration had driven him to make this move.

Since his return to Austin, Rutgers had been unfinished business that had to be resolved.

"McCall? Is that you?"

"Hello, Higgins," Stone said to the officer manning the desk. "Long time no see."

Al Higgins's mouth slammed shut, then he grinned. "Hell, man, what'dja do, go get a quack to suck the fat outta your gut?"

"Cute, Higgins."

"Well, when you left here, you looked like warmed-over piss."

"That's why I quit drinking, smoking, and eating junk. You oughta try it sometime."

Higgins turned red as he peered down at his distended belly. "Didn't know you were back in town."

"You do now."

"What brings you down to headquarters?" Higgins asked in a suspicious tone.

"Actually, I came to see the captain. Is he available?"

"Is he expecting you?"

"Nope."

"Then you can't—"

Stone leaned toward the desk sergeant. "Come on, Higgins, if my memory serves me correctly, you owe me one."

Al flushed, then paled. "You haven't changed one iota, McCall; you're still an abusive sonuvabitch."

"Yeah, right, Higgins. So can I see the captain?"

"You can try, but I figure you won't get anywhere near his office."

Giving Higgins a mock salute, Stone sauntered into the main offices, where no one seemed to notice him until he was just about to the door of Rutgers's office. Then someone hollered, "Hey, you, wait up."

Stone stopped, turned, and faced Officer Riley Bishop, who blinked first, then narrowed his eyes. "Well, I'll be damned."

"Save it, Bishop," Stone said in a clipped tone. "I'm here to see the captain."

"He won't want to see you."

Stone ignored him and raised his hand to knock on the door marked CAPTAIN WILLIAM RUTGERS.

"Hey, you can't do that!" Bishop yelled.

"Watch me," Stone said, then rapped once and opened the door.

Bill Rutgers stood at the window. When he heard the door open, he pivoted. Stone watched his jaw drop, then stay that way as if frozen.

Stone grinned. "You're not seeing things, Rutgers. I may look different, only I'm not. I'm still *your* worst nightmare."

The muscles along Rutgers's jaw bulged into knots. "How the hell did you get in here?"

Stone shrugged. "Walked."

"Don't you get smart with me. I can have your ass hauled out with the snap of my fingers."

"Only you won't," Stone drawled, then sat down on a chair in front of Rutgers's desk and stared at his old boss.

The captain hadn't changed, except that maybe his belly was bigger and his hair thinner. Otherwise, the scar on his temple still stood out, and the nicotine stains around his nose and on his fingers were still there.

"Say what you have to say, then get out."

Stone crossed one leg over the over. "Actually, I don't have much on my mind. I just thought I'd let you know I was back in town." Stone scrutinized him more closely, noticing that a fine line of sweat covered his upper lip. "But you already knew that, didn't you?"

"Yes."

"Ah, that's too bad someone had to go and spoil my surprise."

Two long strides brought Rutgers to his desk, where he glared at Stone. "I don't know why you're here, but again, say what you have to say and get out."

Stone stood. "I came back to prove my innocence, Rutgers."

"Ha, now that's a good one." His eyes started at the top of Stone's head and ended at his feet before settling back on his face. "You're dirty, McCall, always were and always will be."

Stone bolted out of the chair and was in Rutgers's face before Rutgers knew what was happening. In fact, he was so close, he could smell Rutgers's soured breath. "And that's a load of bullshit, too! You and Fletcher Whitmore cut my legs out from under me. And when I find that *you* were shitting close to Whitmore's porch, I'll bring you down with him."

"Why you . . . you," Rutgers spluttered, his face turning purple with rage.

For a minute Stone thought he might have a stroke and felt a twinge of conscience. But only for a moment.

"Get a grip, Cap. I'm outta here." Stone walked to the door, where he paused. "For now, that is." He winked. "Like I said, your worst nightmare's back in town."

After his uninvited guest had left, Rutgers just sat there, inhaling one cigarette after another, feeling as if his head had a buzz saw inside it.

He hadn't even bothered to get up and chew ass for letting McCall get inside the building, much less into his office. But that would come later, after he'd regained his composure.

"Dammit to hell," he muttered, then clamped his mouth shut. If anyone heard him talking to himself, they'd think he'd gone off the deep end. Maybe he had. When the officer had told him Stone was back in town, he'd prayed that he'd been mistaken.

No such fuckin' luck.

Reaching for the already saturated handkerchief, Rutgers mopped his brow again, then placed his hand on the receiver of his private line. He should call Whitmore; he should have called him already. Talk about going berserk that McCall was back in town . . . why, that old man would piss in his pants for sure.

Rutgers drummed his fingers on the desk. While he'd love to be the one who told Whitmore, he was having second thoughts. Maybe he ought to let Whitmore find out on his own, like he had.

Whitmore hadn't done right by him anyway. He'd done what Whitmore asked him to do, then when he'd asked Whitmore to lend him several thousand dollars, the old man had given him only a paltry thousand. So let Whitmore take his own lumps.

Rutgers smiled at the thought. Before this was over, he hoped Fletcher Whitmore was the one who took the hosing down.

# Twenty-two

"Don't you dare hurt my mamma!"

The man shot her a nasty glance. "Get out of the way, kid, before *you* get hurt."

"Please, Nat, run on back to your room. I'll be all right."

Natalie's wide, frightened eyes bounced between her mother and the man. "No, Mamma!" she cried. "He'll hurt you again!"

"Get her outta here!" the man bellowed, then reached in his pocket and pulled out a switchblade knife.

"Oh . . . my God . . . oh my . . . God," her mother whimpered, cringing against the wall, her hands over her gaunt face.

Natalie hadn't planned to do it. But the sight of that knife had triggered something inside her. She lunged at the man, and even though he backhanded her and she sailed across the room, that didn't deter her.

This time she ran like a torpedo and jumped on his back. Again he shook her off, then turned and pointed the knife straight at her.

"No!" her mother screamed. "Don't hurt my baby!"

Natalie stood paralyzed. . . .

\* \* \*

Like a frightened deer frozen in front of car headlights, Natalie shot straight up in bed, her heart banging so loudly in her chest that she feared it might crack her ribs. Shuddering, she took several deep breaths, which did little to settle her heart rate or stop the sweat from pouring off her.

Oh, God, she cried silently, would that nightmare ever end? Was she going to be plagued with it for the rest of her life? She had thought that she'd never have another one after she'd married Phillip, and she hadn't, until now. Even his tragic death hadn't triggered one.

Reaching for a handful of tissues from the table beside her bed, Natalie dabbed at her face, neck, and arms, then peered at the clock. The digital showed six A.M. She might as well get up and go in to work early.

She took another deep breath and lay back down. But she didn't dare close her eyes. The thought of seeing that same picture in her mind was too terrifying to contemplate. She shifted her body into a fetal position, telling herself that everything was going to be all right. But when no relief came, she tossed back the covers and bounded out of bed.

A minute later she was in Clancy's bedroom, bending over her, kissing her on the cheek, reveling in the sweetness and soothing tranquillity of her baby.

Natalie then walked to the window and stared into the inky blackness. Thank God, she felt much calmer and could think more rationally, able now to attribute the nightmare to the hectic and stressful week she'd endured.

The subtle but vicious conversation she'd had with Stanley had started her downhill slide. Stone's phone call hadn't helped any, either. She shuddered, praying that the fire he had started inside her had burned out. Sex could never be a substitute for trust.

Then yesterday, her disappointment over her inability to make any headway had increased. She had thumbed back through some of the articles on Phillip's death, not knowing what she'd been looking for until a certain name had grabbed her attention.

Scott Timpson. She realized that he had been the journalist who had not only written several articles about Phillip's campaign and his death, but who had shown empathy toward the family during that terrible time.

Could that mean anything? Was it possible that he knew something that might help her? Deciding he just might, she had contacted the journalist and had an appointment with him this morning.

Feeling excitement replace her fear, she stepped into the shower.

"I heard you wanted to reopen the investigation," Scott Timpson said shortly after they met at a coffee shop near her office.

Unable to hide her surprise, Natalie asked, "How did you know that?"

He smiled. "Come on, Mrs. Whitmore, you know the answer to that. I'm a newspaperman. I make it my business to know everything."

She had liked the news journalist on sight. He was tall and gangly, with a salt-and-pepper mustache that was precisely trimmed and sharp blue eyes that seemed to look through her. Maybe that was why he'd been the recipient of a Pulitzer Prize—he had special insight that enabled him to go after what he wanted and get it.

"Then you know that I want to reopen my husband's case because I don't think his death was an accident."

"Yes, I do know that."

"So, do you agree with me?"

"Before I answer that, tell me why you sought me out."

"Because of your articles in the paper. Their tone told me you had an insight into my husband that few others had."

"Mmm, that's interesting."

"I'm right, aren't I?" Natalie asked, then sipped her coffee.

"Yes, I did, and that's why I'm curious as to why you're just now approaching me."

Taken aback by his bluntness, Natalie lowered her cup back to the saucer. "For one thing, for a long time I couldn't bring myself to read any of the articles, so I didn't pick up on the relationship. Second, investigating a possible murder is out of my field, Mr. Timpson."

"Make that Scott."

"All right, Scott. Anyway, I thought the best way to handle such a major undertaking was to let someone else do the work, such as a private detective. The problem with that is I can't seem to find one who suits me."

"So you decided to have a run at it yourself?"

"Yes, which I know sounds crazy. But since I made the decision to dig for the truth, to pressure the law into reopening the case, if you will, I've felt a desperate urgency that I can't explain."

Scott let out a sigh, but he didn't say anything.

"So do you know anything that can help me?"

"Maybe, maybe not, although your husband and I got to be quite good friends."

"I'm sorry, I didn't know that."

"He was a good man whose life was cut far too short. I know he could've made a difference in this country, if only . . ." Scott stopped and shifted his gaze.

"Go on, please." Natalie didn't try to suppress the eagerness in her voice.

"If only something hadn't been ripping him apart inside."

Natalie rested her arms on the table and leaned forward, her eyes piercing. "Do you have any idea what that something might have been?"

Scott was quiet for another moment, during which he toyed with his mustache. "No, I'm sorry to say I don't."

Natalie's spirits deflated, and she bit down on her lower lip to stop it from trembling. "Me either, and that's what I'm having difficulty coming to grips with. I just didn't push him hard enough to tell me what was tearing him up inside, as you said."

"Don't beat up on yourself for something you had no control over. He was a man who seemed to guard his privacy, and I think he had his reasons for not telling you, perhaps your safety, for one."

Natalie paled and almost blurted out the fact that she'd been threatened, only to curb her tongue at the last minute. For now it was best that she play her cards close to her chest.

"There's one thing I do know that might help, something apparently you didn't know."

"What?"

"Phillip was considering dropping out of the race."

Natalie gave him an incredulous look. "Did he tell you that?"

"Not in so many words, but the insinuation was there, especially after he became so troubled."

Natalie lifted her cup, only to put it back down as her hands were shaking so. "Oh, God, what a mess. I wonder if his father knew."

"No way."

"So if he was thinking about withdrawing, then something terrible had indeed happened."

"Something dangerous to him both physically and politically would be my guess."

"What about the cop who shot him?" Natalie asked with difficulty. "Do you think he was somehow involved?"

"That's another mystery that's never been solved. Some thought he was dirty because of his reputation as a rebel, while others thought he got the shaft." Scott's lips turned down. "The latter, I have to say, were in the minority."

Natalie pursed her lips. "Well, that mystery is about to end. I'm not going to stop until I find out the truth."

"Bully for you. If I can be of any further help, don't hesitate to call me."

Natalie stood, then paused. "Can I ask you a rather blunt question?"

"Sure, why not?"

"As both a friend and curious investigative reporter, why didn't *you* pursue this case? From what you've said, you were bound to have smelled a rat, if you will."

"Fletcher Whitmore convinced me that wasn't the thing to do."

Natalie gave him another incredulous look, her thoughts reeling. "And you listened to him?"

"He can be a very convincing man." Scott shrugged. "Need I say more?"

"No," she said bitterly.

As if suddenly uncomfortable with the turn of the conversation, Scott peered at his watch, then looked back up at her. "Sorry, I gotta run. I have another appointment."

"Thanks for meeting me," she said without looking at him.

As if he sensed she was upset, he patted her on the hand and said, "I'll do some checking on the cop. If I find anything, I'll give you a call."

Back at the office a few minutes later, Natalie was still seething. Fletcher's powerful reach had long and dangerous tentacles. Was there no end to the lengths he would go to protect the almighty Whitmore name?

How could she have not seen that before now? Because she had thought he loved her as much as Martha did, she told herself. And tonight she had to face Fletcher and the rest of the family at a barbecue.

Natalie stared at the pile of paperwork on her desk, battling down a deep sadness.


The grounds looked lovely in the late evening light. Although it had rained earlier in the day, by noon the sun had come out and the temperature had risen to the boiling point. Still, no one complained.

Natalie, dressed in jeans and a sleeveless cotton shirt, made her way back to the festivities, having taken Clancy inside after she'd fallen asleep from exhaustion.

"Did you get her in bed?" Martha asked with a smile, patting the bench beside her.

Natalie sat down. "Actually, she was a little fussy, so I gave her a baby aspirin."

"Oh, my, I hope she's not coming down with something."

"I'm sure she'll be okay in the morning."

"I can tell you her problem," Daniel chimed in from across the table. "She's too much a little busybody."

Natalie batted her hand at him. "If you say 'like her mother,' I'll throw something at you."

Daniel chuckled. "Now, would I even think such a thing?"

"Let the rest of us in on what's so funny," Fletcher demanded from his position at the head of the long picnic table that sat among the manicured lawn and tall trees.

Seated on one side of Fletcher were Stanley, Paula, and Daniel, while on the other was Ben Byers, his wife, Nellie, and Martha.

Off to the right of the table was a huge black barbecue pit that was still pumping the air with a delicious odor, despite the fact that everyone had already eaten their share of smoked sausage, beef brisket, and pork.

Natalie felt stuffed, so much so that she'd unbuttoned the top button on her jeans. To her surprise, she had enjoyed not only the food, but the shindig as well. Everyone seemed to pretend that nothing had changed, that Natalie had not fallen out of grace with the family.

Well, let them think that, Natalie told herself. As long as she lived under Fletcher's roof, she wanted the peace to continue, fragile as it was.

"Hey, everyone, listen up," Fletcher said, standing and *ping*ing his glass with a knife. Following a silence, he went on, "I have an announcement to make."

"What else is new, Daddy?" Daniel murmured.

Everyone laughed.

"I heard that, son."

Daniel merely grinned.

"I'm serious," Fletcher responded, his eyes seeking and then stopping on Natalie.

Oh, great, she thought, forcing herself to return his stare without flinching.

"Natalie, I'm deeding the north acreage, which comprises a thousand acres, to Clancy, with you as trustee. Now, I'd like for everyone to seal Natalie's good fortune with a toast."

Natalie was so flabbergasted by the announcement that she couldn't have moved if she'd wanted to.

Paula, however, had no such problem. She lurched to her feet and cried, "No! You can't do that!"

Red faced, Stanley tugged at her pants leg. "Shut up and sit down."

She glared down at him, her features cast in stone. "Goddammit, did you know about this?"

Stanley's face turned redder, but he didn't say anything. He merely stared at his daddy with unvarnished hate in his eyes.

"Sit down, Paula," Fletcher said, his voice low and controlled.

But Natalie knew that control was on a short leash. She saw the clenched jaw and knew he was furious as well as embarrassed by Paula's outburst.

But then so was she, only not about Paula. What on earth had possessed him to do such a thing? She knew he had a motive, and that motive had to benefit Fletcher. She didn't know what was behind it, but whatever it was, it had backfired.

"Natalie, what do *you* have to say?"

On unsteady legs, Natalie rose and felt everyone stare at her with undisguised curiosity. "What do you want me to say, Fletcher?"

" 'Thanks' would be nice."

"I know that land was promised to Stanley," she said with pointed softness.

"Damn," Daniel muttered as if he realized that the shit was about to hit the proverbial fan.

Natalie ignored him and waited for Fletcher's reply.

"Well, I'll make it up to Stanley. He won't suffer; I promise you that."

"Why are you doing this?" Natalie asked. "What's the point?"

"Why, I thought that'd be obvious," Fletcher said. "It's a bribe, honey, pure and simple. The land and all the wealth that it'll bring you in exchange for backing off the probe into my son's death."

Martha cried out, then slapped her hand across her mouth.

Paula jumped up again, glowered at Fletcher, then ran toward the house.

Daniel cursed. Stanley continued to glare at his father. Ben Byers and his wife shifted uncomfortably on their seats.

Natalie shook her head, then said, "Sorry, Fletcher, there's no amount of money that'll make me change my mind. The sooner you face that, the better off you'll be." She stood, then turned and stepped over the bench. "I'm going to bed. Good night, everyone."

"Goddammit, girl, don't you turn your back on me!" Fletcher yelled. "I won't tolerate you disobeying me, either, you hear?"

Natalie kept on walking.

# Twenty-three

Three men were due to meet again in back of the posh Austin club, as they had before.

"Sir, are you alone this evening?" a tuxedo-dressed waiter asked the man as he took a seat at the round table.

He didn't bother to look at the waiter. "You're obviously new here."

"Yes, sir, I am."

"Where's Wagner?"

"Uh, he's been assigned to another room, sir."

Cold eyes turned toward the young man, who seemed to be shrinking inside himself. "Go tell him he's just been reassigned—to me. Got it?"

The waiter swallowed so hard that his Adam's apple seemed to go into spasms. "Er, did I do something wrong? I mean—"

"Get the hell out of here and just do what I told you. Now!"

The young man pivoted so fast that he almost tripped on his feet. Finally he regained his balance and tore out of the room.

A few minutes later another man walked into the room,

smiling. "Sorry, sir, there seems to have been a mix-up. I didn't know you were coming." Without adding anything further, the waiter placed a mixed bourbon and Coke in front of the man.

Without looking at him, the man nodded. Only after he heard the waiter leave the room did he turn around. That was when the men he was meeting strode through the door.

"Don't ever be late again."

Ralph stared at Lewis as if to say, Oh, no, not another thorn up his ass.

"Sorry, boss," Lewis said, looking as if he might mess in his britches at any moment.

"Well, I'm not sorry," Ralph said with unexpected boldness. "Things happen. Besides, we're not two dogs off the street that you can kick around at your whim. We have as many smarts as you do and can go anywhere and get another job."

"Hey, Ralph," Lewis said, his eyes darting from one to the other while he grabbed his big-bowled pipe and jammed it between his lips, "take it easy, okay? The boss didn't mean anything by that."

The boss's features were devoid of expression, but his eyes were those of a dead man's as they looked both men up and down. "If either of you crosses me again, you'll be real sorry." He paused to let that sink in, then said in an altogether different tone, "Now, if you will kindly have a seat, we'll get down to business."

"What might that business be this time, boss?" Ralph asked, his voice having turned as soft as melted butter.

"The same as before, gentlemen. Natalie Whitmore." He paused. "And now that damn cop, Stone McCall. He's been snooping around the old warehouse and asking questions, which spells more trouble."

"You tell us what to do and we'll do it," Lewis said, his voice eager.

The first man smiled.

* * *

Natalie couldn't wait to pick up Clancy, not because she was concerned about the new baby-sitter, but because she needed to hold her baby.

While the day had not been disastrous, it hadn't been all that great, either. She'd almost sold a house, but the young couple had gotten cold feet and backed out. She also hadn't been able to get the barbecue or Fletcher's bribe off her mind. One minute she was angry enough to confront him again, and the next she wanted never to see him again. The latter wasn't possible, she knew, so she shut the thought down.

As long as Martha was alive, she could never keep Clancy from the ranch, which meant encountering her father-in-law. Also, thoughts of what Scott Timpson had told her about Phillip's plans to resign from the campaign hounded her night and day, compounding her guilt. She had to find out what made Phillip consider such a drastic measure. Politics had meant more to him than she had.

If only ... No! She wouldn't punish herself anymore. To do so was a waste of time; she couldn't go back. Her only alternative was to go forward, which in one respect she had.

This morning she had signed papers on a town house that was close to the baby-sitter's modest home and the office. Signing on the dotted line should've made her feel better, but it didn't; there was so much work to do before she could move, she and Clancy would have to remain at the ranch.

"Swell," she muttered, nursing her pounding left temple and her bad humor, until she saw Clancy standing inside the glass front door with her tiny nose pressed against it. When the child recognized Natalie, she jumped up and down and clapped her hands.

Natalie's headache fled along with her bad humor. She raced up the walk, and as soon as Margie Chase, the sitter, unlocked the door, Natalie bent and scooped her daughter into her arms and gave her a bear hug.

"Mommy!" Clancy cried, then grinned her toothy grin.

After kissing her on the cheek, Natalie faced Margie, who was tall, dark haired, and attractive.

"What are you doing here, Mrs. Whitmore?" Margie asked.

"Call me Natalie, won't you?" she said, laughing as Clancy tried to remove her earring.

"All right, Natalie, but again, I'm surprised to see you."

Confused, Natalie stared at her. "What are you talking about?"

This time it was Margie who looked confused, then almost embarrassed. "Well, I wasn't expecting you, that's all."

"Margie, you're not making any sense. Of course you were expecting me, unless you wanted to keep my child overnight, which wasn't part of the deal." Natalie smiled.

Margie shook her head. "No, you don't understand. A man called and said that you'd given him permission to pick up Clancy and that he would be arriving shortly."

Natalie stiffened while ice filled her veins. "A man called?" she repeated in a choked voice.

"Uh-huh."

"You . . . you weren't going to let him take Clancy, were you?"

"No, not until I called you and verified it. In fact, I was about to do just that when you arrived. Still, I figured the call was logit because—" Her voice ceased, as if she'd just noticed Natalie's white, stricken features. "You mean you—" Again she stopped in midsentence, her own color fading.

"That's right. I gave no one permission to pick up my child."

"Then who? I mean—"

"I don't know," Natalie said, a rising panic underlying her words. "But I'm sure as hell going to find out."

A short time later Natalie pulled into the garage at the ranch and got out, then stood by as Daniel pulled in beside her.

"Hi, sis," he said, climbing out of his Mercedes, his briefcase in hand.

After shifting a sleeping Clancy onto one hip, Natalie leaned against her car and stared at Daniel.

"Jesus, what's wrong? You look like someone just cut your throat."

"I think that was *his* intention."

"He who? What the hell are you talking about?"

Natalie looked around as if the walls in the garage might have ears.

"Natalie, tell me!"

She took a deep shuddering breath, then told him what had just happened.

When she finished, his face mirrored hers. "You don't really think Clancy's the target, do you?" Disbelief colored his voice.

"No, I think the crazy's just trying to scare me." Natalie paused. "But if I find out otherwise, I'll do whatever it takes to protect my child."

"Jesus," Daniel said again.

Clancy stirred; Natalie patted her on the back until she quieted down.

"Who do you think was behind that and why?"

"My first thought was Fletcher."

Daniel frowned. "That's what you said when you received that phone call, which so far has been an empty threat. Anyway, I don't believe it's Daddy. He'd never hurt a hair on Clancy's head."

"Not Clancy, but me."

"No, you're wrong." Daniel rubbed his chin. "Look, what do you say I take care of this? I'll see what I can find out. It's obvious someone besides Dad doesn't want you meddling. From the looks of you, you're in no condition to think straight, much less do anything." Gently he squeezed one of Natalie's shoulders. "I promise nothing's going to happen to you or Clancy."

"Look, Danny, I can't keep letting you get me out of trouble. I'm not your responsibility. Besides, this is my fight."

"Yes, you can, and it's my fight, too."

Natalie reached up and kissed him on the cheek. "Don't ever change, Danny. I don't think I could stand it if you did."

Daniel didn't respond verbally, but she felt his eyes track her all the way inside the house.

Thank God, Clancy was still asleep when she reached their quarters. Natalie put her in her bed, then stripped and climbed in the shower.

A few minutes later her body felt refreshed, but her mind remained in turmoil. Daniel meant well, she knew, and she trusted him with her life, but she couldn't stand by and do nothing herself, especially when she couldn't quiet the terror festering inside her.

So what should she do? she asked herself, walking into the kitchen to brew a cup of coffee. Maybe she should consider— No. To think about letting *him* back into her life was suicidal.

Or was it?

Natalie's breath caught suddenly, and she almost strangled on the sip of coffee she'd just taken. What if Stone had called the baby-sitter? When she could breathe again, her heart rejected that thought, remembering the "ant" incident at the park.

While she rejected any thought of him hurting her or Clancy, she couldn't see herself approaching him. Yet she couldn't accomplish her mission alone. She could see that now. She needed professional help, but the thought of baring her soul to any of the private detectives she'd interviewed was also intolerable.

In spite of what he said, Daniel couldn't help her. Deep down she felt that he didn't want her to probe into Phillip's death any more than the other family members did. She didn't want them to turn against Daniel because of her. She couldn't live with that.

So, again, should she work in concert with Stone? At least she could keep an eye on him and *use* him. But there were dangers she couldn't ignore.

What about that volatile sexual pull and tug between them? Could she deal with that, the most dangerous of all? First, though, she had to make the commitment to pick up the phone and call him.

Should she? She stared at the phone, likening it to something evil. God, she didn't know. One thing she did know: she was too exhausted to make that decision now. Tomorrow would suffice.

Tomorrow she would also buy a pistol.

# Twenty-four

"Please, have a seat. Mr. Fenley will be with you shortly."

"Thanks," Stone said to the secretary, then sat down.

"May I get you a cup of coffee?" she asked in an impersonal but pleasant tone.

Stone smiled absently. "No thanks; I'm fine."

She nodded and closed the door behind her. Stone's eyes perused the room, which was a typical Department of Defense office, he thought. Jason Fenley's desk was made of maple and too large for the size of the room. The three chairs, arranged in a semicircle in front of the desk, added to the closed-in feeling.

Stone hated that feeling. Give him the wide-open spaces any time. He didn't know how he'd endured his cubbyhole at the station for as long as he had. Maybe it was because he was only in it to do paperwork.

He got up and walked to the window, trying to blend his impatience and excitement into a useful tool. He had hoped for this interview with this agent from the Department of Defense, but when an earlier appointment had been canceled, he'd figured he wouldn't succeed. But then he'd called again, and voilà! here he was in the nation's capital, which was as hot and humid as the Texas hill country.

Stone glanced at his watch. Waiting was not his strong suit. Soon he'd be pacing the floor. Then he heard the door open behind him.

He swung around and stared into the face of a man with cherubic features and a thatch of thick brown hair. But there were deep grooves around his eyes and mouth, and he had a slight tic in his left shoulder that was noticeable. Both underscored the years and experience behind the now smiling face.

"Sorry to have kept you waiting," Jason Fenley said, extending his hand.

"No problem." Stone shook his hand, then dropped it.

"Good," Fenley responded, making his way behind the desk to ease onto his chair. "So you've come to ask about Texas Aero Industries."

"Yes, but first I want to thank you for seeing me. I know how busy—"

Fenley interrupted him with a wave of his hand. "Nailing assholes is part of my job."

For a moment Stone was stunned by the man's words. He didn't look like the type who had balls. He hid a smile, then said, "Well, I still feel I owe you, considering I'm an ex-cop." He stressed the "ex."

When Stone had made the appointment, he'd told the secretary the gist of who he was and what he wanted.

"Your background's your business, Mr. McCall. Again, my business is nailing bastards whose greed causes other people harm." He paused. "That's why you're here, isn't it?"

"Absolutely."

"Then let's get down to business."

"Okay. Obviously, your agency hasn't been able to get enough evidence against Texas Aero to make it stick and put them out of business."

"That's right, I'm sorry to say."

"Why?"

"Why?" Fenley smiled with no humor. "Because they're slicker than owl shit, that's why."

Stone smiled, but Fenley didn't.

"I hate losing, Mr. McCall."

"So do I. That's why I returned to Austin. I intend to clear my name, but doing so involves that company. The only problem is I haven't been able to tie any of my loose ends together to make a solid case."

"How can I help you?"

"By telling me exactly what you know about those people and how they operate."

"That would be my pleasure."

"Before you have your say, though, I want you to know that I visited with a mechanic at Tex-Air in Dallas who told me they bought a lot of their plane parts from Texas Aero, but as soon as their contract ran out, they wouldn't buy any more."

"That's smart," Fenley said, his fleshy mouth narrowing into a thin line. "Texas Acro's parts are a pile of crap, which we feel accounted for the crashes of two small jets."

Stone whistled. "You mean two crashes were actually attributable to the company?"

"Our investigation strongly suggested it. It showed that some of the parts were definitely substandard but were sold as high quality. But there's another kicker: the navy contracted with them, and the landing gear on several of their fighter jets collapsed when they landed on aircraft carriers."

"Then how the hell are they still operating?"

"Because as often happens, we haven't been able to prove it yet. But if I had my way, the doors would be locked and the key thrown away. Unfortunately, word came from, quote, 'on high,' unquote, to scrub the investigation."

Stone whistled again. "So have you—"

"Stopped our investigation?" Fenley said, finishing Stone's sentence. "No, but we have other cases right now that are just as pressing, if not more so." He shrugged. "Still, if I get the chance to tighten the noose around that company's neck and jerk it, then I will. Believe me.''

''Oh, I believe you all right. I think I might be able to help you jerk that noose so tight that it'll strangle them out of business and into a coffin.''

Fenley raised his eyebrows. ''Oh, really? You know something we don't know?''

''I'm getting there, one step at a time.''

''You'd best be careful. As I found out, those people have the connections to play hardball.''

''That's my game. In fact, that's the only way I know how to play.'' Stone gave him a cold smile, then stood.

Fenley followed suit. ''I'm not supposed to do this, but, like you, I'd really like to hang these bastards. I'll have my secretary photocopy some of our investigative files. You take 'em and look 'em over, then forget where you got 'em.''

''Thanks, sir.''

''Good luck.''

''Thanks again,'' Stone said, extending his hand. ''You've been a big help.''

''The more pieces of the puzzle you have, the better off you are.''

''Right, and you've definitely added to my count. Besides, it's nice hearing it from the mouth of a fed.''

Fenley laughed. ''I always thought you cops looked on us as something less than pond scum.''

''I'm an ex-cop, Mr. Fenley.''

''Ah, right.''

''Again thanks for your help and time. I'll be in touch.''

''See that you do, Mr. McCall. See that you do.''


Stanley Whitmore sat on the deck of his home, which overlooked the acreage adjoining the big house, and tried to mop up the sweat as quickly as it oozed through his pores.

''This heat's a goddamn pain in the ass,'' he said.

''Stop whining about the heat, for God's sake,'' Paula

responded in a hissing slur. "If anything, you ought to be whining about what your back-stabbing daddy did to you."

"Don't remind me." Stanley's tone was bitter.

"Don't remind you! Have you completely lost it? Surely you're not going to sit on your dead ass and let Fletcher get by with that?"

"Shut up," Stanley muttered.

"I won't shut up! He promised you that land, and you should have it. Didn't you tell him we were trying to have a baby?"

"Well, now that's a good question. Only problem is I'm not sure whose baby the brat would be."

Paula's jaw dropped, but then she lifted her head defiantly. "I don't know what you're talking about."

Stanley gave her an ugly grin. "Sure you do, honey. And so does Natalie."

"Why, that bitch!"

"No, you're the bitch, and if I ever hear of you humping that bastard foreman again, I'll wring your scrawny neck, you hear?"

"Well, if you had any balls, I wouldn't—"

"Interesting conversation."

They both whirled around and saw Daniel standing in the doorway. Without taking her eyes off Daniel, Paula asked her husband, "What's he doing here?"

"I invited him."

"You invited him?" Paula screeched. "What on earth for?"

"Because I was hoping he would talk to Daddy on my behalf."

"What about it, Danny boy? Will you help your little brother?" Paula's voice was full of sarcasm.

Daniel looked from one to the other, a distasteful expression on his face. "The two of you are pitiful, you know that? Gnawing and snarling over that piece of land like hungry dogs."

Paula stepped closer to him and bared her teeth. "Look, you wormy bastard, that kind of help I . . . we can do without."

"Shut up!" Stanley said again, only this time with more force.

"Both of you shut up," Daniel said, walking farther out on the deck and sitting on a chair under the umbrella. "Why the hell are you out in this heat?"

"I do my best thinking outside," Stanley mumbled.

Daniel rose to his feet. "Well, I don't. So if you want to talk to me, you'd best follow me inside."

A few minutes later found the three of them sitting in the living room with the air-conditioning surrounding them. But no amount of air could cool their body temperatures.

"Would you talk to him, Daniel?" Stanley finally asked, a wheedling edge to his voice.

"What makes you think he'll listen to me?"

"Well, he sure listens to you a helluva lot more than he does me. Half the time he treats me like some addled-brain idiot—"

"Well, at least you get his attention," Daniel said in a faraway voice, as if he were talking to himself.

"Oh, swell," Paula ranted. "Now, both of you are sniveling while little Miss Goody Two-shoes walks in and claims the big prize right out from under our noses."

"Natalie was just as shocked as you were," Daniel said.

"So fucking what?"

"Paula! Watch your language."

"Kiss off, Stanley. Your brother's a big boy."

Daniel's features squinted in fake pain. "Let her have her fun." His voice dropped an octave and he added, "But just remember the stakes are mighty high."

Paula glared at him but didn't say anything else.

"You know why Daddy's doing this, don't you, Daniel?" Stanley asked.

"He told us why." Daniel's tone was soft and even. "He's trying to bribe Natalie."

"That bitch!" Stanley jumped out of his chair and pounded a fist into the opposite palm. "I wish Mother had never brought her to the ranch."

"How can you say that after the shape Mother found her in?" Daniel demanded, his eyes narrowing.

Paula turned toward her husband, a sneer on her face. "You're wasting your time talking to him. He's always been her loyal slave, and I don't see that changing."

"If you don't shut the fuck up, I'm—" Stanley began.

Daniel stood. "No need. Paula's right. I'm not going to betray Natalie, even though I feel Daddy's wrong. I think the land should be yours, but that's not my decision to make."

"She's not even blood kin, for chrissake!" Stanley wailed.

"Look, you heard her say she wouldn't accept it. What more do you want?"

"And you believe her?" Stanley held up his hand and laughed. "Don't answer that. You don't have to. Of course you believe her, but I fuckin' well don't."

Daniel looked him up and down, his features grave. "That's your problem. As it stands now, she's got enough troubles without you and Paula adding to them."

Paula laughed again. "She's finally stepped in someone's shit besides our family's, huh? That thought sure does my heart good. In fact, it makes my day."

Daniel walked to the door, where he paused. "I suggest you both back off and leave her alone."

After he had left, Paula turned to Stanley and asked, "Are you going to let that prick of a brother *and* your daddy tell you what to do?"

Stanley stared back at her out of eyes that were as lifeless as cold marbles. "Go to hell."

Stone arrived at his condo around six o'clock that evening, feeling as if he'd been ridden hard and stabled wet. A trip from Austin to Washington, D.C., and back in one day had been grueling.

But now that he'd showered and slipped into a T-shirt and running shorts, he felt like a new man. Too bad his mental spirits weren't in sync with his body.

He made himself a balogna sandwich, but the minute he

took a bite, he made a face. It tasted like sawdust. But then what could he expect when he'd left the salad dressing off the bread?

"To hell with it," he mumbled, slapping the bread back on the plate.

He thought about his daughter for a moment and smiled.

"Oh, Daddy, really, how could you even think about eating balogna?" he heard her say as clearly as if she were standing in front of him. "That's just too gross."

Suddenly Stone had the urge to call Sally and ask if she wanted to come over. But then he scratched the idea. As much as he wanted to see her, he needed to work, to go over what he'd learned to date, then try to make sense of it all. He had to concentrate alone.

Stone eyed the sandwich one more time, babbled a curse, then shoved the plate under some papers. Out of sight, out of mind, he told himself, except where Natalie was concerned.

He winced. Even her name triggered that reflex, especially when he thought about that blasted phone call. He hadn't meant to call her; he'd just done it, like he'd done so many stupid-ass things in his life. But since he couldn't see her, he'd wanted to hear her voice, which had only made matters worse by deliberately playing on the sexual attraction between them that couldn't be forgotten or ignored.

His ploy hadn't worked. She had seen through him, which was a good thing. Maybe now he could stop thinking about her with his zipper down.

Leaning back on his chair, Stone closed his eyes and forced his mind to shift into business overdrive.

Texas Aero Industries' gig was manufacturing faulty spare parts. He knew it, but had Phillip Whitmore known it? Was that the "trouble" he'd hinted about to Natalie? Stone's gut instinct told him yes, trouble that in the end had cost Phillip his life.

"But why?" Stone whispered, his eyes still closed.

Phillip Whitmore should've been a valuable commodity to whoever was behind his death, especially as he'd been a shoo-in for that U.S. Senate seat. So again, why would someone kill him? Perhaps he had wanted out and was about to "rat."

That scenario seemed the most logical conclusion, for Phillip would have then become a liability rather than an asset, which meant he had to be stopped.

Stone opened his eyes and massaged his forehead, then the back of his neck. There were more unanswered questions than answered ones.

What he did know was that both deaths, Phillip's and that of the man in the warehouse, were connected. When he found out why the men had been targets and who had targeted them, then the pieces of the puzzle would come together automatically, and he'd be vindicated.

And the first thing he was going to do was confront Rutgers again, kick his ass, and watch him beg for mercy.

Stone was so immersed in that intriguing thought that he didn't realize the doorbell was ringing until it sounded as though someone were sitting on it. Still, he sat scowling for another long moment.

"Okay, okay. Give it a rest, will ya?" He stalked to the door and, without even bothering to consider who his unwanted visitor might or might not be, flung it open.

"Hello, Stone."

He swallowed the words "Oh, shit" and instead stared into the uneasy face of Natalie Whitmore.

# Twenty-five

His tongue was dry as plaster while the blood rushed in a warm tingle through his veins.

"May . . . I come in?" she asked, avoiding his eyes.

"Of course." Stone coughed to try to clear the gruffness from his voice, then moved aside.

Lord a-mercy, if someone had told him this would happen, he would've called them a fool. But the excited havoc her presence had incited cooled quickly when she stepped into the lighted living room and he took one look at her face.

Her color was pale, though in every other way she appeared as lovely as ever. He knew he was staring like an idiot, but his eyes couldn't seem to stop soaking her up. She had on a peach silk shirt, pants, and multicolored sandals. Her hair, though slightly mussed and looking as though she'd just made love, added to the sexual voltage that was still shooting through him.

Christ!

"Aren't you going to ask why I'm here?" she asked in a husky voice, that pouty lower lip seeming to quiver.

Realizing that the door was still open behind him, Stone shut it, then leaned against it, taking a deep breath. "Okay, so why are you here?"

This time she didn't dodge his eyes. She peered into them. "I've reconsidered."

"And?" Stone reeled at this sudden turn of events but forced himself to move cautiously. He didn't want to spook her at the gate.

"I think that maybe we should call a truce after all and work together."

"Maybe? That doesn't sound like you're real sure."

"I'm not," she responded with a sudden and spirited honesty.

She was strong willed, but with soft edges. He admired that in a woman. Dammit, he admired everything about this woman, which was the problem. For a moment he wished she weren't involved in this investigation, much less the heart of it. But then he'd stopped wishing a long time ago. For him there never had been a Santa Claus, and he didn't figure there ever would be.

"So have a seat and we'll talk."

She nodded, then followed his hand as he waved it toward the couch. She made her way there and sat down on the end, as though ready to scurry if the situation warranted. At least she hadn't already done so, he thought, which was something to be thankful for.

"How 'bout a Coke or some coffee?"

She shook her head and with that gesture exposed a small perfect ear with a diamond stud centered in the lobe. For a second he was captivated by the thought of running his tongue . . .

He jerked his gaze off her and swallowed an expletive.

"Is something wrong?" she asked, her brows drawn together in a frown.

"No, nothing's the matter." His tone was rough, but he didn't give a damn. With her in touching distance, things could turn from sugar to shit real fast.

Natalie stood. "Look, perhaps I should—"

"No, don't go. Please. I'll get you some coffee. Okay?"

She looked undecided, then sat back down. He gave a sigh of thanks, knowing he'd almost blown it by his abruptness.

She looked more uncomfortable and upset than she had when she'd first arrived. He'd best keep a tighter rein on his emotions or she'd walk for sure.

Feeling her eyes track him into the kitchen, Stone upped his pace, expected at any moment to hear the click of the front door. He was all thumbs when he tried to fill the coffee cups.

"Shit!" he yelped as he poured half of the hot liquid on top of his hand instead of into the cup.

Finally he turned and made his way back into the living room. She watched with eyes large and so deep that he could swim in them.

Determined to keep his hands steady, he eased down beside her and set both cups on the coffee table.

Natalie reached for hers, lifted it, and after blowing on the liquid, took a sip. Then, lowering the cup, she said, "Your place looks nice."

He felt a flush creep up his shadowed face. He wondered if she noticed it. "It's messier than it usually is," he lied.

She let that pass, and he was glad.

"Did Sally have a hand in the decorating?"

"How did you know?"

Her face lost that guarded look for a moment; he even thought she might smile. He held his breath.

"I didn't, actually. It was more or less a guess."

"Well, you're right. And she got those goddamn bunk beds that she wanted."

This time she smiled, and he felt his groin tighten. Forcing his eyes off her bottom lip, he reached for his coffee.

When he looked at her again, the smile was gone and her body had stiffened. Could she have read his mind?

"Look, I really didn't come here to make small talk."

"That's all right," Stone said, his tone light. "You're allowed. No one's keeping score."

"That's not the point."

He shrugged. "Okay. Whatever you say."

"And just so you'll know, I don't intend to apologize."

The tension dissolved into a weary silence as they stared at each other.

"I didn't expect you to," Stone said finally.

"I insist on ground rules as well."

"Which are?"

"I don't want you to touch me." She paused. "Can you handle that?"

"Can you?"

The tension turned almost lethal, and their eyes spoke volumes.

"Yes," she snapped. "So are you still interested in our pooling our resources, so to speak?"

"Absolutely," he drawled, unable to keep the sarcasm hidden.

She flashed him a sharp look, then said, "I don't know where to start."

"Anywhere you'd like."

Natalie picked up her coffee cup and gripped it with both hands. "Okay, first off, I want you to know where I stand, that I haven't changed my mind about . . . certain things."

"I'm a big boy. I can handle that."

"I went along with the . . . my family's belief that Phillip's death was merely an accident, that you . . ." Her voice trailed off, and she swallowed hard.

Stone remained silent, refusing to help her. She had set the ground rules; she could take her lumps.

"Anyway," she finally went on, "they contended that you hadn't used good judgement, all right, but that you didn't have an ulterior motive for shooting Phillip."

"Yeah, right." Stone's tone was as hard as his eyes. "If they really believed that, then why did Fletcher Whitmore use his influence to have Internal Affairs deep-six me? But go on; that's another story in itself, one we'll get to later."

Although Natalie looked uneasy, she went on, "As I've already told you, I suspected something had happened, that Phillip was hiding some terrible secret." Her voice thickened, but she quickly regained her composure. "And when I finally got my head on straight, so to speak, I had to know what awful circumstances had driven him to seek counsel that day.''

She paused and played with a piece of her hair.

Stone took that moment to say, ''I wasn't going to ask because I told myself it didn't matter, but it does. Why did you change your mind about me, about our working together? It's obvious you still think I gunned down your husband on purpose.''

She didn't flinch, but she didn't answer him, either. Instead she looked at him through sad, deep eyes.

Stone didn't respond, either, though he wanted to grab her and force her to say that she no longer thought that *he* had intentionally killed her husband. But he didn't; what would that solve?

She'd already said she wasn't about to apologize for having accused him of being a dirty cop, out for his own gain. Nothing he could say or do at this point would change her mind. Again, though, she was here, so there had to be some doubt. Or was that just wishful thinking on his part?

''I came here because you have the expertise and the contacts that I don't have.''

Her soft, unexpected words brought him back to the moment with a jolt. ''So you get what you want and bust my balls at the same time. Is that what this is all about?''

''I must've been out of my mind to think this would work,'' she spat in disgust, then scrambled to stand up.

God, he was dumber than a brick wall. Would he ever learn to keep his mouth shut? ''Look, I was outta line, okay? It won't happen again.''

She tried to relax, though she remained upright and stiff, while another dead silence permeated the room.

After a moment Stone broke. ''Tell me everything that went on before Phillip went to see his attorney. Did something actually happen that you know about?''

Her tongue came out to moisten that lower lip. He groaned inwardly, then forced his mind back on business.

''Yes, he received a mysterious phone call and then later

went to meet someone at midnight. Both times there was fear in his eyes."

"But you couldn't get him to tell you anything?"

"Nothing, except that everything was going to be all right, that he'd take care of it."

Stone scratched his chin. "Anything else?"

"There was a possibility that he was going to quit the campaign."

"Quit the campaign? Who the hell told you that?"

Natalie explained about meeting with the newspaperman.

Stone shoved all five fingers through his hair. "You're right; it sounds like your husband *was* sinking in some kind of quicksand." After a moment of quiet thought, he asked, "What happened when you told your father-in-law about your investigation? Did he have a coronary?"

"And the rest of the family as well, but mainly Fletcher, as you guessed."

Natalie then explained about his offer of the land in the form of a bribe.

"Dammit, one of these days that man's—" Stone broke off when he saw the streak of pain that crossed her face. Or was it anger? There was something going on that she wasn't telling him, but he didn't feel now was the time to press the issue. As it was, their truce was on shaky ground.

"So was there anyone else at that enlightening dinner party?"

"The business manager and the family attorney."

"So it's no secret what you're up to?"

"No."

"How 'bout threats, other than the phone call."

"I received another hoax call, this time at the baby-sitter's."

After she explained, Stone cursed. Surely she didn't think he'd had anything to do with *that* phone call?

"No, I don't."

"So you read my mind?"

"No, I read your eyes. Besides, I know you wouldn't ever do anything to hurt Clancy."

"Thanks for that vote of confidence, anyway."

There was a long, unpleasant silence.

Natalie rubbed her head as if she had a headache. "I'm not sure this—"

"Yes, goddammit, it is a good idea, but by the same token, you might as well know I'm not going to pull any punches or walk on any eggshells around you, because I'm innocent.

"I'll admit that I haven't always gone by the book, that I've pushed the rules to the limit, but I was a damn good cop, regardless of what you, Rutgers, or anyone else thinks." He paused and tried to get control of his rattled temper. "Speaking of Rutgers, have you heard anything else from him?"

She frowned. "No, but I wasn't expecting to."

"But I'll bet the second you left his office, he picked up the phone and called Fletcher Whitmore."

"So what are you saying?"

"You'll find out soon enough."

Natalie took a deep breath and straightened her spine. "So what's your side of the story? Let's hear it."

Their eyes met for a minute—his unreadable, hers distrusting.

"I was in the bank making a deposit when I saw you and your husband come in. I also saw two men enter the bank right behind you. I knew they were up to no good. Sure enough, one pulled a pistol, and instead of aiming at the teller, he aimed at your husband.

"The shooter saw me with my pistol out, fired at me, and hit me in the forearm." Stone pointed at the scar on his arm. "See for yourself. Anyhow, his bullet spoiled my aim, and I shot your husband."

"What about the bank holdup?"

"A setup. Pure and simple, to get your husband."

"Oh, God," she whispered, turning away.

"I know how painful this must be for you."

"No, you don't, but I didn't come here for your sympathy."

He drew in his breath. "Okay, if that's the way you want it."

"That's the way I want it."

"Well, as long as we're baring souls—" his tone was low and harsh—"you might as well know that while I just happened to be in the bank that morning to make a deposit, I had placed one of our undercover detectives in Phillip's campaign headquarters."

"You mean as in spying?"

"That's one way of putting it."

*"Why?"*

"Because he was the most visible of the clan, and he obviously ran the family business. And because an incident that happened at a warehouse across town necessitated an investigation into the Whitmore family holdings."

When she looked blank, Stone went on, "There's a warehouse across town that a company by the name of Texas Aero Industries had leased. Does that name ring a bell with you?"

"No."

"Well, to make a long story short, they make substandard parts for airplanes, then sell them to commercial carriers as the real McCoys, which has cost innocent lives."

"What does that have to do with any of this?"

"A man was shot to death there."

Her hand went to her heart. "I'm sorry, but I still don't understand what that has to do with Phillip."

"You will."

She clamped her lips together and waited.

"One of my men arrived on the scene just before the man died. He was strangling on his own blood, but he still tried to talk." He then told her about the man whispering the name "Whitmore," then finding the business card in his pocket.

She gasped. "Surely you're not suggesting that Phillip or any member of his family was involved in that murder or in anything else concerning that company?"

"That's exactly what I'm suggesting."

Natalie's eyes flashed fire. "That's absurd!"

"That's the *truth*!"

"Why, that man's death could've been related to something outside the company."

"I checked him out, and while he was heavy into gambling, he—"

"See, there's your answer," Natalie cut in, her voice low and throbbing.

"I disagree."

The sounds of the hot night beat around them.

"I don't give a damn what you say." Her eyes reflected her misery.

For a moment he almost backed down. But he couldn't. He'd warned her that he wouldn't pull any punches. "Think, Natalie, about what I just told you. So the bottom line remains the same. Your family *could be* involved in murder and responsible for the continuing loss of innocent lives as well."

"No! This time you're not only out of line, you've crossed it." Natalie lunged to her feet. "I refuse to listen to another word of your psychobabble!"

# Twenty-six

It wasn't so much what she said as how she said it that caused Stone to snap.

He grabbed her and jerked her against him. "Psychobabble, huh? Is that what you call murder?"

"Let me go!" Natalie struggled against his unyielding strength. "How dare you accuse my family of murder when you still haven't convinced me that *you're* not the real murderer?"

"I'm not a killer, and you damn well know it! Or you wouldn't be here." He felt his control slipping in more ways than one. He ached to shake her, yet the lust that the delicate scent of her rose perfume activated was just as strong.

Sucking in his breath, he added, "And deep down you know it could've been your *husband* the dying man was talking about."

With her free hand she reached up and slapped him. The contact sounded like the discharge of a pistol.

He should've seen it coming, only he hadn't. His blood boiled, and he reacted out of both anger and lust, grinding his lips into hers. It was a hard, punishing kiss, but he didn't give a damn. He'd had about all he could take of her body against his, of her breasts pressing into his chest.

Only after he heard her feral moan did he realize what he was doing and pull back. "Don't you ever hit me again!"

She stared up at him, her eyes filled with astonishment and horror. "I . . . I didn't . . . " She stopped speaking and licked her full bottom lip. "It's just that I'm . . . so mixed up and frightened; I don't know what to believe anymore. If only I'd forced Phillip into—" Her voice cracked and faded into nothingness.

Stone felt like a heel. "Hey, don't beat up on yourself," he pleaded as he watched a lone tear make its way down her cheek. Again his reflexes took control: he leaned over and licked that tear off her cheek.

He heard her breath catch even as she stiffened and turned away.

"Natalie." The crack in his own voice was the catalyst that drew her eyes back to his. Color invaded her face as if his hot gaze actually burned her.

"I want you. I want you so much that—" He paused, unable to go on. After a moment he muttered, "Oh, what the hell!"

He knew it was inevitable that this moment would come to pass. Again. Every time they were together, the tension between them rose to the boiling point.

Greedily, Stone's lips once more devoured hers. But what had been punishment was now searing passion. She moaned again, but this time he knew it was a moan of pleasure.

His tongue rediscovered her mouth, probing, seeking, claiming. The sweetness of that mouth, the feel of her body, built such an explosive pressure inside him, he thought he couldn't stand it. It was all he could do not to throw her on the floor and fuck her into tomorrow.

"I want to touch you," he panted while tasting and tugging on her bottom lip. "All of you."

He placed his fingers on the top button of her blouse, then

hesitated, looking at her. Though her eyes were wide and her face taut, she didn't try to stop him.

Without removing his gaze, Stone jerked the shirt out of the waistband of her pants and touched the skin underneath.

She moaned again, and her eyes fluttered closed.

"Oh, God," he murmured, basking in her softness. But he wanted more. He wanted to touch, to suck, those breasts that had driven him as crazy as that pouty lower lip. He bent his head for another kiss, then slid his mouth down her exposed throat to her breasts, where, through her bra, he captured a nipple.

"Stone, no," she whimpered, clutching his shoulders and shaking all over.

He looked up, his face twisted in agony. "What do you mean, no?" he asked, his voice thick.

"I can't . . ."

He let her go so suddenly, she would have fallen had he not grabbed her wrist and steadied her.

"If that's the way you feel about it, then fine," he lashed out.

Only "fine" was the last thing it was. Every time he kissed her, he felt as if the top of his head were going to come off. Now that he'd tasted her skin, he didn't know how he could continue to work. . . .

Suddenly he returned to reality with a thud, and his passion subsided. Work, hell! This latest fiasco had probably severed that before it ever got started.

He voiced the thought. "So, have I axed the deal?"

She looked at him for what seemed an interminable length of time, while he held his breath and felt sweat cover his body.

"No," she choked, "you haven't axed the deal."

She should have given it more thought. No, she should not have given it *any* thought. She should've scratched the idea from conception and hired a private detective, and that would have been that. But no, she had to conjure up a rational reason for seeing Stone.

Even at that, she had once again underestimated her attraction to him and his power over her. She had managed to excuse the first two times he'd kissed her because she hadn't known who he was. Now that she knew, she had done the same thing, only worse. Not only had she let him *touch* her, she had encouraged it. Then she had behaved like an outraged virgin, which did nothing to hide the brutal truth.

She had wanted him to make love to her even though he could have killed her husband intentionally. That thought both terrified and appalled her. She felt as though she'd been given a lighted stick of dynamite and, instead of dropping it and running like hell, had stood still and watched it explode.

In light of what Stone had told her, how could she have been so stupid? So careless? He had as good as implicated her family in murder, for heaven's sake.

Yet when she'd awakened moments ago, her thoughts had been on Stone, tasting his lips, feeling his callused hands on her body, his mouth on her breasts. And that terror had hit her again as she'd wondered if she would ever be able to put her thoughts back into the right perspective.

She jumped out of bed, showered, and dressed, which cleared her head somewhat. She couldn't undo what was already done, nor could she overlook the fact that her body might betray her again at any time.

The blame began and stopped with her. She had thought she was stronger than she was, that she had stymied that heated side of their relationship. But she had failed, and the worst part about it was, she couldn't walk away.

He knew more about the case than anyone else, and she intended to use him just as he was using her. He didn't trust her any more than she trusted him.

That cold fact was no consolation as her growling stomach sent her downstairs toward the kitchen and the smell of frying bacon.

She hadn't planned on entering Fletcher's study. But when

she found the door open, it just happened. She stared at the top of his desk, which was littered with papers, and felt her pulse jump.

Should she take a look-see?

She shouldn't, she knew. She hesitated, then made her way around the desk to the large, high-backed chair. She didn't sit down, however, but shoved it aside and stared at the papers on top.

Her spirits deflated as she realized that nothing in sight bore the name of Texas Aero Industries. She'd probably have gone into shock if she'd found something. While she didn't doubt the family owned the warehouse, she had to believe they weren't involved with the company itself. Still . . .

"What do you think you're doing?"

Natalie froze outwardly, but inside her heart plunged to her toes. She turned around and stared into her father-in-law's narrowed eyes.

"I . . . er—" She paused and ran her damp hands down the sides of her slacks, feeling as though she'd just stolen a package of gum at the grocery store and gotten caught.

Fletcher walked farther into the room. "If you're looking for the deed to that property, then it's okay."

Natalie drew a quick breath. "Actually, I—"

"Hell, let's go outside on the veranda and talk about it."

Feeling as if she had no choice, Natalie followed him, her mind in an uproar. She didn't know what to expect. She had thought she knew this man so well, only to learn that she didn't know him at all.

After they sat down on the plush furniture on the veranda, Josie brought them iced coffee. Natalie grabbed her cup as if it were a lifeline, then looked around her. The day was starting out to be clear and hot, though at the moment a nice breeze was blowing. She watched two bluejays splash happily in the birdbath.

"So are you going to take my offer?" Fletcher asked, easing back on the chair and watching her from under bushy white eyebrows.

"Don't you mean bribe?"

He shrugged, apparently unaffected by her abruptness. "Call it what you like. The land's yours and Clancy's."

"Only if I kowtow to your wishes."

"That's about the size of it."

"I don't want it, Fletcher."

"Sure you do."

"No, I don't, but I don't intend to argue with you."

"Good, because I don't want to argue with you, either. I'll have Ben draw up the papers so it'll be a done deal. Hell, I'll even put it all in Clancy's name, if that'll satisfy you."

"It's still the same."

"What's still the same?"

They both turned and watched as Daniel sauntered through the French doors, coffee cup in hand. "Good morning," Natalie said, relieved that she was no longer alone and on the proverbial hot seat with her father-in-law.

"Take a load off, son. Maybe *you* can talk some sense into this woman's head."

Daniel grinned, then winked, as if trying to relieve the tension that was more stifling than the heat. "So what's she done now?"

"Caught her snooping around my desk."

Natalie flushed, then ground her teeth together. Damn Fletcher! He was enjoying embarrassing her. But she had no intention of letting either of them know how she felt. She showed no emotion.

Daniel, however, had no such reservation. "Are you serious?" he asked, staring at her with raised eyebrows.

"Yes, he's serious," Natalie answered in a soft tone.

"I told her that if she was looking for the deed to that land, then that was all right. If that wasn't the case, however, then . . ."

Fletcher let his words play out, but Natalie picked up on the veiled threat. Nevertheless, it didn't stop her from asking, "What does Whitmore Enterprises have to do with a company called Texas Aero Industries?"

For a moment no one said another word. Only the birds and the crickets made any noise.

Fletcher was the first to speak. "Why do you want to know?"

Daniel glanced from one to the other with a concerned look on his face. "Mind telling me what the hell's going on here?"

"You'll have to ask Natalie that," Fletcher said, his voice low and even.

But Natalie knew she'd struck a nerve because one was ticking in his jaw. She didn't know whether that made her feel better or worse. She feared the latter. She didn't want them to have anything to do with that company. She wanted to prove Stone wrong.

"I don't see the need to repeat my question," she said, her gaze now resting on Daniel.

"I'm with Daddy. Why would you even ask a question like that?"

"Because I want to know the answer."

"The family business need not concern you."

She refused to back down now. "If it has anything to do with Phillip's death, then it does concern me."

"Bullshit!"

"Now, Daddy, calm down and let's talk this through rationally."

"There was a murder at the warehouse," Natalie said, "What do you know about that?"

"Jesus Christ!" Fletcher bellowed, then jumped up. "Who the hell's been filling your head with such garbage?" He paused and looked down at Natalie, then at Daniel. "You'd best talk some sense into her head."

Although he didn't add the "or else," Natalie knew that was what he'd meant, especially when he glared at her before stomping off without another word.

A silence greeted his abrupt departure.

Daniel finally sat beside Natalie and picked up one of her hands. "Natalie, Natalie, what have you gone and done now?"

"Please, Danny, don't patronize me." She jerked her hand out of his. "I'm not in the mood."

"And I'm not in the mood to let you make a fool out of yourself, even if it's in front of family."

Natalie bowed back. "What's that supposed to mean? You aren't denying someone was murdered at that warehouse, are you?"

"No, I'm not. It was in all the papers for God and everybody to read. But while we own the property, we sure as hell didn't or don't have anything to do with what goes on there."

"What about Phillip?"

"What about him?"

"Did he have anything to do with Texas Aero? After all, he ran the family business."

Daniel laughed. "Honey, someone's been leading you down a primrose path, and like Daddy said, it's all garbage. So, for heaven's sake, put it out of your mind."

"Are you telling me the truth?"

"Have I ever lied to you?"

"No."

"Then, there's your answer."

"But Danny, you don't have that much to do with the family business. How could you know—"

"I know enough to be sure about that."

"So you're saying I should forget it?"

"If 'it' is the murder at the warehouse, then the answer is yes."

Natalie sighed. "You can bet Fletcher won't forget that I brought it up."

"Yeah, he will."

"I don't think so."

"Look, when you've satisfied yourself once and for all that Phillip's death was a tragic accident, then everything will return to normal."

"Nothing will ever be normal again," Natalie said flatly, thinking about Fletcher's deep-seated hatred of her.

"Oh, yes, it will, because you're not going to find anything."

"How can you say that? You know I've been threatened, and you know something was bothering Phillip. You even said that yourself."

Daniel gave her an indulgent smile. "Honey, something bothers me just about every day, but that doesn't mean I'm involved in murder. For chrissake, Natalie, think about what you're saying. For the life of me, I can't figure out where you came up with this."

She didn't intend to tell him, either. "You're right, let's just forget it, okay?" Besides, she reminded herself, Daniel was caught in the middle of something he knew nothing about. It was selfish on her part to keep him involved.

His smile widened as he took her coffee cup out of her hand. "What do you say we go look at that town house before we both head for work?"

"All right," she said, standing.

"Hey, don't get so excited."

"Sorry, it's just that—"

"Sis, please, just give it a rest. Everything's going to be all right. This'll blow over, you'll see."

Natalie knew better, but she kept that thought to herself.

# Twenty-seven

"What you're telling me is that this land is not worth anything to the buying public." It wasn't a question, but rather a plain statement of fact.

The surveyor, Rip Menefee, shook his bald head, then tried to smile. He couldn't quite pull it off. "That's about the size of it, Mrs. Whitmore, at least in my opinion."

Natalie tried to ignore the enormous weight that seemed to land with a thud on her chest. Wasn't anything ever going to go right again? Then, furious at herself for whining, she straightened.

"I wish I had better news," Menefee was saying, watching her with close scrutiny.

"I wish you did, too. I was counting on this deal to be very lucrative."

He smirked. "Well for the a—er, I mean, the bozo who's responsible for this waste of valuable land, it has been lucrative."

Natalie looked across the huge tract that was in the process of being cleared for a nursing home and a host of family dwellings. Many of the prospective buyers were ready to plunk down money.

But she had just been told that she could forget that, which made her ill for more reasons than one. She needed this deal; she'd been working on it since Miracle Realty had decided to list large tracts of land for both commercial and suburban developments. More than that, she had counted on the commission to refurbish her town house.

The money that was sure to be left over, she planned on setting aside for her future, a future that included owning her own real estate agency.

Now that hope of a windfall had just gone down the drain, putting both her present and her future plans in jeopardy.

"So what do you think I should do, Mr. Menefee?"

He scratched his bald head again, leaving tracks where he'd smeared the sweat. "I reckon you'll have to go to the cops. Dumping toxic waste is a felony."

"I know."

"Has the owner even so much as hinted that this land is contaminated?"

"Not hardly."

"Nah, I guess he wouldn't. Pretty dumb question, huh?"

"Not really, because some people don't know how to lie, but Mack Gates is apparently a master at it. He certainly had me convinced that this was the deal of a lifetime for the both of us."

"It would've been, if you hadn't hired me."

Natalie held out her hand. "And I'll be forever indebted to you, too."

"Glad to help. I'm just sorry I didn't have better news."

"Me too. But I'll keep you posted."

That conversation had taken place yesterday, and Natalie was still trying to decide the best way to handle the delicate and dangerous situation. She hadn't even told Lucy yet that the deal was a wash.

Tears pricked her eyes as she leaned back on her chair at the office and stared out the window. It was only eight in the morning, but the sun was already beaming in the window with bold intensity. She expected the mercury to climb past one hundred today, which would put everyone's nerves on edge, especially hers.

She couldn't blame her agitation on the heat, though. Hers went far deeper than that. She hadn't heard from Stone in three days. During that time, she had tried not to think about the volatile exchange between them, but she couldn't help it.

The fax she had received from Scott Timpson yesterday afternoon hadn't helped any. The contents, though skimpy, had been both disconcerting and upsetting. There had been nothing about his personal life—only the standard stuff about his education, which she didn't care about. But what she did care about was the tidbit Scott's newspaper nose had unearthed.

Stone had been implicated in another questionable shooting that involved a suspect who wasn't armed but whom Stone had shot and killed. Later, however, a man had been picked up on an unrelated charge, and for a trade-off, he'd confessed to knowing who had taken the gun from the murder site. Stone was subsequently cleared.

Still, Natalie found the incident both disconcerting and upsetting. It made Stone look trigger happy. While that incident further deepened her mistrust of him, she also knew that Stone, with his sexy, rough voice, his lust for life on the wild, shady side, remained a lure she couldn't resist.

She shivered.

"Cold, honey?"

Startled by the unexpected interruption, Natalie jerked her head up, then felt her heart sink. Mack Gates was the last person she wanted to see.

"How did you get in here, Mr. Gates?"

"I told you to call me Mack." He winked. "Especially since we're gonna be working together so much."

Natalie stood behind her desk. "Again, how did you get in here?"

"Hey, the front door was open."

"I don't believe—" Natalie's words dried up in her throat as she remembered that when she'd entered the office, she'd had a gallon of bottled water in one hand and her briefcase in the other. She'd slammed the door shut behind her with her foot, thinking that she'd lock it later. Later had never come.

Gates chuckled. "It's okay; we all make mistakes."

Natalie didn't respond to his good-humored chuckle. It was all she could do not to order him out of her office. She had never liked the man. Until this morning she hadn't been able to put her finger on why. Now she knew. He was as lecherous as he was dishonest.

He had coal black hair and washed-out blue eyes and might have been handsome were it not for excess weight around his waist. He looked as if someone had put a hose down his throat and aired up his middle.

"So, did you get the survey completed?" he asked, taking a seat without an invitation.

"Yes."

Gates lifted an eyebrow at her sharp tone. "Is something wrong, Mrs. Whitmore?"

"You know damn well there's something wrong."

His unlined features remained blank as an empty chalkboard. "No, I'm afraid I don't know any such thing. I thought this deal was progressing right on target. Suppose you tell me what's going on?"

"What's going on is the deal's off."

He looked as if she'd sucker-punched him in his distended belly. He paled, then his face turned fuchsia. "What the hell kind of talk is that?"

"The truth, Mr. Gates."

"Well, honey, you might think the deal is off, but I got news for you. You can't renege now."

"Oh, yes, I can, especially since you've committed a crime."

He threw back his head and laughed, which should've shaken his belly, only it didn't. It must be made of cast iron, she thought, just like his conscience. But she doubted he had a conscience.

"I don't know who filled your pretty little head with that bullshit, but it's wrong. *You're* wrong."

"I wish that were the case, only it's not," Natalie responded with calm assurance. "The surveyor uncovered your nasty little secret."

Gates leaned toward her desk, his mouth tight. That was when she saw the glitter of sweat on his forehead. He wasn't as cool and unconcerned as he looked, though she would have to admit that he hadn't so much as flinched when she'd dropped her bombshell.

"And just what might that little secret be?"·

"The land is poisoned with toxic waste, which makes it a lethal health hazard."

He still didn't so much as flicker. "That's a pile of crap."

"That's exactly what it is, and you were going to pass that pile of crap off as prime land where the elderly and families would reside." She leaned forward. "And you were going to use me and this company to do that." She pulled back, but her tone didn't thaw one iota. "I don't like being duped, Mr. Gates."

"And I don't like being blindsided, Mrs. Whitmore. Nor do I like being accused of something that's not true, regardless of what you've been told." His features softened, and he gave her a conspiratorial smile. "So why don't we just forget this conversation took place and go on with business as usual?"

"Sorry, I can't do that."

"So what are you saying?"

"I'm going to the authorities."

This time he flinched, and his pupils contracted with shock. "I wouldn't do that if I were you."

"If you don't have anything to hide, then you shouldn't mind."

"Again, I wouldn't do that."

"There's nothing you can do to stop me."

"Maybe not, but believe me, I can make you sorry. No one, certainly not a sanctimonious bitch like you, is going to mess up the deal of a lifetime. *Comprendé*?"

Quick, raw fury darted through her. "Get out, Mr. Gates. As in *now*!"

Ten minutes later Natalie was still trembling with both disappointment and rage, mostly rage. But there was pride mixed in as well. She had stood up to him and called his hand. As far as his threat . . . well, she didn't take that seriously for a minute.

After all, he had a legitimate business and was even a deacon in his church. What could he possibly do to her?

The phone rang beside her, and she jumped. On the second ring, she picked up the receiver. "Miracle Realty. Natalie speaking."

"Are you busy?"

Her trembling intensified, but for a different reason. Stone.

"So when can we get together?" he asked when she didn't say anything.

The silence deepened.

"Natalie, are you there?"

"Yes."

"You haven't changed your mind again, have you?"

"No."

"Good. So, have you heard anything since we last talked?"

Talked? Was that what he called that hot kiss they had exchanged? She smothered a sigh. "Yes, but . . ." She was evasive on purpose. "I'd rather not talk about it now."

"When?" he pressed.

"Look, it's a bad time."

"How 'bout I give you a call later, then?"

She heard the exasperation in his voice but couldn't help it.

"That would be better," she said.

"Ciao."

Stone slammed the door on his car and walked toward his condo. His mind was on Natalie as he bent to pick up the newspaper, which he unfolded and read as he walked up the steps to the door. While he fumbled for his key, he noticed a distinct odor, one that he'd smelled many times in the past as a cop, though normally in the winter.

Natural gas. Hell, if the gas smelled this strong outside, what would it be like inside his house? Worse, all it would take to turn his condo into a tinderbox was for the hot-water heater to ignite. He knew better than to open the door.

It was an inconvenience, but he'd have to walk down to the manager's office and report this, then get the gas shut off before the entire complex went up.

As he walked into the office, he saw the manager sitting at her desk, pecking at a computer.

"Val, we got a problem."

"What's that, Stone?"

"I have a gas leak—pretty strong, too. You need to get the gas people out here pronto."

"Okay, I'll take it from here." She found the number on her Rolodex and picked up the telephone.

When the gas company employee arrived thirty minutes later, Stone was sitting on the curb, reading the paper. He handed the man a key, then returned to his paper, still searching for something worth reading.

It didn't take long before the skinny redheaded gas man joined him on the curb again. His eyes were wide, and he lisped when he spoke.

"You're Mr. McCall, right?"

"Yes." Brilliant observation, Stone thought, since he'd given him the key.

"Have you been working on your heating system?"

"In summer? No, why?"

"Then we better call the police, 'cause somebody has. The couplings ain't just loose; they're all undone. Your place would have exploded if I hadn't got here when I did."

"You sure you know what you're talking about? There shouldn't ever be anybody else in the house but me."

"Well, I don't know 'bout that, but I know 'bout gas couplings, and yours are loose."

"So you're saying they didn't just come loose all by themselves, then?"

"No, no. Uh-uh, no way. Somebody diddled with 'em, and that's why I wanna call the cops. That could have blown you sky high, smooth up!"

Stone wasn't ready for that yet. "Give it a rest, Junior. I was a cop for years; if I want them, I'll call them." His mind was going ninety miles an hour, for apparently his house had been burgled. How else could anyone get in and mess with it?

"First of all, is it fixed now? Can I go back inside yet?"

"Oh, yes, sir, it's fixed all right. I tightened them couplings and even used some Loktite to be sure."

"Okay. One more time . . . you're sure this couldn't have happened unless somebody tampered with it?"

"Yes, sir. That's the only way. It took somebody turning them couplings with a wrench. Those suckers just don't come undone on their own."

After the gas man left, Stone opened all the windows and turned on the ceiling fans, then sprayed with the room air-freshener that nearly gagged him. Sally must have bought it; mixed with the natural-gas odor, it made the room smell like rotten roses.

He plopped down on the couch to think about this. Hell, there wasn't any way around it. Somebody had intentionally planned to blow him "smooth up," as the redheaded fella had told him.

But why? He knew why. He'd put somebody's nuts on a hot plate. Where they'd been picking on Natalie before, now they were turning their attention toward him. Well, nifty enough. He'd see if they could take it as well as they dished it out.

The fire was going up under the hot plate, and he'd see who squealed first.

# Twenty-eight

Mack Gates belched, then farted.

"Shit, Mack, you're about the crudest bastard I know."

Mack shrugged his massive shoulders at the same time he rubbed his belly. "When you gotta, you gotta."

His partner, Stu Roach, glared at him. "Besides being crude, you're a real piece of work. Here we are sitting here with our hands tied while that bitch is squeezing our balls."

How had he been so unlucky to have to face Stu so early in the morning? Mack asked himself. He'd gotten to their office early in order to assess the situation. After making coffee, he'd sat behind his desk, only to look up and see Stu standing in the door, wringing his hands like a goddamn idiot. His first mistake had been telling his limp-wristed partner about the botched land deal.

But Stu had known something was wrong and had kept whining until Mack had blurted out that the huge deal was in jeopardy. Stu's whining had turned into a wail which hadn't stopped.

"Will you just simmer down, for god's sake!" Mack said. "I'm not convinced she's going anywhere. Remember I was there and saw her face when I more or less threatened her."

"What's this 'more or less' shit?"

"Okay, so I leaned on the 'more' side a tad heavier."

Stu's black, bushy eyebrows drew together and formed a menacing frown. "We need this deal or the business is going down the tubes. But more than that, I don't want to go to jail."

"So she goes to the authorities." Mack rubbed his distended belly, belched again, then reached for the package of Tums he kept with him twenty-four hours a day. "So fuckin' what?"

"Are you crazy, man? The EPA'll bury us under that jail."

"Not if we swear we didn't know the land was toxic when we bought it."

"That won't wash. We both knew that old man stored and sold tons of batteries there, and for years, too."

"Yeah, but what we didn't know was just how lethal that could be. Besides, Charles is a damn good attorney."

"Charles is full of hot air."

"That's your opinion," Mack said, his tone icy. "I happen to have complete confidence in him."

"You're not really worried about what that bitch can do to us?"

"More pissed than worried. Still, I don't intend to let Mizz High-titties get away with anything, if I can avoid it."

Stu's full lips formed a smirk. "What do you plan to do, put a muzzle on her?"

Mack didn't answer right off. He wanted to fart again, but he didn't dare. He didn't think it wise to agitate his partner any further. Already Stu was a loose cannon and couldn't be trusted not to squeal to save his own ass.

"Actually, that's kinda what I had in mind."

Stu's smirk turned into a grimace. "You're as full of hot air as Charles."

"I wouldn't count on that. Like you said, not only do we have a business to protect, but it's our asses as well. And I'm not about to let Natalie Whitmore ruin either."

"I hope you know what you're doing. You know the Whitmores have long and powerful tentacles in this city and the entire state."

Mack's washed-out blue eyes lighted. "She's not a Whitmore; her dead husband was. How much weight can that carry?"

"Probably not much," Stu said, rubbing his chin. "Still, I wouldn't underestimate her."

"I don't intend to. On the other side of that coin, she'd best not underestimate me, either."

Stu stood. "I gotta go and see a client. Hopefully, I can concentrate. Keep me posted. And for chrissake, don't do anything stupid. That goes for Charles, too."

The second his partner left the room, Mack reached back into his pocket and tossed two Tums into his mouth. God, but his stomach juices tasted like stale puke.

If and when his wife found out he'd botched the biggest deal of his career and that the millions of dollars she had counted on might not come about, she'd be furious. Sweat poured off Mack's face, and he belched again, despite the Tums. He couldn't lose Lois. She was the thing wet dreams were made of. But he didn't kid himself. The only reason she'd married him was for his bank account, which she had helped dwindle. He hadn't minded and still didn't. As long as she rode him and pumped him dry every night, he didn't care. Only he did care, he just now discovered. The prisons nowadays were full of perverts. The sweat rolled down his face and onto his girth.

What a fucking miserable start to the day, he thought, staring out the window at the black clouds rolling in from the west. Like he'd told his partner, he'd muzzle Natalie Whitmore. He had no choice.

Only problem was he'd have to figure out how.

"Why can't I come live with you, Daddy?"

Stone gripped the receiver so hard, he feared he might snap his knuckles in two. "You know why, honey."

"No, I don't."

He heard the mutinous tone in Sally's voice and tried his

best to defuse it, but he wasn't good at that sort of thing. He was improving, though, and was proud of himself. He and Sally had developed a close relationship, especially since he had moved into the condo. Still, when she tugged on his heart to live with him, he felt that old insecurity churn inside him.

He wished that were possible, only he knew it wasn't, not now, anyway. Besides, his ex-wife would never allow Sally to live with him.

"Daddy, are you there?"

"'Course I am, honey. Look, you know I love you—"

"Daddy, puleecse, I know that. Why do you think I want to live with you?"

He smiled at his daughter's dramatic use of the word "please," while grappling for a comeback to her logic. "Sally, it's not that simple, and you know it. First off, your mother has custody."

"So?"

"Hey, kiddo, put a stopper in that mouth, okay? And listen up."

Sally was quiet; nevertheless, he heard her exasperated sigh through the phone line. He imagined the look on her face as well; a smile touched his lips. Boy, was he ever learning the art of manipulation.

"You know your mother would never hold still for such a move."

"Maybe if you talked to her."

Stone choked. "Come on, you know better than that. She'd be devastated if you even mentioned such a thing."

"I already have."

For a minute Stone was shocked speechless. "Before you talked to me?"

"Well, I just thought I'd test the waters."

Stone held his breath. "And?"

"She went ape-shit."

"Whoa, kiddo, watch your mouth! You're not too old to get it washed out with soap, you know?"

"Oh, Daddy, puleeese. Everyone at school uses that word."

"Not my daughter."

"Oh, all right," she conceded, "I'm sorry."

"That's better. Now, back to the subject at hand. Let's give the move a rest for now. You know I'd love to have you here, but now's not a good time. I still have a lot to prove to myself and to you." He paused. "After that, we'll see."

"What about Natalie?"

Stone flinched visibly. He had wanted the subject changed all right, but not onto Natalie. She was just as much a handful of thorns as Sally's efforts to move in with him. "What about her?" Caution altered his tone.

"Are you still seeing her?"

"Seeing her? I don't know what you mean. And don't you dare say 'please' in that obnoxious way of yours, either."

Sally giggled. "I just thought you two were an item, that's all."

Teenagers! Had they always been this lippy? He didn't think so. On second thought, he always had been because he'd had no choice. His dysfunctional family life had made him that way.

"Forget that. We're no item. She's just an acquaintance."

"Okay, Dad, whatever you say."

"That's what I say, you little minx."

"Just so you'll know, I liked her. And I 'specially like Clancy."

"Me too. But right now I gotta get to work or I'm going to get fired from this new job. Then where would I be?"

"In big trouble."

"Right, kiddo. I'll call you soon."

"Daddy, you do want me to live with you, don't you?"

He heard the uncertainty in his child's voice and felt another tug on his heart. "Of course I do, but I don't want you to get your hopes up. I can't see your mom ever letting that happen."

"We'll see," Sally said airily. "I'll talk to you later."

Long after Stone replaced the receiver, he remained behind his desk in the insurance office and stared out the window.

Yet he wasn't cognizant of anything going on below him on the busy street.

Sally had made a remarkable recovery, and for that he was thankful. He just hoped she didn't dig her heels in about the change of address. If so, he'd deal with that when the time came.

Now he had other things on his mind, such as the new fraud case that Larry had dumped in his lap yesterday.

"Take this and run with it," Larry had said, dropping a file in the middle of his desk.

"What is it?" Stone asked, thinking it looked like the Austin phone directory and much too important for him to handle.

"Jewelry, my friend."

"As in the kind that sparkles?"

Larry grinned. "You got it. As in diamonds, rubies, et cetera."

"Mmm, I always did like that stuff, only I couldn't ever afford any of it."

Larry chuckled. "Well, the skinny here is that the owner of one of the city's largest stores said he was burglarized and that millions in fine jewels were taken."

"Sounds legit enough to me."

"They all sound that way. At first."

"So you're wanting me to play cop and make sure?"

"That's about it, which we do in all cases. But there's something about this one that bothers me. See what you can dig up on the owner. If you save our asses big bucks on this one, you'll be up for a big bonus."

Stone grinned. "Ah, now you're singing my kind of music."

"Thought so. Oh, by the way, how's *your* investigation going?"

"Slow, but hopefully sure. I went to see Rutgers."

Larry's cauliflower ears wiggled and his eyes lighted. "And?"

"I'm sure by the time I left he was pissing in his pants."

"So you shook him up a little?"

"I'd say a lot." Stone's good humor fled. "If I find that he was involved in my dismissal, I'm going to nail his ass."

"Did you tell him that?"

"Yep."

"Damn, I wish I'd been a fly on the wall."

Stone shrugged. "We'll see what happens."

"Yeah, I guess we will."

That conversation had taken place with Larry two days ago, and he'd hardly cracked the file. Now, following Sally's unsettling call, his mind was blown to smithereens. If only she hadn't mentioned Natalie. Hell, who was he trying to kid?

Natalie was never off his mind, especially since he'd spoken to her on the phone. Had she changed her mind about joining forces, as he'd accused her? Or had something else happened? He didn't know, but he knew he had to see her again.

When he wasn't with her, he was miserable. When he *was* with her, he was also miserable.

He pounded the desk with his fist. "Shit."

Wasn't that a helluva state to be in?

# Twenty-nine

"Thanks, Mary, I'll be back in touch."

Mary Emerson nodded. "And please don't wait too long. I'm dying to get started on your place."

"Me too, only there's a lot going on in my life right now. What I wanted to do this evening was make sure you were available."

"I'm available, believe me. That house needs help."

Natalie smiled. "I know, and I'm a realtor, not an interior decorator."

"That's why you've got me." She smiled. "And I'm cheap, too."

"You'd have to be or I wouldn't be here."

Minutes later Natalie made her way down the sidewalk of one of Austin's busiest streets. She often wondered why Mary didn't move her office from this area, as it was always so congested; then she dismissed the thought. Mary's business was not her concern.

But Mack Gates was, she thought as the slimy creep's face jumped to mind. The following morning she had a meeting scheduled with her attorney, who then planned to call the local FBI office. Eventually the EPA would get in on it, which meant Mr. Gates just might end up in prison.

That image buoyed her spirits, only to have them wilt again when her mind switched to Stone. They hadn't gotten together because he hadn't called her back. She figured he was not happy with her since she'd been so withdrawn on the phone.

She had picked up the phone to call him several times, only to hang up, facing the truth about herself. She wanted to see him all right, and not just about business, either.

She wanted to feel his arms around her. She wanted to feel his lips on hers. She wanted him to touch her all over. . . . Oh, God, why couldn't she stop thinking about him in that way?

Pushing down the brewing panic inside her, Natalie upped her pace until she approached the intersection. She couldn't be like some of the college kids walking along the Drag, as this section of Guadalupe was called. She didn't have the nerve to walk out into the street, dodging cars to get to the other side. She preferred to wait for the light to change.

Stopping at the curb amid a throng of UT students who apparently shared her views about challenging the cars and trucks, she was scarcely aware of the kids around her or the stifling heat radiating from the asphalt.

The wait seemed interminable, for traffic was still heavy at seven in the evening. In that moment she felt something hit her in the middle of her back. A hand. She could feel every detail of it in that instant: the sweaty palm, the long fingers spread wide apart.

"Excuse me," she said, trying to angle her head to see which kid was rude enough to push her.

The open hand pushed again, harder this time, and she felt herself being shoved into the street, in the middle of a traffic lane.

The unnerving squall of protesting rubber sounded close, too close, and she felt the heat from a car that swerved wildly into the other lane to miss her. Sheer terror caused bile to flood the back of her throat as she looked up at a car only inches from her head.

Natalie heard a man's voice shouting above the country station playing on his car radio, "Crazy bitch! Are you fuckin' nuts?"

She stood on the yellow line marking the lanes as cars hurtled past on both sides. As if she were in a daze, she saw the refrigerated van approaching, its wheels over the line, straddling both lanes as the driver raced to beat the yellow light.

She couldn't move, couldn't react, as if she were waiting for the truck to flatten her on the street. For some reason the name painted on the van was emblazoned in her mind. She knew she would die thinking about PEARSON INSTITU-TIONAL MEATS.

Everything seemed to take forever. Her eyes were on the driver now; she could tell the instant he took his eyes off the changing traffic light and scanned the road in front of him. She could see *his* eyes widen when he saw her, then she shut hers tightly, steeling herself for the impact.

She heard the squeal of locking brakes, the heart-sickening sound of the van sliding toward her, its tires losing traction on the pavement, riding now on a cushion of melted rubber.

The PEARSON INSTITUTIONAL MEATS truck stopped inches from her body. Natalie could have reached out and touched the Ford emblem on the grill.

The driver flung open the door of the car and jumped out onto the Drag. "Jesus, lady! Are you crazy or what?"

Natalie could hear every word he said, but she couldn't respond. She felt as if her entire body were encased in cement.

She felt another hand at her back and stiffened. The hands moved to her forearm, and she looked into the concerned eyes of an older campus policeman. Only then did she feel blood surge through her veins.

"You'll be all right, ma'am," he said. "Just lean against me. That's right. Now, let's get out of the street."

Once seated on the front seat of his car, she took a deep,

gulping breath of the cool air blowing from his air-conditioner vents.

"Ma'am, do you feel like you're going to pass out?"

Natalie shook her head. She feared throwing up more than passing out.

"You want to go to the hospital? I could have you there in a jiffy; it isn't far."

"No!" Natalie whispered, shaking her head again.

"Can you tell me what happened back there?"

Natalie forced her eyes open and looked at the policeman. She licked her cotton-dry lips and between chattering teeth explained, "I . . . felt a hard hand on my back, twice. The next thing I knew, I was out in the street."

"So you think someone pushed you?"

"I know they did."

"Accidentally or deliberately?"

"I don't know." Tears welled up in her eyes.

"Well, later, when you're feeling better and have time to rethink what happened, maybe you'll think of something, come up with an answer. If so, you'll need to report it to the city police. I'm with UT, and technically this didn't happen on campus."

Natalie nodded.

"Meanwhile, you're in no condition to drive."

"But I have my car."

"Forget driving. I can take you home; you can get your car tomorrow."

Natalie didn't hesitate. Later, she couldn't understand why she gave the officer the address she did. At the time, she just blurted it out, then let her head fall back against the scat and closed her eyes.

She must have dozed off, for the next thing she remembered was hearing the policeman say, "We're here, ma'am. Want me to get out with you?"

"No . . . thanks, I'll be fine."

"You sure?"

Natalie wasn't at all sure, but she said so anyway. "I'll be fine. Thanks for all your help."

She felt his eyes on her even as she rang the doorbell, shaking all over.

The door finally opened, and she stared into Stone's shocked face. "My God, what happened to you?"

Natalie tried to answer, but she couldn't get the words past her numb lips. Now that she was facing Stone, the emotions charging through her ranged from fear to relief.

It was obvious he hadn't been expecting company. His hair was more disheveled than usual, a dark stubble roughened his jaws and chin, and he was dressed in a pair of running shorts with no shirt. Even in her rattled state, she couldn't help but notice the thick hair on his chest or that he had the body of someone in excellent physical condition.

She hated to think how she appeared to him. When it came to her, disheveled was too tame a description. But that didn't matter; she hadn't come here to impress him. She'd come out of desperation.

Stone took her hand and led her into his living room.

She looked up at him through glazed eyes. "Stone—"

"Shh, just take it easy for a minute, get your sea legs."

Before she realized his intention, he stopped, folded her into his arms, and held her, not passionately, but protectively, as if she were a child in need of soothing.

Natalie clung to him, feeling his strength and using his gentleness to try to erase from her mind the horror she'd endured.

"Whatever it is, it's going to be all right." Stone pressed her face against his shoulder. "Just try and get a hold of yourself."

She didn't know how long he held her, his hand caressing her hair. In tiny increments Natalie felt her fear subside and her composure return. She began to question her sanity in coming here. The old doubts and mistrusts suddenly reared their ugly heads. What if she had run straight into the arms of the enemy?

Shuddering, she pulled back, and when she did, he dropped his arms. And though she knew his letting go of her was for the best, she still felt a momentary sense of loss.

"Sit down," Stone said with gruff abruptness, "while I get you something to drink."

"Thanks," she whispered, and sank onto the couch behind her.

Without looking at her again, he hurried toward the kitchen. She wanted to close her eyes, thinking that when she opened them again, this would all be a bad dream. But she knew better, knew if she shut them, she'd relive the incident once again.

Stone returned shortly with two glasses of iced tea. After handing one to her, he placed his on the coffee table, then sat next to her. She noticed he had put on a T-shirt. She lowered her head and sipped her tea.

"Are you up to telling me what this is all about?"

Natalie lifted her head and saw the baffled expression on his face, as if he were trying to figure out what the hell was going on.

She crossed her arms over her chest and peered into his probing eyes. "Someone tried to hurt me."

"Hurt you?" His forehead grooved into a frown. "How?"

"I was standing on the curb of a busy intersection and someone pushed me into the oncoming traffic."

"Godamighty!"

"In fact, I was pushed twice."

Stone raked his hands through his hair again, lurched off the couch, then muttered a harsh expletive.

"The officer who brought me here just happened to be in the vicinity and saw the commotion. He insisted on helping me, though I told him I was fine."

"Well, you're sure as hell not fine."

He was right. She was far from fine. Now that she had

painted him a detailed verbal picture, she felt both violated and frightened.

"Did anyone around see who pushed you?"

"I don't think so. It all happened so fast and there was so much chaos."

"Any idea who would do such a thing?" His eyes probed deeper.

"Well, two incidents come to mind, but—"

"Forget the 'but' and just tell me."

She returned his stare and thought inanely that he looked like a wild animal ready to pounce on its prey.

"This is probably crazy, but I've been dealing with a client who I think has a few screws lose."

"How do you mean?"

In a slow, methodical voice, Natalie explained about Mack Gates, but without mentioning his name.

"But you haven't gone to the authorities yet, right?"

"No, I'm planning to see my lawyer first thing tomorrow."

"Well, that bastard's certainly a candidate."

A chill moved down her body. "I'll admit he gives me the creeps." She stopped, then opened her mouth, only to shut it again.

"Go on." His tone was clipped, and again she sensed the suppressed anger inside him.

"Still, for some reason, I never really took him seriously. Oh, I know he'd do anything to keep the land deal alive, but m—" She paused. She couldn't say that terrifying word.

"You're wrong. Those are the kinds of bastards who'll kill without remorse. I saw 'em every day for years."

"Well, the deal is dead, and he knows it."

"So don't underestimate him, you hear? Desperate people take desperate measures."

Natalie passed her tongue across her dry lips. "I know."

"Which makes what happened to me even more significant."

Her heart lurched. "What are you talking about?"

"Some asshole broke into my condo and messed with the heating unit."

"I'm not sure I'm following you."

"Gas escaped in lethal doses, which could've blown the condo and me to smithereens, if I hadn't been careful, that is."

"Oh, my God," Natalie whispered.

"At first I wasn't too concerned—"

Her eyes flared. "Not concerned! Why, that's crazy. You could've been killed."

"I know that, but when I was a cop that was part of my everyday existence, so you don't think about it. Now, though, I know we've unnerved someone to the extent that the game has turned deadly."

"What are we going to do?" she asked in a small voice, thinking about that gun she'd promised herself she was going to buy but never had.

"A few minutes ago, you mentioned something else. Let's hear that."

Natalie wished she'd screened what she'd said more carefully. Now it was too late. She knew she should tell him about the conversation with Fletcher and Daniel, yet she was reluctant. She feared he would read more into that exchange than was warranted.

By the same token, she couldn't ignore that someone had tried to hurt them both. Besides, she knew Stone would never let her get by without telling him. He looked about as coiled and dangerous as she'd ever seen him. She'd hated to have been a criminal who got in his way. This man didn't like to be thwarted.

"After you mentioned Texas Aero Industries, I found myself in Fletcher's study. There were a bunch of papers scattered on his desk. I just kinda looked through them."

"And?"

"I got caught."

He swore.

# Thirty

Some of Natalie's spunk returned. "Look, that's not my expertise, you know."

"Hey, simmer down. I didn't mean anything by that."

"Yes, you did, but it doesn't matter."

"You're right. All that matters is what you said to him. Please, tell me you lied."

"I can't because I didn't."

"Why the hell not?"

"Don't yell at me."

"I'm not yelling at you."

Natalie's chin jutted. "Yes, you are."

"Jesus, women!" A tense silence followed Stone's outburst, then he said without a trace of emotion, "So why didn't you lie?"

"Because I didn't feel I had a reason to. I just wanted to test Fletcher's reaction to the name, that's all."

"And what was his reaction?"

"He let me know real quick that the Whitmore business was none of *my* business."

"And you didn't take offense at that?"

"Not really, because I don't believe Fletcher or Daniel—"

"Daniel? How did he get in on this?"

"He came in while Fletcher and I were talking."

"That's great. That's just great."

"If you think Daniel had anything to do with any of this, either, you're dead wrong." Her tone was scathing. "He's my best friend and ally."

"That so, huh? Then why didn't you go running to Danny boy tonight?"

Natalie's face turned pale. "Maybe I'll just do that," she snapped, knowing that she'd made a fool out of herself for coming here again. God, would she ever learn?

"Sorry," Stone responded, his features dark and moody. "As usual, I let my mouth overload my ass."

His blunt apology caught her off guard, and Natalie couldn't think of anything to say, especially when he was looking at her as if he could devour her.

Her heart skipped a beat, and she shifted her gaze.

He cleared his throat, then said, "What about Stanley? Remember he was plenty pissed about that land deal."

"And so was his wife, Paula, who has her own ax to grind against me."

"How's that?"

"I caught her in the barn with the foreman."

"Doing what, making whoopie in the hay?"

"Exactly."

"So taking that and all the other shit into consideration—the threatening phone call, the baby-sitter scare, the land deal, getting caught in Fletcher's office—surely you must know that your family or someone close to them is involved."

Natalie shook her head, feeling her blood pressure rise again. "Not murder, though. I refuse to believe that."

Stone's eyes drilled her. "If you hadn't thought that, then why did you rifle through Fletcher's desk?"

Stone was right. Her actions belied her words. One minute she was defending her family, the next she was close to accusing them herself. But she blamed Stone for planting that evil seed she couldn't ignore or dismiss. Damn him.

"What I did was harmless," she said defensively. "Anyway, I was more curious than anything."

"I wanted you to be curious, only I didn't want you to get caught."

"Well, at least I'm doing something," she fired back.

"So am I. I'm snooping, too. The only difference is that I'm not talking to anyone who's a suspect, except maybe . . ."

"Who?" she pressured, not about to let him off the proverbial hot seat.

"Rutgers."

"Ah, so you went to see him?"

"Yeah, I took a walk on the wild side and decided to shake him up a bit."

"And did you?"

"Yep. That sonofabitch cost me plenty, and I intend to make him pay. You wanna know something else? My gut tells me that Fletcher Whitmore has Rutgers under his boots."

Natalie winced against the bitterness in his tone and suddenly realized that nothing had been resolved. They were basically still on opposite sides of the fence. Again, she had made a grave mistake in coming here. Thank God nothing had happened.

She stood, then took a deep breath. "I should go."

"Why?"

"Because," she said uneasily.

He looked at her, then said in a thick tone, "Why did you come here, to me?"

Natalie sucked in her breath as their eyes met and locked. The tension was back, in the room, in his face, in every line of his taut body.

"I don't know."

He stepped closer. "Oh, I think you do."

"I have to go." She heard the desperate note in her voice. "Is that what you want?"

His voice was harsh, even as his warm breath caressed her face. Her heart upped its pace. She was sure he could hear it. She removed her gaze.

"Natalie?"

"Yes, that's what I want to do," she mumbled.

He tilted her chin and forced her to look at him. "You don't mean that. You came here because you want me as much as I want you."

She shook her head. "No, that's not true."

"Then go," he said abruptly, and stepped back. "I won't stop you."

Natalie hesitated, which proved to be her downfall. A hot flare leapt into his eyes, and he grabbed her.

"Stone, I—"

"Shut up," he rasped against her lips. "You talk too god-damn much."

Her body swayed against his arousal, and he was convinced that she wanted him as much as he wanted her. Still, he had to have proof.

"Natalie, sweet Natalie." His hold tightened, and he felt her lips, soft and pliant, tasting like the sweetest of strawberries, quiver beneath his.

He pulled back, stared into her eyes, his own eyes questioning. He didn't want to push himself on her. Not this time. When he buried himself inside her, he wanted her full and eager cooperation.

"Yes," she whispered, answering his unspoken question.

"Are you sure?" His voice came out sounding scratchy, as though he had a sore throat.

"Yes."

The tiny word seemed to have come from the depths of her, and he knew she meant it, which made his knees almost buckle beneath him. He had lusted after women in the past, but never to this extent. He actually ached to become part of her, to blend his flesh with hers, his hardness into her moist softness.

"I want to touch all of you." Those broken words were spoken against her lips while his hands slipped to her buttocks, cupping each cheek, crushing her still closer.

He heard her moan, trembling, and he knew that she'd felt the full extent of his arousal.

She moved against him, and this time he groaned, feeling as if he'd been hit with a bolt of electricity.

Natalie pulled back and peered up at him through widened eyes. He saw the hesitancy he'd so feared. But there was something else as well: passion. If he hadn't seen that, he didn't know what he would've done.

He had to have her. Looking at her, he traced the tip of his finger around her lips, lingering a tad longer on the pouty lower one.

"I know how you feel. Seeing you and knowing I couldn't . . . shouldn't have you has been hell. I felt like a continuous stake was banging in my gut."

"Stone?"

"Shh, let's don't talk."

"It's too late for words, isn't it?"

The husky tremor in her voice and the dewy softness of her eyes caused that banging in his gut once again. He lowered his head and crushed her lips into his.

Her arms looped around his neck and clung while his mouth plundered hers, tongues meeting and tangling in sweet discord.

Unable to depend on his own legs to hold him upright as the all-consuming fire raged inside him, Stone eased her backward toward the couch. Once the backs of her legs touched the cushion, he lifted his head and, without taking his eyes off her, lowered her down.

"Stone, what—?"

He stopped her halting words by tracing her lips with his tongue. He didn't want to taint the moment with questions or recriminations. Both would come later; he was sure of that. For now, becoming a part of her was all that mattered.

"I want to see your breasts, touch them, feel them."

Her only reaction was to swallow convulsively and nod.

With frantic gentleness, he opened one button then another on her silk blouse, exposing the low-cut, lace bra. She clamped down on her lower lip and watched him flick the catch in the middle. Instantly her breasts, with their rosebud-colored nipples, filled his vision.

A groan escaped him as he leaned down and circled one nipple with his lips and sucked on it. Small mewing sounds erupted from deep within her, and she dug her fingers into his shoulders as if urging him to move to the other breast.

Stone needed no second invitation. Transferring his lips to it, he suckled until it, too, was torrid and wet. Still, he didn't stop. Dropping to his knees, he bent his head and tongued his way down her flat stomach.

"Stone, Stone," she wailed, burying her head against the cushions, her eyelids fluttering shut.

Only after he began urging her skirt up did her eyes open. Again there was a question in them.

"Lovely," was all he could say, his gaze already transfixed on the wisp of nylon that rode low across her stomach and around her hips.

He lowered his head again and dipped his tongue into her navel. She jammed her fingers into his hair and made more mewling sounds that became louder when his tongue slid down the nylon to finally stop between her thighs.

For a moment he tongued her there, feeling her warmth seep through the flimsy material.

She bucked against the intrusion. "Stone!"

His name came out an agonized cry. "I know, I know. I'm about to make it all better."

With that promise, he pulled the panties down and off, only then to part her thighs and ease a finger inside her, along with his tongue.

"Oh . . . oh . . . my . . . God!" she whimpered as both finger and tongue worked their magic.

Soon, he cupped her warmth while an orgasm shook her. Once she regained control, she looked up at him, her eyes filled with an emotion he couldn't decipher.

"Was that good for you?" he asked in a hoarse voice.

"You . . . know it was." She paused as if struggling for her next breath. "What about you? I mean—?"

"I know what you mean. But making you come, watching you, satisfies me."

"But you want more, right?"

"Yes."

"So do I."

With a boldness that shocked him and even seemed to shock her, if her shaking hands were any indication, she reached out and unzipped his pants. His penis, hard and throbbing, spilled into her hands, sending shock waves spiraling through him.

He gasped, fearing he might explode. God, but her hands on him were so soft, so warm, and felt so damn right.

"Let's go to the bed," she said.

He helped her to her feet, then with another bold move Natalie circled him with her hand and led him toward the bedroom. Once there, they fell wordlessly onto the bed.

"I want to make you come, too," she whispered against his lips.

His body hot from need, Stone spread her legs and thrust into her.

"Oh, yes," she cried, lifting her hips.

"I want you on top. I want to see your face when *you* come again."

Stone rolled over onto his back, taking her with him. Seconds later he placed both hands on her breasts and watched her as she sat atop him, her eyes glassy, her hair wild, her body glistening in perspiration.

She was the loveliest thing he'd ever seen and the sexiest, because she was so unaware of either.

"I've wanted to fuck you like this for so long," he ground out, beginning to move, first slowly, then faster.

She matched his pace until their bodies exploded in a simultaneous orgasm. Afterward, she fell across him and he held her for the longest time.

"Stone?"

"Mmm?"

"Are you asleep?"

He chuckled. "Hardly."

"What does that mean?" she asked, rolling off him and onto her side.

"It means you were about to smother me to death."

She chuckled, then scooted her buttocks against his stomach. Her action brought a groan from him as he clasped an arm around her waist.

"I could take you again, you know, especially with that beautiful ass squirming against me."

She sighed but stopped moving.

After a moment Natalie felt his entire body stiffen. She angled her head so that she could see his face. It was pale and his lips were gray.

"Stone, what's wrong?" If he said he was sorry, she couldn't bear it. She didn't want to think about what they had done, not at this moment. Later, but not now.

"How did you get that nasty scar down your back?" he asked.

He touched it, then traced it with his tongue. Even under that gentleness, she flinched, feeling a panic of old.

"Natalie, did someone hurt you?"

"Yes."

"Who?"

"I'd rather not talk about it."

"Natalie, who did that to you?"

"A man. He . . . he cut me with a knife."

# Thirty-one

Stone cursed, then rolled her over on her back.

"Stone, please," she begged in a muffled tone while craning her neck.

"What man?"

The lamp in the corner of the room allowed her to see the fury in his eyes.

Her voice quivered. "I told you; I don't—"

"But I do."

"Why do you want to know?"

"Dammit, I want to know everything there is to know about you."

Silence.

"He . . . he was one of my mother's boyfriends."

"Afterward, what happened to the sonofabitch?"

"Nothing."

"You mean your mother didn't press charges?"

Natalie laughed a bitter laugh. "Not hardly."

"Jesus. You mean he got away with that?"

"Yes." She turned onto her back and touched his face. "Don't worry. It's all right now." Only it wasn't all right, and it never would be. But she had to pretend. Otherwise she wouldn't have survived.

Stone voiced her thought. "No, something like that is never all right."

"What would you have done to him?" she asked in a light tone, hoping to remove that fierce look on his face and lessen the tension holding his body rigid. She didn't like where this conversation was heading.

"You really want to know?"

She smiled, but it lacked sincerity. "Yes."

"I'd have yanked his balls off and stuffed them down his throat."

"Stone!"

"Well, you asked."

"I don't believe you."

He shifted, and when he did, she saw that deadly look in his eyes. Her breathing faltered, and she reminded herself again that this man played by a different set of rules—his own—and that he had a dangerous side. She knew he would have carried out his threat.

"Does that upset you?" he asked.

"Sort of."

His only response was to pull her close against him and hold her for a while.

Finally he asked, "Will you tell me about it?"

"I just did."

"No, you didn't," he contradicted with rough gentleness. "You just stated the facts. I want to know how you got into a situation where some sadistic bastard would do such a thing."

"Stone, really, my past is not something I like to think about, much less talk about."

"Maybe it's time you did both."

"Since when have you become a licensed shrink?"

"I haven't. Besides, it doesn't take one of those weirdos to figure that out."

She chuckled, but again it was hollow.

"What happened to your daddy?"

"After I was born, he walked out. He didn't want the responsibility of a squalling brat, or at least that's what my mama said. From there she started drinking, then got hooked on drugs."

"So back to the boyfriend. I want to know what happened."

"It's an ugly story."

"I'm sure it is."

God, she couldn't believe she was even thinking about telling him the dark secrets of her past. But this man had an uncanny way of getting what he wanted from her, which once again was both terrifying and titillating.

*You're sick,* she told herself.

"Natalie."

The soft but firm use of her name forced heretofore unspoken words through her lips. "My mother was a prostitute who dragged me with her from one hovel to another. Each place she picked up a different man."

Stone muttered his favorite expletive. "Did any of them ever touch you? I mean—"

"Rape me? Is that what you mean?"

He didn't say anything. Instead he looked as if he'd been gutted.

Again she touched his face. "None raped me, but there were several near misses."

Stone's relief was obvious. "So, go on."

"This particular brute, more violent than most, was going to cut my mother." Her lips trembled and her eyes filled with tears, but only for a moment. She gritted her teeth, then went on, "I jumped him, and he . . . he cut me."

As if he could feel her pain and was determined to soak some of it into his body, Stone pressed her closer, then whispered, "Is there more?"

"After that, I was shuttled from one foster home to another."

"What happened to your mother?"

"Three months before my tenth birthday, she died from syphilis."

"Jesus! So you stayed in foster care until the Whitmores took you in?"

"No, I was in a church juvenile home, having been sent there after I got into trouble."

"How?"

"I was with a carload of older teens when the vehicle jumped a curb, ran over two people, and severely injured them."

"Lord, it's amazing how you survived."

"I wouldn't have, if it hadn't been for Martha. I credit her with saving my life as well as my sanity."

Natalie couldn't bring herself to mention Fletcher. As traumatic as her past had been, time had healed much of that pain, though some scars would remain the rest of her life. But Fletcher's betrayal of her had come as such a shock and the wound was so fresh that she couldn't talk about it.

Besides, to do so would give Stone more ammunition to further implicate her father-in-law in the mishaps against her. Fletcher might be a wolf in sheep's clothing where she was concerned, but a murderer he was not.

"She must have been some fine lady," Stone remarked into the growing silence.

"And still is. The church home was her favorite charity, and when we saw each other, it was love at first sight."

"That's easy to believe."

"And it breaks my heart that I've hurt her with this investigation."

"On the other hand, you have to be true to yourself."

"And I have Clancy to think about, too."

He was quiet for a moment, then said, "I feel better. You've just filled in that empty blank that your file didn't show."

Natalie pulled back. "So you probed into my background?"

"Yep, and I'll bet you did the same with me."

"Sort of," she said, flushing.

" 'Sort of my ass.' "

"Okay, so I'm as guilty as you are. But remember, turnabout's fair play."

"Ah, so it's my turn on the hot seat?"

"Exactly."

"Well, my past isn't much tidier than yours. In my case, my mother died when I was young and my daddy raised me." Stone paused with a scoff. "If that's what you could call it. He drank like a fish and only worked when we didn't have food in the house."

"I can't believe what parents do to their children."

"Anyway, I survived, even worked my way through school because I had dreams about being a cop. So through gut-hard work, aided by a stint in Vietnam as a weapons specialist, which later enabled me to get an education, my dream came true.

"Soon after, I got a job with Austin PD, married, then right off the bat had Sally."

"Why did your marriage fail?"

"Connie and Sally came home one day and found my daddy slumped over the wheel of my car, dead from a bullet in the head."

Natalie sucked in her breath. "Oh, my God, how horrible."

"The horrible part is that the bullet was meant for me. And for a long time I wished to hell it *had* been me."

"Why were you the target?" Her voice was barely audible.

"A two-time felon I had put behind bars with my testimony gained an early release. He'd sworn all through the trial that he'd get even with me. But hell, I'd heard that threat so many times before, it went in one ear and out the other."

"Only this man meant it."

"Yeah, he meant it," Stone responded in a bitter tone.

"I gather your wife couldn't cope."

"That's an understatement. She was already disillusioned with our marriage. That tragedy gave her an excuse to take Sally and haul it. And that's exactly what she did."

"And you blamed yourself," Natalie said softly, placing her hand on his chest.

He covered it with his. "Did and still do," he responded in a miserable tone.

"What happened to the man who killed your father?"

"The bastard's still in the pen, hopefully for life. Not a pretty story, is it?"

"I guess everyone has baggage. Some drop it and some carry it with them."

"Well, I'm sure as hell going to drop mine or die trying."

Her stomach revolted at that thought. "You don't mean that."

"Damn straight I mean it. I want my life back, for Sally if nothing else."

"That's good, but it should be because you want it, too."

"I do. Why do you think I'm busting my balls trying to find out what really happened that day in the bank?"

"I'm leaving the ranch," she said out of the blue.

One eyebrow shot up. "As in moving?"

"I've bought a town house, which goes toward dropping a big piece of my baggage. It's really the perfect place—three bedrooms—the whole nine yards."

If she hadn't been so busy patting herself on the back, she might have noticed his silence. It was only after he spoke that she picked up on the veiled censure in his tone.

"So really you're going to move out."

"Yes, but somehow I gather you don't think that's the thing to do."

"I'd rather you stayed, at least for the time being."

"Why?" Now her voice was tense.

"I need you inside that house. You're my Trojan horse, and if you leave, I'll never get another drop of information on your family from the personal perspective. Yet on the other hand, I want you to move because I think it's wise."

"I'm moving, Stone, but not because I feel threatened by my family or because I feel duty bound to spy for you."

"You're pissed at me, aren't you?"

"Yes and no."

"Dammit, woman, but you're hardheaded."

"So are you."

"When will you move?" he asked following a deep sigh.

"As soon as the house is ready. It needs a lot of work. In

fact, I was coming from an interior decorator's office when the incident happened."

"So you won't be moving right away?"

"No, but don't you dare——"

"I know," he cut in. "You're going to tell me to butt out about your family. Unfortunately, I can't."

Still, to her relief, he did change the subject.

"By the way, you never told me the scumbag's name who screwed you on the toxic waste property."

"Why do you want to know?"

"Dammit, Natalie, just tell me, okay? The sonofabitch threatened you."

"My attorney'll take care of the problem."

"What's the matter? Are you afraid I'll yank that guy's balls off and stuff 'em down his throat?"

"Yes."

Stone laughed, then kissed the top of her head.

He so rarely laughed that when he did, it sent her pulse rate skyrocketing, forcing her to ask herself again how this multifaceted man had so much power over her.

"Name, Natalie," he said in a tone that brooked no argument.

"Mack Gates."

"Thanks. Now that wasn't so hard, was it?"

"Do you think he's . . . he's the one responsible for pushing me?" Her tone didn't conceal her fright.

"I don't know; that's what we're going to find out. No doubt your snooping has put a crimp in his style. It won't be long until we find out what the hell's going on. Meanwhile, you be careful." He paused. "I wish . . ."

"Wish what?"

"That I could protect you."

"That's not what you were going to say, was it?" Her voice shook.

"No."

She waited for him to continue, her heart in her throat.

"I wish you'd move in with me."

# Thirty-two

Natalie stared at him in amazement. She hadn't suspected anything like that, and to hear him actually say it was mind-boggling. "That's not possible."

"I know." His voice was curiously sad. "But nothing would give me greater pleasure than to go to sleep making love to you and wake up doing the same. You admit we're good together in bed, don't you?"

"I've ... never been touched as you touch me. Phillip never—"

"You mean you and Phillip never had oral sex? Is that what you're trying to say?"

"Yes," she responded in a weak voice, color surging into her face.

"Somehow that figures." His eyes darkened while he stroked her breasts, then kissed her with a hot passion. "I'm glad I was the first on both counts," he whispered at last, spreading her legs and entering her with an unexpected and not-so-gentle thrust.

She gasped, then clutched at him while he guided them to a fiery and desperate orgasm, which left them both more exhausted.

"I know you had sex or you wouldn't have Clancy," he said out of the blue.

Natalie moved her head so that she could see into his eyes. "What are you getting at? Of course we had sex."

"But not good sex."

"I thought so, until—" Her voice caught.

He outlined her swollen breasts with his finger. "Until what?"

"Until now. Again, the way you . . . you touch me, make me feel—it's so different."

"I know. I feel the same way." He kissed her again. This time it was a hot, almost angry kiss.

She responded with the same fervor, only then to say, "But sex isn't everything."

"What does that mean?"

"I think you know."

"Yeah." Stone's mouth twisted. "You're saying that you still don't trust me, right?"

They stared at each other, and it seemed as if in that moment, they crashed back to earth with a thud.

"I have to go. It's . . . getting late."

"And the family'll be wondering where you are, right?"

"That's right." Her head came up in defiance, hearing the sarcasm in his voice. "So will my daughter."

The scowl on Stone's face tempered, but only for a moment. "You never answered my question, you know."

"Okay," she whispered through lips still tingling from his kisses, "I don't trust you."

Natalie stirred the cup of French vanilla coffee, took a sip, then smiled at Clancy, who was still sitting in her high chair at the table.

Josie was catering to her every need. "You're spoiling that child rotten," Natalie told her.

"Why, that's what they're for." Josie grinned as she tickled Clancy on the bottom of her foot.

Clancy laughed out loud.

''My, but someone is having a good time.''

Natalie turned and watched as Martha walked into the room, looking lovely as always, except for the sadness that seemed always to lurk in her eyes. Natalie knew she was responsible for that sadness to some degree, and it grieved her. But she'd gone too far to back off now.

Yet she missed their closeness and longed to hug her.

''It's this child, Miz Martha. She's on a roll this morning.''

Martha smiled, walked over to Clancy, and kissed her on one messy cheek. ''How's my girl?'' she asked, looking at Clancy as if she could eat her up.

''I don't intend to keep her away from you.''

Martha's head jerked up, and for the longest time silence filled the room.

Josie broke it. ''Why don't I take this young-un and get her cleaned up and ready to go?''

''Thanks, Josie,'' Natalie said, her eyes on Martha. ''I'll be up shortly.''

When the two women were alone, Natalie saw that Martha's lower lip was trembling. And for the first time in a long while, she rushed to her and wrapped her arms around her.

''I understand, really I do,'' Martha whispered, pulling back.

''I pray that's the truth, because I wouldn't hurt you for the world.''

''I just don't want to lose you.''

''You won't, unless you want to.''

''I don't understand.''

Natalie had debated about telling Martha that she'd overheard her and Fletcher's conversation, but now she felt the time was right. ''I know how Fletcher feels about me.''

Martha's face paled. ''I don't know what you're talking about.''

''Yes, you do. But I'll refresh your memory anyway. Remember that morning you and Fletcher were in the breakfast room talking about Clancy and me?''

This time Martha's face turned red and she appeared uneasy. "Yes."

"Well, I overheard that conversation."

"Oh, my God."

"That's what I thought, too."

Martha looked terribly distressed. "You have to understand that Fletcher didn't mean what he said that day. He was just angry and hurt and was blowing off steam. He adores you; you've got to believe that."

"No, he doesn't, but that's all right. Or at least it doesn't matter any longer. I'm finally taking charge of my life and Clancy's, and that feels damn good." Natalie's features softened. "But that doesn't mean I don't love you. I always have, and I always will. That'll never change."

Martha grabbed her, and they clung to each other.

"Maybe I'll have a look at your town house soon," Martha said, breaking free.

"I'd like that very much."


When Natalie arrived at the office two hours later, she remained in a melancholy mood, especially as she'd just come from her attorney's office.

"You don't worry about Mack Gates," Perry Bell had told her. "I'll contact the proper authorities, and we'll go from there."

Natalie looked at Perry and wondered how he bore up under the vigorous schedule he kept, especially as he looked as though a puff of wind would blow him away. He had been a customer, and after selling him a home, she'd asked if he would represent her if she ever needed an attorney. He'd said yes, which had been a blessing as she had learned to trust and respect him.

"Until the accident, I wasn't worried about him, at least not my safety," she said at last. "I was sure that Gates was nothing but a bag of hot air."

"He might be; at this point we don't know."

"But what I do know is that the deal fell through. And I'm sorry to say, it was one I had counted on so much."

"Thank God you found out in time."

"Oh, I know." Natalie grimaced. "To think, if that nursing home—or any other home, for that matter—had been built on that toxic mess . . . well, it's just too horrifying to think about."

"My advice is for you to go on about your business, and I'll be in touch. But so you'll know, I expect Gates to fight this tooth and toenail."

"What you're saying is that things might get nastier?"

"Yes, both in and out of the courtroom."

"I'll just have to deal with that, then. Besides, Gates is just another in a long string of problems."

Now, as she thumbed though a mountain of paperwork that she needed to take care of, Natalie found her mind wandering again into dangerous territory. Stone McCall.

She'd hadn't seen him since they'd made love, nor had she heard from him. Yet every time the phone rang, her heart jumped. She wanted to talk to him and she didn't. She wanted to make love to him again and she didn't.

Initially she had thought she could overcome the crazy sexual attraction she felt for him, mistrusting the man himself and what he stood for. Yet she had seen a need in him that had matched the need in her. They were both the walking wounded, which was why it had been so easy for her passion to override her judgment.

That had been inevitable. Since that first kiss, she had feared the final outcome. Still, she had tried to convince herself that the heat of the moment had made her act irrationally.

She knew better. Instead she had acknowledged the weakness in herself and finally given in to it. No doubt she had made love to the man who had taken her husband's life. But she couldn't run from the question that haunted her then and haunted her now.

Could she live with that?

# Thirty-three

In order to keep his thoughts clear of Natalie and how it felt to be sheathed inside her tight warmth, Stone worked nonstop. More than anything, he knew that he'd fucked up real good by sleeping with her. Kissing her several times was one thing, but making love to her was another.

What they'd shared, hot and volatile as it'd been, wasn't just sex. He recognized that. It was much more. He just wasn't prepared to face that truth or sort through it.

Still, it had been a mistake. He had broken an unwritten rule; cops didn't get involved with suspects. And even if he was no longer a cop, he thought like one, especially now that he was working on his own case. But he'd sleep with her again; he knew that, too. He also knew that a future with her beyond this investigation was out of the question.

In their case, no matter how good, how hot, how satisfying the sex was, if there was no trust, then love . . .

Jesus! Love didn't enter into this, even if he wanted it to. Who was he kidding? She wasn't about to fall in love with a has-been, alcoholic cop even *if* she trusted him, which she didn't. What they had was a physical addiction that in the end would explode into tiny pieces. He just hoped he could walk away with his body and soul intact.

He refused to dwell on that now. Hell, he'd slept with her. He couldn't change that, nor would he if he could. What they had shared had been some of the best moments, not to mention the best sex, of his life.

He couldn't dwell on that, either. He had to hold on to his sanity so that he could keep his mind on track.

Damn, but it was hot, he thought, then realized he'd been sitting in the stifling car like an idiot. He cranked the engine, then loosened his tie.

"Ah, to hell with it," he muttered, jerking off the tie.

Now that he'd talked with the jeweler about the burglary at his store, he no longer needed the tie. Besides, since he'd been roughing it in New Mexico, he'd forgotten just how bloody uncomfortable tight collars were.

Stone pulled out into the traffic, certain that Larry would be pleased with his assessment of the jewelry theft. He didn't believe the owner for a second, especially when he had looked at the scene of the crime through a cop's eyes.

He'd be willing to bet that the little weasel Avery Winston had indeed staged the break-in, probably paid someone to do it. There were plenty of accomplished thieves on the street looking for a way to make a fast buck. But proving that Mr. Winston had broken the law was not his job. Unfortunately, though, without that proof, the insurance company would be forced to pay. Larry was supposed to get the police report on the robbery and have it waiting on his desk.

First, though, he had two personal calls to make.

A few minutes later Stone was facing a black-haired woman with a square face, who looked at him from behind her desk with a pleasant smile on her face.

"May I help you, sir?"

"Is Mack Gates available?"

"Not at the moment. Do you have an appointment?"

"No, is that necessary?"

"Not really, Mr. . . . "

"McCall."

She smiled. "All right, Mr. McCall. If you'll have a seat, I'll let him know you're here."

Stone nodded, then made his way toward the two chairs with a table in between them, sensing that she was dying to ask him why he wanted to see Gates. However, she didn't. Maybe it was because of his demeanor. He hoped so. He hoped he hadn't lost the edge that immediately intimidated people and put them on the defensive.

Stone sat down but couldn't remain seated. He was too keyed up, feeling as if he could whip a bear with a switch. Before he had decided to come here, he'd called his good buddy on the force and asked him to run a check on Mack Gates.

Stone hadn't liked what he'd read, but more than that, he hadn't liked what Gates had said to Natalie. He just wanted to get a whiff of this man personally to see if he smelled anything foul. If the sonofabitch had pushed Natalie in front of that truck or had someone else do his dirty work, then he deserved an attitude adjustment and maybe even a facial make-over, not courtesy of a plastic surgeon, either.

"Mr. McCall, Mr. Gates will see you now."

He shook his head as if to clear it, then said, "Thanks."

When he opened the door, Stone saw the overweight man standing behind his massive desk, smoking a cigarette through what looked to be an ivory holder. Stone almost laughed; Gates reminded him of the quintessential pompous asshole who needed to be brought down several notches.

"Mr. McCall, right?" Gates asked, then extended his hand.

Stone ignored it, then watched as Gates narrowed his eyes while a bright flush stole up his face. "That's right."

"Are you here about acquiring some land?"

"Nope."

Again Gates seemed taken aback by Stone's nonchalant but combative tone. His eyes narrowed this time into tiny slits. "So just what can I do for you, Mr. McCall?"

"You can tell me about Natalie Whitmore."

Stone watched Gates's Adam's apple convulse and his face turn white. "Who the hell are you?"

"Let's just say I have Ms. Whitmore's best interests at heart."

"You a cop?"

"What difference does that make? Don't you think a civilian can kick your fat ass?"

Color returned to Gates's face as Stone walked closer to his desk. "Look, I don't have anything to say to you."

"That's fine, but you've got one hell of a lot of listenin' to do."

Gates straightened, which made his belly stick out that much more. "I don't know who you are, mister—cop, private dick, or jackshit—but I don't have the time to listen. So if you'll excuse me, I have things to do. I'm a very busy man."

Stone didn't plan his next move; it just happened. The cop within him roared to life, or at least that was the excuse he used later. At the moment, however, rage sent him over the edge.

Reaching across the desk, he grabbed Gates by his godawful flashy tie. Gates's huge belly slammed against the desk, and the cigarette holder flew out of his mouth as Stone pulled him up nose to nose. "You can't listen real well when you're running your mouth. So shut up and learn something."

"Let go of me!" Gates squawked, his jaws quivering.

Stone jerked harder on the tie until Gates's eyes bulged, then swung him violently from side to side, then up and down, until the air went out of the man like a deflating beach toy.

"Now that I have your attention, we're going to discuss Ms. Whitmore's accident."

"I don't know what you're talking about," the man managed to say, though not much air was getting into his lungs.

"That possibility is all that's saving you right now," Stone said, his voice deadly calm. "Someone pushed her out in front of a car, Gates, and *you're* the sonofabitch who made a threat against her life."

Gates looked terrified. "I . . . I didn't . . . don't know anything about that."

"That's good, then; it'll keep you alive and kicking. But you did threaten her."

"No, I wouldn't do anything like that."

"Liar."

"Okay, okay. I threatened her, but I didn't mean it. I was just pissed, that's all."

Stone tightened the tie a little more. "And now *I'm* pissed. Here's something you need to understand, and try to get it the first time. If Natalie Whitmore shows up again with so much as a hair out of place or a run in her panty hose, I'm coming over here again."

He paused, and his voice grew even more menacing. "And when I do, Gates, I'll pull your fucking head off!"

"I . . . didn't hurt her."

Stone shook him for effect, then said, "Ah, so you're getting the idea that Ms. Whitmore's welfare is important to your lifestyle?"

"Yes, sir." Gates's voice was a hoarse whisper.

Disgusted and feeling as though his hands were soiled by having to touch this man, Stone let him go as suddenly as he'd grabbed him. Caught unawares, Gates toppled backward like a bloated whale. Missing his chair, he hit the floor with a thud.

Stone rounded the desk and stood over him. "And if I find out later you had her pushed into that street, I'll *show* you what it feels like to be run over by a truck."

The hot sun struck him in the face; Stone grimaced against its onslaught but didn't miss a step as he made his way back to his car. Once inside, he started the engine and basked in the air-conditioning that struck him with the same force that the heat had a moment ago.

He didn't pull out of the parking lot immediately. Instead he assessed the situation. Gut instinct told him that Mack Gates hadn't been responsible for the "accident" that could have killed Natalie. But then his gut instinct could always fail him. He didn't think so, though. Gates had looked totally blank when he'd mentioned the incident, and he didn't think the man was that good an actor, especially when someone had a choke hold on his throat. But if Gates wasn't the culprit, then who the hell was?

Hell, at the moment, the suspects were too many and too diverse to list in his head. But he'd put his money on one of the Whitmores or someone from Texas Aero who had a lot to lose if this investigation progressed. He couldn't forget about Captain Rutgers, either. That sonofabitch had Teflon for skin that could easily be scratched.

Right now he had another person he hoped to see. Through his new employer, who luckily handled Texas Aero Industries' workers' comp, he had managed to locate a person who had been hurt on the job at the warehouse. The man had received his unemployment for a while, then gotten fired.

Often, disgruntled ex-employees were a good source of information. Stone hoped that would be the case with this one.

Thirty minutes after he left Gates's office, he pulled up in front of a small, rundown frame house in a neighborhood that looked to be a haven for drug dealers. He'd seen too many of them not to recognize the underlying tension and evil that hovered there.

Swallowing a sigh, he got out of his vehicle once again and, ignoring the sweat that saturated his shirt, made his way up the walk.

Only after he reached the first step did he hear the voice.

"Stop right where you are, buster."

Stone pulled up short, cursing that his mind hadn't been more focused. If it had, he would've noticed that the chair on the porch was occupied.

"Whatcha want?"

The man, who looked to be in his early sixties, had a voice that sounded like rough sandpaper, which meant whiskey had probably eaten away at his vocal cords. His face was wrinkled and menacing as well.

What caught Stone's attention and held him transfixed was the man's leg, which was straight out in front, propped on a can, and covered with sores. Two flies were feasting on those exposed wounds. Stone's stomach, which was normally made of cast iron, revolted, the same as it had the day he'd watched the man scratch that pimple. He looked away.

"Did you hear me?" the man asked in a snarling tone.

Stone put his foot on the step. "Yes, and I'd like—"

"I told you. Stay where you are!"

Stone took his foot off the step. Hell, for all he knew the man could have a gun hidden beside him. "Hey, no problem. I just want to talk to you. Are you Travis Norton?"

"It's 'cording to who wants to know."

"Stone McCall."

"That be you?"

"Yes."

"Whatcha want with me?"

Stone held out his hands to show that they were free. "Just to talk, that's all."

"About what?"

"The warehouse where you used to work."

"How'd you know about that, mister?" The man's voice now dripped with icicles, and his face shut down as though a thick curtain had fallen over it.

"From the insurance records."

Stone tried his best to curb his frustration. Getting information from this man was going to be like pulling teeth. But then, he'd encountered more hostile witnesses; still, he'd have to proceed with caution.

"You the law?"

Stone watched as another fly landed on the man's foot, and as before, his stomach did another somersault.

"No, I'm not a cop."

"Then git off my property. I don't have to tell you nothing."

"Hey, Travis, what's happening?"

Stone whipped around, watched as a wiry, gray-haired man ambled around the corner of the house, then stopped in his tracks.

"Didn't know you had company," the man said to Norton.

"He ain't company, Clyde. In fact, he was just leaving."

Stone turned to Clyde. "You by any chance work for Texas Aero Industries, the same as your friend here?"

"Yeah, but what's it to ya?"

Stone looked from one to the other, reached into his pocket, and pulled out several bills. "The way I figure it, it might be worth your time to find out."

# Thirty-four

His hands fascinated her. Natalie stared at them, thinking how strong they appeared on the steering wheel in comparison with how gentle they felt on her body. She pinched the bridge of her nose to keep from sighing out loud.

"What's wrong?" Stone asked, cutting her a quick glance.

She responded with a question. "How do you know anything's wrong?"

"I heard your sigh."

"No, you didn't." Her tone was huffy.

Stone chuckled. "Gotcha."

"Daddy, what are you laughing about?" Sally asked from the backseat.

Natalie gave Stone a quelling look, daring him to say another word, before shifting her gaze to a sleeping Clancy in the car seat.

They had been to eat an early dinner at a local pizza parlor and were now on the way to take Sally back home. It had been a fun time for all.

Sally adored Clancy, and vice versa. Natalie knew that for someone on the outside looking in, they would appear to be the average American family. Her heart rolled, and she hated herself for thinking such a crazy thought because it was not going to happen. She didn't love him, nor did he love her.

For heaven's sake, she didn't even trust him.

"It's nothing, honey," Stone was telling Sally when Natalie forced herself herself to pay attention.

Sally didn't pretend to smother her sigh. "Sure."

Stone chuckled again before giving Natalie another glance. "How's Clance doing?"

Natalie peered down at the exhausted child and smiled. "She's dead to the world."

"We had a cool time, didn't we, Nat?" Sally asked, unbuckling her seat belt, then moving to the edge of the backseat.

"That we did," Natalie responded.

"Here we are, sweetheart," Stone said, pulling into the drive.

Sally's mouth turned down. "Shoot, I wish I could go home with you."

Natalie looked at Stone, whose features seemed to pale. "I know how you feel, but we've been over this before. Maybe one of these days."

"I know. I know."

Sally's tone was petulant. Still, Natalie couldn't help but feel sorry for the teenager. Again she thought of how much Sally reminded her of herself in many respects and how little in others. At least Sally had parents who loved her, even though they weren't together.

"I hope I'll see you again soon," Natalie said, smiling.

"Me too." Sally scrambled out of the car door that Stone now held open. "Stay cool, okay?"

Natalie laughed. "I'll keep that in mind."

Stone stood by the car until his daughter was in the house, then came around and climbed back behind the wheel.

"You're lucky, you know," Natalie said as he cranked the engine.

His eyes roamed over her. "We're both lucky."

"You're right, we are." She heard the catch in her voice and knew she was reacting not from what he said, but from the way he was staring at her with those piercing green eyes that had the ability to make a person squirm, make *her* squirm.

He didn't say anything until they reached his town house, for which she was thankful. Each time they were together she felt that same sensation, as if she were on a cliff whose edge was crumbling. She never knew when she might make the deadly slip, which terrified her on the one hand and excited her on the other.

A short time later Stone maneuvered his car alongside hers, then turned toward her. "You're coming in, aren't you?"

"Oh, I don't—"

"Please." His eyes burned into hers.

Natalie averted her gaze, knowing that if she did go inside, they would end up in bed. "Look, Stone, I don't think—"

"I won't touch you, if you don't want me to."

Their eyes met, and she went weak all over; if she hadn't been sitting down, her knees would have buckled. God, when he looked at her like that and spoke to her in that sexy gruff voice, she couldn't think. She could only feel.

"We need to talk."

She licked her lower lip. "About what?"

"The investigation."

Her pulse quickened. "You found out something?"

"Sort of."

"What does that mean?"

"Come in and find out."

"Oh, all right."

He got out, and when he opened the door on her side, he reached for Clancy. "I'll take her."

Once he had the baby in his arms, he pressed her tiny face against his chest, then kissed the top of Clancy's head. Suddenly Captain Rutgers's words jumped to Natalie's mind. *You shouldn't trust him.* Did she really believe that? The man who held and kissed her child appeared as trustworthy as a Baptist minister.

"Thanks," she murmured, her thoughts switching from Stone to Phillip. She tried to picture Phillip holding Clancy against his chest, but the image wouldn't come. Maybe it was because Phillip would never have let go of his emotions to that extent.

Guilt stabbed her, and Natalie forced her eyes away from Stone. How could she betray her dead husband with such thoughts? What kind of woman was she?

She answered her own question: Lonely and frightened that nothing in her life would ever be right again.

With that thought on her mind, she followed Stone inside his condo and into Sally's bedroom, where he placed Clancy in the middle of the lower bunk bed. They stood over her a minute and watched as her eyes fluttered and she made a sucking noise with her tiny rosebud-shaped lips.

"She's perfect," Stone said in a low, husky tone.

"Is that how you felt about Sally when she was this age?"

He grimaced as if she'd struck a nerve. "Yes, only I wasn't around to show her. I was always working, then later, drinking."

"Don't be too hard on yourself. At least you're trying now."

"Only after she nearly died."

"It's never too late."

Her soft response drew him around, and again their eyes met and held. Then they both turned and made their way out the door. Only after they had reached the living room and sat on the couch did Stone speak.

"You want anything?" he asked, looking miserable.

"No."

"Well, I damn sure do."

He reached for her and sank his lips onto hers, greedy and demanding. Her response was instantaneous and hot. She groaned against the onslaught of warring tongues and a hand surrounding, then squeezing a breast.

"God, feel how much I want you!" He pulled back, grabbed her hand, and placed it on his crotch.

Even through his jeans, she could feel his hardness. She

could hardly ignore her own raw ache to feel that hardness inside her.

"Stone, please . . ."

"Please what?" he muttered against her lips. "Make you come?"

She froze.

As if he sensed she were no longer responding, he pulled back. "What's wrong?"

"Everything. This . . . us. You said you wouldn't touch me."

"Only if you didn't want me to. And I know you do."

"No, you're wrong."

He cursed.

She ignored it. "You told me you had something to tell me about the case."

"That can wait, but this . . . we can't," he pressed. "You want me. I want you. Why can't you accept that and go with your feelings?"

"Because I can't."

He rubbed the back of his neck in a jerky, frustrated manner. "You still don't trust me, do you?"

She didn't say anything.

"What's it going to take, Natalie? Maybe I oughta give you a gun and let—" He broke off with a curse.

The color drained from Natalie's face, and she flinched as if he'd slapped her. "I'm going home. I should've never come in here."

"Look, I'm sorry, okay? I stepped way out of line, which seems to be a habit I can't break."

"I won't argue with that."

"But dammit, you don't know how much I want you! And what's worse, I know I'll never have you!"

Another warm feeling spread through Natalie, but she forced herself not to react. If she gave in now, they would both be lost. And sorry. This physical thing between them had to cease.

"I—"

She didn't get any farther. The phone rang, and Stone cursed again at the same time he lifted the receiver. "McCall," he muttered harshly.

Natalie would have left the room and gotten Clancy, but she didn't. Stone's reaction to the voice on the other end of the line alerted her that something was going on, something she should know about.

Did that call have anything to do with what he'd learned but hadn't told her? She stood still and watched as he replaced the receiver.

"Who was that?" she asked with unwavering bluntness.

"It has to do with what I wanted to discuss with you."

"So tell me."

Stone jammed a hand inside one pocket of his jeans. She didn't dare let her eyes look at the result of that action. She suspected he was still hard. And she was too vulnerable.

"I went to see a fellow yesterday who used to work for Texas Aero until he got hurt, then fired."

"So he had an ax to grind?"

"That's what I had hoped, only it didn't pan out."

"Why?"

"For one thing a buddy came strolling around the corner of the house who also used to work at the parts factory and all but told his friend to keep his mouth shut."

"And did he?"

"Yep, even though I pulled out a wad of bills and tried to entice them."

"Obviously they didn't need the money."

"I wouldn't say that. Norton, the one I went to see, needed medical attention in the worst way."

"What do you mean?"

"Believe me, you don't want to know."

"That bad, huh?"

Stone took a breath. "Worse than bad. What I suspect is that he was scared to say anything."

"So, has he changed his mind?" Natalie asked, confused and showing it.

"Yep. I'm supposed to meet him at a bar not far from his house."

"You know the place?"

"No, but I can find it."

"I'm going with you."

"No, you're not."

"Yes, I am."

"What about Clancy?"

"We'll drop her off at Lucy's."

"What if Lucy's not home?"

"She is. Tonight's her night to wash."

"Terrific," Stone muttered.

Natalie almost smiled. "I'm ready when you are."

His only response was a hard glare.

"Dammit!"

"I feel the same way," Natalie said, her own frustration rising after they had been sitting for an hour in the parking lot, waiting for the man to show up. Stone had gone inside first thing to see if he was already there, but there had been no sight of him.

"Why don't we try his house?"

"Forget that."

"Why?"

"Because you're with me."

"What difference does that make?"

"Hell, woman, it makes a lot of difference. You never know what some Looney Tune's going to do, especially if he's running scared to start with."

Her eyes widened. "You think someone actually knew you went to see him?"

"Looks that way."

"This is getting scarier by the minute."

"I second that."

Natalie folded her arms across her chest as if to comfort herself. "Then what do you suggest?"

"I suggest we blow this joint, go somewhere, get a glass

of iced tea, and plan our next move, then pick up Clance at Lucy's."

She didn't argue with him, though stopping anywhere for tea was the last thing she wanted to do. However, one look at his face told her he was on a short fuse and she'd best not light it.

Once they were seated inside the coffee shop with two frosted glasses in front of them, Natalie asked, "So where do we go from here?"

"I was hoping you could tell—"

Natalie sucked in a loud breath, stopping his words cold. Then, after a moment, he demanded, "What's the matter? You look like you've seen a ghost."

"Worse."

Stone angled his head as if to turn.

"No! Don't!"

"Why the hell not?"

"Because my brothers, Daniel and Stanley, are at the register checking out."

"Shit. Have they seen you?"

"Not yet." Seconds after Natalie had spoken, her stomach twisted.

"Natalie?"

"They just saw me."

"And?"

"They're headed this way."

"Damn! Get ready; I can smell a shitstorm coming."

Natalie couldn't move. She couldn't breathe, either, nor could she find the saliva to say a word. She felt like an animal that had been caught in a vicious trap.

Daniel was the first to reach the table. She took one look at his face and knew what he was thinking, even if he didn't know who Stone was. No matter whom she'd been with, it would be viewed as a betrayal to Phillip's memory. She remembered the time he'd grilled her about her "client."

"Natalie, what—" Daniel broke off suddenly and transferred his gaze to Stone.

Stone stood.

"Do I know you?" Daniel asked, his tone rigid.

"Maybe," Stone drawled.

"He looks familiar," Stanley chimed in, punching his brother in the ribs. "He reminds me of that—"

"Shut up, Stanley," Daniel ground out between clenched teeth. "I'll handle this."

Stone remained formidable, like a cold slab of granite. Yet there was a mechanical smile on his lips.

"Why don't you introduce us, Nat?" Daniel asked.

Natalie felt as if she might shatter into a million tiny pieces, especially when she saw rage darken Daniel's eyes as they remained focused on Stone.

"His name is . . . Stone McCall," Natalie said in a flat tone.

"My God!" Daniel spat. "You're the cop who shot my brother!"

# Thirty-five

Natalie strove to look her best. The lilac linen suit was cool yet classy. She needed an uplift. When she walked downstairs this morning, Fletcher would be waiting for her, possibly Daniel as well. It wasn't Daniel she was worried about, even though she knew he wasn't happy with her, either.

He'd been furious and his hostility toward Stone almost tangible. Still, even in the darkest moments, she felt she could count on Daniel to stick by her. He wouldn't fail her now.

His seeing her with Stone had been a shock; she could understand that, which was why she'd been reluctant to let anyone in the family know that she'd joined forces with him in the investigation. But in defense of herself, she had met Stone under false pretenses and had become smitten with him before she knew who he was.

What a mess, Natalie told herself again before taking one last look in the mirror, then walking into Clancy's room and kissing her sleeping daughter good-bye.

It wouldn't be long before they would be moving into the town house. The interior decorator and the carpenters had already started remodeling. But she wasn't able to do all that she wanted to because she was short of cash. If only that land deal hadn't fallen through.

Just thinking about Mack Gates sent up a red flag. Immediately she shook off *that* thought and left the room.

Maybe she wouldn't run into Fletcher, after all, she told herself. Maybe he would be riding in the pasture. She feared that was merely wishful thinking. He'd be downstairs drinking coffee, and unless she sneaked out the back entrance of her apartment, she couldn't avoid him. She thought about doing just that, but only for a moment. She wasn't afraid of Fletcher or any member of her family, regardless of what Stone thought. Unless Stanley or Paula . . . No. She wouldn't think along those lines, either.

She'd much rather think that the threats against Stone and her stemmed from someone at Texas Aero who had a lot to lose with their faulty parts scam.

Before Natalie reached the bottom of the stairs, the smell of coffee hit her in the face. She paused, squared her shoulders, then made her way into the kitchen. Fletcher stood looking out the window in the breakfast room, his back to her.

As if he sensed that he was no longer alone, he twisted his head, which enabled him to see over his shoulder. When he saw who it was, he made a full turn.

Neither said a word. Natalie was too taken aback by the extent of his open expression of rage. It blazed from his eyes and contorted his features. She had known he'd be angry, but what she saw went beyond anger.

Preparing herself, she took a deep, steadying breath. She knew she was in for a brutal battle. Fletcher didn't waste any time, either.

"How could you?"

"Fletcher, I know what you're going to say—"

"No, you don't," he cut in. "You don't have the foggiest goddamn idea."

Natalie walked to the coffeepot and poured herself a cup of coffee, but when she noticed that her hands shook, she set down the cup. She didn't want Fletcher to know that he'd already rattled her composure.

"How the hell could you do something like that?"

Natalie counted to ten and turned around. "Fletcher, if you'd just calm down—"

"Don't you tell me to calm down!" he shouted. "You're the one who's in the camp with the enemy."

"That's your opinion," she said with as much calm as the situation would allow.

"And I'm entitled, too. He shot my son and your husband, for chrissake! But apparently you've forgotten that," he added with a jeer, "or don't give a damn. Which is it?"

She refused to stoop to his level by answering the question. But she felt the stab nonetheless, and it cut deeper into that already festering wound. But again she refused to fight in the trenches.

"You've always held firm to the fact that Phillip's death was an accident," she challenged.

Fletcher glowered at her with such intensity that his bushy brows and mustache seemed to stand on end. "And I still believe that, but it doesn't take away from the stark reality that that bastard killed my son!"

Again his words pierced her heart. "I know that, Fletcher. And it's a tragedy *we* both have to learn to live with. It's also why you can't ignore Stone McCall and the part he played in that tragedy."

"The hell I can't!"

"So, you do what you have to, and I'll do what I have to, which means that I'll do what it takes, and with whomever it takes, to find out what really happened to Phillip."

"Goddammit, he was in the wrong place at the wrong time! That's what happened."

"Is it, Fletcher? If you really believe that, then why are you acting like a crazed man just because I'm working with Stone? Furthermore, why did you have him fired?"

"I didn't have McCall fired. His John Wayne antics did that for him."

"He doesn't believe that."

Fletcher gave a brutal laugh. "Oh, really? Well, just because he doesn't believe that, then I guess that makes it so."

Natalie ignored his twisted brand of sarcasm. "He thinks he was on to something and that was the reason he was dismissed."

"And obviously he thinks that 'something' had to do with Phillip."

"Yes."

"That's bullshit, and you know it."

"No, I don't know it. But what I do know is that even though you don't think he shot Phillip on purpose, you still want him punished."

"That's right, because he shouldn't get off scot-free for what he did."

Natalie's mouth was painfully dry. "There's no reasoning with you, is there?"

"No, goddammit, not where McCall and this crazy notion of yours is concerned."

For a moment she couldn't answer and stared sightlessly at the ceiling.

Fletcher had no such problem. He was on a vicious roll. "Let's just speculate for a second that you're right and that Phillip wasn't shot accidentally."

Natalie jerked her eyes back on her father-in-law, aghast.

"Having said that, has it ever crossed your mind that McCall could've had something to gain by killing Phillip? Huh? Have you asked yourself that question? Have you asked *him*?"

"Yes!"

"But the bastard denied it, to cover his own ass, then convinced you that Phillip was involved in something evil that got him killed. Well, again that's bullshit and I ain't buying!"

"Look, Fletcher." Natalie's voice was tired. "We can stand here all morning and sling verbal shots at each other, which won't change anything."

''So, tell me, are you sleeping with him?''

Though her stomach plunged to her knees, she hit back hard. ''That's none of your business!''

''Like hell it isn't! Everything that pertains to Phillip's wife and child is my business. And don't you forget that!''

''What's going on in here?''

''I second that.''

They both whirled around at the sound of unexpected voices. Martha and Daniel stood in the doorway, troubled expressions on their faces.

Natalie felt ill, but there wasn't anything she could do but stand firm. She'd gone this far and couldn't back down now. Still, the reminder that she was all alone against her family was a bitter pill to swallow.

''I just asked Natalie if she's sleeping with Stone McCall,'' Fletcher said, his tone now casual, as if he'd said the sun were shining.

No one was fooled. Martha looked perplexed, her eyes bouncing back and forth between Fletcher and Natalie, finally resting on Natalie. ''What's he talking about?''

''Natalie had dinner last night with the cop who shot Phillip,'' Daniel said in a low voice.

Hurt filled Martha's eyes. ''Is that true, Natalie?''

''Yes, it's true.''

''Oh, no,'' Martha whimpered, tears springing to her eyes. ''Why . . . I mean . . . I don't understand. How could you? And sleep with him . . .'' Her hand went to her chest as if she were having a heart attack.

''Shh, Mother,'' Daniel said, and placed an arm around Martha's trembling shoulders. ''Of course, she's *not* sleeping with him.'' Although Daniel's expression was a trifle hard, his voice was calm. ''It's all part of Natalie's plan to find out what happened to Phillip. Isn't that right?''

Natalie threw Daniel a grateful smile, though she sensed he'd like to throttle her as well.

Natalie forced herself to turn to Martha, which was hard, as she had seen condemnation mixed with the tears. ''That's right," she said in a soft voice. "We've been working together on the investigation." At least part of what she said wasn't a lie.

Fletcher scoffed. "Investigation my ass."

"Calm down, Daddy," Daniel said.

Natalie gave Daniel a weak but grateful look. "Thanks, Danny, but this is my fight."

"Yeah, and all for nothing." Fletcher's breathing was hard and heavy. "What beats me is how the hell you can stay in the same room with McCall, much less defend him. Answer me that, will you?"

*Because I love him*, Natalie almost blurted out, only to catch herself in time. Her face flamed, and she spoke quickly to mask her alarm. "When I first met him, I didn't know who he was. Then, after I learned, he convinced me that we should work together."

Fletcher threw back his head and laughed a loud, harsh laugh. "That's the biggest pile of crap I ever heard."

"Fletcher, please." Martha's voice quivered. "I can't stand to see you and Natalie at each other's throats like this."

"Well, then Natalie best get her shit together and stop all this nonsense."

"I'm *not* backing down." Natalie's voice was a coiled whisper.

The room fell silent.

"Then I guess you're going to have to make a choice," Fletcher said, squinting at Natalie.

"Which is what?" she asked, a sinking feeling in the pit of her stomach.

"Oh, I think you know, but I'll spell it out. It's McCall or this family."

"No, Fletcher!" Martha cried.

"Daddy," Daniel said, "surely you don't mean that."

"The hell I don't!" Fletcher's militant stance and eyes were unyielding. "So who's it going to be, Natalie?"

Natalie didn't say a word. Instead she turned and walked out of the room.

*   *   *

Fletcher surveyed his empire. God, he loved every inch of this soil, had put everything he had into making the ranch what it was today. That sweat and toil had paid off. He had more land than he would ever see and more money than he could ever spend.

He was seventy years old and should be in his prime, enjoying life to the hilt. Instead he'd never been more unhappy in his entire life. He blamed Natalie for a good portion of that unhappiness. Hell, the son he had hoped would be president of the United States was dead, and nothing was going to bring him back. But nothing was going to tarnish his name, either.

Fletcher nudged his horse into a full gallop. By the time he reached the shade tree at the bottom of a hill, he was panting as hard as the animal. He leaned over and rubbed the horse's mane, then dismounted. For a moment he thought his legs might not hold him upright.

He muttered an expletive, then walked to the tree and leaned against it. After jerking off his Stetson, he mopped his brow with the back of his hand. But the heat didn't bother him; he'd acclimatized himself to it long ago. In fact, he welcomed it, thinking of it as a way to empty poison from his system.

Fletcher cursed again just as the sound of a vehicle reached his ears. He stood straight, stared into the distance, and watched as a maroon truck lumbered up the bumpy road toward him. He glanced at his watch. Good, right on time. But then, *he* knew better than not to be.

The driver pulled beside the tree and killed the engine. By the time Fletcher reached him, he was already out of the truck.

"You wanted to see me?"

"Sure did."

The man scratched his head. "I hope nothing's gone wrong. I tried to make certain those—"

"It isn't about work. At least not that kind of work."

The man dug deeper into his scalp. "So what's up?"

"I have a special job for you."

He grinned. "Hell, ain't they all special?"

"Only because you're a greedy bastard."

"But I always get the job done, don't I?"

"Yep."

"Okay, so whatcha want me to do?"

Fletcher proceeded to tell him. Then, just as the man started to get back in his truck, Fletcher said, "Oh, by the way, Dave, if you ever screw my son's wife again, your nuts are mine."

Dave gulped. "Yes, sir."

Stone was positive he could take on a prize-fighter and whip him, but since no fighter was available, he'd settle for someone at Texas Aero. Of course, he had no intention of whipping anyone, unless he was forced to. Now was not the time to lose his cool, especially while he was still fishing for information on one side and his enemy on another.

He considered someone at that warehouse to be his enemy and suspected that someone under the Whitmore roof was in cahoots with them. He just didn't know who. After that showdown at the restaurant, he felt it wouldn't be long before the scumbag showed his final hand.

Too bad Natalie was in the middle. Maybe she had dodged the bullet this morning. Maybe she'd managed to escape old man Whitmore's wrath. He doubted that, but one could always hope.

Putting Natalie out of his mind for the moment, Stone made his way inside the office part of the warehouse. He had no plan of action. He'd come here on a wild hare, mainly to shake them up, to see if the rotten apple was on this tree.

"I'd like to see Mr. Shankle," he said to the harassed-looking receptionist behind a cluttered desk.

Larry had given him the name of the man who handled the insurance and who Larry thought might run the company, too. Stone knew better. Ralph Shankle was just a lackey, but it didn't matter. Word would get around.

"Name?" the receptionist asked in a disgruntled tone.

"Stone McCall."

"I'll see if he's available."

A few moments later she said, "You can go in."

Easy enough, Stone thought, opening the door, then striding through as if he knew exactly what he was doing.

Ralph Shankle stood behind his desk, a cold expression on his face. "What the hell do you want?"

Stone was put off guard, but he didn't show it. "Ah, so you know who I am?"

"You're not welcome here, McCall."

Mmm, so this company had at least felt that apple tree shake. Good. "Aren't you being a little premature?" He watched Shankle, but he wanted to turn away. It wasn't that the man's pockmarked face made him wince, but rather the look in his eyes. This man was evil, had no conscience. He'd dealt with scum like him who dressed in the best suits money could buy and worked behind a desk in an office fit for the CEO of Texaco. But they were still scum.

"No, I don't think I'm premature at all. You see, I don't give a damn why you're here."

"Then why did you see me?"

"I just thought you ought to know that this company's on to *you*."

Stone scratched his chin. "Mmm, that's interesting. If you have nothing to hide, then there's no problem."

Ralph laughed. "Oh, we don't have anything to hide. It's you who seem to have the problem. If my memory serves me correctly, you're the one who lost your job with the police department."

Stone ignored that deliberate dig. Besides, he had one of his own. "Killing that employee was your first big mistake."

"Get out, McCall! And keep your nose out of our business."

Stone sneered. "You don't frighten me, Shankle, or your boss, either. I've whipped tougher men than both of you. And if you think you've heard the last of me, think again."

Stone stopped at the door, turned, and smiled. "Tell your boss, whoever he is, that I hope he sleeps well tonight, because the prison mattresses aren't all that thick."

# Thirty-six

Natalie felt drained. Her confrontation with Fletcher had started the day off wrong. In fact, she'd had to quell the urge to pack a quick bag, grab Clancy, leave the house, and go to a motel. Then when she thought about what such a knee-jerk reaction would do to Martha, she had cooled her temper and swallowed her pride.

Besides, when she left the ranch she would walk out, not run as though she were in the wrong.

Forcing her mind off that incident and onto her work, Natalie rubbed her forehead. She had met with her attorney, the land surveyor, and a government official from the EPA. Mr. Mack Gates was in trouble, but how much remained to be seen. She felt responsible as well. She should have known all was not right, that one didn't get something for nothing, especially from a low-life like Gates.

Now, as she prepared to leave for the day, she tried to shrug off the doldrums, but she couldn't. Stone also played a major role in her inability to bounce back. She felt a crushing need to see him, to feel his arms around her, to feel his strength seep into her bones, as she imagined his hands all over her flesh, his mouth, hot and open on hers . . .

"Stop it!" she cried out loud, then asked herself why she was doing this. If only—

The phone on her desk rang. She jumped, then forced her breathing to settle before she reached for the receiver.

"Miracle Realty, Natalie."

"Hi."

This time she almost stopped breathing altogether. "Hi."

"What's wrong?" Stone asked.

"How do you know anything's wrong?"

"Because I know you."

She let those intimately spoken words pass. "Well, you're right, it's been a bad day."

"Did Fletcher confront you?"

"Oh, yes."

"Dammit, I wish I could've been there."

"No, you don't."

"Look, I want to see you."

The undercurrents, the meaning behind those words, were unmistakable. Heat stirred in her lower stomach.

"Will you pick up Clancy and stop by?" he asked when she didn't respond.

"I don't have to get Clancy today. The baby-sitter's keeping her overnight. She's having a party for her niece and wanted Clance to stay."

"Then *you* stop by."

Again, the need to see him was like a fever pushing her onward. Still, she hedged.

"I—"

"I'll see you in twenty minutes."

He hung up, leaving her holding the receiver with nothing but a dial tone in her ear.

She made it only as far as the door before Stone slammed it shut and grabbed her.

"If I can't have you again," he whispered in a thick voice, "I'd just as soon be dead."

Exhilaration, like a raging fire, leapt through her veins. "I feel the same way," she managed to say.

With quick but unsteady fingers, Stone discarded her blouse and bra, then inched her back into the bedroom and onto the bed. While she watched, he scrambled out of his clothes. Once they were cast aside, her eyes crawled over his naked body.

"You like what you see?" His voice sounded like gravel.

"Yes," she whispered.

He leaned over her, his own eyes greedy and devouring. "And I like what I see, too," he said, kissing her lips, the sides of her breasts. She moaned with rising desire when his tongue lingered on her nipples, wetting them, drawing circles around them.

Another bolt of fire spread through her as he suddenly lifted her lower body and removed her slacks and shoes, but not her panties.

"God, you're lovely," he whispered, his jaw rigid against her cheek, seemingly spellbound by the gossamer string of nylon that barely covered her.

She nestled her fingers in the hair on his chest and drew him down. But instead of kissing her, he pressed his lips against the inside of her ankles, her calves, and her thighs.

"Oh, yes, yes," she said, and began to move.

"Oh, yes, what? Tell me what you want."

"You! I want you." Her movements turned savage, and she wanted him to rip off her panties, wanted to feel his tongue probe and plunge anywhere and everywhere. She wanted to be possessed, to be filled to capacity, to have all of him, nothing withheld—now, hotly and totally.

"You're torturing me!"

Her cry seemed to send him careening over the edge. He ripped off her panties, spread her legs, then thrust into her wet warmth.

She gasped. She clung. She took. She gave.

"I love you, Natalie," he rasped. "Can you feel how much I love you?"

"Yes! And I love you, too!" she responded, sinking her teeth into his shoulder.

She could never get enough of him.

Afterward they were too exhausted to move or talk. Or maybe they didn't want to talk about the fact that they had spoken of love. She knew she didn't—but not because she hadn't meant it. She had, and she felt he had, too. Fear and uncertainty were the culprits behind their silence. Their love was as fragile as a thread and could break at any moment.

"Natalie."

"Mmm?"

"Are you all right?"

"Of course, why?"

"I just didn't want to hurt you. I couldn't wait, and you're so small and tight . . ."

She kissed him, which was all the assurance he needed.

"I have to know what Fletcher said to you," he said after they were lying quietly in each other's arms.

She turned so that she was facing him and told him the gist of the conversation.

"I can imagine the look on Fletcher's face when he heard *my* theory concerning the murder."

"It was a nasty scene all right. He . . . he said I had to make a choice between you and the family."

"Are you okay with that? I mean . . ."

"Am I going to stop seeing you?"

His mouth twisted in pain. "Yeah, I guess that's what I mean."

"No."

The silence lasted for a long time.

"Who do you really think is behind all that's happening to us?" Natalie finally asked, her lips aching from his hard, desperate kisses.

"Are you asking for a list?"

"Yes."

"An unedited list?"

"Yes," she said in a small voice.

"Okay, here goes. Someone at Texas Aero is my best guess. But then I'm not ruling out Fletcher, or Stanley, or anyone else involved with your family, including your sister-in-law and that foreman. They all have their reasons for wanting to hurt you, both physically and mentally."

"What about Daniel?"

"Nah, I don't think so. Danny boy just doesn't seem to have the stomach for violence."

"Well, at least we agree on that."

"But not on the others?"

"I still say my family's not responsible. I don't care what that guard said before he died."

"Well, if you're right, but I'm not saying you are," Stone amended quickly, "then our perp is definitely someone at Texas Aero, whose chain I just rattled, by the way."

"You went there?"

"Yep," he said, then filled her in on his conversation.

Natalie thought for a moment, then said, "It's too bad we can't add Mack Gates to that list."

"Well, we sure as hell can't rule him out when it comes to your so-called accident. Anyway—" Stone stopped.

"Anyway what?"

"I kinda took care of Mr. Gates."

Natalie's eyes narrowed in suspicion. "What did you do?"

"I gave him an attitude adjustment."

"How?"

"I threatened to beat the shit out of him if he ever came near you again."

"You're kidding?"

"I don't kid about things like that," he said flatly. "You should know that by now."

Her mind raced. "So where do we go from here?"

"Head on. I told myself I wasn't going to stop shaking that tree until the rotten apple fell out of it."

Natalie smiled at his analogy. "And you'll be waiting."

"You got that right. And I pity that poor bastard, too."

Natalie stared into those deep green eyes, cold as ice, and

once again felt frightened at what she saw. But then he spoke, and all the ice melted under the warmth of his voice.

"Don't worry. It's going to be all right. Now that I've found you, I'm not going to do anything to fuck that up." He paused with a lopsided smile. "Speaking of fucking . . ."

Adrenaline shot through her, and she pressed her breasts against his chest. "It's my turn now."

"Natalie?" He sounded as if he were choking.

She turned away a second and looked out the window. The moon hung swollen in the sky. A perfect night. She faced him again and smiled, then ran her hand down the darkness of his stomach, to his rigid penis.

When she took him in her mouth, he cried, "Oh, please, don't stop!" She didn't.

A while later, Stone kissed her at the door. "I hate for you to leave."

"I hate to leave, too."

"Then don't."

She touched his lips. "We both have work to do."

"I know," he said, trapping her fingers and kissing them. "Call me when you get to the ranch, okay?"

"Okay."

She felt his eyes on her until she got into her car and drove off.

The car parked down the block pulled onto the street behind her, a satisfied smile on the driver's face.

"I don't like this at all."

The man stopped his pacing and glared at his partner. "I told you I'll take care of things."

Ralph, who had shaved off his beard, leaving his pock-marked face open to public scrutiny, rubbed his jaw. "Only you haven't."

"Ralph's right," Lewis put in, calmly tamping the tobacco into the big bowl pipe, then lighting it. "From the get-go, the operation has been one fuck-up after another."

"So what are you saying?" the man asked. "Surely you're not trying to usurp my position?"

Ralph and Lewis stared at each other before refocusing their attention on the boss. Ralph spoke up. "Not if you'll get this matter wrapped up, especially where McCall's concerned. He's the real threat."

"McCall doesn't scare me," the man said.

"He sure as hell scares me," Lewis said, puffing hard and fast.

"Yeah, me too," Ralph added. "He's a crazy bastard! You know that. Surely you haven't forgotten that he nailed us with the insurance company when he talked to that janitor at the old warehouse?"

"That's far from over," the man said.

"Right now, that's not the fucking point. I'm telling you McCall's getting too goddamn close, which is something you should've been aware of and taken care of."

"I've been busy." The man's tone was frozen.

"So have we, trying to keep the company from going belly up *and* trying to keep out of prison."

"No one's going to prison."

Ralph smirked. "If you don't jerk a knot in McCall's pecker and the Whitmore dame's pussy, we sure as hell will. You noticed I said 'we.'"

The man's eyes narrowed. "Are you threatening me?"

"Ah, hell," Lewis said. "This kinda talk's gettin' us nowhere."

The man ignored him. "Because if you are," he continued, his eyes locked on Ralph, "you'll be making a big mistake."

"Now who's threatening who?"

The man went on, "I can kick you back under that rock I let you crawl out of."

Ralph locked his arms across his chest, his features and voice equally menacing. "Maybe so, but you can bet your ass we'll drag you back under there with us."

# Thirty-seven

Stone sat in the parking lot of Texas Aero's warehouse and waited. He probably shouldn't be here, but since he'd already shaken this tree once, he figured he might as well shake it again. He was making headway, jabbing the right people. He had sensed that from his prior conversation with Ralph Shankle.

He had sensed, too, that Ralph was up to his kneecaps in the airline parts scam, though he didn't think he was the brains behind the operation. That was why he'd decided to return. When a rat got cornered, it never failed to squeal.

Stone tapped his fingers on the steering wheel and watched the changing of the shifts a few yards in front of him. He'd been there for about thirty minutes, and during that time he'd had to fight off thoughts of Natalie.

He still couldn't believe that he'd told her he loved her. Hell, he couldn't believe that he actually did love her. But it was true. He couldn't deny it any longer. He also believed that she loved him and had finally come to trust him, though he hadn't asked about the latter. As to a future with her . . . well, that remained to be seen. They both had a mission, and until that mission was completed, nothing could be settled.

Meanwhile he planned on enjoying not only the succulent delights of her body, but her sharp mind as well. Besides Sally, she was the best goddamn thing that had ever happened to him. He was desperate to hold on to her.

At first Stone didn't pay any attention to the Lincoln that turned into the parking lot at the warehouse, until the driver got out. Stone jerked upright, his pulse tingling. Pay dirt!

He watched Ralph Shankle step out of his highfalutin vehicle before getting out of his own. It was Shankle's car that caused Stone's blood to boil—a car that was paid for at the sacrifice of human lives. Maybe the government hadn't been able to prove that fact, but he was convinced that Shankle and his boss were guilty of murder by manufacturing inferior airplane parts, then selling them as standard ones.

The thought of this sonofabitch or anyone connected to this illegal operation threatening him and Natalie sent that boiling rage pumping harder through his veins. Upping his pace, Stone reached Shankle before he entered the building. Stone looked around and was relieved to see that for the moment no one else was close by.

"Shankle."

The burly man swung around. When he saw Stone, his eyes narrowed, but surprisingly his tone was halfway pleasant. "Ah, McCall, so we meet again?"

Stone was put immediately on the alert. After the way this man had reacted to him the other day, he didn't trust him as far as he could throw him, which wouldn't be far.

"Yep, looks that way."

"So what's on your mind this time?"

"Same as before, the truth."

"Look, McCall, what's it going to take to get you off my back?"

The irritation was back in Ralph's voice, Stone noticed, hiding a smile. Perhaps the rat was showing signs of squealing.

Stone shrugged his shoulders in a nonchalant manner. "I just told you, Shankle, the truth. It's that simple."

"And just what would that be, you reckon?"

Stone longed to cram that smirk down Ralph's throat, but he kept his cool. "You can start with telling me why one of your former employees was killed and why he whispered the name Whitmore before he died."

Ralph blinked, but not before Stone saw the fear that crept into his eyes. "Now, what makes you think I'm going to tell you any more than I did the last time you invaded my space? In fact, I could have you thrown off this property with little effort."

"I don't think so."

Perhaps it wasn't so much what Stone said, but the way he said it that turned Ralph's face a sickly shade of white, making the pockmarks stand out like wads of cellulite.

"Okay, McCall, I get your message."

"I'd be real surprised, but I'm listening."

"I thought as much. So let's stop blowing smoke up each other's ass and get down to why you're really here." Ralph dug in his pocket, pulled out his wallet, opened it, and lifted out a handful of bills.

The hair on the back of Stone's neck and arms stood out. "What's that for?"

Ralph stretched out his money-filled hand to Stone. "Oh, come now, we both know you're as dirty as the rest of us. So why not take the money and—"

He never got the rest of the words out of his mouth. Stone grabbed him and lifted him off his feet so fast that Ralph didn't seem to know what hit him until Stone slammed him into the wall of the building, then bounced him against it several more times.

"Why you—"

"Shut the fuck up," Stone said, "before I add to the damage already on your face."

Ralph hung suspended with his face looking like an overripe watermelon about to burst. He opened his mouth to say something, but Stone's hand had a lock on his throat that made speaking impossible. He reminded Stone of a guppy, opening and closing its mouth.

"No one calls me a dirty cop and gets away with it!" Stone slammed him against the wall again. "And I don't take bribes!"

Ralph yelped as he shook his head from side to side.

"I never have and I never will! Understand?"

Ralph's eyes bulged, and he yelped again.

"It seems that you're just not a quick learner, Ralphy-pooh, but maybe your boss is." Stone let him go as suddenly as he'd grabbed him.

Ralph's knees buckled, and he slithered to the ground.

Stone was tempted to kick the living shit out of him, but he controlled himself when Natalie's face jumped before his eyes. He didn't want to blow that by going too far, which had been his problem in the past.

"You tell your cronies that it's only a matter of time until I gather enough evidence to shut this place down and put scum like y'all out of business."

With that, Stone turned and walked back to his car. He didn't bother to give Ralph Shankle a second look. Hell, he hoped he was puking his guts out.


Across the street, a man smiled as he got back into his maroon pickup. He couldn't wait for the old man to see what he'd gotten. McCall was about to get his balls yanked off, and that bitch Natalie was about to get her snatch sewed up.

He snickered. Natalie was the one he wanted to see get her comeuppance. Teach her not to go rattin' on other people.


Natalie had talked to Stone only once since they had confessed their love, but the conversation for the most part had been all business. He'd told her he was going to the warehouse to see what he could find out. She had told him to be careful, to which he'd responded, "Don't worry. I have something to live for now."

She recalled those words again, and a warm feeling flooded her system. She didn't know how this mess was going to turn out, but she knew that her trust for Stone was strengthening every day, which spoke well for a future with him.

She wouldn't think about that now. Instead her mind was on Phillip. For some reason she felt the need to backtrack again, to remember everything Phillip had said and done before his death.

After working hard on another land deal that she hoped would be as lucrative as the one that had fallen through, she had taken the day off. Also, she was tired and needed to spend time with Clancy. Thank goodness Fletcher had avoided her, as had Stanley and Paula. Only Daniel and Martha had treated her with love and decency.

She had spent the morning in the pool with Clancy. Now, after putting her exhausted daughter down for an early nap, Natalie continued to search her brain for something that she might have missed.

Nothing new came to mind. Frustrated, she took a shower and dressed. She needed to move from the ranch. That was another problem pulling at her. In fact, she should have moved a long time ago, money or no money. But love and loyalty for Martha and Daniel had kept her here, a mistake she now regretted.

Her presence had torn the family farther apart. Besides, Fletcher had made it clear that if she continued to see Stone, he didn't want her there. She was surprised he hadn't already ordered her to leave.

Thrusting aside that disturbing thought, Natalie opened an old jewelry box to look for a pair of earrings that matched her outfit. Inside she found a tiny key.

"Wonder where this came from?" she mused out loud.

She clutched the key in the palm of her hand, her mind clicking. After examining it, she realized it was a bank lockbox key.

She clutched it to her chest like a lifeline. Since it wasn't hers, it must have been Phillip's, which meant he had placed it there for safekeeping. She didn't know why, but she intended to find out. Now.

She placed the key in the side pocket of her purse, where she kept her Kleenex; then, without so much as a backward glance at herself in the mirror, she walked downstairs to the kitchen. Josie was there.

"Lordy, child, what's the matter? You look plum tuckered out."

"I am, but that doesn't matter. Clancy's asleep, Josie. Would you be a dear and keep an eye on her?"

"Sure 'nough. But where you goin' in such an all-fired hurry?"

"To town. I'll be back after a while." She kissed Josie on the cheek, then headed toward the front door.

"Nat."

She had her hand on the knob when she heard Daniel say her name. She pivoted and smiled. "Hi."

He didn't return her smile. "Were you going out?"

"As a matter of fact, I was. Why?"

"Would you mind joining us in the living room?"

Natalie's lips twitched. "Why so formal, brother dear?"

"Come on, Nat," Danny said, stepping closer. "I'm serious."

"I can see that."

He held out his hand, gesturing that she should precede him. She sighed. "All right, but only for a sec. I have something I have to do."

She walked into the room, only to pull up short. The entire Whitmore clan was there. What was even crazier was that it was the middle of the afternoon. But the hostility was so thick, it reminded her of an early morning fog—gray and dismal.

She bristled. "What's going on?"

"What does it look like?" Fletcher asked, stepping out of the shadows, his face grim.

Natalie looked around and felt her heart sink. "It looks like I'm about to be convicted without a trial."

"You're exactly right," Fletcher said in a cutting tone.

# Thirty-eight

Natalie glared at her father-in-law, then made a helpless gesture with her hands. "What's your problem this time?"

"I don't have a problem," Fletcher shot back. "You do. I demand that you come to your senses and start behaving like a Whitmore."

"I don't know what you're talking about," Natalie said, her eyes circling the room, looking for a friendly face. When she found Daniel, even he looked sheepish. "I won't allow you to treat me like this. You don't own me. And you don't own Clancy."

"The hell I don't!"

"Fletcher, please, calm down. You promised you wouldn't get riled."

Martha might as well have been a piece of wood, for all the attention Fletcher paid to her.

"Mother's right, Daddy. This needs to be discussed in a civil manner."

"Butt out, Daniel. As usual, this is none of your business. She's ripping this family apart, and I won't stand for it another minute, nor will I stand for her consorting with the enemy."

Natalie would have laughed at his choice of words if the

situation hadn't been so tragically serious. "Is that what you think I'm doing?"

"Hell, I *know* that's what you're doing."

"And just how would you know that?"

"I have proof you didn't come home the other night."

Raw fury almost strangled her. "Have you been spying on me?"

"You're damn right, especially after I found out that you were seeing that murdering cop."

"Look, Fletcher, we've already been over this, and I'm not about to get raked over the coals again. I'm tired."

"Well, so am I," Fletcher exclaimed. "And sick, to think that you, Phillip's wife, actually slept with McCall, then crept out of his house like a thief in the night."

"You've gone too far this time, Fletcher."

"I don't think so," he drawled in an ugly tone. "Anyway, I ruined him once and I can again."

Natalie reacted as if she'd been kicked in the stomach. "So Stone was right. It was *you* who put pressure on Rutgers and the department to fire him."

"You're goddamn right I did."

"You lied to me!" Natalie cried.

"And I'd do it again. But you have no right to act sanctimonious. You lied to me about your relationship with him."

Natalie's eyes flashed with anger. "Damn you, Fletcher!"

"Damn *him*, you should say. To my way of thinking, McCall got what he deserved, especially when he made himself out a saint at my son's expense." He paused and wiped the sweat off his forehead.

"Not only that, the bastard's a renegade, plays by his own rules. Well, when he shot my son, he made the biggest mistake of his life, and I made him pay."

"Just like you're making me pay, guilty or not."

"For chrissake, Natalie! Look at the facts."

"What I'm looking at is how low you've stooped, how despicable you've become."

"Maybe so, but you can blame yourself for that. You were

caught red-handed, sneaking out of his house in the middle of the night. I could've stood you reopening the case, because there's nothing to find, no conspiracy, no nothing. But sleeping with the man who shot my son is something I won't tolerate."

"I'm with you, Daddy!" Stanley put in, giving Natalie a gloating look, as if to say, "You're getting what you deserve."

"My personal life is my business!" Natalie cried.

"How can you say that after what we've done for you?" Fletcher demanded. "Why, Martha saved your life. And how do you repay her, by betraying her love and—"

"That's enough, Daddy," Daniel said again, this time with steel in his voice.

Fletcher shot him another glare but for once seemed to listen.

"Look, sweetheart," Daniel said, concentrating on Natalie, his tone soft and cajoling, "Daddy didn't mean—"

"Like hell I didn't!" Fletcher cut in.

Daniel ignored him and went on in that same tone, "What we're all concerned about is the fact that you and/or Stone McCall obviously think that someone in this family is involved in something illegal, that *we* had something to do with the making of faulty airplane parts, which is just not the case."

He paused. "If there was and still is a cover-up at that factory warehouse, then McCall's the one who's involved, who's guilty. Again, all Daddy did was lease them the building. It's your lover who's on the take."

Natalie folded her fingers into a tight ball. "I don't believe that."

"Maybe you'll believe this, then." Fletcher reached down, picked a packet up off the coffee table, and thrust it at her, a triumphant look on his face.

When Natalie hesitated, he said, "Go on, open it. See for yourself."

Though a coldness swept through her and she had to bite her lip to keep her teeth from chattering, Natalie did as she was told. The envelope contained a colored photograph of

Stone and a man she didn't recognize. The stranger had a wad of bills in his hand, and that hand was extended to Stone.

She looked up, her head buzzing with confusion. "I don't understand."

"Sure you do," Fletcher said. "But I'll explain anyway. That guy who's giving McCall money is a honcho at Texas Aero. His name is Ralph Shankle, and he runs the factory. It's obvious that he's paying off McCall."

Natalie dropped the picture and staggered backward. "How did you get this?"

"How do you think I got it? I also had McCall followed."

Natalie's face turned red, and she stifled a scream, no longer able to cope with all that was happening. She wanted to stop up her ears, stop the drumming in them, race out the door, and pretend that she had dreamed all this. But she couldn't pretend, not when the ugly truth had just slapped her in the face.

"Don't you see, sweetheart," Daniel was saying, "McCall has apparently used you to try to soil our family's good name because of what happened to him. And, again, if there *is* something illegal going on within that company, then the police will find it out. And if McCall's involved, which I think he is, up to his armpits, then they'll nail him, too."

Natalie shook her head. "No, I don't—"

"Ah, hell!" Fletcher hissed. "She's made up her mind that lover boy can do no wrong, which tells me she's made her choice."

"But the man said Whitmore before he died," Natalie fired back, desperate.

"Ah, hell," Fletcher said, waving his hand. "Who knows what was on that fellow's mind at that moment. Anyway, the police have linked his murder to a huge gambling debt he owed." His stare was rigid. "But I'm sure you and your lover already know that."

Natalie wanted to deny everything that Fletcher had thrown at her, but she couldn't. Oh, God, had Stone indeed used her as her father-in-law had said? She groped to sort through

Fletcher's accusations and Daniel's explanations, but she couldn't. She'd never been able to completely bury the old seed of mistrust against Stone, and it rose to the surface.

"We love you, Nat," Daniel said. "You're still part of our family. Don't throw that away."

"Surely we've proved our love and loyalty," Martha added in her own sweet but persuasive way. "Don't let this man destroy all our lives."

Tears flooded Natalie's eyes as Martha's words sank in, breaking her heart. But she couldn't worry about Martha now. Her thoughts were filled with Stone. Again, had Stone duped her, used her for his own agenda? If so, then he didn't love her, had never loved her.

Dear Lord, she wanted to believe in his innocence, but the photograph was damaging. He had never convinced her or *proved* that her family, including Phillip, had ever been involved in anything illegal.

So what was she telling herself? Was she saying that Stone was indeed the enemy? Doubt in Stone flooded like hot bile in the back of her throat, bringing with it a blind, searing anger at the possibility that he had made a fool out of her, not once but twice.

"Natalie, say something," Daniel said, coming over and placing an arm around her shoulder. "Please."

Her body felt pummeled into numbness, but somewhere she found the strength to turn and run out of the room.

"Let her go!"

Fletcher's harsh cry reached her ears, and she increased her pace.

"Knock, knock."

The sound of a voice instead of an actual knock on the door brought Natalie's head up. Scott Timpson, the newspaperman, stood in the doorway of her office, a frown marring his rail-thin face.

"Hey, I'm sorry. I didn't mean to frighten you."

"You didn't," Natalie said, fighting for composure.

"You couldn't prove that by the look on your face."

"Please, come in and sit down." Her smile was lame. "But I only have a second to visit."

"That's okay. I was in the neighborhood and thought I'd drop by and ask how things are going."

"Not good."

"I'm sorry I wasn't more help."

"You were a lot of help, only it just hasn't come together yet, and I'm not sure it ever will."

"What about McCall? Ever decide how he fits into the puzzle?"

Natalie turned away for fear he could see through to her broken heart. "Yes and no." She didn't want to tell him that she was about to leave the office and confront Stone. She had wanted to do that last night, but she hadn't had the strength or the courage. But this morning, she did.

"Well, I have a little more information on him, if you're interested."

Natalie twisted back around to look at him. "What is it?"

"Shortly after he was promoted, he was accused of taking bribe money that he supposedly used to pay off debts and bad checks his money-hungry wife had racked up."

Natalie's fingers, interlaced, twisted back and forth. This was not something she wanted to hear, not now, not when her trust in Stone had already received a mortal blow and not when she feared for both her life and Clancy's. Yet she remained convinced that Stone would never hurt either of them. But then maybe she was kidding herself because she still loved him, fool that she was.

At that moment, however, she had something more important on her mind.

"How did you find out this information about Stone?" she asked, her eyes darting to the clock.

Scott shrugged. "I just kept digging, that's all."

"Did anything come of the charge?"

"No, even though Internal Affairs looked into the matter. Either the charge was bogus or McCall was able to beat it."

"Thanks for telling me, Scott," Natalie said, standing.

He rose as well. "Are you sure you're all right?"

"No, I'm not sure about anything, but I have to go."

"No problem. I'll walk out with you."

She gave him another lame smile. "I'd appreciate that."

Natalie had no idea what she was going to say. She only knew that if she didn't confront Stone, she could never live with herself. She realized the photograph in and of itself was not proof positive that Stone had done anything wrong. And if she had ever completely overcome her mistrust of him, she wouldn't be here now. But the picture, coupled with Scott's information, had been the catalyst bringing those doubts back to life.

She rang the doorbell and waited.

Shortly, Stone threw open the door, dressed in an old T-shirt and worn jeans. His hair was mussed as usual, and his face was shadowed by a day's growth of beard. Physically he had never looked better, and once again it hit her just how powerfully attracted she was to this man, even knowing that he had taken her husband's life.

God, what kind of woman was she?

"Hi, babe," he said, his face lighting up. "I was just about to call—" He broke off, his features dimming. "Hey, what's wrong? You look . . ."

"Sick. Is that what you were about to say?"

He frowned as she rushed past him and didn't stop until she reached the center of the living room.

"Yeah, that's as good a word as any." His frown increased as his eyes swept over her, his confusion obvious. "What's going on?"

"Why did you lie to me?"

"Lie? What the hell are you talking about?"

"This is what I'm talking about!" She whipped the photograph out of her purse and threw it at him. It fluttered to the floor face up.

His eyes narrowed, then he leaned down and picked it up. She watched him, gauging his reaction.

"Where'd you get this?" he demanded, rising to full height.

"From Fletcher."

"I see."

"Is that all you have to say?"

"You believe what this implies." It wasn't a question, but a harshly spoken statement of fact.

"Actions speak louder than words." Her voice, sharp and labored, seemed to come from someone else's throat. "There's more, I'm sorry to say. A newspaper friend of mine came to see me."

When he responded with only hostile silence, she told him the gist of that conversation.

He gave a harsh laugh. "How the hell am I supposed to defend myself?"

"You could try."

"Why? You've already made up your mind."

Though his tone was softer, the accusation still carried a stabbing punch. "So defend yourself. I'm listening."

"Yeah, right."

There was such a pained air of defeat about him that Natalie felt an overwhelming urge to reach out a hand to him, only to steel herself against any such compassion.

"I won't deny I went to the warehouse," Stone was saying, "or that I had a confrontation with a honcho named Ralph Shankle, who did for a fact offer me a bribe to back off, just as the picture shows. But what happened next, Fletcher's flunky failed to capture on film."

"And just what was that?"

"I showed the fellow exactly what he could do with his money."

"Meaning?"

"I didn't take the goddamn bribe! What I did take, or threaten to take, was a piece of the asshole's hide."

"Then why wasn't that in this picture?"

His face registered contempt. "You figure it out."

"So you're saying that whoever took the picture deliberately left off the fact that you turned the bribe down?"

"That's exactly what I'm saying."

What he said made sense. Dared she believe him? Again? She wanted to. Oh, God, she wanted to more than she'd ever wanted anything in her life. Yet she believed Daniel, too.

"I love you, Natalie. You've got to believe that I'd never do anything to hurt you."

"I want to believe that," she whispered.

"Only you don't, do you?" He seemed to deflate. His eyes turned dull, and his mouth curved down.

"I—" The words froze in her throat while her heart was filled with ice, her mind with self-loathing. She ached to trust him, only . . .

When she didn't go on, he flinched. "You said you loved me."

She didn't say anything.

He gave her a cold, insolent smile. "You may have trouble loving me, but we both know you haven't had any goddamn trouble finding your way into my bed."

The color drained from Natalie's face. "You don't have to be crude."

"Don't I? You tell me how the hell I should be, then."

Natalie made a helpless gesture with her hands. "This is no good."

"You're damn right it isn't. So why don't you just get the hell outta here."

She jerked as if the words had been a whiplash. "What?"

"You heard me. Go, dammit! Love without trust will never survive, Natalie. And it's obvious that your family has won your trust and I lost it." He turned his back, then stood silent for the longest time before adding in a dull tone, "Lock the door behind you."

Moving like a robot, Natalie walked out, feeling as if she would choke on all the unsaid words.

# Thirty-nine

Natalie couldn't seem to pull herself out of her depressive state of mind. Even though she knew she had done the right thing by confronting Stone, she couldn't quell the battle that raged within her. Her spirits were even blacker because she missed him, missed his hot kisses, his intimate touches, his being deep inside her . . .

She rarely let her mind slip into that side of their relationship. The pain was unbearable. In addition to losing Stone, she had thrown a kink in her determination to solve the mystery of Phillip's death, which forced her to take another look at her motives.

What if Phillip's trouble had stemmed from his campaign and nothing else, as the family believed? Should she back off? Should she let the past stay buried, heal the wounds, and go on with her life?

Questions with no answers.

The underpinnings of her life had received a severe blow; she couldn't ignore that. As a result, she wondered if it was worth the pain to continue.

During the week since she had walked out of Stone's condo, she had depended on Clancy, her work, and Lucy to get her through the long days. But the nights—they were intolerable. Many of them found her pacing the floor or on the balcony, watching the stars. Once she even moved Clancy to her bed.

The morning after she'd had that confrontation with Stone, Lucy had demanded to know what was going on.

"Heavens to Betsy, kid, did someone sock you in the eyes last night?"

"Do I look that bad?" Natalie went through the motions of a response, though she didn't care how she looked.

"Worse."

Natalie smiled without feeling. "You certainly know how to make a person feel better."

"Ah, come on, you know I didn't mean that like it sounded. It's just that I'haven't seen you like this in a long time, like someone had hollowed you out inside."

Natalie turned away, thinking that Lucy's assessment was perfect.

"It's Stone, isn't it?"

Natalie nodded. "How'd you know?"

"Only a man has the power to make a woman feel lower than duck shit."

This time Natalie laughed. "You're just the tonic I needed. Thanks."

"I've also got a pretty stout shoulder."

Natalie was tempted to blurt out everything that was weighing on her heart, but she didn't. Some things were just too personal to share. Besides, before she could bare her soul, she had to sort things out on her own. Her feelings and her intentions were still too muddled.

"I know, Luce, and I appreciate that. Believe me. But right now—"

"No offense," Lucy said. "I gather the investigation's not going well, either. Can you tell me what's happening there?"

Natalie's eyes sparked. "I know I'm—we're close, but nothing's broken open yet."

"Have you talked to Daniel?"

"Some."

"Sounds to me like you need to unload on him. If anyone can help and advise you, it's him."

"Maybe you're right."

"At least he can wipe that stark, pained look off your face."

"We'll see."

"By the way," Lucy said, changing the subject, "I've been wanting to discuss something with you."

"Sounds serious."

"It is," Lucy said, then paused.

"Well?"

"I want to sell the business."

Natalie blinked. "Excuse me?"

"I knew you'd be shocked. I am, too, at myself. Still, I've mulled it over for months, and I'm sticking to my decision."

"But why? I mean . . . ?"

Lucy rose, walked to the window, and for a moment kept her back to Natalie. Then she swung around. "Boredom and/ or restlessness." She shrugged. "You know, since my marriage fell apart, I haven't wanted anything to do with men. But through the intense counseling I've been getting, I'm ready to flap my wings again."

Natalie smiled, got up, and hugged her. "Praise the Lord."

"Well, anyway, I have a friend in Colorado who wants me to come there and live, told me she had the perfect hunk already picked out for me." Lucy shrugged again. "End of story."

Only for Natalie it wouldn't be the end, but the chance for a new beginning. She could barely contain her excitement. This was what she had dreamed of, the chance to own her own agency.

"So what do you think?" Lucy asked. "Am I crazy, or what?"

"No, you're not crazy, or what. I think it's a wonderful idea, though I can't bear the thought of losing my best friend."

"Ah, you won't lose me. Anyhow, I'm not going to jump

off the deep end here, so don't worry. I plan to take my time in finding a buyer."

"I just might have a buyer in mind."

"Oh, really? Who?"

"I'll tell you later, okay?"

Suddenly Natalie pulled her thoughts away from that conversation. As much as she'd like to dwell on the thrilling possibility of purchasing the agency, now was not the time for such dallying, especially when she looked at her appointment book for the afternoon.

She had two houses to show, plus she had work to do on the land deal. If this deal worked out, she would have enough money to make a down payment on the agency. She had opted not to tell Lucy as yet because she couldn't handle anything else at the moment, not when her personal life was in such a mess.

The phone jangled. Natalie gave a start, then her mouth went dry. Stone? If only . . . No, she wouldn't do this to herself.

She reached for the receiver. "Miracle Realty, Natalie speaking."

Silence.

"Hello," she said with an aggressive agitation in her tone that she couldn't control but was ashamed of.

"If you value your life and your kid's," a muffled voice said, "then you'll back off your investigation. Now."

Click.

In a matter of seconds Natalie's body went from hot to cold. She felt shocked, numbed into immobility. Oh, God, she couldn't comprehend how someone could hurt an innocent child. She rubbed her temple, trying to come to grips with the fear that had a tight squeeze on her heart and made breathing difficult.

Stone? Could he have been the caller? No. Again, her gut instinct told her that he'd never hurt Clancy. But would he hurt her? No. Then who was this vile person who kept tormenting her?

It didn't matter now. She had to get Clancy. She was top priority.

Forty-five minutes later Natalie tucked Clancy's teddy bear in her arms, then leaned over and kissed her on the cheek. She'd been sitting by Clancy's bedside for over an hour, her mind reeling the entire time.

The tap on the door startled her. She turned around to face Martha, who appeared pitifully unsure of herself.

"Hi, come in," Natalie said, and to her dismay heard her own voice crack.

"I hope I'm not interrupting. I just er . . . wanted to see Clancy for a minute."

Natalie smiled through unexpected tears; then, angry at herself, she reached for her purse, opened it, and yanked out a tissue. Then she saw the key. Oh, no, she moaned silently, wanting to kick herself. While wallowing in self-pity over Stone, she'd forgotten to go to the bank and see if the key actually was to a lockbox, and if so, what significance it might have.

"Natalie?"

She knew she must look like an idiot. "I'm all right, Martha. Look, would you keep an eye on Clance for a while? I need to run back into town."

Martha's face brightened. "I'd love to."

"Thanks." Natalie squeezed her shoulder.

Martha trapped her hand and gazed up at her, tears swimming in her eyes. "I love you."

"And I do you, too," Natalie responded, then left before she broke down and boo-hooed like a baby.

"Thank you, Mr. Kane."

"Any time, Mrs. Whitmore," he said in a nasal tone. "After all, the Whitmores are our most valuable customers."

Natalie wasn't sure that was true, as she'd had to cut through massive red tape before she was allowed into the lockbox. Now, though, she had the box in front of her. She sat down and lifted the metal lid. She didn't know what she expected to find, but not papers that had TEXAS AERO INDUSTRIES emblazoned across the top.

The back of her neck tingled, then she broke out into a cold sweat. What did this mean? Was she about to uncover the answer to Phillip's death?

Her hands shook so much that she had difficulty in removing the papers. Once they were spread onto the table and she'd perused them, her excitement dimmed. They were nothing more than invoices clipped together. Then, on closer examination, a horrifying truth jumped out at her.

Phillip had signed them.

"Oh, no. Please, God, no," she groaned.

The worst-possible scenario had come to pass. She lifted her head, a combination of anger and fear threatening to choke her. Phillip *had* been part of Texas Aero, a vital part, it appeared.

Damn him! She wanted to scream. But most of all she wanted to crawl in a hole and never come out. How could he have fallen into such a vile trap? Her heart started pumping again, harder.

Unless he hadn't known that the operation was illegal. Was that possible, or was she merely hoping against hope? Natalie forced herself to thumb back through the invoices. Nothing else leapt out at her, just the unvarnished truth that Phillip had indeed been involved. Still, there could be something else here that might prove his innocence, she told herself with frantic intent. Or his guilt, she amended, only she didn't want to look on the dark side.

She decided to take the invoices to Stone—only to return to reality with a sickening jolt. She couldn't go to Stone. Not now, not ever. She was on her own, and the pain was so overwhelming, she almost wanted to die. Then Clancy's sweet face came to mind, and she stood and squared her shoulders.

# Forty

"Come on in, Danny."

Natalie didn't turn around, but she felt his presence behind her even before he placed his arm around her shoulders.

"What's going on? Are you sick?"

She gazed up at him, her features drawn. "Yes and no. It must be mental telepathy because I was just about to see if you were home."

"What's the matter?" Daniel asked with urgency, his hold on her tightening. "I haven't seen you cry since—"

"I'm not crying."

"Well, you're damn close to it."

Natalie was too tired to argue. Blinking, she got up and walked to the bed, kissed Clancy again, then motioned for Daniel to follow her.

Once they were out of the room, he said, "Let's go out on the veranda. Believe it or not, there's a breeze."

"Where're Martha and Fletcher?"

"Gone to Stanley's for dinner." He gave her a lopsided smile. "Paula's cooking a meal."

"Paula, cooking?"

"Yeah. But it's merely a ploy in a long line of many to

butter up the old man. And I suspect she's also trying to patch the torn remnants of her marriage."

"That's a poetic way of putting it, but I don't feel sorry for either of them."

"Me either."

"So we have the house to ourselves?" Natalie asked.

"Except for Josie, who's already fixed supper and retired to her rooms." Daniel propelled her toward the French doors that led outside. After they were seated he asked, "Want me to get you some iced tea?"

"No thanks."

"What *do* you want, then?"

"Answers, Danny, but you already know that."

"That's too bad, because there aren't any more answers to the questions you're asking."

"Two terrible things happened to me today."

"Jeez, I'm sorry, sis."

"I received another threatening phone call."

Daniel's jaw went slack. "And I can't for the life of me understand what the hell's going on."

Natalie was silent for a moment, letting her gaze roam over the grounds aglow with colored annuals. Usually the flowers made her feel better, soothed her spirit; but not now.

"You keep telling me, along with Fletcher, that Phillip's death was just an accident, that the family had nothing to do with Texas Aero or the murder there, yet Clancy and I keep getting threatened because I've asked questions that no one wants answered." She gave Daniel a sharp look. "Does that make sense? Of course it doesn't, and I'll tell you why."

"I'm listening."

"Y'all were wrong about Phillip."

Daniel stroked the side of his chin. "How so?"

"He *was* involved with Texas Aero. I have evidence to prove that."

"Oh, come on, that can't be so. Look—"

She held up her hand. "Don't, Danny."

"Okay, Nat, have it your own way. So what do you want from me?"

"Advice and help. Not just a pat on the head and condescending platitudes, but honest to God help in finding out who Phillip was working with. When I know that, I'll know who's behind the threats."

Daniel made a face. "I'm sorry, but I'm finding it real hard to swallow that my brother was involved with that company. Yet I can't deny that you've apparently shaken someone up at Texas Aero or maybe McCall—" He broke off, his eyes narrowing on her.

"McCall what?" she pressed, then waited for his answer with dread, knowing what he was going to say.

The late afternoon was stirred by a gentle breeze that brushed her cheek, rippled her hair, but failed to cool her off either outside or inside.

"Are you still seeing him?"

She was silent for another moment.

"No."

Danny raised his eyebrows. "Is that the truth?"

"Yes."

"Then the pictures did the trick?"

"The trick?"

He flushed. "Well, you know what I mean. Surely you understand where I'm coming from. The thought of that bastard touching you—"

Natalie held up her hand. "Don't, Danny. Don't say anything else, okay?"

"Sorry."

"Just help me find out what's going on. And trust me that I'm right about all of this."

"How can I help? I'm no private eye. Hell, I'm just a teacher."

"I know, but you could talk to Fletcher, tell him about Phillip. You can also convince him that someone is a threat to Clancy, which will spur him into action."

"I wouldn't count on that. He'll more than likely just rationalize that away, like he's done everything else."

"Tell him anyway." Natalie's tone was mutinous.

"Okay, okay. Just don't go ballistic on me."

"Thanks," Natalie whispered in a bleak tone. "But I have to tell you that I feel about as desperate as I've ever felt."

Daniel took one of her hands in his. "I've never let you down, have I?"

"No."

"Well, I won't now, either. Is there anything I need to know that you haven't already told me?"

"One thing."

"What?"

"I'll be right back."

"Where—"

His words were lost as Natalie rushed inside to her bedroom. Moments later she bounded back down the stairs and onto the veranda.

"Natalie, you're acting crazy."

Daniel sounded exasperated, and she didn't blame him. But she figured it was easier to show him than tell him. She thrust a folder into his hand.

He looked down at it, then back up at her. "What's in there?"

"Invoices."

"Invoices?" he repeated.

She nodded. "That's the evidence I told you I had. I just want you to look at them and tell me if you see anything besides Phillip's signature that's significant."

"Where did they come from?"

"Out of a bank lockbox."

"I don't understand."

"Neither do I, but apparently Phillip thought they were important. He hid the key in an old jewelry case of mine; I found it accidentally."

"Has anyone else seen them?" Daniel asked.

"No. I was going to show them to Stone the night I saw the pictures."

"All right, I'll have a look at them, but don't count on me for any miraculous insight."

She leaned over, kissed him on the cheek, then smiled sweetly. "Because you love me, you *are* miraculous."

"You've been a real asset to this company. I'm impressed with your work."

"That's reassuring," Stone responded.

Larry Meadows's mouth turned down. "You sure as hell couldn't prove that by listening to you."

"What does that mean?" Stone asked, but he knew. He found it hard to get out of bed every morning, much less show any enthusiasm for anything. Losing Natalie had changed his life yet again. He felt as if a vital part of him were missing; he felt he'd been gutted, like a goddamn catfish.

"It's the investigation, isn't it? It's eating you up."

"Yes to both questions," Stone said, bypassing his feelings for Natalie.

"Hell, man, what's going on? I thought things were coming together, that you were rocking and rolling."

"I thought so, too, only . . ."

"Only what?"

"Things went to hell in a hand-basket real fast."

"What about the Whitmore woman? Does she still figure into this?"

The knot in Stone's stomach twisted. "No."

"Okay, so you don't want to talk about her?"

Stone didn't say anything.

"Well, I'm available, if you need someone to throw darts at."

Stone forced a smile. "In that case—"

"That was purely a figure of speech, asshole."

This time Stone's smile was genuine, only it didn't last long. "Have you ever felt you were this close to something, only you couldn't quite grasp it?" Stone's voice was fierce.

"That's the way I feel about this case. I'm missing something, dammit, but I can't nail it."

"What about Rutgers?"

"He still sticks in my craw because he's responsible for getting me kicked off the force. But as to his actual role in anything else pertaining to the case, I don't thinks he's a key player."

"Sounds like you're sorta chasing your tail."

"That's it in a fucking nutshell."

Larry yanked on an ear. "I don't know if this will be of any consolation, but you were on dead center about the jeweler."

"Ah, so the sonofabitch did engineer the burglary himself?"

"Yep. Your report was right on target."

Stone lifted his eyebrows. "You didn't . . ."

"Nah, we didn't tell Rutgers how we knew, but we did put pressure on him to have his men lean on the little creep until he sang like a canary at a cat concert. Just so you'll know, if things don't turn out the way you want, you have a full-time job here—a damn good one, if and when you want it."

"Thanks, Larry. I'll certainly keep that in mind, but first I have to finish the job I started."

Larry got up and walked to the door. "All I can say is that I pity the poor bastard who's guilty. I've always said I wouldn't want to meet you in a dark alley, and I haven't changed my mind."

"Thanks for nothing, asshole."

"Anytime." Larry laughed, then shut the door behind him.

Stone got up, walked around the front of his desk, then leaned against it, thinking about how easy Larry's life seemed. At times like this he actually envied him.

He wished he could laugh with that kind of freedom. But then laughter had never come easily to him. In his job as a homicide cop, there hadn't been much to laugh about. Only since he'd been around Natalie had that changed somewhat. Now his life once again was headed down the toilet.

"Dammit!" he muttered just as the phone rang. He didn't get excited. He knew it wouldn't be Natalie. It was over between them, and the sooner he came to grips with that, the sooner he could begin to heal.

"McCall," he snapped into the receiver. After a moment his knees went weak, and he clung to the desk. "Tell her to hold on. I'll be right there!"

The instant the automatic door opened to admit him into the main lobby of the hospital, Stone's stomach revolted. He'd hoped that he'd never have to travel this road again, though logically he knew better.

Still, having to come here again so soon and under such frantic conditions was something he could have lived without for the rest of his life.

By the time he reached the intensive care waiting room, his ex-wife, Connie, and her husband were sitting on the couch, looking pale and grim.

Stone didn't waste time on platitudes. "How is she?"

Connie stood and faced him. "I don't know. We're waiting for the doctor. They're working on her now."

"What the hell happened?"

"Please, Stone, for Heaven's sake calm down."

"Jesus, Connie, how can I calm down when she might be d— " He choked on the word again, as he had the time she'd had the wreck.

"She's not going to die," Connie retorted, glaring at him.

"Of course she's not." Stone heard the panic in his voice but wasn't surprised. First Natalie, now Sally. He was drowning, yet everyone was still pitching water on him. "What happened?"

"She started having severe stomach cramps and vomiting like you've never seen."

Stone cursed. "Did the doctor give you any indication of what might be wrong?"

"No, but you can ask him yourself."

Stone swung around and stared at the tired-faced doctor

walking toward them. Again platitudes were cast aside as he demanded, "Is she going to be all right?"

The doctor smiled, which seemed to send some of the blood back into his face. "Yes, now that we took care of that abdominal obstruction."

"Thank God," Stone muttered.

Connie sagged against her husband, then asked, "Was it a result of the wreck?"

"Yes, but as I said, we were able to take care of it without surgery. In a few days she'll be fine."

"Can we see her?" Stone asked.

"Of course," the doctor said, "but only two at a time."

"You go ahead," Stone said, looking at Connie. "I'll wait."

The upheaval in Natalie's life was taking its toll. She was miserable. She grieved over Phillip's and Stone's duplicity but had no one to blame but herself for the latter. From the beginning she had known she was playing with fire. The fact that she'd gotten burned should not have come as a big surprise. She'd gone to his house, given him every chance to make some sense out of all this. Instead he'd kicked her out of his life.

Still, she was desperate to bring this probe into Phillip's death to closure. It had turned into a monster that had a stranglehold on her life.

"Mommy."

She peered down at Clancy, who was sitting on the floor, surrounded by toys, and grinned. "Mommy's here, darling."

Seemingly content to hear her mother's voice, Clancy picked up her doll and began pulling on the hair. After watching her a moment, Natalie turned her thoughts inward again. She hadn't gone to work today. She had felt the need to pack, as her condo was almost ready to move into. She had worked until an ache in her shoulders had forced her to rest.

So she decided to get out the invoices and look at them again. She had given Daniel the originals but kept the copies she had made for herself.

Now, as she sat cross-legged in the middle of her bed, she scrutinized every word on the invoices. The documents had to do with the actual sale of parts to various airlines, which in themselves were no big deal. But the question that wouldn't die inside her head and heart was, had Phillip known that the operation was illegal and the parts *defective*, or had he been duped by someone he knew and trusted?

Ten minutes later Natalie cried out in stunned disbelief, "Oh, my God!"

The first time she'd looked at the invoices, she had flipped through them like a deck of cards, disappointed that nothing concrete had leapt out at her, certainly not any inconsistencies in the signatures. Each of the seven was signed with only one word: Whitmore. Now, under such close scrutiny, she noticed that four had actually been signed by Phillip; the other three had been signed by someone else.

The difference was minimal, but there nonetheless.

"Oh, my God," she said again, her words rivaling the sound of her pounding heart. The other signature she knew as well as she knew Phillip's.

*Daniel*.

The other signatures were his. The ramifications of what she had discovered immobilized her with stark panic. Were Daniel *and* Phillip both involved in the illegal scam? If so, was Daniel still involved? And if he was, then who would stand to lose if Phillip not only wanted out, but threatened to blow the whistle on the operation? Daniel again.

And he had the invoices.

With her heart now lodged in her throat, Natalie scrambled off the bed, grabbed Clancy, and took her downstairs for Josie to watch.

"Mommy!" Clancy cried when Natalie turned to leave.

"I'll be right back, sweetheart. Josie'll play with you."

With that, Natalie turned and raced back upstairs. She had to get out of the house. Now! She was in the process of reaching for an empty suitcase when she heard a tap on the door. Because she didn't want to talk to anyone, she didn't say a word, praying they would go away.

"Hey, Nat, you'd better be decent 'cause I'm coming in."

Natalie froze as the door opened and Daniel strode across the threshold.

# *Forty-one*

"Good Lord, Nat, you look like you've seen a ghost."

Outside, Natalie could hear birds chirping, could visualize them swinging through the treetops. That peaceful image did little to change the inside climate. In the deathly quiet of the room, cold rage pumped through her, settling in her ears.

"Natalie, for God's sake, say something!" Daniel took a step closer.

She cringed and would have backed up if she hadn't been too shell-shocked to move. Licking her paste-dry lips, she whispered, "When . . . when did you get home?"

"A few minutes ago. Why?"

The look he gave her was one of puzzlement, but otherwise nothing about Daniel had changed. He remained the same steady, soothing person he'd always been. No! That was all an illusion, she told herself. Or was it? Was he guilty as sin, or had he, too, been duped by the owners of Texas Aero?

She *had* to believe the latter, or she didn't think she could hold up. She'd lost so much in life already. The thought of losing the one person whom she had always loved in the purest sense of the word was incomprehensible.

"Natalie, please, tell me what has you so upset now. Did you get another threatening phone call? If you did, I'll—"

The shake of her head stopped his flow of words. "No, it's not that."

"Then what is it?"

"Daniel, we've always been honest with each other, right?"

He frowned. "What the hell kind of question is that?"

"I'm serious. Answer me."

"Okay, we've always been honest with each other." He lifted one eyebrow, then smiled. "So, are you happy now?"

"No."

"Jesus, Nat, you're not making any sense. This mess with Phillip has you so strung out that you're going to snap."

"I—" She couldn't go on. There were no words to express the turmoil inside her.

Daniel walked over to the chaise longue and sat on the edge of it, his smile widening. "I'm here, and listening, as always. Has something else happened?"

Natalie stared at him, trying desperately to see underneath that inquisitive but unthreatening demeanor, wondering what evil, if any, lurked there.

"Nat, if you don't tell—"

"Danny, what are *your* ties to Texas Aero?"

Natalie had to hand it to him. If he had something to hide, he knew how to mask it. No muscle, anywhere on him, so much as twitched. "Tied as in connected, is that what you mean?"

She nodded.

"I know nothing about those people or their operation."

Pain ripped through her, so intense, she thought she might faint. But she didn't. Somehow she managed to keep her face blank.

"Hell, Nat, you know where my interests lie."

"I thought I did, Danny."

"Look, you should get some rest, back off this crazy venture of yours." He cocked his head. "But for my sake, what's this third degree all about? I mean, if that bastard McCall isn't putting you up to this—"

She gave a savage shake of her head. "He has nothing to do with it."

"Then let it go, for God's sake. Get a life."

"I can't."

"Nat, there's a limit to even my patience. So this had better be good."

"You're lying to me, Daniel."

He chuckled, then shook his head. "I must be in heap big trouble for you to call me Daniel in that tone. You only did that one other time that I remember, after I—"

"Stop it."

His eyes crinkled at the corner. "You're serious about all this, aren't you?"

"Dead serious."

"Okay, so what, pray tell, have I lied to you about?"

"You think this is all a joke, don't you?"

He stood, and when he did she noticed that a nerve was throbbing in his throat. She'd never known that to happen before. Apparently she'd found a chink in his armor. She didn't know whether that made her feel more relieved or more frightened.

"No, Nat, I don't think this is a joke. I just think you're going through a rough time and need a punching bag." He stuck out his chest. "So, go ahead, punch all you like."

Again, she ignored his attempt at humor. "Tell me why you lied."

"About what?"

"*Your* involvement with Texas Aero."

"I told you—"

"Don't!" she cried. "Don't you dare deny that again!"

"What's the bottom line, here, Natalie?"

"The invoices, damn you! You've always been 'Dr. Whitmore'—too academic to get involved in the family business. I believed you until now. What's *your* signature doing on Texas Aero's invoices?" She thrust the papers at him.

He didn't take them. Instead they both watched as the sheets fluttered between them, then landed face up on the carpet.

"Are they copies of the ones you gave me?"

"Yes."

"Well, I haven't had a chance to look them over," he responded in an offhand tone, "but I will."

Natalie laughed around the tears of pain and sadness building inside her. "You really are something, you know that?"

"Do you realize what you're saying and who you're saying it to?"

She took a deep breath and stiffened her shoulders. Yet her eyes were dark with sorrow. "Yes, and that's why it breaks my heart."

"One more time, what are you talking about?"

"The invoices, Daniel. I finally figured out what there was about them that Phillip thought was so important, important enough to hide in a safety-deposit box."

"So, don't keep me in suspense."

She gazed hard at him. "Your signature is on three of them."

"So what?"

She laughed again. "Is that all you have to say? God, it was you who duped Phillip, wasn't it?"

"I'd be careful if I were you."

"Careful. Oh no, not anymore. I'm through being careful where you're concerned. I'm not about to settle for anything less than the truth."

This time he laughed, an ugly, bitter laugh. "The truth, huh? You want the truth . . . well, go get it from someone else because I've about had enough of your shit."

Natalie's features turned glacial. "You can't walk away that easily, not this time."

She caught a hint of struggle in his eyes before they turned menacing. "Make no mistake about it, I can do any fucking thing I please because you're not calling the shots."

"Then who is, Danny? You? Are you calling the shots?"

He lunged toward her. "You're goddamn right I am!"

She gasped, then threw a hand over her mouth.

He chuckled. "Oh, so now you're going to play the shocked, desperate sister. Sorry, honey, but that won't work. You opened this can of worms. Now you're going to stand still while they crawl all over you."

"How could you, Danny?" Her voice quivered.

"How could I what?"

"Betray your brother, betray us all."

He sneered. "Phillip was an idiot who lived in his own goddamn dream world. Yet when I told him about the parts factory deal and how much money we stood to make if he went in with us, the greedy bastard jumped on it."

"You mean he knew about the scam they were running?" She could barely get the sickening words out of her mouth.

Daniel's features twisted in an ugly expression of mockery. "Phillip? No way! When he found out, he wanted no part of it."

"But Phillip wouldn't keep quiet, right?"

"That's right. The bastard was going to rat on the operation. And I—we couldn't allow that to happen."

Natalie's mind scrambled to come to grips with the horror of the moment, a horror that seemed to have blindsided her despite her suspicions. But being suspicious and hearing the brutal truth were two different things.

"I know what you're thinking."

"You don't have any idea what I'm thinking!" Natalie shot back.

"Turning me in, you know, won't bring Phillip back."

Natalie was frantic. First Phillip, now Daniel. How could she not have known? She hadn't wanted to, she told herself. She had survived her childhood and a portion of her adulthood by shutting out painful things, thinking that if she did, they would go away.

"If you want, I'll even cut you in on the deal. Goddamn, but it's lucrative."

"Does . . . does Fletcher know?" Natalie asked in a frail whisper.

"No, so why don't we keep this our little secret. It would kill Mother and Daddy both if they lost another son. Besides that, they'd never forgive you for ratting on *me*."

She couldn't believe what she was hearing. Daniel was sick and needed help. How had she not seen that? Blinders. She hadn't wanted to probe beneath the surface. But then in her own defense, who would have ever thought that sweet, gentle Daniel had a Jekyll and Hyde personality?

"You're saying that I should just forget about this?" she asked, stalling for time so that she could think.

"If you're smart, you will."

"And if I'm not?"

"Surely I don't need to remind you that I'm not the only one involved."

He spoke in such a blasé tone that he could've been discussing the heat. He had tipped over the edge into insanity. Think, Natalie, think!

"So what are you saying?" she finally asked.

"You know what I'm saying, but if it'll make you feel better, I'll spell it out. If you go to the authorities, you could be putting yourself in more danger, and Clancy as well. The men I work with play for keeps."

Natalie's blood curdled. *Clancy!*

Daniel grinned, though his eyes were vacant, dead. "All you have to do is keep your mouth shut, and nothing will happen to either of you."

She didn't dare trust him to mean that. On the other hand, how could she *not* trust him? But what of the innocent people who could possibly suffer untold horrors from the continued use of substandard airplane parts? Could she live with their blood on her conscience?

"So what's it going to be, Nat? Do we have a deal?"

Her vocal cords had turned to chalk, but still she managed to speak. "Of course, Daniel," she lied. "We've got to protect the family name."

His face contorted, and the muscles in his body all seemed to grow rigid. And for what seemed the longest time, they stared at each other, the years rushing through their heads like a kaleidoscope.

"I'm not going to turn you in, Danny," she said in a cajoling tone.

"I'm sorry, Nat, but I don't believe you."

Before she could say another word, he pulled a pistol from his jacket and pointed it straight at her.

# Forty-two

Stone stared at his face in the mirror.

"Jesus!" he muttered, thinking he looked like he used to after he'd been on a drunk. His eyes were sunk back into his head, and he needed a haircut. He didn't care how he looked. His feelings were what were important, and he felt like shit.

He wished he had been coming out of a drunken stupor. At least the emotional and physical pain that hammered at him would be tolerable. If only he'd pleaded his case harder to Natalie. If only the mistrust between them hadn't been there from the onset. So many if-onlys.

The bottom line was he'd lost her. He'd gambled and lost. Yet he knew he had to pull himself back together; he had no choice. At one time he could wallow in self-pity. Now he had Sally to consider.

Still, it was hard because he wanted Natalie so much that he ached all over, even his teeth. He smiled without mirth, thinking that if he'd stop gritting his teeth, maybe they wouldn't ache. Though he longed to spend every night for the rest of his life buried inside Natalie's tight warmth, what he really wanted from her encompassed so much more than sex. He wanted to take care of her and Clancy. He wanted to love them, be responsible for them in every sense of the word. He had never wanted that responsibility in the past, but now he did. He felt he was ready for it.

Only he would never get the chance.

And while that ripped him apart, he couldn't ignore the cold fact that he was worried about her and Clancy. They were in danger. He didn't know from whom as yet, and consequently his "take-charge" mentality was taking a severe beating.

Dammit, he didn't trust any of the Whitmore bunch, nor did he trust anyone at Texas Aero. But pacing the floor and whining wasn't going to net results. Maybe if he went to see Natalie again. That thought stopped him in his tracks. Would that help or make matters worse?

Hell, they couldn't be worse, he told himself. Besides, what did he have to lose? Not a damn thing; he'd already lost his heart.

Stone shoved his fingers through his hair, then scrambled out of his jogging shorts into jeans and a clean shirt. He was at the door when the bell suddenly chimed. He pulled up short, then cursed. He wasn't in the mood for a vacuum cleaner salesman.

He jerked open the door, a scowl darkening his face. "I'm not—" His words dried up as he tried to recall where he'd seen the man who stood on his porch, leaning on a cane.

The cane jogged his memory, made him drop his gaze to the man's foot. Though now encased in a sandal and devoid of sores and the extra added attraction—flies—Travis Norton's wound still hadn't completely healed.

Stone shifted his gaze back to the man's face. "What brings you here?"

"Er . . . Mr. McCall, is it?"

"That's right."

"Could we talk?"

"It depends on what you have to say. I don't like being played for a fool, Mr. Norton."

The man's ruddy face lost some of its color. "Sorry I stood you up, but—" He stopped.

"But what?"

"Can I come in and sit down?" Norton asked.

Stone saw the sweat pop out and settle in the deep grooves on his face. Apparently the man was in pain. "All right," Stone said begrudgingly, stepping aside. "But this had better be good."

"Oh, it's good, I promise." Norton paused, turned, and stared at Stone. "Uh, that is, if the money's still there."

"Have a seat, Mr. Norton, and we'll see."

Once the man had all but fallen down onto the sofa, Stone, too restless to sit, stood against the fireplace, an elbow crooked on the mantel for support. He wanted to get into his "cop mode" and grill the man quickly and unmercifully, then get rid of him so that he could go to Natalie. But he knew that if this man was willing to talk, and apparently he was, considering the effort it must have taken for him to come here, he'd have to use patience in dealing with him.

Looking at Norton now, Stone thought he appeared about as uncomfortable as a preacher approaching a hooker.

"Why didn't you meet me when you were supposed to?" Stone asked in a neutral tone.

Norton's eyes flickered from one part of the room to the other before coming back to Stone. Still, he didn't look directly at him. "I was scared."

"Scared of whom?"

Norton angled his neck, giving Stone a clear view of his dirty bald head. "How much money you offering?"

"It's according to what you have to tell me."

Norton licked his cracked lips. "Lemme see some green stuff or I ain't talkin'."

"Don't play games with me, Mr. Norton. Like I said, after that fiasco the other day, I'm not in the mood for any horseshit. If you were smart, you'd be as afraid of *not* talking to me, 'cause I'm liable to take that cane and whip your ass for wasting more of my time."

"All right," Norton said with a gulp.

"So back to my original question: Why were you afraid to talk?"

"I'm not lookin' to push up daisies, that's why."

Stone almost smiled. "You really think someone would kill you if they knew you talked to me?"

"Yep."

"What made you change your mind?"

"I need the money real bad."

Stone didn't ask why. He didn't want to know. If the man gave him anything he could use, then he'd gladly pay him. But that was a big "if."

"So, I'm listening," Stone finally said.

Norton cleared his throat and looked around as if the walls might have had ears.

"Norton!"

"I overheard Mr. Whitmore talking to two men in the factory."

"Which Mr. Whitmore?"

"Daniel."

Stone looked as stunned as he felt. "Are you sure about that?"

"Yep. I may not be smart, but I kin see."

"Okay, so you can see. But how do you know Daniel Whitmore by sight and name?"

"'Cause I seen him there several times. And a buddy told me who he was."

Again Stone felt as if he'd been sucker-punched in the gut. "So what were he and those two men talking about?"

"Killing someone."

If he'd had false teeth, Stone would have lost them. Yet he didn't believe a word this man said. It was just too farfetched. "Ah, come on, Norton, you can do better than that."

Norton looked confused, which increased Stone's frustration. "If you're making this up . . ."

"I'm not. I swear it."

If the stark fear that radiated from Norton's eyes was for real—and Stone knew it was—then the man was indeed telling the truth. Christ! Who would have ever thought that wimp, Daniel, had the balls to plot anyone's murder? But then it was that kind of person who was the most dangerous.

"Who were the other two men?" Stone asked.

"Don't know for sure. I couldn't see them, but one sounded like Ralph Shankle who runs the factory."

"Did you overhear that conversation before or after the man at the factory was shot?"

"Afterward."

"Do you know why the man was murdered?"

"Sure do."

"Tell me."

"He caught on to what was going on and wanted in on the action."

Stone kneaded the back of his neck, "How do you know?"

"He told me."

"Will you testify to that in court?"

"What's in it for me?"

"Staying out of the slammer, for starters. Since that murder has never been solved, withholding information is a felony, Mr. Norton."

Norton's face lost its color, but when he spoke his voice was bitter. "Okay, I'll testify. But nothing better not happen to me, you hear?"

Ignoring that threat, Stone asked, "Do you know who actually pulled the trigger?"

"Nope."

"If I find out you're not being straight with me, I'll be back to see you, and you don't want that, I assure you."

Norton looked terrified. "I swear that's the truth."

Stone pulled out his wallet and removed several hundred-dollar bills. "Here, take them, but expect to hear from the law soon." He paused with narrowed eyes. "And you'd best be at home when they come calling."

Norton gulped again as he rose to his feet. "I ain't going nowheres."

The second Norton lumbered out the door and into his

pickup truck, Stone dashed into his bedroom, his heart pounding, his body drenched in sweat. Natalie! He had to warn her about Daniel. He called the office, but since it was Saturday, he feared she might not be working. He was right; he received a recording.

"Damn!"

His next thought was to call the ranch, but he decided against that. What Natalie didn't know at this point was a built-in safety net.

He rummaged through the bottom of his closet until he found the box, then reached inside and removed the pistol. He straightened and, with a grim set to his shoulders, raced out the door.

Later, Stone didn't know how he reached the ranch without getting a ticket. He'd exceeded the speed limit every chance he got. Once on Whitmore property, he proceeded with caution up the long, circular drive. But instead of pulling up in front of the house, he stopped a ways from it, angling his car off the drive into a wooded area.

From there he made his way on foot, only to stop in his tracks when he saw a black woman sitting on the front porch, a child in her arms. Clancy. Thank God, she was out of the house.

"Hello," he said, forcing a calmness in his voice he was far from feeling.

The woman jumped, and the child whimpered "Shh, it's all right," Josie whispered, glaring at Stone. "Who you be, mister?"

"A friend of Natalie's."

The woman, who Stone figured was the housekeeper, stared at him with open hostility. "What you want?"

"Is she home?"

"Yes."

"Alone?"

She snorted. "That ain't none of your business."

"Who's with her?"

"Look, mister—"

"Dammit, answer me." Though Stone never raised his voice, she got the message.

Fear widened the woman's eyes. "Mr. Daniel."

Stone's gut twisted. "Who else?"

"Nobody. Miz Martha and Mr. Fletcher, they be gone." She pulled Clancy closer against her heavy bosom. "You the law?"

"I want you to listen to me real carefully, okay? I want you to take Clancy out of the house. Both of you leave, then call the emergency number 911; tell them to send the sheriff."

Her black eyes widened until they seemed to take up her whole face. "Oh, Lordy me," she whispered at the same time she seemed to gasp for her next breath. "I can't—"

"Do it. Now!"

"Yes, sir." Josie got out of the swing just as Stone strode past her into the cool foyer, where he paused and listened. Nothing. He stepped deeper into the house. When he reached the foot of the stairs, he heard the voices and began to ease up the stairs, heading toward them. The door to what he assumed was Natalie's apartment was ajar.

He paused outside, pulled his pistol, and listened as Natalie said in a broken voice, "Oh, Daniel, put that gun away. We both know you're not going to use it."

Stone groaned inwardly, realizing that he'd arrived just in time. Something had obviously happened that had brought them together in this lethal situation.

"That's where you're wrong, Nat," Daniel responded.

Stone inched forward so that he could see them without them seeing him. His gut clenched when he saw Daniel's gun pointed at Natalie.

"What happened, Danny?" she asked in a broken voice. "How could you be part of something so destructive and evil?"

Daniel laughed.

Stone thought he sounded mad, which frightened him even more. "Money, my love, and power."

"But you have money. And why do you need power? I don't understand."

Atta girl, keep him talking, Stone thought, his own mind searching for a way to defuse the situation without anyone getting hurt, especially Natalie. He didn't give a damn about Daniel or himself. Natalie and Clancy were his only concerns.

"Of course you don't understand," Daniel was saying. "You've always been treated like you could walk on the goddamn water, while I've been treated like pond scum."

"Oh, Danny, that's not true."

"Yes, it is!" His voice sounded an octave higher.

Stone inched closer.

"First it was Phillip who got all the attention, always the fair-haired wonder boy, then Stanley, then you and Clancy. So you see, there never was a time for *me*! I never got anything, except a pat on the head from Mamma and a tongue-lashing from Daddy."

Stone saw Natalie visibly wilt, as if all the life had been drained out of her. It was all he could do not to storm the room and beat Daniel Whitmore to a pulp. But he couldn't do that; the risk to Natalie was too great. Still, he couldn't wait much longer to make his move. Daniel was becoming more unstable by the second.

"I loved you, Danny." Tears streamed down Natalie's face.

He laughed again. "Well, I never loved you. From the first minute you stepped through the door, I hated you."

"Oh, God," Natalie sobbed. "Did you have anything to do with Phillip's death?"

"Hell, I'm the one who ordered the sniveling bastard killed."

Natalie cried out, which seemed to shake Daniel. Stone watched, drenched in cold fear, as Daniel shook the gun in Natalie's direction. She backed up against her escritoire, whose writing lid was down. Daniel began to back toward the door, closer to Stone, still unaware that he and Natalie were no longer alone.

There was no way Stone could announce his presence, not

while Daniel had a pistol; Natalie would make a ready-made hostage. No, it would be too easy for someone to get hurt. He would have to do something to disarm this creep.

Of course he could just shoot him out of hand, but he'd already killed one Whitmore—even if it had been an accident—and he didn't want to do that again. Worse, he would never shoot Daniel in front of Natalie, nor did he want bullets flying in the room with the woman he loved.

Stone tensed, then charged into the room, his shoulder striking Whitmore in the small of the back, scything him like Kansas wheat.

"Stone!" Natalie's terrified cry filled the room.

Daniel's pistol skittered across the carpet, coming to rest against a table. His body out of control, Stone continued forward on his stomach until his shoulder slammed against the couch. He felt his whole arm go numb as he watched Daniel regain his feet, then lunge for the gun.

Stone's arm was slow in obeying his commands, for the pain was intense. Daniel's pistol was already coming up.

He had misjudged, miscalculated. Now both his and Natalie's lives depended on the whim of a madman, one who was already lining Stone up in his sights and tightening on the trigger.

Out of the corner of his eye, Stone saw Natalie grab something from her desktop and fling it at Daniel. The heavy cutglass paperweight struck him in the face, and his gun hand came up involuntarily to protect himself.

This was the break Stone needed; his own pistol was now centered on Whitmore's chest, and he yelled at the man in his best command voice.

"It's over, Whitmore! You'll never get a shot off."

"Please, Danny," Natalie pleaded, inching toward him. "Give up the gun."

"No, dammit! I won't go to prison."

"Come on, Danny, please."

He gave Natalie a sick smile, then held out the pistol. Stone's knees sagged in relief, only to watch in horror as

Daniel suddenly jerked back the pistol and gave a bloodcurdling laugh.

"Put the gun down, Whitmore," Stone demanded in a low, controlled tone. "Make this easy on yourself."

The room drummed with a second of silence.

"Danny, please," Natalie begged again.

"Whitmore, what's it going to be?" Stone watched as Daniel faced him.

Their eyes met at the same time Daniel pointed the muzzle at his own temple.

"No!" Natalie screamed.

# Forty-three

### One Year Later

Natalie smiled at her precocious daughter and shook her finger at her. "Mommy told you not to do that."

Clancy had been playing in the sandpile and had taken a liking to dirt. When Natalie had brought her in to bathe her, her lips were still covered with it. Now, after she wiped Clancy's mouth one more time, she lifted her and took her into her bedroom for a nap.

"Promise me you won't eat any more dirt or Mommy won't let you play in the sandpile again."

Clancy's lower lip protruded. "Daddy eats dirt."

"Clancy Whitmore, that's not so, and you know it!"

Clancy giggled as Natalie laid her on the bed. "Shh, settle down now and go nap, nap a while, then I'll take you to see Gram and Papa."

"Daddy go too?"

"No, Mommy and Daddy have work to do around the house. Besides, Gram and Papa want you all to themselves." Natalie leaned over and brushed Clancy's glowing cheek with her lips, "Sleep tight and don't let the bedbugs bite."

Clancy giggled again, then grabbed her teddy bear and shut her eyes. Natalie remained on the bed until her daughter's breathing was steady.

Once she closed the door behind her, Natalie made her way into the bright, sunny kitchen in the new condo, poured herself a cup of coffee, then stood beside the table in the breakfast room.

She sipped the hot liquid before putting down the cup and looking at her watch. She had expected Stone back an hour ago. She wondered what he was up to now. That thought brought a smile to her lips, something that had been rare until their marriage six months ago.

Occasionally she would pinch herself just to prove that she wasn't dreaming, that she and Stone were indeed man and wife, sharing their life with Clancy, who had called him Daddy from day one of their marriage. And Sally was part of the household as well, spending as much time with them as she did with her mother and stepfather.

Natalie was also thankful that life was finally beginning to settle into a normal pattern. Before that, they had suffered through a living hell—Daniel's death. Even now she couldn't think or talk about that horrible moment when Daniel had taken his own life without drowning in bittersweet tears.

Such a tragic waste, she thought again, biting her lip to hold it steady. She missed him terribly and knew that she would grieve over what happened for the rest of her life. But blessedly for her, most of the details were sketchy in her mind, as Stone had grabbed her the second she'd screamed and buried her face in his chest, refusing to let her see the final seconds of Daniel's life.

Afterward there had been no need for words between her and Stone. He had become her strength, had kept her sane through an insane time. But then she'd had to be strong for Fletcher and Martha, who had been dealt the most crushing blow of a parent's life, the loss of two sons.

Ralph Shankle and his partner, Lewis Melton, were tried and convicted of fraud, and their company was shut down.

The trial had been another nightmare, especially as Stone had had to testify.

During that time Natalie had been in another courtroom as well, testifying against Mack Gates for his attempt to sell land that was filled with toxic waste.

While she knew that Fletcher's and Martha's suffering would never end on this earth, Natalie felt that letting them see Clancy whenever they asked had been their salvation.

That gesture had also gone a long way toward healing the breach between them and bringing the family back together. Still, there was a long way to go.

"My, but you're serious."

Just hearing her husband's voice sent a warm feeling through Natalie. She twisted her head and watched as he strode toward her.

"I was just thinking," she said in a melancholy tone.

He put his arms around her and nuzzled her neck. "Every time you have to go to the ranch, you get like this."

"I know, but I can't help it. It breaks my heart to see Fletcher and Martha. They're still so broken."

"It's rough, no doubt about it. At least they have Stanley," he added, turning her in his arms, trapping a tear, then licking it.

"Ah, Stanley." Natalie gave him a quivering smile. "He continues to be a piece of work."

"A manipulative one, if you ask me."

"That side of him comes from Paula."

Stone rubbed his chin. "I can't believe they're still man and wife."

"Me either."

"I figure it's because you turned down the land that Fletcher offered you, insisting that it was rightfully Stanley's."

"I had no choice, Stone. I told Stanley and Fletcher all along that I didn't want that land, but they wouldn't believe me."

"Well, now Stanley believes it, and he's in hog heaven."

"Paula's trying to get pregnant."

Stone rolled his eyes. "God, I pity the poor child."

"You're awful."

"Only you love me anyway, right?"

Her eyes darkened. "Right, and so does daughter number two."

"By the way, where is Clance?"

"Napping, after eating dirt."

Stone threw back his head and laughed. "Uh-oh."

"She said, 'Daddy eats dirt.'"

"Lord only knows where she got that."

"I can't imagine. When you two get together, I'm not surprised about anything."

They both laughed before Natalie sobered again and asked, "So how did your meeting go?"

"Would you believe Rutgers asked me to come back to the force?"

"Yes. Even that bozo knows a good cop when he sees one."

Stone had discussed Rutgers with her before he'd gone down to the station to confront him. He'd debated the best way to handle his ex-boss, whether to raise a stink or not. Natalie had listened to the pros and cons but in the end had told Stone it had to be his decision, that only he could tie up that loose end.

However, that was before Martha had come forward with a canceled check for a thousand dollars made out to Rutgers and signed by Fletcher.

They had both been dumbfounded that Martha as executrix of Daniel's estate had come forward with such damaging evidence. Natalie suspected that it was part of Martha's way to begin gluing the broken pieces of the family back together.

After that, Stone's decision had been made.

"So what happened?" Natalie asked, following the lengthy silence.

"Summed up, I told him to eat shit and die."

Appalled, Natalie cried, "You didn't!"

"Well, not exactly in those words, but close to it. Rutgers

had decided that he wouldn't take early retirement after all. He told me he intended to sit back and wait until he could draw full pension." Stone paused and smiled. "That's when I slammed the check down on his desk and said, 'Think again.'"

Natalie's lips twitched. "I assume that was after he offered you your job back."

"Of course."

She blew out a breath, then frowned. "I'm sure that was a low blow he wasn't expecting."

"Are you saying I shouldn't have nailed his ass for what he did to me?"

"No, absolutely not." She grinned. "I'm just sorry I couldn't have been there."

He chuckled. "Well, I could've gone after his badge and gotten it. Instead, I decided to put the fear of God in him and let it go at that."

"But you have no regrets, right?"

Stone looked out the window and was quiet for a minute. "At times I expect I will, especially when I see Fletcher and know that he and Rutgers took an unnecessary chunk out of my life. But on the other hand, Fletcher's getting paid back twofold."

"You can say that again," Natalie responded.

"And even I don't believe in kicking a dog while he's on his belly. Well, maybe some dogs. . . ."

She smiled, but only fleetingly.

"So what about you and Fletcher?" Stone asked, his tone tentative. "I know that the things he said behind your back continue to tear you up inside."

"Martha said he didn't mean them."

"Do you believe her?"

"I'm not sure, but right now it doesn't matter. Anyway, he apologized for some of the things he said to me. But the other . . . well, one day, when the time is right, I'll bring it up. Right now, I just feel sorry for him. He's a pitiful, broken man who, like you said, has gotten back as good as he's given."

"We all change, that's for sure. At one time, I would've cleaned his clock for what he did to you, but—" Stone broke off with a grin.

"Now you're a tamed pussycat," she finished for him.

"Speaking of which . . ."

"Stone, you're awful!" Yet she couldn't stop the heat that suddenly gathered between her legs. "And have a nasty mouth, but then you know that."

He lifted her hand and kissed the palm while his eyes delved into hers. "Are you complaining?"

"Never."

"Good. Now we can get down to the main business of the day."

"And what is that?" Natalie murmured, still quivering inside.

"My surprise."

"Surprise?"

"Yep. In the form of land. I've always wanted to own my own ranch, have a few head of cattle, maybe even a garden. So, I talked to a friend of a friend who has a hundred acres available for a great price." His eyes were anxious. "So what do you think?"

"Well, I guess since I now own a real estate agency, I might be able to handle the paperwork."

He grinned, then looked anxious again. "You really wouldn't mind moving back to the country someday when we can afford to build a house?"

"Of course not, silly. Home is wherever you are. Besides, I think it'll be fun to have our own place to mold and shape like we want."

He leaned over and kissed her hard and deep. Then, looking at her, he said in a thick voice, "When I first met you, there was this big hole inside of me that I never thought I could fill. Then I fell in love, and that hole is more than filled; it's running over."

"Oh, Stone, I love you more than you'll ever know. And I'm so sorry about so many things."

"Shh. We've never discussed those black days, and I don't intend to start now. The future's ours." His sober features spread into a wide grin. "Speaking of the future, why, I can see you now, branding the cattle, working the land, all the while barefoot and pregnant."

"And walking ten feet behind you as well, right?"

"Well, now that you mention it . . ." He grinned.

She poked him in the ribs.

"Ouch!"

"That's just to remind you of your place, Mr. McCall."

"And what about your place, Mrs. McCall?" His voice sounded rusty now.

She went warm all over. "I prefer the top."

"I know you do," he whispered, sliding his hand up her skirt. "And practice, you know, makes perfect."

She pulled back and looked at him. "Here? Now?"

"Why not," he said, shifting her so that he could unzip his pants. "Now, for you, my love," he added, then proceeded to lift her skirt.

"Oh, Stone!" Natalie's cry of delight came when he sat on the nearest chair and eased her down on him.

"God, but you fit me like a glove."

"Our bodies were made for each other."

He moved, and their eyes locked. "I could spend the rest of my life like this," he ground out.

"Me too."

He unbuttoned her blouse, unclasped her bra, and freed her breasts. "Maybe we'll make a baby now," he whispered, tonguing a nipple.

Natalie clutched his head to her as their movements increased ever so gently. "I'd like that."

His eyes were hot and wild. "Would you, really?"

"I can't think of anything I'd like better than to have your child growing inside me," she whispered.

"Then let's stop talking and get serious."

A long and loving silence filled the room.

THROUGHOUT THE NEXT YEAR, LOOK FOR OTHER
FABULOUS BOOKS FROM YOUR FAVORITE WRITERS
IN THE WARNER ROMANCE GUARANTEED PROGRAM

WIN A ROMANTIC GETAWAY FOR TWO

To show our appreciation for your support, Warner Books is offering an opportunity to win our sweepstakes for four weekend trips for two throughout 1996.

Enter in February and March to win a romantic spring weekend to Hilton Head, South Carolina;

Enter in April, May and June to win a gorgeous summer getaway to San Francisco, California;

Enter in July and August to win a passionate fall trip to the blazing mountains of Vermont;

Enter in September, October, November and December to win a hot winter jaunt to Sanibel Island.

To enter, stop by the Warner Books display at your local bookstore for details or send a self-addressed stamped envelope for an application to:

Warner Books
1271 Avenue of the Americas
Room 9-27B
New York, NY 10020

No purchase necessary. Void where prohibited. Not valid in Canada.
Winner must be 18 or older.

WARNER BOOKS. WE'LL SWEEP YOU OFF YOUR FEET.
★★★★